THE

HAZARDS

OF

HUNTING

WHILE

HEARTBROKEN

THE

HAZARDS

OF

HUNTING

WHILE

HEARTBROKEN

a novel

To Denise—
Thanks for
cheering me on!
all best,

MARI PASSANANTI

Copyright © 2011 Mari Passananti

ISBN: 978-0-615-49364-0 (pbk.)

for Julian

acknowledgements

Many thanks to my amazing editor, Jennifer Fisher, whose keen eye and ability to see the forest and the trees at the same time made *The Hazards of Hunting While Heartbroken* a much better book.

Thank you to my cadre of earliest readers, and especially to Annette Widener Stafford and Lisa Mogan, who read draft after draft, enthusiastically and without complaint. Thank you also to Wendy Walker, for her relentless encouragement, and to Sharon Bially and Lauren Belliveau, who basically forced me to think outside the box.

Thank you to Anja Passananti for her insights into the world of the young, cosmopolitan and fabulous. Thank you to Regina Starace—I love the cover.

Deepest gratitude to my parents, Riitta and Vincent Passananti. Without their support and encouragement, this book wouldn't have made it out of my laptop and into the world. I'm grateful beyond words to Maria Porto—without her I'm certain this book never would have happened. Finally, thank you to Rick Howes, for putting up with all my ups and downs with good humor and more than a little panache.

ONE

No kid dreams of growing up to become a headhunter. It doesn't rate up there with astronaut, veterinarian or firefighter, especially in the minds of the young and unstoppable.

For as long as I can remember, I wanted to travel, paint huge canvases and study the old masters at some Italian art institute whose name I can no longer recall. My parents urged me to aim "higher." They dreamed of their only daughter studying medicine, or at least law, and preferably at an Ivy League school. We compromised. I won a scholarship to Princeton and declared myself an art history major. With a decade elapsed between me and college, I'm not remotely near where I expected to be by now, even though I've tried to do everything right. Maybe that's part of my problem. It's amazing how often "right" is mere shorthand for "safe." I am one of those women who is always doing what she's supposed to be doing, even though I see my closest friends taking chances, following their dreams and reaping the rewards.

Ten years ago, I was sure that by my late twenties, I'd manage or perhaps even co-own a prestigious gallery. I'd be married and devoted to my best friend, with whom I'd make an adorable baby at some hazy date in the medium-term future. We'd entertain interesting people in our fabulous but unpretentious loft. None of those things happened, even though I'm now two years, seven months and four days beyond thirty, single and earning my living by meddling with the careers of others. Yet I've never stopped and asked myself, *Zoë, is this the life you want instead?*

At least not until now.

Maybe it's bad karma to complain, since there are millions of people in this world worse off than I.

But still. I cannot believe this is my life.

In the middle of our routine pre-interview phone call, Niles Townsend informs me, "So they wanted me to, uh, you know, in this plastic cup, right there in the doctor's office, and the special room they use is so close to the nurse's station that I got stage fright." I have no idea how to respond. Niles interprets my silence as permission to continue his tale of woe. "And then Susie, my wife, got hysterical, since they needed the sample, because she was ovulating."

I glance down at the street as some woman about my age, who probably has the *exact* life she wants, steps into Valentino, her designer dog firmly secured under her arm.

"So that's why I need you to cancel my meeting tomorrow morning, Zoë," Niles says.

The word "cancel" snaps me back to the task at hand. I try to spit out a generic yet thoughtful response. "Niles," I say gently. "We've been through this. Cutler and Boone was really excited about you, and more importantly, I think you'd be very happy there. But honestly, they're beginning to find you a bit unreliable. If you make me cancel tomorrow's meeting, that'll make three times you've put this off. We need to make them feel like *you* want them. It's kind of like dating that way."

Niles sighs loudly into the phone. "I hear what you're saying, but Susie's eggs can't wait. She actually called the doctor yesterday and asked if I should, err, bring my own materials tomorrow. You know, in case I get stage fright again. She thinks it might help, and her nurse actually suggested this magazine that..."

"Niles," I snap, "Too much information!" What I want to say is, I'm not your therapist, I'm your headhunter, so kindly limit your remarks to your job search. But of course I can't say that, because, as my boss frequently chirps, "That would upset Niles Townsend. And Niles Townsend is too important a client to be upset in that manner."

I hear his mobile phone ring in the background. "I need to take this, Zoë. Go ahead and re-schedule this thing, okay? Thanks." He's gone before I can beg him to re-consider.

I peel off my headset, rub my temples and swivel in my chair. I flinch at the sight of Carol Broadwick storming through the bullpen towards my desk. She opens her mouth to say something, catches herself and asks me how I'm doing in a put upon tone, as if I've insisted on diverting her from important business. Carol views pleasantries and small talk as a complete waste of time, but she's been making a limited effort since her latest consultant advised her to take an interest in her employees.

She does not care that I spent Saturday night eating chocolate in front of an infomercial for a handheld trouser press, until my friends stormed my apartment to drag me out. So I say, "Fine. Thank you for asking."

Before I finish getting the words out, she launches into a tirade. "I just hung up with the managing partner of Cutler and Boone. He wanted my assurances that Niles Townsend would be there tomorrow. Frankly, they were much hotter for the little creep before he started acting like the process was all about his *needs*. So I want you to remind him that it wouldn't hurt to show up a couple of minutes early and look like he's interested. But you know what to do." She gives me a fake smile and starts to turn on her Chanel heel to stomp away.

I decide to confess. If she hears it from me, she won't be blindsided by a call from a pissed off client. Which would put her in a fouler than normal mood, which in turn would wreck everyone's week.

"Wait a second," I say. "I actually could use your advice on this one."

She rotates back to face me, and I realize I've said the magic words. Carol's fearsome, especially if you don't know how to handle her, which normally involves the right cocktail of competence and deference, garnished with carefully timed reliance on her inestimable experience.

I give her the short version of my conversation with Niles. When her eyes begin to narrow, I reassure her that I did my level best to impress upon him the extreme importance of showing up.

"Let's call him together, and that way you can learn to sort these things out for yourself," she suggests with an indulgent smile. Ganging up on Niles over his procreative problems sounds unwise, but based on the garish way Carol has applied her eye shadow and lipstick this morning, she is going to have a manic day.

I'm not stupid enough to rush her inevitable meltdown. Or direct it at myself.

Instead I follow her couture clad form across the bullpen into her office. She installs me in one of her imitation Louis XVI chairs and I watch in mixed horror and admiration as she calls Niles and formulates a plan to save both his interview (as well as the company's six-figure commission) and his marriage. She makes it look so easy.

Though she's unbearable most of the time, there's a reason why she's the unchallenged doyenne of the city's recruiting world.

"Niles, we think you're great," Carol explains indulgently. "Everyone you met during the first round at Cutler thought you were great. Your client list is enviable, without question. But here's the thing. Cutler doesn't hire a lot of laterals. And you can't swear on a whole stack of Bibles that all your clients will go with you. I know it says here you have $6 million in portable revenues a year, but realistically, I'm looking at this, and I think it might really be closer to $2 million. So I'm thinking it might be better to not piss them off. And by that I mean you ought to act like you give a fuck."

She drums her manicured nails on her desk and I watch the overhead light sparkle off her huge diamond rings. Carol wears one on each hand, in honor of each ex.

The speaker phone crackles but Niles says nothing. Probably because Carol isn't wrong. Niles represents big banks that go through lots of mergers and take government money. It's not the most stable roster of clients.

Which is why he ultimately agrees to Carol's proposal. "My wife will hate it," he grumbles.

"She'll like the seven figure salary you'll bring home once you start at the Cutler firm. Zoë will be there tomorrow at 8:30," Carol announces triumphantly. She hangs up without giving Niles a chance to regroup.

The taxi pulls up in front of 311 Park as it starts to drizzle. I check in with the concierge and ride the elevator to the floor right below the penthouse. Niles is waiting, fully dressed in his suit—thank God—but pacing the Oriental carpet like a caged animal. "Good morning," he says, without making eye contact.

I remind myself this must be more embarrassing for Niles than it is for me. Not that it helps much. I can't bring my gaze off the floor as I hand over his fetish magazines—the ones I was foolish enough to purchase at my regular newsstand this morning—and the sterile cup I procured for $1.99 at CVS last night.

Niles tells me to have a seat in the den off the main foyer. I park myself in the nearest chair and whip out my BlackBerry. The walls are lined with books, many of which might fascinate me under normal circumstances, but not today. I don't need to nose around and risk inviting elective conversation. Even before today, I was afraid of saying the wrong thing to Niles. He's one of those men who holds forth with no filter, but acts annoyed if anyone beneath him, such as myself, presumes to question his narrative.

I suppose he's entitled.

Niles Townsend is a very successful forty-two year-old Yale-educated litigator, whose clients include some of the biggest household names in the financial services industry. To say he's uptight would be like saying it's a bit brisk at the North Pole. He wears three-piece suits with color-coordinated pocket squares, even on Fridays. He's on the board of the Episcopal Philanthropic Something-or-Other. He (and his wife) believe he could earn more at a rival law firm where there's no territorial senior partner to impede his ascension to the top of the litigation department.

Cutler & Boone is a perfect fit for Niles. I need to believe he wouldn't miss the possible conception of his child for a lesser law firm. Still, I have no idea how to act in this situation, so I perch uncomfortably on the edge of the sofa and pick up yesterday's newspaper from the coffee table.

Niles disappears down the hall for almost forty-five minutes. No, it doesn't just feel that way. What if he doesn't emerge in time for his interview? If he does suffer from impotence or performance anxiety, I'm unconvinced that a stack of magazines featuring garishly made up plus sized women who enjoy each other will cure him. But what do I know?

I consult my watch again. If he misses his appointment at Cutler & Boone after all this I might cry. Carol will lose it and perhaps even fire me in her frustration. I'd be totally screwed, a pariah with no job, no reference, no life plan. I start to panic. Should I check on his progress? I could send a text reminding him of the time. *No*, the little voice in my head screeches.

Finally Niles emerges with the cup. He's managed to lose the tasteful brown bag in which I delivered it.

"Susie said to tell you to put the sample up your shirt. It's not good for it to go below body temperature."

I suggested yesterday that perhaps Susie should carry her own damn semen. I was told that would be impossible; she had scheduled an acupuncture treatment to stimulate receptive energy in her womb or something like that.

Niles shoves the cup at me. I gingerly test that he's fastened the lid securely. He waits expectantly. I un-tuck my blouse and slip the warm cup against my skin. It takes a phenomenal effort not to recoil. I know there's a layer of medical grade plastic between me and the semen, but still. Couldn't we have done this exercise last month, when we had that monster heat wave?

Niles, duly assured his seed won't suffer frostbite, grabs his briefcase and we ride down the elevator in excruciating silence. His car service is waiting, but he doesn't offer me, or his sperm, a lift, even though we'd pass the hospital on his way. Not that I want to spend more time with him. At least he'll be at Cutler's offices early.

Finally a cab stops and I slide in, cradling the cup like precious cargo. I'm afraid to take it out from under my shirt. What if they take its temperature at the clinic and find out I disregarded Susie's orders?

Today unquestionably marks a new professional low. Still, I remind myself how grateful I was when Carol plucked me out of the gallerina job from hell some three plus years ago. After the insanity of the art world, there's not much Carol can throw my way that I can't handle. In retrospect, she probably knew all along that if I could handle my boss at the gallery, where she was a frequent customer, odds seemed good that I could hack it at Broadwick & Associates. And while Carol's mercurial at best, at least she's never punished me for rain on her birthday. Nor has she ever forced me to return a latte because it wasn't frothy enough. Though I'm sure the thought crossed her mind after watching my former employer instruct me to do exactly that, on the fateful afternoon when Carol stomped into the gallery to pay six figures for an enormous orange monstrosity for her living room wall.

Given the state of the economy, I should be more thankful I have a job in the first place, and even more grateful that it's an occasionally lucrative one. The phone doesn't exactly ring off the hook with people wanting to hire me, like it does for rare superstars like Niles Townsend. But I still can't wrap my head around the fact that I'm in stop and go traffic with his sperm up my shirt.

I try to distract myself by calculating my share of the commission in the event that the Cutler firm hires Niles at a million plus a year. It's a masochistic pastime. Even if he gets through today, a hundred things could still cause the deal to implode. And even assuming I manage to earn this huge paycheck, most of it will have to be earmarked for rent. I'm still in denial about how much more expensive my life became the day Brendan, my former fiancé, moved out.

The cab lurches to a stop at a red light. The cup jabs against my stomach. I hold my breath as I double check the lid. I try to focus my mind's eye on the Jimmy Choo boots Carol pointed out to me on one of our recent "motivational walks." My boss adores material displays of success and expends a fair amount of energy trying to instill a similar ethic in all of us, so that we'll need to work harder to feed our spending addictions.

We finally arrive at the hospital. The cabbie gives me a strange look as I extricate myself from the car without removing my hand from under my shirt.

The hospital's elevator stops at almost every floor on the way up to the clinic on the 27th. I worry that the sperm might expire. When the receptionist finally whisks it away, I feel my whole body relax for the first time since yesterday afternoon.

It's a temporary sensation. In the cab on the way back to work, I contemplate the sickening possibility that I may have gone through this exercise for nothing. What if Niles, traumatized by the morning's events, bombs at his interview? It's not a far fetched worry, considering how my luck's been running lately.

A half hour later, I step off the office elevator at Broadwick & Associates to be greeted by Jessica, whose role here at the company is unclear, but who's been with Carol since she started twenty years ago. Carol semi-affectionately refers to Jessica as the Town Crier, a moniker the latter almost eagerly lives up to. Jessica has a pretty face attached to a giraffe-like body. Her legs are too long for normal-sized clothes, so her pants always hit above her ankles. I wonder why she doesn't wear more skirts.

"Someone's got a secret admirer," Jessica taunts in a playground voice. She's pointing at a tasteful arrangement of pink roses on the reception desk and waving a florist's card at my nose.

"Lucky Sibyl," I reply, assuming she means the receptionist, a doe-eyed twenty-two-year-old waif who garners more than her fair share of male attention.

"Not Sibyl," Jessica laughs. "You! Those are for you. And just look at the card." She hands it over. "Someone wants to take you on a da-ate."

I'm starting to seethe. "Who told you it was okay to read my mail?"

"It wasn't exactly addressed to you," Jessica pouts, and crosses her arms over her chest.

I read the envelope, and she's not lying. It's addressed to "The Beautiful Woman Whose Desk Faces Out the Fifth Floor Window (Madison side)." Unless the sender's blind, that has to mean me. The only other person whose desk faces out that window is Marvin, a middle-aged recovering lawyer with a growing paunch and a shrinking hairline.

I tear it open. "You've been looking sad lately. Drink? P.S. I'm across the street, one floor up from you." I flip the card over, hoping for more, but there's no name, just a 212 phone number.

I can't help it. I dash across the office to my desk and peer out. There's no one in the windows across the way.

Of course it's possible the florist made a mistake. Maybe the flowers and note were intended for someone else entirely. Somewhere, down the block, two nearly star-crossed souls have missed each other due to a mislabeled delivery. Some hapless man who made this bold gesture keeps pacing to his window, wondering why the object of his affections isn't even bothering to look at him. He's dejected, then despondent, then enraged. Maybe he'll get a gun and mow her down for ignoring him. I'll read about it on the front page of the *Post*, and somehow it'll be my fault, because I took delivery of roses intended for some other woman.

Jessica is squinting out my window like a sailor scanning the horizon for land. She's on her tiptoes, which makes her pants rise even farther up her calves. Finally satisfied that I wasn't lying when I said he wasn't there, she demands, "Are you going to go out with him?"

"I think it might be just the thing, you know, to get you out of your funk," adds Marvin, who lives for office gossip. "Are you sure you've never seen him?"

"I spend most of my time looking down at the street. And I'm not in a funk."

"Sure you are," Marvin cajoles, and the others nod their agreement. "Not that I can blame you. Anyone whose fiancé calls off the Wedding of the Year with less than a month to spare is entitled to a bit of a sulk. So are you going to go out with him?"

"Let's just watch and see if the mystery man appears," I say, with as much authority as I can muster. While I want to press my nose to the glass and stare up at the windows of 749 Madison until I spot signs of life (preferably hot, masculine life), I force myself into my chair, and try to look busy.

Of course I can't concentrate. My right brain is galloping at break-neck pace to places it has no business going and my left brain is powerless to stop it. What if everything, including my humiliation at the hands of Brendan, happens for a reason? Maybe I was supposed to waste my twenties in a holding pattern so I could meet the man of my dreams by virtue of coincidental office geography on this exact day. Maybe I needed the emotional scarring of a cancelled wedding to prove my worthiness for real love. I wonder what he's like. What does he want from life? Maybe we're each others' long missing puzzle pieces, meant to fit together. The little voice in my head shrieks at me to pull myself out of my death spiral into fantasy land and Get. A. Grip. She tells me he is probably horribly flawed. Socially inept. Whiny. Blighted by bad breath, ear hair and stooped posture. He's damaged, desperate and eager to blame a woman for his sexual deficiencies.

No. Life cannot possibly be so unfair that it would charge back and kick me again just as I'm working to pick myself up and dust myself off. I've been a good person. I don't deserve more rotten love luck. Isn't it enough that I got dumped a week before my wedding? Or that my first and only post-break-up Match date failed to mention he was quadriplegic—after he told me he enjoyed skiing and hiking, *and* arranged to meet me at a basement restaurant with no handicap access? Instead of bringing me out of my slump, that date sent me home panicked that I am a horrible person because I had the audacity to think, that no matter how angry the poor guy was at the world, I deserved a heads up on his condition.

I tell the little voice that there's no harm in nurturing a little hope. That shuts her up.

Oh please, I beg whatever higher power determines such matters, please let him be at least a little cute and a lot nice.

TWO

He doesn't appear. Not during the lunch I scarf at my computer, pretending to work, but stealing furtive glances across the street and up. Not in the tiresome afternoon hours that drag by.

With every passing minute in which the mystery man fails to show himself, I become increasingly convinced there's been a mistake. The flowers must have been meant for someone else, in some other window, on some other block. But a small, okay, maybe a not-so-small, part of me still wants a glimpse of this secret admirer. Not that I'm even considering his offer. He could be a serial killer. Normal guys don't send roses to women they don't know. And even if they do, things like this only end well in the movies.

But curiosity is natural, right? I'd be a freak if I weren't a little interested. I just want to see him, and then I'll get right back to work. I congratulate myself for suppressing the urge to call my best friend Angela and hash out all the possible outcomes. When you work in a bullpen, everyone knows your business. You don't need to go broadcasting your innermost thoughts for public consumption by making unnecessary personal phone calls.

Still, I check my make-up at fifteen minute intervals for the rest of the day, and run a brush through my hair way more frequently than usual. If my secret admirer decides to appear, I might as well look nice. I kill way too much time alternately staring out the window and at my own reflection. I hate how my make-up mirror magnifies every pore, but in the good news column, I've always loved my round blue eyes. Plus my hair is looking good these days, despite Carol's frequent snarky remarks about it. Maybe the expensive salon I now patronize on Angela's advice isn't a luxury after all. Her genius of a hairdresser convinced me to add subtle layers, because "they would emphasize my heart shaped face and good cheekbones." He was right, and my new haircut is the most flattering one I've ever had. Too bad it doesn't

hide my nose. It's what I would change about myself if I could trans-
form one thing. I've never liked it. I think it resembles one of those
bad early-eighties ski slope nose jobs. Lucky me: I was born this way.
I didn't pay a one-trick surgeon thousands of dollars for the effect.

I snap the compact shut and check the window again. Nothing. I
spin my chair the other way and tell myself I will return all four calls
on my list before looking again.

I'm not the only one who spends the better part of the afternoon
watching. Carol is tied up in meetings outside the office for most of
the day, so Jessica doesn't need to fabricate an excuse to hang by my
window. She keeps buzzing around my desk, twittering, "Still not
there!" As if I need clarification.

Marvin, on the other hand, takes it upon himself to do a bit of
recon. At lunchtime, he marches right across Madison Avenue and
uses what he calls his "immeasurable deductive powers" (meaning he
consults the building directory) to discover that, if indeed the flowers
came from an occupant of that particular building, the sender works
at Takamura Brothers, a very prestigious advertising agency.

As soon as Marvin delivers his report, Jessica skulks over and
says, "You know, all advertising execs are jerks."

"Don't you think that's slightly unfair?" I ask, as I quietly admit
to myself that I'm more than a little excited to know more about my
mystery man.

Jessica ignores my admonition and adds the zinger. "And *so* many
of them are gay!"

"Now that's mean," Marvin says. "Obviously, if Mister X here were
gay, he'd be sending flowers to me, not to Zoë."

That makes sense. But what if Jessica's right? What if I've wasted
most of my work day staking out a gay man who doesn't know he's
gay? One who makes overtures towards anonymous women because
he knows the odds of an actual connection are remote? Or worse, one
who knows his sexual preference but won't admit it? I've been down
that road once and have no desire to travel it again. And did I mention
I work on commission? If I don't close deals, Carol doesn't pay me.

Thankfully, Sibyl's perky cheerleader voice pages Jessica to reception. As she strides away, Marvin wheels his chair close to mine and
rests his hand on my knee. He leans in to whispering range, and his
tie, a green number flecked with pink flamingoes, falls towards my
lap. "Don't listen to her. She's jealous of you."

"That's ridiculous," I sniff. "Who in their right mind would be jealous of me?"

"I never said she was in her right mind," Marvin laughs as he pushes himself back in the general direction of his desk, which is roughly behind mine in the bullpen. "I have to get back to the grind. Bills to pay and all that. But call me if hot stuff makes an appearance."

By five in the afternoon, I've abandoned all pretenses of working and I'm staring out the window, willing him to appear. By 6:45, I reluctantly tear myself away because if I don't leave now, I'll be late for Angela and Kevin. As I re-touch my lipstick for the hundred fifty-seventh time today and shut down my computer, there is still no movement in the windows across the way.

I take the elevator down to the lobby only to realize I've forgotten my coat. Running back up will make me late, but there's an autumn chill in the air, which is strange and unseasonable for the week after Labor Day. It makes me think it won't be long before I'm going to work and heading home in the dark.

I retrace my steps and head back up. The lights in our reception area have been dimmed for the night, but a few of my colleagues are still hard at work. Thankfully, I bet Jessica's gone. She's never around much after five. I'm fumbling for my key card when the doors fly open in my face and Marvin almost mows me down.

"He's there and he's gorgeous!" he announces breathlessly. "So I raced out here to see if I could catch you."

We practically smash into each other as we try to crush through the doors at the same time. "Wait!" I yell, then stop myself and lower my voice. "I can't go running over there. Try to look casual." I smooth my hair and my skirt and walk to my desk, using every iota of self control to force my gaze away from the windows. I scoop my coat off the back of my chair and whirl around, nonchalantly, I hope, to put it on. As I do so, I steal a glance across the way. He's in the window, standing up and talking on the phone. He's got his sleeves rolled up and his tie loosened.

Marvin didn't lie. He's the most stunning man I've ever seen. He's got those chiseled cheekbones I thought only existed in Renaissance art and on models in Armani fragrance advertisements. His dark hair is slicked back in New York fashion, but not too severely. It's hard to tell how old he is from here, but I'd guess about forty. I wonder whether that's too old.

He sees me and smiles. It lights up his whole face. I smile back. He waves. I keep smiling, like an idiot, and then, having no experience with such scenarios and having no idea how to keep a silent, trans-Madison Avenue flirtation going, I shoot him what I hope is a coy look, and hurry out of his line of sight.

"That's it, baby!" Marvin calls after me. "Make him work for it!"

I'm not sure that's what I'm doing. It feels more like running away, but I turn towards Marvin and give him a little wink.

"Three Bellinis," Angela announces authoritatively to our waiter, a college-age Adonis, who looks like a recent import from Italy. She flips her cascading brunette locks and gives him a practiced smile to soften her bossy tone.

"*Certo,*" he replies, and flashes a smile back at her. I don't speak Italian but I'm going to go out on a limb and guess that means something close to certainly. Before he can step away to fill our order, Kevin says, "Actually, make that two Bellinis and one Beck's." He hands over his credit card so the bartender can start a tab, which Kevin will pay when we decide to close it out. The best thing about my job is that, if I do well with candidates like Niles, I'll be able to stop my friends from subsidizing so many of our outings. Neither one of them has ever tried to make me feel badly about our economic gap, but after all these years, I still suffer pangs of guilt and anxiety when they pick upscale places. And if I'm being honest, it was much easier to ignore the disparity when I was engaged to Brendan. He almost always paid for both of us.

As the waiter, thus reinstructed, retreats, Kevin explains, "It's bad enough if someone sees me in here. I can't be drinking a Bellini to boot. The Councilman is supposed to be a man of the people."

"Supposed to be is right," I say. "No man of the people I know avoids Hamptons traffic in his own helicopter."

Angela nods her agreement and her diamond earrings (two carats, each ear, a gift from a deposed Burmese prince) sparkle in the soft light of the bar, which is festooned with more candles than a Diptyque store.

Kevin frowns. He manages the mayoral campaign of a Democratic Councilman, and freakishly popular former prosecutor, from Brooklyn. He's one of those obscenely wealthy politicians who claims to understand the average voter, because he drinks beer and occasionally takes the subway, when the cameras are watching. He's also the frontrunner, by a healthy double digit margin, which is why Kevin can skip out of work and meet us for cocktails.

Angela rolls her eyes and says, "Right. Now remind me again, where did you go to school? Wasn't it a little place called Princeton? And, just incidentally, what kind of suit is that you're wearing?"

"Zegna," Kevin admits grumpily. "But I got it at the outlets."

Angela and I laugh. Kevin's not a snob, but he's definitely a clothes horse. Always was, and always will be. No wonder Brendan suspected he was gay. Women, on the other hand, generally seem to appreciate Kevin's super stylish European newscaster look. He picked up most of his fashion sense from his first roommate, a pretty, wispy guy with a penchant for makeup, cross dressing and sexual partners of both genders. Kevin brought him home to Summit, New Jersey for Thanksgiving freshman year, in a calculated move to horrify his Catholic parents.

In his line of work, I don't think it would matter if Kevin did prefer men. What's important is his ability to help the candidate connect with as many people as possible, so Kevin's rightly concerned about his populist image. We're perched on micro-suede covered stools around a marble topped table in the latest of a string of fashion cafes to open in New York. I can't even remember which designer owns this particular establishment, but whoever the proprietor is, he's banking on the notion that, whatever the market's doing, people aren't ready to cut back when it comes to either entertainment or image. The waiters are from the old country, and the walls display a rotating collection of photographs by Mario Testino. The portions of what limited food they serve are minuscule, and around eleven, once the post-work crowd disappears, velvet ropes spring up on the sidewalk outside to discourage the under-primped from even trying.

Angela tells me that, after midnight, they suspend this pretty blonde girl from the ceiling. She wears a pink fairy costume, complete with glittery wings. She has a "magic wand" and taps people on the shoulder to admit them to the VIP room upstairs. Sometimes she taps a series of people and sings, "You. You. And You. Not You. Not You. You."

You get the idea. We're here because Angela, my best friend and assistant associate shoe editor at *Vogue* magazine, has declared it *the* new place for the fall. And now, at just after 7:30, it's mostly full of young, conservatively dressed professionals. I can sip my aperitif comfortably, knowing we'll be long gone before the Fairy Door-Mother flies out on her trapeze to judge my accessories.

The bartender returns with our drinks. Two champagne flutes and a bottle of beer.

"A man of the people would drink Bud," Angela says.

"You are so not tricking me into asking if they have Bud." Kevin pours his imported lager into a glass, takes a sip and loosens his tie.

Angela asks me, "How's it going with Niles?"

Niles Townsend is married to her cousin. Angela referred him to me when her cousin confided that he was feeling put-upon and underpaid. That's the only reason I'm working with him, a fact Carol reminds me of almost daily. Usually, I'm only entrusted with the careers of more junior people. But I'll say this for Niles: the man can follow directions. Angela told him to be sure to ask for me, and, for better or worse, he did. I think he was a little shocked when he did the math on my college graduation year, but he seems to have forgotten his hesitations. As this morning's events illustrate, he's altogether too comfortable with me now.

"Fine," I answer. "He's considering various possibilities."

"Well, get him something that pays well," Angela advises. "My cousin's eyeing this mansion in Westchester, you know, for the six children she wants."

I resist the urge to share my knowledge of Niles and Susie's fertility problems and say, "I'll do my best, but, you guys, something really strange happened at work today."

"What's Carol done now?" asks Kevin. It's a legitimate question. Her antics can be pretty amusing, especially when viewed from a distance. "Did she make you all *feng shui* your desks again?"

"No, nothing like that. It's not Carol at all, actually." I recount the saga of my mysterious admirer, starting with the flowers, and ending with my glimpse of him. I mention that he's gorgeous at least seven or eight times. I produce his unsigned card from my purse and slap it onto the table as evidence.

"But I don't know what to do. Is it too weird? I should just forget the whole thing, right?"

"Wait a second," Angela says. "Let me try to understand. He's gorgeous. He works for one of the most prestigious ad agencies in New York—no, not in New York, in the world. Which happens to pay its people a ton of money. He sent you flowers. He called you beautiful."

She ticks off each point on her French-manicured fingers. "Call me crazy, but I am failing to see the problem."

"Maybe it's too soon," I stammer. Kevin starts to say something in support of this argument but Angela cuts him off.

"It's been three months. Which would normally not be a huge amount of time. But in your special circumstances, there's none of the maybe-we'll-get-back together nonsense. Brendan's embracing a whole new life. You need to move on as soon as possible, and you've sworn off the Internet. So I can't think of a better way than a whirlwind romance with a secret admirer. Let the guy spoil you a little if he wants. It would do you good."

"Don't rush her if she's not ready," says Kevin.

Angela shushes him. "You should call him, but not tonight. I mean, you want him to know you're interested, but you can't afford to look too eager."

I digest her counsel with the last sip of my first Bellini. The gorgeous waiter replaces it without being asked.

"He's probably a psycho. He could be some kind of deranged deviant. Or he could have chronic bad breath. Or a heinous accent. Or a tiny penis." Kevin rattles off a laundry list of potential pitfalls. "I'm not so sure. These things only tend to work out in the movies."

"That's what I thought!" While I know what I want to do, I have no idea what I *should* do. I hate it when my two most trusted advisers disagree.

Angela snaps at Kevin, "Penis size is irrelevant here. What Zoë needs is to be taken out on the town, shown a good time. It's not like she has to sleep with him on the first date. Some of us have more patience than you."

"Don't give me that look. If women want to come home with me after one dinner, that's my business. It's not like you haven't done it."

"I have not," Angela sniffs and flips her expertly highlighted mane so the lightest pieces fall to frame her face. She re-crosses her legs daintily, and positions herself at an angle so that most of the bar can see her over-the-knee python boots. Kevin raises his eyebrows. "First dates that last a whole long weekend don't count," she explains with a laugh.

I clear my throat and say, "I'm going to call him."

This snaps Kevin and Angela out of their side conversation. "Not now!" they say in unison.

"Of course not now," I say. "Tomorrow. In the afternoon. Definitely not before then."

Angela nods her enthusiastic approval. Kevin shrugs his conditional acceptance and changes the subject to work. I briefly consider sharing the Niles Sperm Saga, but divulging that level of client confidence would constitute grounds for immediate and summary firing. Even if Carol happened to be in one of her best, most medicated moods when she found out.

For now at least, it will have to remain one of our few secrets. The three of us have shared almost everything forever. Angela and I were roommates as college freshmen. I was impressed with her immediately, and I know she found me a bit sheltered for her taste, but I won her over quickly. By which I don't mean I dazzled her with my charm, but that day one of college life was way less intimidating when faced with an instant friend, provided courtesy of whoever matched roomies at the office of student life.

That first night, the resident assistants led everyone in our dorm through a series of hokey ice breaker activities. Kevin was not so slyly checking out Angela, as was every guy in the circle. We played this game where every person had to say three things about themselves, two true and one false. The rest of the group had to try to deduce the fake statement. Kevin correctly surmised that while Angela had indeed read the entirety of *War and Peace*, by her own volition, and she won her high school talent competition handily, with a belly dance performance that scandalized the administration of her small town school, she had never, ever gone back and changed the answer on a test once she'd marked her choice.

Angela was mildly impressed, and Kevin was completely smitten. He became her first collegiate kiss later that night, but things between them fizzled when the upper class guys arrived on campus two days later. Kevin, being boyish and fickle, took the let down in stride and turned his attention to me. We realized we had tons in common, but I didn't want to spend my freshman year tied down to the first boy who spoke to me, even if we were freakishly and instantly in tune to one another. I suppose I was blinded, too, by the steady parade of hot older boys who came by our room every day, mainly in search of Angela. But somehow, during those first weeks at Princeton, we three slightly lost kids forged a bond that's lasted through our four years there and beyond.

I'm thrilled we all ended up in New York, that Kevin lives in the apartment across the hall, and Angela's a short cab ride away. I can't imagine my life without these two, even though keeping up with them financially is impossible.

I bet it hasn't occurred to either of them that, if I want to stay in my place, I will need to do more than cut back on restaurant spending. I'll have to start shopping for a roommate. I've been putting it off, hoping to produce more commission checks out of thin air, because sharing the apartment with some random feels like such a huge step back. I'm too old for all the nonsense that comes with breaking in a new roommate, and I feel like a bit of a loser for not being able to swing the place by myself.

Which is all the more reason I cannot risk losing my job over a good story involving Niles' bodily fluids, so I'm relieved when Angela changes the subject and starts going on about how her latest intern can't walk in heels and that it's strange that human resources doesn't see that as an automatic disqualifier for employment at the world's most recognized fashion magazine.

My worries about Niles must conjure him up, because I have a message from him on the way out of the bar. As I watch the night shift glitterati trickle in, I listen to Niles explain to my voice mail that he's not a pervert and he wants to make sure this morning's events remain strictly confidential. He says he only agreed to the scheme because his career is the most important thing in his life. Which you'd think would be strange to hear from a man who's spent the past several months talking about impregnating his wife. But his priorities aren't my problem. Thankfully people like him exist in droves, or I'd be unemployed.

THREE

Super Hot Secret Admirer Guy is at his window when I arrive at work the next morning. He sees me, waves and makes the universal hand signal for telephone. "Call me," he mouths. I need to do it now. If Carol's on a tear, I won't have a free moment once she returns.

I'm reaching for my phone when Marvin comes up behind me and shoves a paper under my nose. I shrug at the man in the window. He nods and makes an exaggerated sad face, like a little kid would make, by sticking out his lower lip.

Marvin cuts right to the chase. "I took the liberty of doing a bit more due diligence. Your mystery man's name is Oscar Thornton. Of course I Googled him. He's a senior vice president with Takamura Brothers. He did a stint at Salonen & Salonen but it doesn't say when. Over the course of his career, he's worked on everything from Major League Baseball teams to vodka to prescription arthritis drugs."

I flip through the sheaf of papers. Oscar Thornton has been quoted in what looks like a wide range of ad industry publications. He donates to the Democratic Party regularly, and he ran the New York Marathon five years ago in a very impressive three and a half hours. That's all Google knows. There's very little in the way of personal background information.

"Does it even say how old he is?" I ask.

"No. But based on his graduation year, he's forty-two."

"A real grown-up," I mutter.

Marvin regards me curiously. He squints and assesses my nascent wrinkles. "What does that make him, nine years older than you?"

"Ten."

"Maybe you need an actual adult. That was part of Brendan's problem."

"Brendan's problem was that he wanted to sleep with men."

"Not true. Brendan's problem was that he was too much of a child to let anyone know who he really was."

I ponder whether this could be true, for about half a second, and wonder how much I should value the insights of a man who's wearing a tie with little whales on it. They're all smiling and spouting spray from their blowholes.

I'm about to say something to this effect when I notice a dark cloud come over Marvin's face. That can only mean one thing.

Carol barrels into the bullpen. Her blouse has come un-tucked, and her eye shadow looks as if it was applied with a paint roller, which can't mean anything good. "Why the fuck weren't you at the *mandatory* staff meeting yesterday?" she demands, visibly pleased at the prospect of making me squirm.

"I was at the fertility clinic with Niles Townsend's, err, you know."

Her expression undergoes a sea change. "Of course you were." The corners of her mouth turn upward into a pinched smile. "How did that go?"

"Fine," I tell her, which isn't exactly the truth, but she's way too volatile to listen to a lengthy rehash. On a well-medicated day, Carol might find humor in my disgusting recount of yesterday morning's endeavors, but this is clearly not one of those days. She's turning away, and I exhale, thinking the crisis has subsided, but then she spins back towards me.

"Those flowers!" she announces.

"Yes?" I can't imagine what I've done wrong with regard to my roses. My desk is made of particleboard—not a surface she'd be concerned about protecting.

"I don't like their *feng shui.*"

I blink at her, confused. We're always moving our desks around. We've positioned the trash cans, to avert bad luck, more times than I can remember. Last July, she abolished all colored pushpins from our bulletin boards in favor of clear ones. She's even ordered pictures of mountains and water for every cubicle on the advice of one specialist. But I'm failing to see what possible problem pink roses could present. They're in water. And water's good for getting rich, if I recall correctly.

"The flowers, Zoë, have too much Yang. Or Yin. Or whatever the feminine one is, and that is *not* good for financial gain. Take them home with you tonight." She scans the room, arms folded across her couture-covered chest. Everyone's off the phone, listening to her, as much because she's too loud to talk over, as because they're interested in what she's saying. "Now everyone get back to work before I start firing people."

I stifle a laugh as she stomps away into the sanctuary of her private office. She's muttering to herself that she could make twenty times the money if she just sacked all of our sorry asses. Her door slams shut and Marvin whispers, "Call him. He looks promising."

Carol's door flies open before I can respond. "Oh, and Zoë?" my boss sticks her head into the hallway and shouts. "Touch up your highlights." She retreats again and the door crashes shut behind her.

If I was a new employee, I'd die of mortification. But she's just being mean. I know this for sure, and not because I had my hair done on Saturday. Carol once had too much to drink at the holiday party and announced to everyone within earshot that she's jealous of my naturally blonde hair. Honestly, I could wear my true color. But I blonde it up a notch, first and foremost out of habit, and also because stylists in New York don't seem to understand the meaning of "just a cut." They blink at you like you're severely limited if you dare to suggest exiting a salon for under $300. Maybe my highlights are dispensable. God knows I should trim some expenses.

As Marvin scoots back to his desk, I spy Mystery Man in his office across the way, working on his laptop.

I fish my make-up case from my top desk drawer, make sure I look presentable, start to dial the number from the florist's card, but hang up after I press the fifth digit. My colleagues may look busy now, but as soon as they catch wind of what I'm doing, they'll circle me like a pack of hyenas.

I decide to go outside and use my cell phone. Carol's yelling at someone on speaker, in her office. Her back is to me, and she doesn't notice me slink by, but her assistant's eyebrows go up as she watches me tiptoe past. I dive into the elevator, descend to the lobby, push through the revolving doors, make sure I don't know anyone within a twenty-foot radius, and dial.

It rings twice before a deep, manly voice answers, "Oscar Thornton."

"Alright. I'll have a drink with you."

"Where are you? I can't see you."

I can't see him either, but I picture him walking to his window and looking for me. I'm glad he can't see me huddled with all the banished smokers by the building entrance.

"I'm outside, on my cell phone. In case you haven't noticed, I don't exactly have a nice private office like you."

"I missed you yesterday morning. I was worried I might have picked a day you were out," he says. "Where've you been?"

Delivering semen for a client. Wait. Maybe I shouldn't say that. "You know, meetings."

He drops the line of questioning and asks, "How about tonight, then?"

My mind goes blank. I was expecting more small talk. He wants to go out tonight? What do I have tonight? What night is tonight? *Think, Zoë.* It's Thursday. I have ZUMBA. At seven. With Angela. I could skip that. I glance down at my navy blue suit. I don't want to meet Oscar in this.

"Are you there?" Oscar asks.

"Uh, yes, I'm here. Tonight could work, but it would have to be later, like maybe around nine-thirty?"

"No problem. I'll see you at nine-thirty at Nobu. Does that work for you?"

"Sure."

"Great. I'll have my assistant make the reservation. See you tonight."

As we hang up, I realize he never asked my name. I've just made a date for tonight, at a very expensive restaurant, with a man who doesn't even know my name.

I palm my phone for a moment, decide calling back to introduce myself might be awkward and head back into the building. Date or no date, I still have the little problem of my rent, which is due in two weeks. So maybe I should get back to my desk.

The newest item in my inbox is a message from Marvin, asking, "So?"

I turn around in my chair. "We're going out tonight," I whisper. He flashes me the thumbs up sign.

Two hours later, I'm in the middle of an in-depth market analysis with a third-year corporate lawyer who doesn't want to understand why he can't have both more money and a more pleasant working environment.

He's telling me for the fourteenth time that he deserves better than this because he graduated from Harvard, when Sibyl parades into the bullpen with a dozen red roses. I pretend not to notice, because this time, I know they're not for me, but they are gorgeous. Long stemmed and perfectly arranged without any distracting baby's breath. Oscar's tasteful pink arrangement pales in comparison.

My eyes nearly pop out of my head when she plops them on my desk. I mouth, thank you, without interrupting the client on the phone, and dive for the card, which is addressed exactly like yesterday's, except this time, nobody's ripped the envelope open on my behalf. As my young lawyer drones on about "feeling undervalued," I read the handwritten missive. It distracts me from the urge to snap at him that he should feel lucky to have a job.

"So sorry I didn't ask your name. Maybe it's nerves. I've never done anything like this before, but I'll be at Nobu at 9:30, waiting and hoping you're still interested. –O.T."

Wow.

But there's no time to savor the only-in-the-movies-does-this-really-happen quality of the moment, because the sound of Carol's voice jolts me out of my little happy place. It's coming through the glass walls of her office, since she's shrieking at top volume. "You cretins can go screw yourselves! I always get my fucking money and if I have to fucking sue you jack-offs, I am going to get full fucking freight for this deal! Who the fuck do you fucking think you are? Fuckers!"

She keeps going like this, and, amazingly, she gets louder with each chain of expletives. Carol curses like a sailor. All the time. And she can use the f-word as every part of speech. It's a wonder they can't hear her across the street at Takamura Brothers.

My client, on the phone, certainly can. Loud and clear. "I'm sorry," he says, "But what the heck is going on over there?"

I've been through this before. I feign ignorance. "What do you mean?"

"Don't you hear that? It sounds like someone's standing next to you, yelling obscenities."

"How odd," I say, hoping I sound convincing. "I don't hear anyone. Maybe you're picking up someone's cellular conversation."

"Maybe," he says, but sounds doubtful. Carol picks that exact moment to come storming out of her office, slamming the door behind her. She's yelling at her assistant now. "Tell that fucking fucker if he calls back he can fucking talk to my fucking lawyers!"

"You seriously don't hear anything?" my client asks. "You seriously don't hear a woman screaming the f-word, over and over again?"

"No. I'm sorry I don't." I glance over at Carol, who's paused for oxygen. I can tell, from extensive past experience, that she's not quite done. She's inhaling through her mouth and snorting the air out through her nose, and her ears are burning bright red. It would be futile to motion at her to lower her voice so I say brightly into the headset, "If you're still hearing another person's conversation, why don't we hang up and I'll call you back in a minute?"

"Okay. Or, actually, let me call you back at four."

Even better, I think as I consult the calendar. She'll be out at a meeting then.

I disconnect just before Carol unleashes another torrent, at nobody in particular. Unfortunately, she stops midstream as her eyes hone in like lasers on my new roses. They're sort of crowding my prior roses. I can only assume that must constitute horrible *feng shui*.

"Zoë!"

"Uh, yes?"

"What did we say about flowers?" she yells. I hear New Girl gasp, somewhere in the back corner of the bullpen.

"Bad *feng shui*. I'll take them all home tonight."

"Very. Bad. *Feng. Shui*," she announces to the entire office. "If anyone loses a deal today, it's because Zoë undermined our balance with nature." I watch her Chanel-suited form retreat and then her office door slams.

Marvin snickers, "She curses like one of Tony's boys on *The Sopranos*, so all of Midtown Manhattan can hear, and Zoë's *flowers* give us bad *feng shui*? This place drives me to drink." He reaches for the secret silver flask in his desk drawer, and I wonder, for the hundredth time in a month, how soon I could get another job that would cover my rent. Not that I think that would be the best course of action for me, career-wise. And most days, I do feel more lucky than not to be here, especially with the economy still shaky. The legal industry, while not immune, hasn't contracted as much as some other sectors, so I suppose my colleagues and I feel somewhat, albeit thinly, insulated against the gloom.

The thing is, even if the economy were booming, I don't know what I'd be doing instead. The commission structure here gives me the opportunity to earn more than I would almost anywhere else. But

Carol is certifiably nuts, and sometimes my clients act even nuttier, so it's nice to indulge in an escapist fantasy now and then. Like three to five times during the average work day.

At just after seven o'clock, when I should be Salsa dancing myself to svelte, I'm instead staring despondently into the abyss that is my closet and wishing Angela wasn't so fanatic about her workout regime. She'd know what to do. When I called to tell her I was blowing her off in favor of a wardrobe-induced panic attack, she graciously offered her own closet, which undoubtedly houses no less than a dozen perfect outfits for this occasion.

Since I don't think it would be wise to try to shoehorn my size six form into any of the items from her size two collection, I'm stuck with what little I already own, and with Kevin, who's not really helping matters.

"Maybe you should go shopping," he says, shaking his head. He holds up a little black dress that would work except that the zipper is torn. New resolution: Fix things when they break. Do not bury them in the back of the closet and hope that tiny tailor gnomes will repair them.

"I can't afford to go shopping!" I wail. "I have to pay the whole rent on this place, starting on the first, remember?"

"Right, there's that," Kevin agrees. "Unless Prince Charming wants to become your new sugar daddy. God knows he's old enough."

I make a face. "He's not going to be any such thing. He's merely a pleasant distraction."

"Yeah, right," Kevin shrugs. He reaches into the closet and pulls out a Pucci scarf, which he immediately dismisses as too funky for a first date with a "grown up man" who's been admiring me in dull business wear. He wraps it onto his head, bandana-style and gets back to work, muttering that all I have is suits. Even though the blue tones bring out his eyes, he looks ridiculous.

I shake my head, and wonder, silently, whether Brendan might have been right about Kevin. I know better than to make any remarks in this vein. It would either irritate him, or set off an explanation I've heard dozens of times before. Kevin is in tune with women because his dad was a total check-out who worked a hundred hours a week, and his mom practically raised Kevin and his sisters alone, and their house was always full of her lady friends. Antics like this one with my scarf are performed to make me laugh, not speculate on his sexual proclivities. Instead I ask, "What are you doing home so early anyway?"

"The Councilman took the night off. It's his anniversary."

I look at him quizzically. Kevin never gives his candidates time off after Labor Day of an election year.

"I know, I know, I'm getting soft in my old age." He adjusts the scarf so more of his sandy-colored hair peeks out. "But I told him tonight is absolutely it."

"You have a rare night off and you're spending it with me, going through clothes?"

"I'm not that pathetic. Maybe if we get done here, I can go for a run. Campaigns make you paunchy." He pats his nonexistent stomach.

"Hardly," I say, even though I know he's fishing for a compliment. "And I still think you're pathetic."

"That's because I didn't tell you that after my run, I'm going out with Lily." He folds his arms across his chest, in a classic male gesture of self-satisfaction.

"Who's Lily?"

"I'm surprised Angela didn't tell you. She's a model. From Slovenia. Or maybe it's Slovakia."

"You know, they're totally different countries."

"I have it written down in my diary." Kevin spent two years in London and picked up the lingo. He likes saying "diary" and "shed-yool."

I hold up a pink sundress that would be perfect. That is, it would be perfect if it were a weekend in July and we were going for sunset drinks in the Hamptons. Kevin grimaces. "It's not saying Nobu to me."

"I know. I'm getting desperate." I study the feasibility of fixing my little black dress with safety pins and change the subject. "Why is a model going out with you?"

"Because Angela told her she should," he grins. "And who knows? Maybe I'll get lucky before she discovers I'm absolutely worthless, in terms of advancing her career."

At least he's honest.

"This is never going to work," I groan. I drop the reliable little black dress in a little black heap on my bed and dive back into the closet. I'm not sure what I expect to find in there.

Kevin picks up the dress and asks, "Just a zipper, right?"

"Yeah. What? Are you going to tell me you secretly minored in home ec or something?"

"I wish," he laughs. "I would have been a hit with all the ladies in the class. But no, I was thinking the dry cleaner across the street could fix this."

I consult my watch. "They close in seven minutes."

Kevin grabs the dress and runs for my door, calling behind him, "The girl in there *loves* me. I'll be back."

He's got one foot out of my bedroom when he remembers the scarf. He turns, whips it off his head and tosses it to me. As I re-direct my focus to my shoe options, I wonder what I'd do without him.

FOUR

In the cab on the way to Nobu I start to second guess myself. I do this even though I know I look good tonight, and that dating is good for me. I'm also fairly sure I'd be a moron if I didn't jump at the chance to go out with a hot, successful man who fell into my lap, but I'm anxious at the same time. What if he's a freak? Or worse, what's if he's perfect, but decides I'm a freak before we finish our first drink? I take a deep breath and remind myself this date is a healthy exercise, a life-affirming leap of faith.

Or maybe I'm getting ahead of myself.

Maybe it's too soon to plunge into something as rash as a last-minute dinner with an older stranger. It would seem more rational to ease into the choppy singles scene waters by consenting to a safe fix up with a friend of a friend, or something in that vein. As much as I want to get back out there, part of me is paralyzed by the prospect of failure at dating. I already feel like I'm under-achieving at work, compared to many of my friends, so why should I risk turning my love life into even more of a fiasco? Not that it would be easy to out do myself in that department. Although, as my mother loves to remind me, and my voice mail when I can't face her chatter, I'm not getting any younger. It really smarted when she tried to re-enroll me in Internet dating last week. The whole idea of meeting men on the web sort of skeeves me after my first failed foray.

But then, it's not like I've suffered one of those normal break-ups, where they say you need a month to heal for every year of the relationship. In the case of Brendan and me, I have a sense of absolute finality most girls take ages to reach, because he's not interested in women. Therefore, no matter what else happens, we will never, ever reconcile. Angela says at least I'm inoculated against wondering whether he was the one who got away.

The cab stops and goes with the traffic that never seems to ease up these days. I feel like I should be eagerly anticipating a first-rate dinner with my handsome stranger, but instead my mind goes where it's gone countless times over recent months, to another fancy dinner.

Brendan didn't have the nerve to tell me in the privacy of our own home. So he took me to the Blue Water Grill. I was expecting a romantic evening to decompress from the wedding insanity that had taken over my life. Seriously, no human being should ever have to lose sleep over the ribbons on her bridesmaids' bouquets, an over-budget ice sculpture, or the fact that her mother and future mother-in-law have a serious difference of opinion regarding the choice of font for her ceremony programs. Our upcoming wedding, a six-figure extravaganza largely furnished by his parents but micro-managed by my mother, had taken on a life of its own. I couldn't entirely disagree when Brendan called it all ridiculous.

He waited until the waiter cleared the salads and took our entrée orders to tell me. Then he just blurted it out. "You're going to hate me, Zoë. But not as much as I would hate myself if I didn't tell you."

I remember stopping my wine glass in mid-air while my mind raced to figure out what he could possibly have to say that would make me hate him. Things had hardly ever been passionate between us. No super high highs and no dreadfully low lows. We were never one of those gooey engaged couples who spent hours staring into each others' eyes. Instead, Brendan and I had a solid friendship, dating back to our sophomore year at Princeton, which I had long since convinced myself would serve as the foundation of a long, contented life. I never imagined our future would look much different from our present. So what could it be? My brain jogged to unsavory places. Maybe he had herpes. Maybe his law firm wanted him to transfer to the west coast. Maybe, due to a premature midlife crisis, he wanted to quit the law firm altogether and sell T shirts to tourists in the park.

Before I could form any of the questions my brain wanted to ask, he just said it. "I can't pretend anymore. I love you, Zoë, but I can't marry you. We need to call off the wedding."

I sat in stunned silence for a second, then used a monumental effort of will to keep from tossing my Brunello into his face. I felt my face crumple and I started to cry.

"It's not what you think," he said, and reached a hand across the table to rest on mine. I brushed him away. "Zoë, if I wanted to marry any girl, it would be you."

"So you're having an early mid-life crisis? Or is it regular, plain old cold feet?" It came out louder than I intended. The diners at the next table turned to look.

"Keep your voice down," Brendan hissed. "It has nothing to do with a mid-life crisis, and everything to do with having the maturity to be honest with myself. Zoë, I'm gay."

"Excuse me?" I heard what he said but couldn't process it.

"I think you heard me."

"And you've just figured this out now? After almost ten years together? After a year-long engagement, two engagement parties, an announcement in the *Times*, hundreds of hours wasted on wedding planning, and RSVP cards trickling in every day, from as far away as Europe and South Africa? *Now* you decide you're *gay*?"

I remember thinking it was preposterous. Inconceivable. Unreal.

"I've known for years. I thought I couldn't do it to my family. I thought I could make it work with you, and maybe if we had a family of our own, playing it straight could make sense."

"And did you ever, for one second, stop and consider what all this would mean for me? That my marriage to my alleged best friend would be a sham? That the person I thought I could trust more than anyone else in the world not only lied about who he is, but didn't contemplate my feelings at all?" I paused for air and forced myself to lower my voice a notch. "Wow. I have no idea what to say, Brendan."

"How about you understand?"

I remember I glared at him and forced myself to keep breathing until he came out with, "Think how hard this is for me. And at least now we won't ever get divorced."

The Brunello flew into his eyes and I ran out of the restaurant, burning with embarrassment over making a scene, humiliated beyond what I ever imagined possible, and terrified of facing my friends and family with the news that I must be the stupidest woman in the Tri-State area, if not on the entire Eastern Seaboard, if I could be with a guy for a decade and fail to deduce his sexual orientation.

My mother denies it, because she doesn't want to support the idea that her daughter's happiness should be tied up with a fairy tale wedding, but my brother tells me *she's* been seeing a therapist regularly ever since *my* break up. I think at times she felt more invested in planning the reception that I did, and I think she nearly died of shame when she had to tell her friends the news. My father reacted in a more circumspect manner, reassured me it was better to know, and never brought up the topic again. My friends all claimed to be as stunned as I was, though I suspect Kevin and Angela may have played up their shock so as not to rub more salt in my open sore.

I'm so lost in my thoughts and horrified at the still fresh hurt that I'm not sure how long it takes me to realize that we've arrived at the restaurant. The cabbie is tapping on the partition, understandably urging me to pay the fare and vacate the back seat so he can pick up a new customer. I apologize, tip him well, and find myself on the sidewalk. Good. Eight minutes early. Time to walk around the block and clear my head. I will not allow my bad break-up to derail my first promising post-engagement date before it starts.

The over-plucked, under-nourished hostess peers down at me from her elevated stand for a good half minute before speaking, and during those thirty seconds, I loathe myself for allowing her to make me feel inadequate. At least I'm in respectable company. Even Angela agrees that a single sniff of disapproval from one of these slinky, black-clad creatures is enough to send almost anyone running to an emergency session with a therapist. Or at least an expensive wardrobe consultation. Thanks to Kevin's sprint to his love-struck laundress, my trusty almost-too-much-but-not-quite chandelier earrings, and the sample size Sergio Rossi's Angela sent my way last week, I have nothing to apologize for. I am the fashion equal of every person here. Amazingly, the hostess's studied frown breaks into a smile when I say I'm meeting Oscar Thornton.

She steps down from her pedestal and leads me through the restaurant to one of the best tables. That must be a good sign. A total psychopath *probably* wouldn't have favored patron status at an upscale restaurant. But it's not impossible. Why did I ever agree to dinner? Does he do this all the time—ask out women he's never met and then take them on expensive dates?

He gets up when he sees me approach and I freeze. What's the etiquette here? Will he go in for the air kiss? Should I stick out my hand and introduce myself? I wish the hostess would stop hovering. For some illogical reason I don't want her to know we're meeting for the first time.

Before we make it across the room, it becomes obvious that practically every woman in the place is watching Oscar Thornton. And with good reason. He's even better looking up close than from across Madison Avenue, and taller. He's broad-shouldered, high-cheek-boned, and he's been blessed with the most soulful brown eyes I've ever seen in my life. He's wearing his suit with a pink, French-cuffed shirt underneath, but no tie. And he's definitely one of those men who can carry off pink. A forty-something blonde woman rolls her eyes when she sees me coming and whispers something to her friend, who actually points at me. For a second I have the sickening feeling that my dress is caught up in my underwear. But that's not it. I can feel the fabric, swishing reassuringly against my legs.

Oscar goes in for the air kiss. I turn my head too fast and he gets my ear. We sit down and wait for the hostess to retreat before I say, "I'm Zoë, by the way."

"Oscar," he says. "But you already knew that. Can I offer you a drink?"

I glance down at his dirty martini, and when the waiter arrives I order a pomegranate one, which should take the edge off my nerves, but which I resolve to nurse. There's no word that fairly describes this Oscar other than "delicious," and I am not about to screw things up by becoming a drunken fool. I search the recesses of my brain for a safe topic. I'm guessing he does not need to hear about my recent humiliation at the hands of my former fiancé.

Fortunately, he speaks first. "So tell me, what goes on over there across the street? I've decided you're either in phone sales, or you're some kind of consultant. Which is it?"

"Well, I suppose both would be accurate. I work for C.R. Broadwick and Associates. We're headhunters. But you really don't know where I work? You didn't check before you sent the flowers? Which are gorgeous by the way, thank you again." If he asks what happened to them, I'll have to tell him I took them home, for fear of inappropriate *feng shui*.

"You're very welcome. So do you like hunting heads?"

Less than five minutes into our first date, and he cuts right to the million-dollar question, which my parents ask me at least every other time we speak. "Not many kids dream of growing up to work in legal search."

"Right. Most toy stores don't carry junior headhunter kits." He nods with flirtatious pretend seriousness.

"I worked in a gallery out of college, which loses its glamour quickly, unless you're lucky enough to own your own place. And the *Wall Street Journal* isn't exactly full of ads that say, 'Art History Majors Wanted.' The money in head hunting is good, and once in a while, I can really help make someone's career, which is nice." I realize I'm on the verge of answering a short answer question with an essay response and stop myself.

"Very few people *love* their work. If you're happy sixty or seventy per cent of the time, you're ahead of the game. Besides, you're young. You've got time to change careers four times, if that's what you decide you want to do."

I listen to his advice, thinking he's so handsome and confident that I could jump him right here. Though he must not feel the same way if he's giving me a speech I could get from a career coach. But I'm not sure where else to steer the conversation so I flip my hair flirtatiously and decide to stick with our safe and serious topic. "So how about you? Do you love your job?"

"Yeah, I suppose I'm part of the lucky minority."

After that, we talk about his job, and I learn that he's the point man for at least half a dozen accounts, and all of those are for household-name products. I'm starting to feel a little professionally inadequate next to him, when he changes the subject and asks where I'm from. Good. More safe territory.

He orders us another round of martinis but makes no move to consult the menu. I realize I've finished my drink and give him the short version of my life. He listens raptly, as if it's the most fascinating thing he's ever heard, when I tell him I grew up in Wellesley, right outside Boston, which was an idyllic existence, featuring excellent public schools, private tennis lessons and long weekends in Stowe and Wellfleet. Then I landed at Princeton and encountered a whole different level of privilege: the kind of kids who use "summer" as a verb, and do so on the Riviera.

My parents now "winter" in Florida, where they can play golf, drive below the speed limit and eat dinner before six. I neglect to mention that my father, a retired math professor, has become obsessed with paint-by-number kits. Every wall in both parental homes is covered in paint-by-number reproductions of the great masterpieces of classical art. Or that my mother gets hippy-dippier as the years go by, but limits her eco-consciousness to certain aspects of her life. She wears only organic clothing and grows her own herbs. But she still gets her nails done every Thursday and insists on driving her gas-guzzling BMW six short blocks to her gym. I do mention that I have an older brother. He's married with kids in San Francisco. I stop myself before blurting that he's probably the most normal member of the Clark clan.

The drinks arrive. "So that's the sixty-second scoop on me. How about you?"

Oscar runs his fingers through his hair and leans towards me over the table. "I'm afraid there's not much to tell. I was born in Utah, but I went to Columbia and haven't dreamed of leaving Manhattan since. I'm forty-two years old, and my wife left me a year ago for a French film producer she met at a charity benefit. Maybe I should have seen it coming. They had this whole Euro connection thing going on."

I must look at him like he's lost me, because he explains, "Olivia was from Andorra. We met at a coffee cart on 53rd Street." He pauses to smile at this memory. "She was on vacation with some girlfriends, but she canceled her ticket home after we spent the better part of a week together. We got married, and while she never complained about it, she never really took to living on our side of the pond. I suppose we'd been growing apart for some time, but it still smarted. Anyway, I came home early from a business trip to London, to surprise her for our anniversary, and the housekeeper told me my wife had gone out. She wouldn't look at me when she said it, and I knew something wasn't right. When she came home the next morning and saw me there, she didn't even try to deny it. She just went to her lingerie drawer and pulled out divorce papers."

He pauses and looks directly in my eyes. I have no idea what to say. If Angela told me some guy shared all that on a first date, I'd say, way too much information. The little voice in the rational side of my brain is yowling "red flag!" at the top of her little imaginary lungs, but I'm blinded by Oscar's looks. Every woman in this restaurant wants my date. I can't toss him aside because he might be on the rebound like me. Or sensitive. Which, if I recall correctly, used to be considered a good thing in a man, at least until the early 1990's or so. I take a huge gulp of my second pomegranate martini and mumble, "I'm sorry."

He brightens. "I believe everything in life happens for a reason, and I don't believe in looking back. But I do want to be upfront about my history. What about you, have you ever been married?"

"No."

"Ever come close?"

"You could say that."

The waiter reappears and provides me with a temporary stay, which is good, because I'm not eager to tell Oscar about Brendan. To an outsider, it might seem weird—no, not weird, *unfathomable*—that I knew a man for fourteen years and didn't surmise he was gay. I still feel like the biggest fool ever. In my defense, Brendan went to great lengths to hide the truth. I found a bottle of Viagra after he moved out. It had fallen behind the bathroom vanity, and in hindsight, explained a lot.

Oscar asks if he can order for us, which catches me off guard because no guy has ever asked me this before. He rattles off a list of requests, and selects a bottle of wine, which the waiter calls a highly discriminating choice. Any thoughts I had previously entertained about offering to pay my share vanish. The rent is more pressing than this stranger's opinion on my post-feminist manners.

The wine, on top of the cocktails, gives me the courage to ask Oscar if he ever asked out a complete stranger before.

"You're the first. And don't get creeped out. I just moved into that office a couple of weeks ago. Everyone's telling me it's time to get back in the saddle, but I spend so much time at work, and I can't bring myself to do Internet dating. So when I noticed you, you seemed so beautiful, and fresh, and *approachable*, that I decided to dip my toe in the water. I figured the worst that could happen would be for you to ignore me."

The little voice in my head squeals, "Line! Line!" but I silence it and smile back at him. The wine feels warm in my otherwise empty stomach and I'm getting lost in his gaze. The sushi arrives, not a moment too soon, and the wine keeps flowing. Another bottle appears and lubricates the conversation.

We actually have quite a bit of those first-date things in common. We both prefer dogs to cats, but neither of us has time for one.

It turns out Oscar's ex-wife now lives with his two ex-Labradoodles in Paris. In addition to both being dog-less dog lovers, we both like to ski, but neither of us gets to go very often. We're annoyed by SUV's, reality television, and clueless people who don't care what's happening in the world. By the time the waiter clears the plates, my first date jitters have developed into a full-blown crush. And he's getting cuter by the minute. Or maybe that's the wine.

We leave the restaurant a full four hours after we arrived. When he steers me out the door, his hand lingers on the small of my back. I expect him to hail a cab, but a black sedan pulls up. "Your chariot," he jokes, as he holds the door. He's so engaging, and gorgeous, that his hokey humor doesn't bother me at all. I slide into the back seat. "Where to?"

In a moment of insanity, I blurt Angela's address. I do this because Oscar seems so perfect. I want to remove the temptation to invite him upstairs and ruin the chance of something bigger, for one night of fun.

"You heard the lady," he says, and raises the privacy screen. He drapes his arm around me and before I fully process what's happening, we're kissing in the back of his limousine. It sure doesn't feel like he's out of practice. His hand rests on my knee before sliding up my inner thigh, and while the voice in my head is shrieking at me to push him away, my body over-rules it and I feel my legs open a little as he pulls his mouth away from mine to kiss my earlobes and neck. He pushes one of my spaghetti straps off my shoulder and his mouth moves down to my collarbone. The hand that's not on my thigh moves up my waist.

Fortunately we arrive at Angela's before my resolve crumbles completely. He walks me to the entrance and plants what feels a lot more like a third date kiss than a first date one on me. Angela's doorman, who has known me for three years, pretends to ignore the show and admits me without comment. I linger in her lobby until the black car disappears from view, then step back outside and hail myself a taxi. The doorman looks at me quizzically but shrugs, and within minutes I'm on my way home.

FIVE

I am so hung over I want to die. I am mortified that my brain, which feels so swollen it could burst through my skull, cannot recall the entire conversation from last night. My memory gap starts around the time the second bottle of wine arrived. I have no idea what we talked about after dinner, but at least I know for sure there was no conversation in the car. It's becoming more and more clear to me that I missed most of the decade wherein I was supposed to be learning the ropes of Manhattan dating protocol because I was with Brendan. Still, I'm pretty sure that drinking enough to lose parts of a first date can make the possibility of a second date somewhat remote. I hope I didn't make a fool of myself.

Both fortunately and unfortunately, my head hurts too much to obsess about how much I screwed up. I can kick myself later, after I guzzle a few liters of water and the Advil kicks in. I briefly fantasized about calling in sick when the alarm went off this morning, but I have three client meetings today. Besides, staying home wouldn't buy me a day of rest. Carol has her assistant call sick employees at various intervals throughout the day, to make sure they're home. She claims to have some "pressing work question," but it's always something that could wait. I make a mental note to cancel my landline, toss back as much water as I can stomach, and haul myself to the shower.

The subway ride is fifteen minutes of pure hell. My head feels like it's in a vice and someone's breakfast smells of onions. I make it to the office by ten after nine, and brace myself for the barrage of questions about my date with the mystery admirer from across the way.

I head straight for the kitchen, where I run into Marvin, who looks too traumatized to remember to ask about my love life. He's frantic, red-eyed, and generally looks like he's stuck his fingers into an electrical socket. "Someone stole our coffee maker!" he finally manages to splutter.

I don't immediately register what he's saying so he elaborates. "It was there last night, and now it's gone. I'm going to Starbucks. Do you want anything?"

I ask him to bring me the biggest coffee he can carry.

Carol struts off the elevator before Marvin can make it out the door. "Good morning, people!" she trills.

She sounds happy. Friday mornings she does yoga. It normally tempers her mood swings for an hour or two. She steers Marvin back towards the bullpen. "People, I have an announcement. Effective immediately, this office is detoxifying. No more coffee! We're all going to drink green tea, which will make us more alert, more productive, and therefore more wealthy."

She plucks a Starbucks cup from New Girl's desk with a gloved hand and deposits the almost-full beverage in the trash bin. New Girl stifles a whimper. Carol turns and retreats to her office, and her assistant starts distributing tea bags from a cardboard box. As soon as we hear Carol get on the phone, Marvin gives me a look and I get up and accompany him to the coffee shop.

Around ten, I receive an email from Oscar, which is odd, because I only gave him my phone number. He must have consulted our website.

"Zoë, I can't stop thinking about what a great time I had last night. You're amazing. Are you free on Saturday? I'd like to cook you dinner. Xoxo Oscar."

Wow. Maybe I'm not so bad at dating after all. Or maybe he was too buzzed to notice that I passed buzzed and rounded the turn into drunkenness shortly after the second martini rolled into the first bottle of wine. I email him back, thank him again for dinner, and tell him my boss reads my email so he should use my Gmail account.

Saturday. I have something Saturday, but in my post-debauched state, I can't remember what it might be. Besides, whatever it is, it can't be as important as a second date with the hottest, most sophisticated man who's ever taken an interest in me. And called me amazing.

Sadly, there's no time to think about the weekend now. I have a junior litigator coming in for a practice interview. We don't normally provide that service, but this poor kid gets loud hiccups whenever he's nervous. Carol says it's part of my job to de-sensitize him to the interview environment. Which is bullshit. We work for commissions. If any regular client kept striking out like this, Carol would say to write him off and tell him, gently, that there's nothing more we can do. But this kid isn't a regular client. A month ago, when Carol assigned me the file, she told me, "He's a V.I.P." When I asked her to please clarify, she got all giggly and told me, "Well, just between us girls, his father is a partner at Silverblum Gatz, and he thinks it's time Junior accomplished something for himself. So he's resolved not to get his son another job, unless he absolutely has to."

I thought that explained it, because everyone, even New Girl, knows Carol would love to get a Silverblum account. The prominent investment bank is one of the few feathers still missing from her professional cap. But there was more.

"And I want to get that dreamy Walker Smythe into bed," she confided. "So you had better do right by his son."

Powerful, wealthy men make my normally frosty boss frisky. So that's why I have blocked off two hours of time, for which I will not get paid, to grill Percival Rupert Lyman Smythe about his law school grades, his woefully limited work experience, and his 2nd Circuit clerkship.

Percival Rupert Lyman Smythe is late, because it's not the receptionist on the phone. It's Niles. His sperm was too cold to spin, or something like that, and they have to try again next month. But in happier news, he tells me that he thinks his meetings went well, and he's ready to fly to Cutler & Boone's LA office to try to seal the deal.

I take down the dates he can't travel due to Susie's ovulation calendar, and promise to set up the trip as soon as possible. If I can't get him out there within a week or two, chances are good the deal will die.

While I'm busy on the phone, Carol's assistant swoops down out of nowhere and confiscates my *venti* Americano-with-two-extra-shots with her manicured talons.

I dash out to buy a replacement and return in the same elevator as the Silverblum guy's kid. Safe. Carol's not quite crazy enough to seize my beverage in front of a client.

Unfortunately, she's hovering over my empty desk when I emerge from the conference room almost two hours later. She's reading my email. Not even surreptitiously. Marvin shoots me a sympathetic glance and mouths, "Lunch?" I mouth back, "Okay," but Carol has other plans for me.

"Zoë, *darling*, are you free for lunch?" she practically sings. Not a good sign. When she calls any member of her staff darling, it's because she wants something. Such as twelve hours of labor on a Saturday.

I can't lie. She's been in my Outlook and has no doubt seen I have nothing planned. Evidently she needs to buy a present for a friend and she wants to use me as a mannequin. Resistance is futile. If I tell her I can't do it now, I'll be out at Barney's with her at eight o'clock tonight. At least it looks like she took her pills today. Her make-up is beautifully blended.

Moments later, we're down on Madison, hailing a cab, which is ridiculous, because Carol has a driver. He parks a block away, because she thinks none of us know about him. Just like none of us are supposed to know she shops for herself during the work day. She has her chauffeur ferry her bags directly from Bergdorf's to her apartment so we won't see.

My throbbing head and I spend the better part of an hour modeling Hermes scarves for my boss and a saleswoman who makes me feel small and unworthy by glaring at my pinstriped pantsuit as if its inferior fibers might somehow contaminate the merchandise.

Her obvious disapproval scandalizes Carol, who barks that I should go to Saks over the weekend to buy something presentable and more age-appropriate. "Ann Taylor is only for girls in their twenties," she explains, in a tone that implies I'm an imbecile. I know better than to object that achieving the age of thirty-two does not automatically render me rich enough to buy couture.

After forty painful minutes, she loses interest in humiliating me and makes a decision. We leaves Hermes with her purchase carefully gift wrapped in their trademark orange, and she "treats" me to a lunch of a side order portion of seaweed salad, no dressing, served with a lengthy dissertation on her new detox diet. In addition to coffee, Carol has banned red meat, white carbs, blackened anything, and all "colored" booze. By this she means, champagne, okay, scotch, no good. She drones on for what feels like an eternity about how she's having her nutritionist and lifestyle guru come in to review the holiday party menu. She's sure she'd be millions richer if she'd only had the foresight to rid her body of poisonous elements years ago. *I'm* sure she'd be millions richer if she stopped hiring these quacks to micromanage her personal life through a series of fads, but she doesn't solicit my opinion, and I'm smart enough not to volunteer it. When she excuses herself to go to the ladies' room, I decide it's safe to whip out my phone and order a turkey club and fries to be delivered to me back at the office.

Kevin must hear me on the landing when I get in shortly before eight at night, because he appears at my door before I can even kick my shoes off. "You look like hell," he says with a grin. "Must have been a successful date."

"Almost too successful. He's too good to be true."

Kevin rolls his eyes. "The guy's in advertising. He makes good first impressions for a living, but I'm glad you had fun. It's about time you emerged from your cave. I bet you shaved your legs for the first time in a month."

"He'd have no reason to touch my legs on our first date," I say, with mock incredulity, though I don't share that my pulse quickens at the mere thought of Oscar's hands on me again.

"Liar," Kevin shrugs. He removes his suit jacket and heads for the couch, where he has to clear away a dozen old magazines to make room for himself. Kevin's right about my apartment. The hibernation and wallowing need to end. Brendan humiliated me, but it's time to get over it. People have suffered more dire embarrassments, although now that I think of it, I don't know anyone personally who has. But that doesn't matter. What matters is that it's high time to clear him and his aftermath from my life. Tomorrow I will start by shoveling out this apartment.

I head to the bedroom to change and yell through the door, "So how was Lily?"

"Nothing between the ears, but her legs go up to them."

"You slept with her, didn't you?" I say, as I emerge in yoga pants and my favorite, threadbare sweatshirt.

"Uh, yeah. Obviously. Never know when I'll get another chance with an international cover girl."

"You dirty dog," I settle on the other end of the couch and curl my legs underneath me. "Was it all you'd hoped for?"

"Nope. She was all bony and she just lay there, like a starfish," he deadpans, and waits for my response. I can't tell if he's joking. My fourteen-hour hangover has compromised my powers of perception.

He gives me a second to try to work it out before he says, "Actually she was totally above average."

I hit him with a sofa pillow as the door buzzes. Kevin goes to the intercom and admits Angela. She's dressed for a rare night at home, in a bright pink warm up suit with the words "Juicy Bling" emblazoned across her butt.

She dumps her gold Prada purse on the counter and demands to know why Kevin hasn't called Lily. "She called me seventeen times today, to ask why you hadn't rung. She said you said you'd call."

"She's boring," Kevin shrugs and reaches for the remote. He clicks straight over to CSPAN. I think he's one of four devoted viewers outside the nation's capital.

Angela tries a new tack. "Of course she's boring. Most models are. Even the bright ones learn early on that nobody wants to hear a human clothes hanger's opinion on anything. And Lily's image is freakishly clean, so I can't imagine it would hurt your career to be seen out on the town with her."

"Nor would it harm your career to keep one of the magazine's most frequently photographed faces happy." He gets up and heads towards the door. "To be continued. I have to write the Councilman's remarks for the municipal employees' union dinner. If your lights are still on when I'm done, I'll knock."

"He's pathetic," Angela says as soon as he's gone.

"How so?"

"He just is," she says, as if she doesn't feel like getting into it. She goes to the kitchen and opens a bottle of wine. Hangover or not, I feel like I've almost recovered sufficiently from last night's debauchery to face alcohol again. We order Chinese food and she masterfully extracts every detail of my date with Oscar while we wait for it to arrive. Or rather, every detail I can recall.

A weird pang of nostalgia grabs me as I start recounting my night. Angela spent hundreds of hours of our freshman year analyzing my life from her customary perch on our bunk beds. She'd arrived at school knowing a lot more about guys and sex than I did, and I eagerly gave her every detail of every encounter, in exchange for her sage advice. Which boiled down to: stop worrying about it, you silly, sheltered, wide-eyed suburban girl, and just do it with one of these boys already.

Angela seemed to be having so much fun, with her disproportionate share of attention from a parade of handsome upperclassmen, that I finally followed her advice right before winter break. I took the plunge with this guy I vaguely knew from my Shakespeare seminar, on his sofa, late one night after a party. It was over in under three minutes, and I ended up pinned under a passed out, drooling frat boy until dawn. When I got back to our room and told Angela it wasn't terrible, but I didn't understand what all the fuss was about, she smacked herself in the forehead and groaned that she didn't mean for me to give it away to someone half in the bag.

These days, she's refined her lines of questioning a bit. She needs to know which waiter we had, what sushi Oscar ordered, and what kind of suit he was wearing. This one I can't answer, but I assure her it looked expensive, probably Italian. She nods her conditional approval and moves on.

When I tell her that I had him drive me to her place, Angela laughs so hard that wine sprays out her nose. "Why on earth did you do that?"

"Because I didn't trust my willpower to hold out if I brought him here."

"Plus he'd never ask you out again if he saw this squalor."

"He already asked, so I'm safe for now."

Angela's face goes white when I gush that he must think I have long term potential, because he's cooking me dinner tomorrow night. "Have you lost your mind?"

She bolts off the couch and lunges towards the calendar in the kitchen. Tomorrow's the tenth. Oh. My. God. I completely forgot Carol's son's engagement party. At the Plaza. She rarely talks about her children, but still. How did it slip my mind entirely?

"And more importantly, did you drop your black dress off at the cleaner's this morning?"

Of course I didn't.

"So let me understand this correctly," Kevin says moments later, through a bad cellular connection. "You want me to cancel on an international super model so I can be your rent-a-date at Carol's spoiled brat's party."

"You said she was boring," I hiss into the phone.

"That's beside the point."

"You said you hadn't even decided whether to call Lily."

"I changed my mind."

Why does he need to be so exasperating? If he can't go, I'll just have to make peace with the idea of facing the festivities alone.

"Kevin, please?"

"I have to go. The Councilman's on my other line." He's gone before I can ask again.

"Don't worry," Angela says, as she tops off her wine. "Lily would never admit to being free on such short notice, and Kevin won't get a better offer. When he calls back, tell him Carol's hired Dave Matthews or the Red Hot Chili Peppers or something. You know, appeal to his sense of collegiate nostalgia."

"If he can't help me out it's not the end of the world. I can say hello to Carol, then hide in some corner and make snarky commentary with Marvin until it's kosher to leave. But what am I going to tell Oscar? I really like him. At least I think he's really hot." Angela laughs at my frankness. "And now I'm going to cancel our second date with less than twenty-four hours' notice. I might as well stand the guy up. And who knows when anyone nearly as interesting will fall in my lap again? I'm guessing sometime around never."

Before Angela can snap at me to stop whining, much less figure out what I should say to Oscar, we both freeze. Someone is banging on the door and we didn't buzz anyone up. Nobody has a key except the super, and he'd never show up and admit himself, unannounced. Nobody but Kevin ever knocks, and he's still across town. Angela lunges for my phone on the coffee table, presumably in case we need to dial 9-1-1.

I peer through the peephole with more apprehension than you'd expect. Brendan's distorted face blinks back at me through the cloudy lens. I undo the deadbolt and open the door, suddenly unsteady on my feet. "What are you doing here?" His surprise arrival makes me queasy and off-balance. I didn't expect seeing him would throw me so literally.

"My therapist says I need to atone," he says.

"So you're atoning by breaking and entering the building and scaring us half to death?" snaps Angela. "Ever hear of calling first? Or better yet, ever hear of the postal service? You could achieve atonement without intrusion, for the bargain price of forty-four cents."

"My therapist says it has to be face-to-face."

He says it so seriously that I start to wonder if he's on something. Brendan's lost weight. He was never heavy, but now he's downright gay-thin. His ribs show through the fabric of his clingy black T shirt, which reads, "D&G: Diet & Gym," and his jeans are skinnier than mine. His conservative barber shop haircut is gone, replaced by boyish tousled brown curls. My jaw drops when I notice that he's wearing a touch of eyeliner. I can't believe I slept with this man for years and didn't see it. Or frankly that nobody else saw it and had the decency to tip me off, either. Though I'm not sure how such a conversation would have gone. But I have to hand it to my ex-fiancé. He was smart enough to fool everyone.

Brendan blinks at me, waiting for some sign that he should continue.

I finally find my voice. "Maybe I'm not in the mood to listen to your apology." I back myself onto the sofa because I really feel as if I might faint. It kills me that he still invokes such visceral emotions.

"You can listen or not, but I have to say it," he says. He crosses the room and sits on the couch next to me. I try to slide away but there's no place to go. I'm out of upholstery.

Angela realizes that I'm not imminently kicking him out, so she excuses herself, "to powder her nose."

I top off my wine, and make a point of not offering him anything.

"You have every right to be angry," he says.

I cut him off. "Angry doesn't even begin to describe it. How about furious, and disgusted, and humiliated? How could you possibly wait so long to tell me? Our invitations were in the mail. We had the trip of a lifetime booked for our honeymoon. There's an unworn Carolina Herrera dress in my mother's closet that I can't look at without bursting into tears. Jesus, Brendan, you *must* have known years ago, and you let me go through with the whole charade." I feel tears starting to well and I fight them back down.

I'd never admit this to him, but part of my malfunction is anger with myself. I don't miss being with Brendan. For better or worse, our friendship ended the day of our break up. What I miss is being half of an established couple, the security of knowing I'll have someone to come home to. Someone who doesn't care if I wear yoga pants and a pony tail most of the time. I also miss knowing that I'll always have plans on Saturday night and New Year's Eve. And that I won't need to face family holidays alone—a poor, pitiable pot without a lid, as my mother would say.

Brendan interrupts my private moment of self-indulgent self-pity. "I'm sorry you're still so upset with me, and I hope time will heal some of your wounds." I can tell by his intonation that he's rehearsed this. Just like he used to rehearse his moot court arguments, and later, his answers to common interview questions, in front of our bathroom mirror, "But I need to tell you that I've been seeing Steve off and on, for the last three years."

"Steve? Who's Steve? Wait, my *hairdresser* Steve?"

Brendan nods uncomfortably.

"Steve, who spent two hours rehearsing my hair and veil so I could marry *you*? Steve whom I've seen *twice* since we called off our wedding?"

He shrugs. "You always knew *he* was gay."

I will myself not to throttle him. Instead I fly off the sofa and start to pace a tiny circle on the carpet, wringing my hands behind my back, to prevent myself from slapping his smug face.

"Until it came down to the wire, I thought I could do it. I thought I could play it straight, and keep Steve and that whole part of my life in a box off to the side, least until my parents died."

"You were planning to marry me until *your parents' death* did us part?"

"Steve was dead set against that and he got me to focus on what I'd be giving up. The holidays, the vacations, and the public recognition of our union." He actually gets misty-eyed saying this last part.

"Your union?" I repeat dumbly.

"We're making it official before the end of the year, and my shrink says I cannot walk down the aisle before I make things right with you."

He's getting married. It feels like he's punched me in the gut. Maybe I do miss him, after all.

"And this is what you call making things right," I splutter through my tears, which are suddenly coming fast and furious. "You show up without warning at *my* apartment and tell me how living a lie was unfair to *you*, without so much as one single thought about how it affected me!"

Brendan sighs loudly. "You know, I'm sorry you're hurting, but can't you see that ultimately, I'm doing you a favor? You're so blinded by your dashed fairy tale daydreams, that you can't see past the fact that our wedding would have been one awesome day kicking off a lifetime of frustration."

"That's not true!" As soon as I hear the words fly out of my mouth, I know that he's at least a little bit right. I can tell by his mingled expression of pity and dismay, that he knows it, too.

"I expected this kind of indignation from my parents, but you? Zoë, we were best friends for almost ten years. One best friend wouldn't want the other to be less than he could be, right?"

"One best friend shouldn't expect the other to overlook his lies. And it seems to me that you can't even call it a real friendship if one person is pretending to be someone he's not. You ruined my life!" I shriek. I know I sound hysterical, but I can't help myself. The emotional side of my brain has completely over run the rational side. "You took my twenties! I wasted my best years as your girlfriend, and I did it gladly, because I thought we were going to live happily ever after. And now I have to start all over, but not you. No, Brendan, you get to stay right on course because you lied to me, and kept a whole different life on the side. Which you now get to continue, uninterrupted, while you leave me to start completely over. You bastard! Get out!"

His face changes. It sort of darkens and clouds over, and I realize that, even though I feel I'm in the right, I've overstepped some serious boundary.

"Technically you can't kick me out. You never took my name off the lease," he says in a voice so calm that it takes every iota of mental fortitude to keep from smacking him.

"Just go. I'll deal with the lease tomorrow."

"Unfortunately, and this part I'm truly sorry about, but you know how my father was eyeing this place as an investment?"

I nod, speechless, but I think I know where he's going.

"As of Monday at noon, he'll be your new landlord, and he has it in his head that he should raise the rent."

The world starts to spin faster. "And you couldn't persuade him otherwise?" I know the answer is no. Brendan has never once in his life stood up to his parents. He's too aware of where his bread is buttered.

"You know I don't pick fights with my father lightly. And think about it, Zoë. You've saved money on rent for several years now, so if he does raise it, it's not like it's going to bankrupt you. And you'll get a better management company. They're already planning to re-caulk your shower..."

His voice trails off as he watches me realize that this speech was also rehearsed. Which somehow makes the fact that he couldn't be bothered to take issue with his dad on my behalf sting more. Especially since he claims he came here to atone or some such nonsense. I grab the arm of the couch for balance. Then it hits me. He's being this way, not out of concern for keeping the family peace, but because he's always been an over-indulged spoiled brat. Yes, he's cultured and worldly and smart, but he's also always had a hyper-developed sense of entitlement. Most of the time he hides it well, under his charm and polish, but ultimately, it's just the way he is, and there's nothing I can say that will change his self-absorbed view of the situation. He feels entitled to have his apology accepted, even if he's dovetailed it with bad news he did nothing to prevent.

Angela picks this moment to emerge from the bathroom. She glares at Brendan, her freshly made-up eyes narrow, and she says, icily, "Since when do you run around, storming into other people's apartments, making threats about caulking, and generally behaving like a ventriloquist's dummy for your parents? The Brendan *I've* known since we were nineteen would be embarrassed to be seen with you."

"And the Angela I knew at school wanted to write for the *New Yorker*, not try on shoes for a living, but I guess we've all changed since then," Brendan shoots back.

"Not nearly as much as you think," Angela snarls. "Because I won't have you threatening my best friend. So if you look the other way while Daddy Dearest gets cute with the rent, there'll be hell to pay."

Brendan regards her stonily, as if weighing whether she's capable of making his life somehow worse. Any residual empathy for my situation has disappeared from his face.

Angela says, "It would be tragic if Steven's salon was somehow connected, in the media, I mean, to an outbreak of lice. Or if the managing partner of your law firm read that you frequently spend three-hour lunches at that massage parlor near South Street Seaport. Don't try to deny it. Bryce, my copy editor, saw you there four times last month. I'm sure we could buy a photo from their security cameras."

"You miserable bitch," Brendan shouts, and starts to rush towards her. I finally find my tongue.

"Get out!" I shriek so loudly that I'm sure all my neighbors can hear. They're saying to themselves, "Don't worry. It's just that poor, sad girl whose fiancé left her at the altar for a hot hair stylist."

Brendan punches the air a few feet from Angela's face and mutters, "You're not worth it."

He starts to retreat, but as he reaches the doorway, he decides to take one last parting shot at me, in a saccharin voice. "You know, Zoë, anger is toxic. I just wanted us both to be happy, even though it was time to go our separate ways."

"GET OUT!"

The door closes and he's gone.

Angela touches my arm as I catch my breath and will myself not to cry. "Maybe it's a blessing in disguise," I splutter. "If the rent goes up, this place becomes a stretch even with a roommate. Maybe I'd be better off finding something else on my own."

"You're right, honey. We're all getting too old for roommates."

"I'll be happier starting fresh anyway," I say, with forced conviction. But my eyes roam the square footage, huge windows and great ceiling height I'll have to sacrifice and I'm not sure—at all—which is the better course.

SIX

"Okay. We're going to go in, have a glass of champagne, say hello to Carol, and get out in under two hours," I say, as Kevin and I emerge from the cab.

He came through, as usual, and showed up at Angela's at 6:30, looking almost too spiffy for a rent-a-date, his suit dressed up with a blue and green striped tie that makes the most of his eyes. To Angela and Kevin's great mirth, I've stashed my second date clothes here for later, because I'm wearing the black dress from Thursday night to Carol's party. After Brendan's intrusion, Angela argued I was entitled to a bit of retail therapy "someplace fun, like MaxMara," but ugly visions of my looming rent bill and ensuing eviction, initiated by my ex-fiancé and my soon-to-be ex-hairdresser, prevented me from indulging.

Kevin keeps saying he finds my latest encounter with Brendan unfathomable. As if that's supposed to make me feel better. Kevin had wanted to keep us both after we called off our engagement, but Brendan made it clear he was starting a new life, one that would include nobody from our old college circle. Which is fine with me, because it annoyed me in the days immediately post break up, when Kevin attempted to provide thorough reports on Brendan's activities. I was relieved when my ex-fiancé put a stop to that and demoted my closest pals to holiday-greetings-only status.

Carol must have four hundred guests at this party. I wonder how many of them are filler like me, people the couple barely know, whom she invited to shore up the appearance of social stature. Filler or not, I'm nervous about ducking out early, until Kevin reminds me that if we stick to the plan, by nine tonight, I'll be back across town, munching hors d'oeuvres with Oscar, and he'll be in his bed with Lily, munching something else altogether.

I grudgingly exchange my $200 check for a glass of champagne. When Carol invited the entire office, except for New Girl, to her son's engagement celebration, Marvin asked if we would be allowed to expense our gifts. His snarky inquiry unleashed a forty-five minute tirade about all Carol does for us and what wretched ingrates we all are. Which I took to mean, no.

An eighteen-piece orchestra is playing *It Had To Be You*, white gloved waiters are passing oysters, and Carol is holding court at the far end of the ballroom. She's sipping champagne, teetering unsteadily on five-inch heels, and she's corseted her size six self into a black dress that ought to be one size larger. Closer to us, a trim but bald man in his sixties and a blonde, who might not even be old enough to consume the wine she's drinking legally, preside over a rival receiving line. That must be Carol's ex. Kevin mumbles that he's never seen boobs that big in real life before. The happy couple are nowhere in evidence. I scan the room for Marvin, Sybil the receptionist, or even the Town Crier, but can't find them. Kevin tosses back his champagne, taps his watch, and says, "Let's get it over with."

We snake through the mob of guests, most of whom are jockeying for proximity to the oysters, and find ourselves at the back of a bottleneck of people waiting to see Carol. When it's finally my turn, I smile broadly and say, "Congratulations. You must be so proud," to which Carol responds, "Did you see his little whore? How dare he bring her here? On *my* night."

A surprisingly meek voice from her left says, "Mother, technically it's my night. Well, mine and Vanessa's. And Dad's been married to Carissa for over a year. It's not nice for you to call her a whore to your friends."

"Zoë isn't my friend," Carol snaps. "She works for me."

Carol's son looks at me apologetically and says, "Mother, I really think it's terrible that you shake down your staff for gifts. Vanessa and I are so blessed. We don't need to take from those who are less fortunate."

Before I can fully process his back-handed sympathies, Carol's focus lasers in on Kevin. "Who's this?" she demands.

I introduce Kevin and she nods approvingly. "So you're not the gay fiancé."

"No, ma'am." Kevin sticks out his hand. "Kevin O'Connor."

Carol places her hand in his as if she expects Kevin to kiss her rings. Her son turns his attention to an elderly relative, and makes no motion to introduce us to his bride or her parents, who are standing by her side, looking left out. I'm about to extricate Kevin and myself, when Carol barks, "Zoë!"

"Yes?"

"Do you think I'd look better with double-D breasts?" She's staring, or actually almost leering, at her ex-husband's latest wife. Carissa does look stunning in an emerald green gown with a plunging neckline that shows off the work of the city's finest plastics guy.

"Uh, no. I don't think it's the look you're going for," I stammer.

"How about you, Keith? What do you think?"

"Um, it's Kevin, not Keith, and I make it a rule never to comment on my friends' bosses' busts."

Carol half snorts, half grunts. Maybe we're about to be excused. More people have trickled in and joined the queue to pay homage to her. She doesn't need to waste any more time on insignificant me.

As if reading my mind, Carol smiles her best normally-reserved-for-clients smile and says, "Thank you for coming, Zoë. I'm *delighted* you could make it."

I tell her I wouldn't have dreamed of missing this party and start to back away. Carol turns to greet some octogenarian named Uncle Albert, but then stops and calls after me, "Oh, Zoë? Go and fetch me a martini, will you? And make sure they put two olives in it."

So much for her detox diet. Our missing coffee maker will undoubtedly materialize on Monday morning. I'm guessing her restrictive regimen was motivated solely by her desire to suck herself into that dress.

I walk past four cocktail waiters, stand in line at the bar for seven minutes, get Carol's drink, carry it to her and wait patiently for her to acknowledge me. She turns and frowns. "Honestly. Can't you do anything right? I said I wanted a cosmopolitan." She rolls her eyes and starts explaining to a man I recognize as the head of one of the city's biggest laws firms that it's simply impossible to get good help these days.

Which is a funny thing for the head of a staffing agency to tell a major client.

Fortunately one of the previously oblivious waiters overhears and assures Carol that he'll be back with her cosmo in a minute. Kevin and I begin pushing towards the exit. I notice Marvin across the room, holding a drink in each hand. I smile and wave but decide there's no time to engage in idle chatter. Oscar will be at Angela's to pick me up in half an hour. As we wait at the coat check outside the ballroom, I hear Carol's ex take the microphone. He's launching into a speech about being a single dad in the city. As Kevin helps me with my coat, Carol's ex says, "I'd like to thank Evan's mother for *co*-hosting this lovely affair, but most importantly, I want to acknowledge Carissa. Without her exquisite taste and tireless attention to detail, we wouldn't be here tonight."

Nervous laughter ensues. For a second I regret leaving before the real fireworks start.

I study myself in Angela's full-length mirror, wishing she was here with her expert eye. Of course, since she helped pick my outfit, it's safe to assume she'd approve. I'm wearing a short, but not too short, black suede skirt with tall boots and a pink sweater. Underneath I've got on the most threadbare, worn-out, washed a hundred times cotton underpants I could find in my bureau. Just a little added insurance so things won't get out of hand.

I don't think I look as if I'm trying too hard, but maybe it's not quite right. Her cats, Ernest and Algernon, watch with amusement as I pull the ensemble off for the third time and change into black pants and a shimmery gold top. I almost fall over, trying to trade my boots for delicate stilettos without sitting, and turn in the mirror again. Algernon yawns sarcastically. I decide to go with the skirt, and consult my watch. Almost 8:45. I need to get downstairs before the doorman spills the news that I am only pretending to live here. I touch up my lipstick and rub myself down with one of many prominently positioned lint rollers. Angela once told me she goes through three a week. I guess that's what she gets for being a couture maven with felines.

When I emerge from the elevators, Oscar is approaching the door looking relaxed and gorgeous in a roll neck sweater, black corduroys and a Barbour coat. Perfect timing. He gives me a chaste peck on the cheek. "You look beautiful."

"Thanks. You don't look so bad yourself." I cringe at how hokey I sound.

He holds the door of a double-parked Mercedes convertible for me. I suppose his driver gets the weekend off.

"You know, you didn't have to come pick me up. You could've given me your address."

"Maybe I'm old fashioned, but I think if I ask a woman out, I should go pick her up. Especially on a Saturday night." He smiles broadly. And sincerely. The skin around his eyes crinkles.

As he starts the engine, I realize I'm more nervous now than I was the other night at Nobu. Maybe because I had such low expectations for that date. Seriously. Things like that never work out in real life. But here we are, embarking on date number two, and I might really like him. Right. It's probably too soon to decide that. At the minimum, I'm incredibly attracted to him.

Desperate not to let my nerves tie my tongue, I ask the first question that pops into my mind. "So, where do you live?"

"Central Park West."

While I'm not surprised, I can't help feeling slightly intimidated. It's more than likely his building makes Angela's Gramercy digs look common, even with her key to the Park. Thank God I didn't give him my actual address the other night.

Traffic's light, even for a Saturday night. Oscar tells me he went into the office this morning, and then went for a long run before he started messing around in the kitchen. He's explaining how busy things are at work lately, but I'm too busy trying to find some flaw with him to listen. He's successful. And gorgeous. And gentlemanly. And he works out and cooks and drives a Mercedes. He is too good to be true.

I can't stop my jaw from dropping when he pulls up in front of the Beresford, which even the most jaded New Yorker would have to admit is an imposing structure. "You live here?" I stammer, as a doorman opens my door and extends a hand to help me out of the car.

"I bought here recently and got a great deal on the place."

"My boss lives here."

"Really? Which unit?"

"I'm not sure."

I've never been inside Carol's apartment, but everyone knows she lives at 211 Central Park West. When she brings it up, Marvin always makes a face and whispers, "She may live in the Beresford, but she's on a low floor."

Oscar says, "I'll have to look for the famous Carol Broadwick at the next owners' meeting." He hands the keys to the doorman, who apparently does double duty as a valet, and we step into the immaculately preserved lobby that's greeted the building's visitors since the end of the roaring twenties.

Dragon-crested elevator doors slide open to admit us, and I wonder whether I should switch from headhunting to advertising. If Oscar, at the tender age of forty-two, can live like this he must be doing something right. And my background in art history would lend itself to the ad business, right? Maybe that's a stretch. He presses the button for the 20th floor. Two down from the penthouse. Definitely not a low floor.

I'm somewhat relieved when the elevators deposit us in a common hallway and not inside his apartment. Not that his apartment isn't intimidating. He's obviously wealthy enough that he doesn't consider a cavernous foyer in Manhattan to be wasteful. He takes my coat and hangs it up in a hallway closet that's three times larger than the one in my bedroom. He's got an amazing, postcard-worthy view of Central Park through huge glass doors that open onto a private terrace. The living room boasts a real stone fireplace. The kitchen has obviously been redone recently, with black granite everywhere. A small glass door on the far end allows a glimpse of a brick wine cellar. The kitchen opens to a formal dining room with more doors onto the terrace. I'm dazzled. I can't help it. I wonder if it's wrong to lust after a man for his real estate.

It can't be *that* wrong. This is New York, after all.

"What a fantastic place. Your view. It's amazing. No, it's *enchanting*." I stop myself from gushing further.

"It looks even more fantastic with you in it." He smiles broadly at me. "Seriously though, I'm partial to it myself. I wish I had more time to spend here. How about a glass of wine?"

I follow him to the kitchen and watch as he retrieves a bottle from the wine cellar. I don't recognize the label, as I'm sure it's not a selection frequently poured by the glass, but I see it's fifteen years old.

He hands me a glass and raises his. "To an utterly *enchanting* evening."

"Don't be mean," I say, with mock indignation, but he's smiling and I am, too. He produces a remote control from one of the drawers and jazz floods the kitchen from surround sound speakers. He adjusts the volume to a background noise level. Maybe my radar should start bleeping trying-too-hard, but because I've never dated a real *grown up* before, I give him a pass. Maybe this is what grown ups do on dates. Not eat in front of the television, like Brendan and I used to do all the time.

For the next hour I sip my wine and pick at a selection of fancy cheeses while Oscar rolls up his sleeves, chats with me about his work and whips up a three-course meal. He's almost too comfortable, like this is date twelve and not date two. I, on the other hand, start to feel self-conscious, perched on a stool watching him work. And I start to panic silently as soon as I let myself wonder how on earth I can recip-rocate. Macaroni and cheese, even if it's my mother's recipe and not from a box, in my shabby kitchen circa 1979 with its view of a dirty brick wall, won't exactly measure up. And then I start to worry about other things outside my control, such as what I'll say if I run into Car-ol in the elevator on the way out of here tonight.

He waves off my offers to help (I may not be a culinary vision-ary, but I could certainly produce a salad) and periodically pauses to top off my wine. I pace myself. He's barely touched his glass, because he's busy with the food. He sets two places across from each other at the breakfast bar. I notice that he sets fish knives. I've never seen those outside of a restaurant. He uses another remote control to dim the lights. He lights a candle and says, "Let's eat in here, if that's alright with you. My dining room feels too stuffy." He ladles out two bowls of lobster bisque and watches while I taste it.

"Your talents are wasted in advertising. You should have a restaurant."

"I'm not interested in working nights, but thank you." He tastes his creation and looks up at me so intently that I start to feel a little uncomfortable in my skin. It's sad to admit, but nobody has ever gazed at me with that kind of overt lust. I don't know how to react, but succumbing to my urge to say that I really, *really* want him would be a significant mistake. Though it could lead to an unreal night.

I wimp out and make PG conversation. "Where did you learn to cook like this?"

"I'm self-taught. One night sometime midway through business school I just got sick of eating pizza and frozen dinners. So I started buying cook books. Once I realized I had a knack for the kitchen, I started tweaking some of the recipes and making them my own. I love to eat and it's the only hobby I can fit into my professional life, unless you count exercise. Pretty sad, right?"

No, it's pretty amazing. "It would be sadder for you to serve your dates Ramen noodles or Spaghetti-O's," I say, with a big smile.

He makes a face like the thought makes him gag. I take another spoonful of the to-die-for bisque. No canned goods here. We eat in silence for a moment.

"Can I ask you something?" He doesn't wait for me to respond. "The other night you said you haven't been married, but you came close. What was that about?"

I knew that sooner or later he'd ask. I don't know many divorced people, but the ones I do know seem to relish the opportunity to delve into other people's romantic misfortunes. I try to think of a positive way to couch my recent history.

"This soup really is great," I repeat.

"Out with it!" he commands with a smile. "It can't be any worse than what I told you on our first date, and you came back for more."

"There's not so much to tell. I met this guy during our sophomore year at Princeton. We hit it off, became completely inseparable, but didn't become an official item until our senior year. We both moved to New York after graduation. He went to Columbia Law School, and his father helped me get the gallery job I told you about the other night. Pretty soon after that, we broke up for a year and a half, but stayed friends."

I thought stupidly, that our enduring friendship was some kind of sign that we were meant for each other.

"You must have stayed more than friends if you almost married the guy," Oscar prods.

"Yeah, we got back together. By the time he graduated and started working at a law firm, we were more like roommates than anything else. But we got engaged anyway. My friends back home were starting to get married. Maybe I felt like I was on the train, and doing what I was supposed to be doing, or something like that. A few months ago we came to our senses and called it off."

I plow my soup around the bowl with the back of my spoon. Everything I just said is true. He doesn't need the gory details.

"I don't get it," Oscar says finally.

"Get what?"

"Get why you'd spend your twenties living with someone who was no more than a nice agreeable roommate. I'm a when-you-know-you-know kind of guy myself. If something feels good but not great, I move on."

I wince at this, and he rushes to add, "But that's just me. Anyway, if this ex of yours was so smart, why didn't he seal the deal sooner? Before you guys drifted apart?"

"Because he was gay."

It comes out before I can stop it. And maybe it's for the best. If I'm going to see where things go with Oscar, maybe I should try honesty. Perhaps not brutal honesty, but truthfulness anyway.

"It happens," he says, utterly nonplussed. "The head of the law firm Takamura Brothers uses for almost all its legal work came out of the closet last winter."

"I know him! He shocked everyone. His wife claims she had no idea. Even Carol Broadwick was stunned. Although in retrospect she says she should have seen it. He always sent such tasteful corporate gifts."

"Right. But the point is, here's a guy who's at the top of his professional game. He's got a wife and three kids, and he's the head of a huge firm with a very macho culture. One day he snaps. He can't live the lie anymore. So he explodes out of that closet and embraces an entirely new life."

"That's exactly what Brendan did, and I thought he was so callous about it. It was like he couldn't believe I hadn't always known. If I take a step back, I can see that he did what he had to do, but in the moment it was like being hit by a bus."

I wonder whether this constitutes excessive sharing on my part, but Oscar is looking straight into my eyes, listening with what appears to be genuine concern.

"At least you didn't marry the guy and have kids. Look on the bright side. You're still young."

"I wasted almost ten years on him. I'm furious with myself about it." I'm about to go into how heartsick and furious I felt when Brendan first dropped the bomb, but the little voice in my head is screeching at me to shut up and stop volunteering too much personal, emotionally explosive information. I manage to bite my tongue, and silently applaud myself for doing so.

Oscar waits a split second, to make sure I'm not adding anything else, before weighing in. "You said this Brendan person was your best friend for at least half the years you spent together. So it wasn't a total waste."

"Easy for you to say."

"I'm divorced, remember? Which tells you I've made my share of relationship mistakes. I'm glad you told me. It's nice to know where you're coming from. And this way I don't have to hear it from some wacky aunt of yours or something, months down the road."

Months down the road. Could he be thinking long term already? Do men do that? I thought that was a female urge. One that should be suppressed, at that. I should ask Kevin what this means.

Oscar clears the soup bowls, deposits them next to the sink and produces a platter with a whole roasted trout and an impressive assortment of vegetables from the oven. As he starts to filet and serve the fish, he asks, "How long have you lived over in Gramercy?"

I can't believe that's it. He doesn't think I'm some emotionally underdeveloped freak who couldn't deduce her former fiancé's proclivities. I also can't believe that I'm about to lie about my apartment, when I just came clean about Brendan.

"Not very long. Brendan and I lived in Murray Hill when we were together." Technically, at least, this is true, and I may be moving in with Angela and her cats if my rent increases thirty-six hours from now.

"I lived over there when I first came to the city from Colorado. Talk about culture shock. I'd been going to college, skiing a hundred days a year, and living with four guys in this huge rental house. Then I come to B-school and I move into a one bedroom, six flight walk up in Murray Hill, with incredibly loud radiators, that I shared with this classmate from Tokyo. We created a second bedroom by ripping the shelving out of the closet."

"Who got the real bedroom?"

"He did."

"Seems unfair." I smile, flip my hair and bat my eyelashes playfully. It's been way too long since I've flirted and it feels great. Especially since he's flirting back, smiling, looking away, mirroring my pose. I almost forget we were discussing his student digs.

"It worked out fine for me in the end. Seiji—that was his name— introduced me to his uncle Hideki Takamura during our second semester, and the rest, as they say, is history. I got my dream job and the first account I worked on was Rossignol. I thought I'd hit the lottery."

The oven timer goes off. "Fifteen minute warning on the soufflé," Oscar says, matter-of-factly. He reaches across the table to top off my wine.

Great. In order to reciprocate, I'm going to need to produce something far superior to slice and bake, or even cupcakes from the corner bakery.

I get out of my seat and offer to help but he waves me away. "I'll just put away the food. The maid will take care of the rest in the morning."

Of course she will.

"Does she normally work Sundays?" It seems cruel and unusual to me to have someone, who probably slaves all week for less than minimum wage, give up her weekend so that Oscar and I don't have to load our own dishes into the dishwasher.

"No, but I pay her double time if I ask her to come in on the weekend. She likes the extra money. She sends it home to Nicaragua. Have you been to Central America?" he asks, leaving no doubt that the subject of his overworked maid is closed.

"I went to Belize once." I don't add that I went there during the year Brendan and I were broken up, with this adrenalin junkie from Melbourne I'd met two weeks earlier, in a no name bar in the Village. His idea of a romantic getaway involved lots of drinking and diving, but not much in the way of spa treatments, gourmet meals or even hot showers. I stuck it out for three nights, because it was the first truly exciting sex I'd ever had in my life. By the fourth day I was so hung-over, un-shampooed, mosquito-bitten and just plain hungry, that I left him for a four star hotel ten miles and a world away. I charged four nights on a credit card. It was the best $2,600 I ever spent. We broke up for good on the plane ride home, then returned to my place for break up sex that made me cry after he left. But Oscar does *not* need to know any of this. He already knows more than I'd planned to divulge about the Brendan debacle.

So I say, "It was nice. Undeveloped, compared to much of the Caribbean."

He says something about being due for some time in the sun this winter, then goes to fetch the soufflé. My eyes bulge in amazement as I take the first bite.

Oscar smiles, clearly pleased with himself. "I had you pinned as a chocolate lover, and I'm happy to see I guessed right."

"You really made this yourself?" If I wasn't so wowed by him, I'd probably seize the opportunity to say something snarky, like most women love chocolate, so you just played the odds. But I feel no such destructive impulses.

"Yes, ma'am. And I can do even better. You'll have to stick around." Another big smile. His eyes sparkle and the skin around them crinkles again. I now understand how sharing a great meal can qualify as foreplay. I will never again mock those articles touting the merits of aphrodisiac menus.

I'm definitely planning to stick around.

We demolish the dessert. Oscar selects a new bottle of wine and we arrange ourselves on the leather couches in his living room. His free hand—the one not holding his drink—reaches across the space between us and touches my arm. Every tiny hair on my body stands on end as he starts to rub his hand down my forearm to my wrist and back up again. There's something skilled about the way he does it expertly, yet almost absent-mindedly at the same time.

He wordlessly takes my glass, sets it on the table, places his own next to it, cups my face between both his hands and leans in to kiss me. His lips barely graze mine and it takes an immense amount of maturity and self-control to keep from launching myself into his lap.

Evidently Oscar lacks comparable maturity and self-control. Before I have time to muster the will to re-commandeer control of the situation, his mouth is on mine and he's easing me back into the couch. I slide down along the slippery leather until I'm more reclined than seated. He kisses my neck and ears and something inside me stirs. I suddenly can't remember why I wasted the summer dejected over Brendan. Oscar moves my hair out of the way and his lips graze the back of my neck. His ex-wife must have been insane to leave him for another man.

He whispers, gruffly, in my ear, "Stay the night."

"Mmmm."

Oscar smells faintly of some cologne I can't name and his mouth tastes slightly of the dessert wine, which now sits abandoned on the coffee table. His hand runs down my side and finds its way under my sweater. He kisses me again, and when he pauses for air, he murmurs, "Let's move to the bedroom."

And while every fiber of my being is eagerly saying, "Yes!" I force myself to focus on my unfit-for-company underwear, or at least on the reason I wore it.

"Not tonight." I kiss him again because I don't want him to get the idea that I'm not interested. Because I *so* am. I'd love to tear off all our clothes and spend the night in his bed, but I'm not going to risk becoming a one-night stand. He's too extraordinary. If I want to keep him interested, Angela counseled, it's imperative to extricate myself from date number two with him wanting more.

SEVEN

When we pull up in front of Angela's building, her doorman is having a heated exchange with a very Nordic-looking man in tweed. He looks about forty years old, and his face has turned red with fury. When the doorman notices us, he asks his adversary to step aside. The Nordic man continues to freak out and steps closer to the doorman, so his nose is inches from the other man's face. He starts screaming, in a pronounced Germanic accent, that he has friends in Washington, and that he will have the doorman's pathetic self deported back to Puerto Rico if he doesn't let him pass at once. I see spit flying from his mouth, illuminated in the darkness by the portico lamps. The doorman stands his ground.

Oscar, who of course has no idea that the crazed Teuton must be my best friend's date, laughs out loud. "Puerto Rico is a U. S. territory. We don't deport there. Not that your doorman looks Puerto Rican to me."

"He's from Brazil, actually."

Oscar double parks and gets out to open the door for me. As if on cue, a window several flights up flies open. Angela leans out, waves her phone maniacally, and screams, "Reiner! If you don't stop disturbing the peace this instant, I'm calling the police."

At this, more lights come on from other units.

Reiner, who appears strangely encouraged by Angela's threat, abandons his quest to throttle the poor doorman and runs out onto the sidewalk so he can see her better.

"Please," he wails. "I just want to come up and talk."

"Forget it! It's over between us," she yells back. "Now please leave before I have to pour a pot of boiling water down on you."

"You've misunderstood, my darling!"

"No, I think you've misunderstood. If you don't leave, I'm calling the cops."

"You know I have diplomatic immunity," Reiner yells, more cold-ly. His imploring tone has vanished.

"That just means they can't charge you. I can still call," says An-gela, petulantly.

I start towards the entrance, but Oscar is rooted to the spot, watching the show. Angela raises her arms to shut the window, and as she does, she notices me standing there. "Zoë! I didn't expect to see you back before dawn. You must be Oscar! I'm Angela, and you really are cute. Sometimes Zoë's taste isn't so great."

Oh, God. She's drunk. Angela never slurs her speech, but you can tell she's had too much to drink when she says something unfiltered.

Oscar actually blushes. Angela leans out the window again. "Hey, Zoë, why don't you and your new lover come up for a nightcap?"

"He's not my new love –" I cut myself off and feel my face go red.

"Sounds great," Oscar yells with a smile, before I can decline on his behalf. He takes my arm and starts steering me towards the en-trance, giving wide berth to Reiner, who's now making motions that suggest he might be about to physically assault the poor doorman.

The doorman turns away from his tormentor to let us through. Reiner screams, "That bitch owes me. Do you have any idea what I've spent on her, tonight alone? Not to mention over the past three weeks. I demand to go upstairs."

His accent gets more and more pronounced as his cheeks get red-der and redder.

"I'm sorry, sir, but Ms. Mancuso made it clear that I am not to ad-mit you under any circumstances. Now I'm going to ask you one last time, to please leave. If you don't I'll have to call the police."

Reiner looks as if he's trying to formulate some persuasive retort, but his brain must come up empty because he lets out an alarming roar and charges at the doorman. Reiner's first punch knocks the old-er man off his feet. His uniform hat skips across the ground like a flat stone over water, before coming to rest on the pavement.

Oscar's there in a flash. He grabs Reiner with both hands and shoves him roughly against the wall. I watch in mingled horror and admiration as he closes his fingers around Reiner's throat, and when he speaks, his voice has lost every last bit of its earlier charm and ten-derness. "I'm not surprised the lady won't allow you upstairs."

Reiner makes a sucking sound, as if he's not getting enough air. The doorman clambers to his feet.

Oscar says, "Now you are going to get the hell out of here and never come back. Because if my friend over here sees you around again, he's going to call me. And I have friends who could care less about your diplomatic immunity. Do you understand?"

Reiner tries to nod, but Oscar's choke hold prevents his head from moving very much.

"I can't hear you."

"Yes." It's barely audible, but it must be good enough because Oscar releases his grip and a very disheveled Reiner slumps towards the pavement. He forces himself onto his feet, and makes his way across the street, his face burning with shame and anger.

We all watch him plod down the block, until he's out of sight. I stand rooted to the sidewalk, stunned at my date's amazing display of masculine prowess, and slightly startled by how fast he resorted to his fists. Even though this Reiner character clearly had it coming.

"Thanks," the doorman says to Oscar. "Even five years ago I would've turned him to pulp, but I'm getting old, and with all the panic about immigrant labor lately, I'm afraid to get physical, even with a prick like that." His eyes move from Oscar to me and he adds, "Sorry, miss. I meant to say even in self-defense."

"It's alright. I'm glad you're not hurt."

"Probably just bruised a bit. You enjoy your evening, miss."

Oscar asks, "Shall we go in? I'm ready for that drink."

As we pile into the elevator, he says, "It must be nice, having a friend in your building." He sounds cool and collected, not at all like a man who nearly beat someone to a pulp mere minutes ago.

"Mmm-hmm." I press the button for Angela's floor.

"Which floor is yours?"

"Not tonight," I say with the best smile I can muster. He pushes me against the wall and kisses me, hard. His little fight doesn't seem to have taken anything out of him. In fact, it seems to have revved him up. I'm glad we're not at my place. He might be hard to turn away under the circumstances.

Angela's waiting at the door, wearing a floor-length hand embroidered silk robe that one of her beaus brought her from a business trip to Asia. It's not like she's uncovered or anything, but I don't know anyone else who would receive her friend's date without getting dressed. She's also sporting the beginnings of a greenish mud mask on her chin.

"Is he gone?" she demands, before I can even make introductions. The treatment on her chin crackles.

"Yes, and I doubt he'll bother you again. Oscar Thornton." He sticks out his hand.

"My hero!" Angela's eyelashes flutter. "Angela Mancuso. Please, come in, have a drink."

To my surprise and relief, Oscar says, "Thank you, but I might beg off. I'm afraid I accepted your invitation under false pretenses. I thought if I got inside the building, Zoë might have me up to her place."

At this, Angela's eyebrows go up. Oscar leans down to kiss me on the cheek. "I'll call you in the morning," he says, and then to Angela, "It was nice to meet you."

"You, too, and thanks for your help with Reiner."

"My pleasure."

We watch him disappear back into the elevator. Angela hisses, "You still haven't told him you don't live here?"

I shrug. "What the hell happened tonight?"

"I need a drink before I launch into it."

I open the fourth bottle of wine I'm about to share tonight while Angela finishes slathering a new kelp-based anti-wrinkle potion on her face.

"That bastard slapped my ass."

I look up from the corkscrew, confused.

"Reiner ran into some prince from Monaco, and instead of introducing me, he told me they had to talk in private, and that I should run off and get him a fresh drink. And then he slapped my butt, as if I was some 1970's Bond girl, and he and the prince laughed like it was the funniest thing ever."

"Why didn't you slap him back?" It's unlike Angela to take anything less than fawning, doting treatment from her dates.

"All the decision makers from *Vogue* were in the room, at least half of the senior management team. I couldn't risk making a scene."

"I thought this baron or whoever was taking you to dinner."

"That was supposed to be later. We had to stop in at the Cavalli men's fragrance launch first."

"Why did you have to go to that? You do shoes."

"Zoë, dear, you're missing the point. Reiner humiliated me. In public. And I didn't know what to do, so I ran outside and got a cab home. I guess he charged out after me."

"Wait, when was that?"

She consults her watch. "Just over five hours ago."

"He was out there with your doorman for five hours?"

"No. There was a shift change. He only harassed Philippe for about three hours. Juan was down there before. But that's not the worst part. My boss called me twice. She's furious. Reiner's family owns, among many other things, a major cosmetics company that buys a lot of ad space in the magazine."

"I'm sorry. That sucks. But what does she expect you to do about it?"

"Her voice mails pretty much insist that I apologize to the insufferable twit."

At this point, I know I'm supposed to commiserate, and ask why she ever went out with Reiner, the Baron from a Mostly Insignificant Country, in the first place. But I'm starting to feel just a teeny bit peeved. Angela will obviously weather this crisis, and she hasn't even bothered to ask how my (much anticipated) big date was. Nor has she even said anything about Oscar. He may not have quite the social connections her suitors boast, but damn it, he is objectively hot. Not to mention he's the most exciting thing that's happened to me in ages, if not in my entire pathetic life. And he just kicked the insufferable twit's butt. He should rate a nod in this conversation.

EIGHT

On Monday morning, Carol shows up in pants. That can only mean one thing. We're about to spend half the day moving our desks. Carol thinks that we get lazy if we sit next to the same person for too long. She also likes to reward the most productive people by giving them views. Unless I can convince Niles Townsend to sign on the dotted line before lunch today, I'll be trading my window on Madison for an interior cubicle.

A year ago, this would have upset me, but now I know it's just part of the circle of life at Broadwick & Associates. Next time I have a good month, I'll be rewarded with better desk geography.

This particular morning, it seems that Carol wants to do more than switch our seats. Without even saying good morning, she barks at Marvin to help her move one of the five-foot grey dividers that encircles New Girl's desk. New Girl, detecting an unavoidable invasion to her personal space, does what any rookie would do, she grabs whatever she can hold, in this case, a purple mug full of pencils, a stapler, and a mouse pad, and cowers in the opposite corner of her cube.

"New Girl!" Carol barks. Her eye shadow is emerald green today, and it looks like it was applied by an eleven-year-old. "You are going to sit next to Marvin from now on. So you can listen to him and learn how to make money."

Marvin scowls at me. He hates training new people. He feels like he has to conform when there's a newbie hovering over his shoulder. No gin from the flask. No offering to fix up recruitment coordinators with eligible real-estate-owning bachelors, in exchange for interviews for his candidates. No making out with those same candidates in the smaller, windowless conference room. Marvin is pushing forty, and there's something about a young corporate associate, fresh from law school, in his first ever French-cuffed shirt, that he can't resist.

Carol grabs the monitor from New Girl's desk without unplugging it. Sparks fly from the surge protector and scatter on the carpet. The screen goes dark. Carol grunts as she carries the seven-year old relic and slams it down next to Marvin's sleek flat screen. The new people always get stuck with the oldest computers. She snaps at Marvin to make himself useful and switch the boxes, by which she means the actual computers, which reside under our desks. Marvin obediently drops to his hands and knees and begins sorting through the cables and wires.

I glance at my own computer screen. There's a new message from Oscar. I feel my face break into a smile before I even read the contents. "What the heck are you people doing?" he wants to know. I look for him in the window but he's not there.

Before I can sit down and write back, Carol appears behind me. "Zoë! Switch desks with the Town Crier."

I was afraid this would happen. Not only am I losing my view, which recently improved with the addition of Oscar, but now I'll sit closest to the Boss Lady. Which means she'll come tearing out of her office about seven hundred times a day, to "bounce things" off me. It doesn't sound so terrible, but truly, it is. Because if she flies out of her office to tell me something, and I happen to be away from my desk, something bad will happen. I'm not sure exactly what, but I know that when Marvin sat there, she actually gave him a twitch. It only went away after three months of therapy.

By eleven, my files, my hard drive, and I are installed at my new desk. I tell myself it could be worse. I still have a window, and I'm looking down on 64th Street, which, while not Madison Avenue, is far from the end of the earth. At quarter past, Carol calls me into her office.

"Close the door," she says, without looking up.

I obediently shut the door and sit in one of her visitor chairs. "How's Niles Townsend? Is he close?"

"I think so. If he doesn't get totally distracted by their IVF treatments, I think it'll be okay. And he'll want to move quickly, so you'd collect the fee by February, or March, at the latest." I'm always careful to refer to all commissions as Carol's, even though my contract entitles me to half the money I generate for the office.

"Well, let's hope his wife is preggers this month, and then we won't have to worry about it. You just let me know if you need help closing him."

"Of course." I'm starting to wonder what she really wants. It's unlike Carol to call one of us into her office to discuss anything but an imminent crisis.

Fortunately, Carol's not the type to let her audience sit in suspense for long.

"Zoë, I need you to do a very special assignment for me."

Not good. Last time I got a "special assignment," it involved looking for an intellectual property lawyer who spoke Hungarian, and who was willing to move to Los Angeles. They don't exactly grow on signposts in Lower Manhattan. Special assignments like that always take at least three or four full days, and they rarely result in a red cent of remuneration. But I'm not an idiot, so I say, "My pleasure."

"You're going to help Janice get into college."

"Excuse me?"

"My daughter needs to get into the Ivy League, and she doesn't have time to write the essays. Did you know Harvard requires *four* these days? In any event, you were an English major at Princeton, so I assume you can write serviceably well."

"My degree is actually in art history. I only minored in English."

"Whatever," Carol sniffs. She reaches into one of her drawers and produces an overflowing manila folder. She slams it on her desk and pushes it in my direction. A few stray sheets fall out in transit. I don't immediately reach for the file. Maybe I'm too dumb-founded.

"Oh, come on," Carol says. "It's not like you don't have your nights and weekends free, and I suspect you need the extra money. So I'm going to give you a thousand dollars for each school, and then an incentive payment of $5,000 for each acceptance, which I'm prepared to double if Janice is accepted, early-decision, to Yale."

"Carol, I don't know anything about your daughter. How do you expect..."

"My Janice is as qualified as any other Spence graduate!" Carol hisses. I strongly suspect she doesn't want this conversation overheard. "Like I said, her schedule is busier than that of most professionals."

She pauses and raises her eyebrows pointedly at me to make doubly sure I register the dig. I sometimes wonder whether she was born mean, or if some traumatizing event in her past soured her previously sunny disposition. "Everything you need to know about her grades and hobbies is already in the file."

I try a different tack. "I'm not sure it's in Janice's best interest to have someone she's never met write her applications."

"Fine. I'll make sure you have dinner with my daughter this week." Carol turns to the intercom on her phone. She jams down on the buttons with such force that she breaks a nail. Once she's done yowling in pain, she barks at her secretary to email her daughter's schedule for the next two weeks.

She disconnects and hands me a spreadsheet. I know before I look that it shows my commissions for the year. I had a great spring, but I've produced virtually nothing since the break-up. Even if the Niles deal closes, I won't see money until late in the first quarter of next year. And all I've got besides him are some junior litigators, who, if all goes well, will barely cover my expenses, and that's if I go extra-lean on Christmas.

"Unless accounting fucked up, you're not in a position to say no. I'm offering you practically free money, Zoë. Don't be an idiot."

Although I fervently wish I could point my finger at inept accounting, the chart doesn't lie. I wordlessly collect Janice's college application file and ask if there's anything else.

"No, that's all for now. Just make sure her applications are mailed with plenty of time to spare, and make me copies of everything. Oh, and obviously this will be our little secret. You don't want any of the rest of them getting jealous over your little side deal, right?"

She's back on the phone before I can get myself out of her office. Back in the bull pen, somebody's left a certified letter from an unfamiliar address in Lower Manhattan on my desk. I tear off the green label where Sybil signed, and rip the envelope open to reveal a one-page document called "Notice of Amendment to Lease Agreement." It explains, in two fairly short paragraphs that Landlord, meaning a trust controlled by my ex-fiancé's father, is exercising the right to amend our lease agreement, and this letter serves as my 30-day notice.

I skip over some legalese until I find the important part. As of December 1, my rent will increase to a nausea-inducing $3,800 per month. Furthermore, I am hereby instructed to transfer all utilities to my name before such date as they are no longer included in my rent.

And then there's the *coup de grace*: Landlord expects me to forward an additional $2,600 within ten days, to cover the "proportionate increase" to my security deposit and final month's rent.

The world starts spinning faster. Why is Brendan's father doing this to me? His family doesn't need the money. The only explanation I can think of, is that he's so upset about his son that he needs someone to blame. And I'm a convenient target. Whatever the rationale, the bottom line is that now I have to move. The increase is too steep, even if I could manage to wedge another person in there. I'm so wrapped up in my fury and indignation that I don't notice the Town Crier skulking behind me.

"Unpleasant news?" she asks with a malignant smile. Today, in addition to her not-long-enough pants, she's sporting a fuchsia scarf that only serves to accentuate her pasty complexion.

Instead of dignifying her question with an answer, I say, "Didn't you move on up to the Madison side of the office this morning?"

"I have important business to discuss with Carol," she sniffs, and clutches the folder she's carrying to her chest, as if I'm about to wrestle it from her grasp. "But what's in the letter?"

"None of your business," I snap. "And if you'll excuse me, I need to do some real work now." I'm too angry to remember that I have to be nice to my co-workers. It's actually in my inch-think employment contract. Something about not fighting, bickering, yelling, or even swearing. Which is a real hoot, coming from Carol.

The Town Crier skulks off, in the direction of her new desk, not Carol's office, as I put on my headset and dial my voice mail.

"Hi Zoë, this is Laura Reynolds. I just finished up at Freedman Zucker."

I hold my breath. Laura is a great candidate and she wants this job. The only problem is that she's about eight months pregnant, but the partners at Freedman swear they're okay with that. She says she wants to start work there after her maternity leave. And I'm not worried about Laura deciding to opt out in favor of raising her kids. She's got two degrees from Harvard, a D.C. Circuit clerkship, and four years in one of the toughest firms in the city under her belt. She wants to be a federal judge. She's what Carol would call a Grand Slam Home Run.

Except now she's telling me, or my voicemail, rather, that her water broke in Lawrence Zucker's office and she's calling from the hospital. Her contractions are "only" six minutes apart, so she wants to know if she should ring Mr. Zucker's secretary and offer to pay for his carpet to be cleaned. Because she really wants the job.

This last statement should be music to my ears, but I'm wondering if Lawrence Zucker, a 65-year-old stickler for propriety, will recover from the shock of having his floor drenched with amniotic fluid. Even if it's the amniotic fluid of a former Federal Circuit clerk, who might, for all we know, be about to give birth to a future Supreme Court Justice.

Carol says Lawrence Zucker used to boast that he never hired women. Even though he's come around a bit, he doesn't strike me as the kind of guy who wants "female issues" thrust upon him, particularly in the sanctuary of his private, professionally decorated office.

I groan and save the message. The next one brings brighter news. Jordan McWendell, a baby corporate associate, has accepted an offer he's been mulling for over a week. He told his firm today, and he starts in two weeks. Which means I'll get my share of the fee in about ten to twelve weeks. So that's good. Even though it's a small commission by the lofty standards of Broadwick & Associates, it'll put something on my blank spreadsheet for the first time in four months.

The rest of my messages involve more mundane matters. I try to call Laura Reynolds, but her cell phone is off. The nurses must have confiscated it. I leave a brief message, wishing her luck and telling her not to stress about the carpet.

Before I hang up, Carol is shrieking, "Zoë! ZOE!"

I dash into her office.

"Call Lawrence Zucker's office and tell them I'll pay to have the rug cleaned."

"Wow. I guess news travels fast." I know Carol makes it her business to be informed, but this time the grapevine seems to have moved at almost super-natural speed.

"Well, don't just stand there, for God's sake, Zoë, get on the fucking phone and fucking fix this."

For a second I feel a rush of misplaced gratitude. Carol's going out of her way to save my (to her) piddly little deal. But of course that's not it. She merely desires to stay in the good graces of the firm's senior management.

Lawrence Zucker's assistant thanks me profusely for the kind offer, before reminding me that, if the cleaning fails to meet Mr. Zucker's expectations, he will expect our firm to replace his irreplaceable, hand-knotted Persian area rug. Which has over a hundred knots per square inch, in case I didn't know.

She calls me back an hour later to say that regardless of the "little incident" this morning, the firm would like to extend Ms. Reynolds an offer. The hiring partner wants to know which room at which hospital she's in, so he can call her to discuss it. I think this is a lousy idea, seeing as Laura could be giving birth as we speak, but I don't dare say so. Let him call and leave a message.

I waste a half hour on hold with our preferred florist, attempting to send Laura and Jordan flowers from Broadwick & Associates. Carol likes to send flowers to our clients for babies, deaths, and successful placements. Then I throw myself into my work for the rest of the day.

Maybe it's fear of bankruptcy that motivates me, or maybe placing Jordan has given me a much-needed boost, but I don't even realize I've skipped lunch until Carol's assistant emails me, from ten feet away, to inform me that I am to take Janice Broadwick for dinner next Wednesday. Of course, she doesn't bother to ask if it works for me, and it really doesn't. I have a once-a-month book group that night, and it's my turn to host, but I know better than to ask her to reschedule.

At half past eight that night, Kevin appears at my door with a pizza, half pepperoni for him, and half anchovy for me. It's one of my secret quirks, which most of my friends refuse to indulge. He's also toting a six-pack of Sam Light. "Have you eaten?" he asks. He hasn't even bothered to go home long enough to change out of his suit. "I need a break before tackling the Councilman's speech for the Chamber of Commerce tomorrow."

In a few more days, Kevin will probably disappear until after the election. The Councilman has a comfortable lead, but that means Kevin has to worry about turning out complacent voters. It's the phase of the campaign where he lives on pizza, blows off the gym, and worries about the consequences after the ballots are counted. He snivels about it, but he secretly gets off on the adrenalin.

"I just walked in the door, but I'm famished." I reach for a slice of pizza as Kevin flips the tops off two beers and hands me one. "Thanks. You're the best."

"I know." He dives into the pizza himself.

"So I've got a question for you. Do guys ever think long term when they first start dating someone?"

"What do you mean?"

74

"Last night, Oscar made some reference to meeting my extended family, months down the line. Does that mean he's already planning a future with me?"

"Maybe. Or maybe he wants to sleep with you. Unless of course, you've already slept with him. In which case it could still mean nothing more than he wants to keep sleeping with you. Which I suppose you should take as a compliment."

I shoot him what I hope is a snarky look. "I haven't slept with him yet. And you're not being helpful. I'm *really* into him, and I want to know if the feeling is mutual."

"There's no one answer, Zoë. Most guys don't think beyond their immediate future, and getting their needs met in the moment. But you can always find exceptions to that rule. Then there are guys who behave like total dogs until the right woman comes along, and makes them fall hard and reform their bastardly ways. So I'm sorry, but there's no easy answer to your question. If there was, and I knew it, I could write a book enlightening the women of the world and retire twenty times over on the royalties." He takes a big sip of his beer.

"Speaking of saving for retirement, I can't hang out long tonight. I need to hunker down and get Janice Broadwick into college." I motion towards the over-flowing manila folder on the counter.

"She has you doing her kid's college applications? Is that even legal?"

"Probably not."

"So why the hell did you agree?"

"Because I don't have much of a choice. I need this job. My rent is going up, a lot, as of December first. If I don't want to tap my already paltry savings, I need to stay in Carol's good graces. Especially with the way the economy's been going. It's not a great time to look around."

"I bet you don't tell your candidates that."

"There's always work for litigators in a down economy. When deals go south, companies sue each other. And demand shoots up for talented corporate regulatory people," I explain, somewhat impatiently. He already knows the recession economics of my business.

Kevin shrugs, like he doesn't agree completely but he doesn't feel like getting into it, and helps himself to another slice of pizza. "It doesn't bother you that Carol's asking you to do something totally unethical?"

"Sure it does, but she did, and now I need to get these done. There's a nice bonus for me if Janice gets into Yale, early decision."

"But it's dirty money."

"Easy for you to say. Last time I checked, you had a nice little trust fund."

"I live within my means," Kevin says, defensively.

"No one said you didn't. It's just that your means and your salary don't have anything to do with each other. I can't afford to go work for some noble cause."

"Well, if you ask me, you'd have plenty of time to look for a better job, even in the private sector, if you didn't have your head in the clouds over Oscar." He spits out the words "private sector" and "Oscar" with equivalent amounts of disdain.

"What exactly is that supposed to mean? Besides, who says I want a new job?"

"You've always said what you do lacks social utility."

"I haven't said that in a long time. And it's not like some do-gooder job is going to pay my bills."

"Especially now that you're trying to keep up with Mister Central Park West."

"I'm doing no such thing. I'm having fun and hoping he has long term potential."

Kevin smirks smugly and chews his pizza. He's really starting to irritate me. I'm tired and I don't feel like having a debate on the moral merits of my various life choices.

"Of course you're competing with him. You even lied to him about where you live. That's twisted."

"And it's also none of your business. Just like it's none of my business that you're shagging Lily the Slovenian hottie, even though you think she's dumber than your parents' golden retriever." This was Kevin's own comparison, after their last date. I see no harm in repeating it back to him.

"Lily went back to Europe. And I wasn't getting all wrapped up in some fantasy relationship. It was just sex. Not like you and your trans-Madison fairy tale. Has it even occurred to you that if someone seems too good to be true…"

I cut him off. He sounds way too preachy and I'm getting a migraine. "I've got lots to do tonight. Maybe I should get to it."

"Fine." He gets up and collects his pizza box, but leaves the remaining beers on my counter. My door slams shut behind him. Across the hall, I hear him slam his own door, too. I can't believe he's so bent out of shape over this. Why should he suddenly care about the details of my dating and work habits? Not that I've had much of a dating life recently. And aside from the odd remark that he wouldn't want my job, he's never been too bothered by my accounts of the day to day insanity at Broadwick & Associates. But I can't waste the evening worrying about this. I have to put in a decent effort with these applications. I'll worry about Kevin's *way* out of character behavior after I've made a dent in them.

I decide one slice of pizza won't hold me, so I order sushi for delivery and tackle Janice's folder. She's included a copy of her transcript and she's completed her basic background information on just one of the eight applications enclosed. She's filled out a chart that indicates her teachers have mailed all her recommendations. And on the first page of the Yale application, she's affixed a pink post-it note: "To Whom It May Concern—For my hobbies and interests, please refer to my Facebook page."

You've got to be kidding me.

I rifle through the stack of papers until I find the instructions. My blood pressure spikes when I read that Yale early decision applications are due in four days. Not surprisingly, Yale wants to know, in a 500-word essay, how studying at Yale will help Janice achieve her life and career goals. But that's not all. After the first question, the admissions committee gets really cute. They want to know, if Janice Broadwick has just finished her 300 page autobiography, what would appear on page 232?

I groan, even though there's nobody to hear me. Then I swallow hard and flip to the final essay question: "John Keats said, 'Even a proverb is no proverb to you until your life has illustrated it.' Please explain a life experience you have had, which illustrates a proverb that has meaning to you."

I think I am going to throw up. I push Keats aside and haul out my laptop. Maybe I'll start with her hobbies and interests and call in sick tomorrow to figure out the proverb problem. I open Facebook and search for Janice.

When the page loads, I stare in astonishment. Carol can't possibly have seen this. A full-color photo shows a bikini- and lei-clad mini-Carol. She's doing a body shot off the chiseled chest of a man, who appears to be at least of college age, possibly older, and who is wearing nothing but unzipped board shorts.

My first thought is that maybe Carol should leave the office before 7:30 p.m. once in a while. That way she might have some clue what her kid is doing with her spare time. My next thought is that I hope admissions committees at elite schools don't monitor Facebook. I put a note on the folder, suggesting to Janice, as gently as possible, that she consider adjusting her privacy settings.

NINE

Carol is utterly unsympathetic when I tell her about Yale's looming early decision deadline. "Honestly, Zoë," she grunts between exercises, "I can't imagine why you always call me with problems. Can't you call me with a *solution* for once?"

I start to apologize, but her Pilates trainer drowns me out with instructions for Carol to engage her abdominals.

"Fine. Stay home and work on Janice's paperwork if you must, but I want that application postmarked before the last possible day." Before she hangs up, she tells me to make sure I remember to call in sick. So my fellow cube farmers won't get suspicious.

It's not worth telling Carol that none of my colleagues would wonder too much about my unscheduled absence from the office. Her paranoid mind would never grasp that. I bet she'll count the sick day against me, too.

By ten o'clock, I'm making headway on the first, and easiest, essay question, when Oscar calls. "I miss seeing you," he says.

"I miss you, too, but I'm not there today. I called in sick."

"That's too bad. I was going to try to ply you with tickets to *Il Trovatore*."

"You mean the Met?"

"The one and only, but if you're not feeling up to it…"

"No! I can rally. I'd love to go."

"You do sound a bit hoarse."

"I'm fine. Really. I'm not sick. I'm stuck at home, doing my boss's daughter's college applications. The Yale one is due in less than a week."

"Seriously? She has you writing essays for her kid?"

"Seriously. The strange thing is, I'm so used to working for an insane person that this latest request didn't even strike me as odd."

"Maybe you should dust off your resume."

"You're not the first person to suggest that. Anyway, by tonight I'll be desperate for a break."

"Fantastic. It opened last week and got great reviews. I'll swing by and pick you up around seven. Oops. There's my other line. I'll see you tonight."

He's gone. The opera. Wow. I must be doing something right this time around if he wants to take me to *the opera*. It's not exactly a low-key, probationary kind of date. A guy has to really like you to take you to the Met, right? Maybe I needed someone like Oscar to come along, to lend a more sophisticated and mature element to my stagnated existence. I'm so preoccupied with congratulating myself on this romantic achievement—making a seemingly perfect guy so serious about me—that it takes me several moments to realize that I have nothing to wear. And I have to write at least two of these Yale essays today, if I want to have any hope of making the postmark deadline. And of course Oscar will be at Angela's promptly at seven. Not here.

By two o'clock, I have convinced myself, and hopefully the admissions committee, that Janice Broadwick will make a meaningful contribution to campus life in New Haven, and that she plans to put her degree to use as an employee of a high-profile NGO, preferably one that helps orphaned, AIDS-afflicted, starving children in Sub-Saharan Africa. She concludes with a paragraph that explains her deeply ingrained sense of *noblesse oblige*, and without actually using those words, I promise, on Janice's behalf, that she will always look at her Yale education as an awesome privilege that will morally compel her to give back to those less fortunate.

I've also emailed Oscar that I will meet him at the Met. Tonight, after the performance, I will come clean about my address. Hopefully, he'll find the whole thing funny. Or maybe he'll be flattered by my reasoning. Or else I'll distract him from my pathetic subterfuge by inviting him up.

Angela has dispatched a messenger from *Vogue* to bring me a dress that she promises will be "to die for." It's Gucci. It's a loaner from the store. Angela swears it will fit. And look stunning. But if it gets damaged, she'll be on the hook for the replacement costs. She says the sales lady knew it wasn't for the magazine. Angela works in shoes, and even if she needed a dress to accessorize a footwear photo shoot, she would never have hired a "fat" size six model.

I'm wasting time, playing with my hair in the mirror, arranging it into up-dos I could never pin into place artfully enough, when my cell phone rings. Carol's assistant, Patricia.

"*Madame* wants an update." We all call the boss lady *Madame* behind her back. I'm not sure who started it, or even why it's funny, but it's a tradition that predates my employment at the firm. "Are you done yet?" she demands.

Carol rubs off on her people. Within a month on the job, every one of her admins loses the ability to speak civilly to the staff.

"I've finished one essay and I've made good progress on the second." Technically, this is true. In that I have started to ponder how anybody could create a 300-page tome about the life of a privileged, but otherwise ordinary, teenager.

"Well, just so you know, *good progress* had better mean *done* by the time Carol gets back from her waxing appointment, or you're going to ruin everyone's week." Patricia hangs up. I decide to write an essay about how Janice's team mates elected her as captain of the school tennis team, which meant beating out her best friend, which in turn sorely tested their friendship. Trite? Painfully so. But it's as good as anything else I can fabricate in under half an hour. I'm certain Janice plays tennis, and I'm about seventy-five per cent sure that Carol bragged about her daughter becoming captain of the team as a junior. As if such an honor had never, in the entire history of the Spence school, been bestowed on one so young.

Decked out in the loaner gown furnished by Angela, I feel transformed and fabulous. I've wrangled my hair into a twist that looks surprisingly elegant, shoved my breasts into a bra that helps make the most of the dress's plunging neckline, and weighted my ears down with sparkling chandeliers borrowed from the legendary accessories closet at *Vogue*. I feel half a foot taller, and even the fact that I have to tramp down five flights in my high heels doesn't dampen my mood. Carol was miraculously pleased with my progress on her daughter's behalf. I feel justified in taking the evening off.

I must have cleaned up better than usual because not one, but two cabs, screech to the curb as soon as I raise a gloved hand. When we reach the Met, Oscar's there, waiting on those famous stairs in his tux, looking incredibly sexy. He's also carrying his briefcase, which seems incongruous with his evening wear, but maybe he came straight from the office. He smiles broadly when he sees me, and meets me halfway down the steps.

"You look incredible."

"Thanks. Unfortunately it's just a loaner. Angela came to my rescue. She said she couldn't have me embarrassing myself at the opera." I feel myself grinning like an idiot over his compliment.

"Come on. You could never do that."

I feel my face flush, and divert my eyes from his gaze flirtatiously. Can he really be as into me as I am into him? Am I that lucky?

On the way to our box, I catch at least four women swooning over my guy. As soon as we're seated, a waiter brings a whole bottle of champagne, which appears to be a big seller here, recession or not. The two other seats in the box are unoccupied when we arrive. Oscar says, "We have it all to ourselves tonight. The firm has these seats and no clients could make it."

Despite all my years in New York, I've only been to the opera once, and that was with a field trip for an art appreciation class in college. We sat in the second to last row of the orchestra, way underneath the first balcony. The music was amazing, but I don't remember seeing much besides the bald head of the man in front of me. This is totally different. Not only do we have an enviable view of the stage, we can see almost every member of the audience, most of whom are busy checking each other out. From the moment the curtain goes up, I'm riveted, even though I don't understand Italian. I lean forward against the railing and take it all in. Though part of me feels like a little kid playing dress up, I could get used to living this way. Halfway through the first act, Oscar slides his hand onto my thigh. As his fingers stroke the fabric, little bolts of electricity shoot through me. I can't wait to be alone with him. It could be the champagne buzz, but I seriously feel like the music is making me want him more. It's so intense, it's practically erotic. I cringe inwardly at the clichés my brain has decided to indulge. I need to get a grip. But, God, he does it for me. If he doesn't come home with me tonight, the frustration might kill me.

The little voice in my head reminds me, in a patronizing tone, that I ought to want more from Oscar than sex. I am too old to let my hormones run amok in this manner. And of course I do want more. He's fantastic. Maybe he's even The One. It's just that maybe, after the summer I've had, I feel the tiniest bit entitled to one of those rare, great shags that leaves you breathless and makes you forget your middle name.

At intermission, Oscar asks me to order some more champagne from the waiter, then excuses himself. He returns right after the new bubbly arrives, and when he sets his briefcase down, I register that he took it with him. Which seems odd, and even somewhat offensive. Why would he worry about me rifling through his work? But maybe he just assumed I'd want to run to the ladies' room. Or maybe he has some hyper-vigilant client who made him promise not to let his files out of sight. I should chill.

By the time the singers come out for their curtain call, it's all I can do to keep myself from jumping all over Oscar right here. It's probably a combination of the decadent outing, the Dom Perignon, and the fact that his hand didn't leave my leg once during the entire second act. After the third or fourth bow, we start to push towards the exits. A couple in their fifties joins the crush from another box and the man smiles at us. "Oscar Thornton," he says, in a tone that conveys pleasant surprise. He has salt and pepper hair, sharp, fiercely intelligent eyes, framed and magnified by black horn-rimmed glasses, and a slight overbite. We all step to the edge of the corridor to let others pass.

"It's been ages!" His wife, a slim specimen with an obvious face lift and a royal blue evening gown declares. She has a teeny hint of a Southern drawl, the commonly encountered variety that's been cowed into remission by years in New York City.

"Bradford. So nice to see you." Oscar shakes hands and kisses Bradford's wife on the cheek before introducing me. "Bradford and Trudy Bainbridge, this Zoë Clark."

I'm so lost in my thoughts about how much I want Oscar right now, and how little I want to chat with this couple, that I miss the fact that the Bainbridges and Oscar have moved past the obligatory small talk part of the encounter. Trudy Bainbridge is blinking her surgically sculpted eyes at me as if I'm somewhat limited, and I realize she's asking, for the third time, how Oscar and I met. Oscar is looking at me uncomfortably. After a too-long pause, I tell her, "He works across the street from me, so I suppose we bumped into each other that way."

Oscar exhales. I can't blame him for not wanting these people to know the details of his romantic overture. Once the Bainbridges excuse themselves, he leans into my ear and whispers, "Bradford manages one of the largest hedge funds in the world. He's got more money than almost anyone in New York, and he's a super nice guy, in spite of it."

"So you believe that wealth and success are incompatible with civility?" I ask playfully, because it seems, based on his apartment, car, and choices of venue for dates, that my guy isn't exactly hurting for cash.

He misses the irony. "Yeah. Most guys in Bradford's position are total jack asses. But Bradford's still married to his college sweetheart, they've got four sons, eight houses, a private jet, two yachts, paintings on loan to the Met, and a family foundation that gives away gazillions of dollars. And he can still talk to anyone without seeming the least bit pretentious."

"That's nice." I'm having a difficult time being interested in anything but the fastest route to Oscar in bed naked. And I really hope he shares that interest.

"Enough about them. Let's get out of here." He grins conspiratorially and I'm fairly certain he's thinking along the same lines I am.

We navigate down the opulent red staircase, under the unreal chandelier, and out across the plaza to Oscar's waiting car. I slide into the comfortable black leather backseat and think it must be nice to travel in style all the time.

"Where to now?" his chauffeur asks.

Oscar turns to me. "Invite me in tonight." It's neither a question nor a statement. It hangs somewhere in between.

"Okay." I'd be ready to squeal with excitement if the moment to come clean wasn't upon me.

"Gramercy," he instructs the driver. I have to tell him. Now. Angela's not going to play along with this insanity by vacating her place, and even if she would, I have no way to ask her out of Oscar's earshot.

"Actually, that's Angela's place. I live a few blocks away."

His head tilts to the side and he looks at me like a puzzled puppy. "But I've dropped you there twice."

I decide to go for the whole truth. "I lied, and I'm sorry. I was so attracted to you that I didn't want to take any, um, chances." I feel myself blush bright red. "I was going to tell you on Saturday, but then I saw your apartment and I was, I don't know, ashamed of mine. It's not even as nice as Angela's, which would be slumming for you."

He raises his hand to my lips. He's smiling. It's going to be alright. "I guess I'm flattered, but seriously, you have nothing to worry about. I imagine that it can't be any worse than my old student digs."

It's nice of him to say that but my stomach still crunches with apprehension as we emerge from the car outside my building, and I rifle through my bag for the key, since there's no doorman to admit us. What if he decides we're socio-economically incompatible? Then again, he already knows I'm wearing a borrowed dress. He must not care that there's no way I can keep up with him.

I lead him up the shabby stairwell to the landing I share with Kevin. One of the overhead lights flickers at us sarcastically, and as if on cue, makes a buzzing sound and burns out. Kevin's home, and I can hear he's watching *The Daily Show*. I hope he doesn't decide to stick his head in the corridor to say hi. Or to continue our tiff from last night.

When I flip on the lights and close my apartment door behind us, Oscar says, "It's not nearly as bad as you made it out to be."

I hang up our coats and ask if he wants a drink.

"Nope." He pulls me in for a kiss. "I just want the highlights tour. Let's see your bedroom."

TEN

I have never had sex like this before. During the last couple of years with Brendan, we did it once or twice a month. It was missionary, routine, and I spent a lot of time contemplating the cracks in my ceiling. Even with the inappropriate guys I dated while broken up with Brendan, it was never this good. Maybe Angela's been onto something all along, with her older men. Though I can't imagine a guy like Reiner giving me four orgasms in one night. My alarm will go off in forty minutes. We finally drifted off sometime after four, but I don't feel the least bit tired. Oscar is asleep next to me. He's got an amazing body. I know he's a runner, but he has more of a rower's build, with broad shoulders, defined muscles and a narrow waist. His tux lies in a tangled heap on my floor, along with the gown, which hopefully wasn't damaged in his hurry to remove it from my person.

Oscar's briefcase rests on my bureau. The luxe leather sports an unsightly scratch, that I don't remember noticing before. What a shame. Maybe, if I close Niles Townsend, and scale down to a studio apartment, I could replace the bag for Oscar as a Christmas gift. Although I suppose the more responsible thing would be to buy a more modest present and stick any surplus income into my 401(k).

I slide out from under the covers to slip into the bathroom and remove last night's mascara and re-apply just enough make-up so as not to horrify Oscar when he rolls awake and sees me. When I slip back under the covers, still naked, he stirs. "Come here," he murmurs and reaches out an arm to pull me down to his chest. I breathe in his scent and wonder whether I've ever felt so content in my life. I feel him getting excited again, pushing against my thigh. He rolls me onto my back and we have another go.

Afterwards, when we're lying entangled and I've silenced my alarm, he says, "This place is actually kind of nice." As if on cue, someone upstairs flushes and water rushes through the ancient pipes behind the walls, which shake from the onslaught. I laugh and say, "It's far from perfect, but it's home for now."

"You're planning on moving?"

"I might have to. My ex's father is my landlord now, and he's raising the rent."

"What a prick."

"You could say that. I should start looking around. Even if I won the lottery tomorrow, it would bother me to write him a check every month. But anyway, that's not your problem. Do you want some coffee?"

"I'd love some, but I need to get out of here. I can't exactly show up at work in last night's penguin suit. What are my chances of getting a cab downstairs?"

I glance at the clock. Not quite 7:30. "Pretty good, if you get out of here within the half hour." I have a full day myself, seeing as Janice still needs to get into Yale, and obviously Oscar has to get to the office, but I still hate that he's bolting without breakfast. I tell myself to stop being ridiculous. It doesn't mean he didn't have a great time. This is just what adults do. They have responsibilities and careers that they do not blow off for carnal pleasures and coffee and Danish.

Angela calls me when we're both on the way to work. "So?" she demands.

"The opera was amazing."

"Obviously. It's the Met. I only have five minutes. I don't want a review of the show, I want to hear about the after hours cabaret."

"We went back to my place and he spent the night."

"So you 'fessed up? How'd he take it?"

"Surprisingly well. I think he saw the humor."

"Or he thought you were a freak, but he still wanted to get in your pants."

"Hmm. Also possible."

"So, out with it. I need the details."

Suddenly I feel uncharacteristically coy. I don't want to give her the blow by blow while walking with the throngs down Madison Avenue. And I like Oscar. Too much to kiss and tell. Or at least tell *all* the details. I'm so happy about what I suspect is my first truly promising male-female relationship that I don't want to mess anything up by saying the wrong thing to a third party. Even if that third party is my best girl friend in the whole world, from whom I normally withhold nothing. No fact has ever been too tawdry. But this feels different. So I say, "Um, I'll fill you in later. I dropped the dress at the cleaners. You should have it back tomorrow. Thanks again. I finally understand why women who can afford it spend tens of thousands of dollars on clothes."

"Well at least part of my job here is done," Angela laughs. "And don't worry, I'll ply you with alcohol and get you to spill the dirt later."

I don't know if it's the adrenalin or some other weird happiness-inducing hormone, but I plow through the work day unaffected by my sleep deprivation. Everything falls into place. I even finish Janice's Yale essays. I'll proofread everything tomorrow, and they'll be ready to send a full twenty-four hours ahead of Carol's deadline. Instead of obsessing about whether I'll hear from Oscar, I feel strangely Zen and satisfied with the way things went last night. Maybe this is a sign of maturity. I silently congratulate myself once more. Adults don't make themselves crazy over whether a guy will call, but I feel an unmistakable surge of excitement when Oscar texts me as I'm shutting down my computer. He says he has a business dinner, but asks if he can stop by later. Wow. He wants to see me two nights in a row. He must really like me. Maybe this is how it's supposed to be. Easy. Or not. Everyone says guys text for sex and call for dates. Maybe he's only looking for friendship with benefits, and I'm reading too much into three great dates. I force myself to wait a full thirty-two minutes before writing him back, and then spend another ten composing, "Sounds great. Call me when you're on your way," which seems like a feeble effort for a person who's spent the day trying to dazzle Ivy admissions officers with her prose.

Fortunately, I have plans to prevent me from spinning like a top in my apartment for the next few hours. Angela wants to meet at the bar in the Four Seasons, ostensibly because she's coming from a meeting around the corner. Really it's because she loves that the waiters recognize her there. As I cross the lobby, I remind myself that I should scale down my tastes to make them more proportionate to my budget. Angela's already waiting, perched on an overstuffed chair from which she can survey the entire room, martini in hand. She's flipping through a folder of papers on the table in front of her.

As soon as the waiter is dispatched with my drink order, a cosmo with Cointreau and Stoli O, Angela launches right into a presentation so slick I suspect she rehearsed it. "I've printed out listings for all the apartments in your price range, and I will clear my Saturday so I can see them with you. For moral support."

"This is great, Angela, but I haven't decided that I'm moving."

"Of course you are. There's no way you're giving your hard-earned cash to that fuckwit. Or his family."

She's right, but her choice of verbiage stings anyway. It crosses that line that, instead of merely sticking it to Brendan, also makes *me* feel like an idiot. "You know that 'fuckwit' was the man I thought I was going to marry."

Angela rearranges her expression to try to look apologetic. She fails. "Well, obviously he wasn't a fuckwit *then*. Only now. Stop changing the subject. Some of these look promising. And while they're not rent control like mine, they're all in my neighborhood."

I leaf through the pages half-heartedly. Moving seems so daunting, and these places sound positively tiny. I hadn't focused on the fact that I'd be scaling down this much. Even with more units available because of the downturn, rents have soared since Brendan and I signed our original lease. And this time it'll be me, alone, on the hook for everything. Maybe I should stop putting it off, post a roommate wanted ad on Craigslist and see if anyone normal responds.

"You know, it'll be good for you to live by yourself," Angela says, as if reading my mind. "You might actually like it. And you're the only person I know who's never willingly tried it. There should be some kind of ordinance against that."

"I had a single for two years in college."

"On-campus student housing so does not count." She takes the folder from me. "I know you're frazzled, so I've gone ahead and made appointments at the ones that look most worthwhile. If there's anything else you want to see, we can call and ask if they'll accommodate."

I have to admire Angela. She's a bundle of efficiency. It's not like she has nothing to do all day. Working in shoes at *Vogue* is on a whole different level than specializing in footwear anyplace else on the planet. Most designers live and die by the magazine's blessing, and since shoes have the second highest profit margin of all products in the fashion industry, Angela's job is way more serious than most people give her credit for.

"So we're starting bright and early at nine on Saturday," she says, taking a ladylike sip from her martini. "You'd better tell Oscar you'll be needing your beauty sleep, since I'm guessing you got, maybe, two hours at the most last night."

"But it was so totally worth it. I feel like I can't get enough of him, and I can't wait to see him again."

Angela smiles. "I'm glad you're finally getting a normal, satisfying sex life. You're *glowing*, for the first time, in, well, forever. But before you drag Prince Charming off to Bloomingdales to peruse the Villeroy and Boch, why don't you get to know him better? You know, see what he's about in the *non*-Biblical sense."

"Since when are you all about raining on my parade?"

"I'm not. God knows I think a talented lover is a beautiful thing, but it's also obvious to me that you crave more than a physical connection. I'm just saying, have fun, but don't be scared of losing the sex if he's not right for you in other ways. You can find other great lovers out there. Great apartments, on the other hand, are rare."

ELEVEN

"I think I should take one of the places I saw today," I tell Oscar glumly on the phone Saturday afternoon. "Angela and I saw eleven apartments, they're all a step down from what I have now, but they'll probably go quickly." Angela kept reminding me, whenever I pointed out tired Formica, dirty windows or creaky floorboards, that these flats all come without Brendan, which is, undeniably, a huge plus. By our fourth appointment, Angela had almost convinced me that these places weren't any worse than hers. So I should stop being a bitch already and pick one. She was right, naturally, but it's still hard for me to wrap my mind around the fact that I won't be able to sustain myself in the lifestyle to which I became accustomed while cohabiting with my fiancé. Excuse me. Ex-fiancé.

"You want to know what I think?" Oscar asks.

"Of course."

"I think you should sleep on it, preferably in my bed."

"That sounds nice."

"How soon can you be here?"

"Give me an hour." I didn't shave my legs this morning because I didn't want to be late for Angela. It's way too soon for Oscar to see me un-primped, and I kind of enjoy the delicious anticipation of knowing I'll see him soon, but not this very minute.

Three hours, seven (yup, seven) leg-shaking orgasms, and one bottle of pinot noir later, I'm feeling better about my real estate problem. Maybe I should just take the cheapest place I saw today, so I can start saving a few pennies. If things keep going this well with Oscar, I'll probably be sleeping here most of the time anyway. I silently chide myself for getting carried away, but it's hard not to with my head on his bare chest and his arm wrapped over me protectively. I want to stay here forever. Unfortunately, my bladder has an alternate agenda. When I come back from the master bathroom, which is bigger than the living/dining spaces in any of the apartments I considered today, Oscar's switched on the news. His expression has gone from sated to stunned in the five minutes I was gone.

"What? What happened?" In the split second before I see the screen, a dozen different doomsday scenarios play through my head. That's what being a modern New Yorker is like. But then I see the picture has nothing to do with attacks, terrorism or carnage, and my jaw drops in surprise.

The banner at the bottom of the screen reads, "NYC Councilman, Mayoral Frontrunner Walter O'Malley implicated in global human trafficking and pornography ring. Details soon."

Kevin must be having heart failure.

"Oh. My. God. My friend manages O'Malley's campaign."

"He already knows. If all the news channels have it, the senior staff will have gotten a heads up," Oscar says. He shakes his head at the screen. O'Malley doesn't seem the type. He's way too image-conscious and clean cut."

I'm not sure I agree. Aren't successful men always in the news for monumental acts of stupidity? Mostly because they think they're too smart to get caught? But I don't feel like getting into a big discussion about it. Especially since I am still naked and have rearranged myself into what I think is an attractive reclining pose beside him on the bed.

My phone rings in my purse. "Do you mind if I see who that is?"

"Not at all." He's riveted to the train wreck on television that is my friend's career.

I slide back out from under the warm and ridiculously luxurious sheets, still naked, and dig for my phone. Angela.

"You heard?" she asks, skipping a greeting.

"I just saw the headline. Was he buying or selling?"

"Neither. The FBI says he invested in the distribution of the stuff, but the materials in question aren't exactly of the vanilla flavor."

"Oh God. Poor Kev."

"I know. It gets worse. It sounds like this ring trafficked under-age girls from as far away as Eastern Europe and Southeast Asia to put them in the pictures and films. As if that's not disgusting enough, the prosecutors are asking questions about where the funds for the upfront costs came from. If O'Malley was even tangentially involved in importing kiddos for perverts, his political future is *so* over. And rightly so."

I glance back over at the TV. They've moved on to a report from their Middle East correspondent. "We have the news on now, and it doesn't say anything about human trafficking."

"It will any minute. I heard it from my sister. I just hung up with her." Angela's sister is married to a special agent in DC. "She never tells me anything about the FBI, but she called to tell me this story was about to break, because she knows how tight I am with Kevin. Even though her husband would flip."

Oscar switches off the TV and rolls on his side to face me. He reaches out to pull me towards him.

"Angela, I have to go. I'll call you back in a bit."

Oscar slides me underneath him, kisses me hard, and reaches his hand between my thighs. I tell myself I can worry about Kevin's career crisis a little later.

Sometime in the wee hours of the morning, I roll awake and register Oscar's absence. Through the wall, I can hear the low murmur of indecipherable phone conversation. I slide out of bed. The door to his study is closed. I knock timidly and try the knob. Locked. He must be deep in conversation because he doesn't acknowledge my louder second knock. I slink back to bed and try to fall asleep.

By the time he reappears next to me, I'm silently squelching a panic attack about him seeing someone else. The little voice in my head says not to be so ridiculous and typical. Oscar is here with me. If he wanted to sneak around, he'd have plenty of hours in his week to do so with zero risk of getting caught. Besides, everything always seems dire at three in the morning.

As soon as I've reassured myself that I'm experiencing a nocturnally induced overreaction, the little voice reminds me smugly that it's not like Oscar and I are exclusive. So I should stop being presumptuous.

At ten-thirty on Sunday morning, Kevin gets one of his lifelong wishes: an invitation to appear on *Meet the Press*. He just never imagined it would happen this year, with this candidate, and certainly not under these circumstances. Oscar and I watch on the kitchen TV.

Kevin looks stunned. He has his lines prepared and David Gregory even feigns mild surprise when Kevin stares into the camera with his exhausted eyes and set jaw, and tells the national audience, "Councilman O'Malley admits to a serious lapse in judgment, because he did not personally vet all his investments over the years. However, he vehemently and unequivocally denies any wrong doing, and he also wants to assure the people of New York that no campaign funds were used for any improper purpose. The Councilman has not been charged with any crime and he is continuing his campaign."

"All publicity is good publicity, right?" I ask Oscar.

"Right. Until someone gets indicted." He pours more coffee for both of us and produces an impressive fruit salad from the fridge. If it weren't obvious he loves being in the kitchen, I'd think he was a total freak for trying so hard. I mean, *after* bedding me. I hope this kind of effort means I'm special. That there's no one else.

He puts four slices of bread in the toaster and starts to scramble some eggs. "Did you ever catch Kevin last night?"

"No." I didn't want to risk calling Kevin from here, in case he's still in the midst of his disproportionate reaction to the stupid college application thing.

"Well, you should call him later and tell him he did a great job on TV. That didn't look easy. And the poor guy doesn't look sleep-deprived. He looks like a torture victim who's been dressed up in nice clothes and foisted into the spotlight with no warning." Oscar stirs the eggs and adjusts the flame underneath them.

"Kevin's always well-dressed. He even keeps a book called *Dressing the Man* on his coffee table."

Oscar nods but doesn't comment, tops off his own coffee again and changes the subject. "What are you going to do about the apartment hunt? Are you going to keep looking?"

"Maybe. Or maybe I should just take one of the ones I saw yesterday. If they're still available. A couple of them would shorten my commute by a few minutes."

"You don't sound enthused."

"My current place isn't anything spectacular, but it's nice, it's home, and it's practically palatial next to anything Angela and I saw."

"Your place is great." Oscar sounds sincere. He serves up two perfect plates of eggs. "It, I don't know, *feels* like you. Not that you don't look fantastic in your present environs."

I feel myself glowing as he leans over the counter to kiss me. Something about his touch makes me feel warm all over. I swear when his mouth touches mine, even my toes tingle. Oscar stares into my face for a moment, looking equally gooey and glowy. I can't believe I was so worried a few short hours ago. Or that I am finally half of one of those sickening new couples who only have eyes for each other. I can't remember ever feeling so besotted, except perhaps as a teenager, when I had a huge crush on the captain of the soccer team. Which tragically went unrequited for the entirety of our tenure at Wellesley High.

Oscar reaches for his coffee and I absentmindedly glance at his briefcase on the barstool next to mine. The leather looks as creamy and luxurious as if he'd carried it out of the shop brand new this morning. It's so inviting that I reach over and stroke it. The bag is exactly the kind of thing Carol would urge Marvin to buy—a status symbol accessory whose price tag cancels out an entire commission check.

"How did you get the scratch fixed so fast?" I ask.

"I didn't. I replaced it. The original was a graduation gift from my favorite professor and mentor. It killed me that I destroyed his present."

"I didn't realize you had such a soft streak." I think I just fell for him harder.

"Yeah, well, it was a foolish use of my funds. One of these things is a waste of money. Owning two pushes the limits of decency."

He shakes his head at himself and changes the TV channel. Numerous pundits are dissecting the O'Malley scandal, and Kevin's performance. We watch until the commercial break. They seem to think the Councilman will weather this storm, not because he should, but because his opponent is basically a wing nut.

I've applied a seaweed mask that promises to arrest the aging process when I hear Kevin in our shared hallway right before eleven in the evening. He's obviously had a long Sunday—he's still in the suit he wore on TV. I rush out to intercept him in my pajamas and embarrassing hot pink slippers with poodles on them, that I'd never wear in front of Oscar. Before he can cut me off, I blurt, "I saw you on *Meet the Press* this morning. You did great!"

"Thanks." His voice is flat and discouraging of further dialogue.

But I forge forward anyway. "I'm so sorry about the Councilman, but with all the publicity, I bet this thing could still catapult your career."

"Wow. You have a powerful grasp of the obvious." He turns the key in the lock. "Zoë, I'm sorry. I can't talk to you right now. Have a good night." He slips into his apartment and closes the door. I hear the television turn on. I stand in the corridor, stunned that he can still be mad at me, over something that's stupid, necessary for my very survival at work, and clearly none of his business. Our other neighbor, a well-dressed but sour forty-something divorcee with severe eye brows and no upper lip, emerges from the stairwell. She looks at me in my green face and flannel costume and sniffs before making a beeline to her door. Her glare jolts me into motion. I retreat to the safety of my own sofa before the tears flood down my cheeks and ruin my mask.

Against my better judgment, I flip open my phone and dial, not Angela, but Oscar. "What's going on?" he asks. I can hear the TV in the background.

"Have you ever been dumped by a friend? Not a girlfriend, but a regular friend. A close one, though."

I hear him turn down the volume. "I can't say that I have."

I press forward. "Have you ever had a friend be disgusted with you over something you've done, say at work, and over-react?"

"I'm in advertising. I'm sure much of my work offends some people."

"You're missing the point. Don't you think it's ridiculous for this friend of mine to get all worked up about me writing college essays for Carol's daughter?"

"So we're talking about Kevin. I don't even know him, but I imagine he's just had the worst career week of his life. Give the poor guy a break."

"But he got mad at me before the Councilman's news broke."

"I don't know what to tell you. Maybe the guy's moody. I don't see why you're so worked up about it."

When I say nothing, he adds, "I'm sorry. That was short. I desperately need a decent night's rest. While you got your beauty sleep last night, I had to jump on a call with some folks in Asia."

"It's okay. I understand." Though I'm not certain I do. I think it's odd he didn't mention the call before. It would've saved me hours of anxiety.

After we say goodnight and hang up I lie awake for a long time, even though I should be relieved he offered an innocent explanation for his late night conversation. Oscar not only seemed nonplussed by my current crisis, he deftly avoided sharing anything about himself when I invited him to do so. Maybe I need to know more about what makes him tick. I should at least acknowledge the *possibility* that sophisticated dates and incredible sexual chemistry might be an insufficient foundation for true intimacy.

Or maybe that's not entirely honest. I had no problem with how things were going until the notion of another woman entered my brain this morning. It's as if things are too wonderful, and I should steel myself against inevitable disappointment. On the other hand, he did say he wished I was there in bed with him, and he couldn't wait to see me again. When I finally drift off, I'm wishing he was with me.

TWELVE

Angela leaves me a voice mail during the weekly Monday morning staff meeting, otherwise known as Carol's favorite forum in which to single out some hapless employee for public humiliation. Once my boss finishes reducing New Girl to a trembling, weeping mess over her failure to properly log some seemingly irrelevant scrap of information into the computer system, we're dismissed, utterly de-motivated, to go forth and spend the week eating our children—Carol's favored shorthand for the practice of poaching our clients.

Angela's message cuts to the point. Kevin is reeling from the weekend's developments, she's having a drink with him after work, he still doesn't want to see me, and she's going to "knock some sense into his useless male brain," because she can't stand her best friends fighting. If that doesn't work, she wants me to apologize to him so we can all move on.

I'm not fighting. Nor should I be the one asking forgiveness. I didn't do anything wrong. He had a hissy fit over something dumb and now he's embarrassed.

Before I can stew long enough to get really upset again, disaster strikes. Carol comes blasting out of her office like a bullet train leaving its terminal and comes to a screeching halt over my desk. She stops so suddenly that she practically ejects out of her Ferragamo pumps. "Yale. Does. Not. Have. Janice's. S. A. T. Scores." She spits each word out between her teeth. The effect sounds like reptilian hissing but makes her look like she's expelling watermelon seeds.

"SAT scores get sent directly by the student." I am an idiot. I hear the words cross my lips and am powerless to stop my blathering, futile self-defense. "Janice would have done that herself when she took the test."

Carol looks stunned for a split second, as if she can't comprehend that I've dared to speak. Out loud, even. "The minutiae of the process could not interest me less, Zoë. The fact is Yale needs the scores and they don't fucking have them."

I have no idea how to go about ordering Janice's SAT scores, but I am smart enough to know she doesn't want to hear anything from me except, "I'll straighten this out immediately. I'm sorry you're disappointed, and I take responsibility." This line is copied almost verbatim from a post-it affixed to my computer screen and everyone else's. It's what we're supposed to say when a client is pissed, whether it's our fault or not. It throws them off their game more reliably than a profuse apology.

Carol, who coined the exact verbiage of the speech, is affected enough to give me a stay of execution. "Thank you." She grinds one heel into the carpet, pivots a hundred-eighty degrees and storms off at a statelier pace than her advance mere moments ago.

Martin sticks his head over one of the grey dividers that demarcate my cube. "What the hell was that about?"

I motion towards the hallway. Once we're across the street at Starbucks, away from the Town Crier's bionic hearing, I spill the college admissions story. I'm embarrassed, but Marvin is unfazed. "I thought if you had to drag me across the street to tell me, it would have been much juicier than that." He frowns into his *grande* nonfat cappuccino with an extra shot.

"Sorry to disappoint." It comes out with more sarcasm than I intended.

"But let me tell you something." Marvin's been around two years longer than me, and he not so secretly relishes the opportunity to assume the old, wise, mentor-slash-oracle role in our relationship. "You're navigating dangerous waters. If Janice gets skinny letters, Carol will fire you in two seconds."

"You think I don't know that?"

"Of course you know it. I just doubt you've internalized it. All I'm saying is that you might want to devise plan B for yourself *before* the Ivies start making their decisions."

I hadn't stopped to think of it that way. I've already been earmarking Carol's "incentive payments" in my head, mainly as an excuse to put off a decision about moving or finding a roommate, but also, at Carol's urging, for bags and shoes. Marvin's absolutely right. Just when I was beginning to think I might have a long and fruitful career working for Carol, it hits me that I probably need to start interviewing. With the economy giving everyone except the city's litigators indigestion, it might be a lousy time to explore the job market, but maybe I should put resume revision on my list of pressing things to do. I can itemize that right under finding a cheaper apartment and patching things up with Kevin.

At six o'clock in the evening, the U.S. Attorney announces he will charge Burt Smealey, who happens to serve as O'Malley's campaign fundraising chief, with trafficking in child pornography. The Councilman holds an almost simultaneous press conference to disown the guy, an old friend and managing director at one of the city's most venerable financial firms. He goes on about how "saddened" he is by the news, how the films in question are truly stomach-turning, and how he will not rest until the children of New York—and indeed the entire world—are safe from exploitation on the Internet. I wonder if the Councilman knew about his aide's involvement. Could he be dumb enough to keep someone with such a seedy side in his inner circle?

There's also a report that one of the girls, who has since turned eighteen, has agreed to be interviewed on television. Angela calls four minutes later to say, predictably, that Kevin cancelled on her.

When I meet her at Per Se an hour and a half later, Angela looks stunning in black over-the-knee boots and a bright pink swirling cape by Emilio Pucci that very few women could pull off. Her eyes are smokier than usual, which means she blitzed through the beauty department on the way out of the office. As I make my way to the bar stool currently occupied by her fresh-from-Italy Fendi bag, I register no less than four men watching her. We air kiss hello, and before I can remove my coat, the bartender appears and tells us that the gentlemen at the end of the bar want to buy us a round.

"Two cosmos. Cointreau and Stoli O, with a twist," Angela pronounces without pausing to solicit my input. "And please tell them thank you."

She must have something on her mind. It's unlike Angela to use a barman as a messenger service. She normally thanks her admirers and benefactors in person, but she hasn't even bothered checking these two out. I take a speedy inventory. They're youngish, under forty. Italian suits that might disguise the very beginnings of a paunch. Tired eyes. A few grey hairs at the temples. Drinking scotch.

If I had to guess, I'd say they're litigators fresh off a trial. It's too early on a Monday night to see Wall Street types or their corporate counsel out and about.

The bartender returns with our drinks. I lean over to take the first sip before daring to pick up my martini glass. Angela raises her cosmo to the men who paid for it. They toast back, but thankfully make no motion to get up. I should be thrilled to meet lawyers in bars. It works for Marvin. He's made many lucrative contacts in dark places. But I'm not in the mood to banter about the legal scene and feign interest in some guy's practice.

Angela cuts to the chase. "Has Kevin called you?"

"No. But I didn't expect to hear from him today." This is true, and I can almost kid myself into thinking it's because he's in the midst of a career meltdown.

"Bastard. I told him he should." Angela takes another sip of her cosmo. "Maybe you should just fall on your sword so we can all move on." Her BlackBerry buzzes. She checks the caller I.D. and silences it. "Damn Reiner. I'm going to have to change this number."

I decide to ignore the aside about her discarded Bavarian suitor. "It might be easier for me to fall on my sword if I knew what the real problem was."

"Um, where did you go to school?"

I look at her blankly. And then I start racking my brain for a reason Kevin could be so pissed off.

"It should be obvious. I mean, it's been obvious to me for *years*."

"What's been obvious?"

She rolls her eyes. "Don't be coy."

"I'm not."

"Seriously? You don't see it? Are you blind? He's crazy about you."

"Kevin?"

"Duh."

"Since when?"

"Probably since forever, but really, truly, since things with you and Brendan started to cool off."

"You mean when Brendan exploded out of the closet."

"Nope. Way before then." Angela re-crosses her legs. A woman in an indescribably dull St. John suit looks at them with what she hopes is disdain but is really envy.

"No way. I would know. He lives across the hall. I see him every day. I've been a regular spectator of his dating life since, well, since he first got a dating life."

"And none of those romances ever work out."

"That has nothing to do with me. Lily the cover girl didn't exactly show long-term potential."

"Stupid. Stupid. Stupid," Angela mutters.

"What?"

"Has it ever occurred to you that Kevin picks the wrong women—placeholder girls, really—because he's carrying some kind of torch for you?"

"Has he ever said anything?"

"He doesn't have to."

"Wouldn't I know if he liked me that way? It's not like we have a lot of secrets."

"And you never thought it was odd, that with his trust fund and all the options that affords, the *perfect* Manhattan flat just happened to be the dump across from yours?"

"You know he likes to play at being normal."

"Not so much when it comes to his personal comfort. He could've easily bought that place at Fifth and Ninth. For example. Now I think you're being willfully blind, Zoë."

"Well, I think you're wrong. Kevin would laugh at you if he heard this. And I'm happier than I thought possible with Oscar. So, Angela, I appreciate that you want everything to be nice and fuzzy between Kevin and me, but I'm not going to torpedo things with Oscar because you invented some crush that doesn't exist."

She raises one perfectly sculpted eyebrow. I wish I could do that. Raise one and not the other, I mean. Although her ability to pluck her brows like a professional is enviable, too. "You and Oscar aren't exclusive, are you?"

"I'm not seeing anyone else, if that's what you mean."

Angela decides to push a little. "Do you know that he's not seeing anyone else?"

"He said he hasn't dated since the divorce and I believe him." Normally I would tell Angela about my nagging doubts, magnified by his wee hours conversation behind closed doors, but tonight I decide it would just take this conversation in a direction I'm not excited to explore.

"No offense, Zoë, but I wouldn't rely so much on your instincts. You missed Brendan being gay, and if you can't see that Kevin likes you, well, then you're just completely clueless."

Angela is usually spot on with her insights into the male psyche, but tonight she's starting to irritate me. Maybe I'm not the guy-savviest girl in New York, but I don't see any reason I shouldn't take Oscar at his word. He and I have no reason to fake the glow we bring out in each other.

The bartender comes over to ask if we want another round. Angela nods her approval, but I interrupt to tell him I'm switching to pinot noir. Normally I don't mind her queen bee thing at all—she's a magnanimous doyenne, at least as far as I'm concerned—but tonight it's beginning to chafe.

When her BlackBerry buzzes again, I check my phone. Two missed calls. One's from work. The other's my mom. She will want to know whether I booked a ticket for Thanksgiving. She'll remind me it's only a few weeks away, and that airfares aren't going anywhere but up. There's no message from Oscar. But that means nothing. He told me to call him after I was done with Angela. He said he'd love to come by.

Sometimes I miss the days before everyone was so connected all the time. Even though I'm not thrilled with Angela at the moment, I'm sure that will pass shortly, and it would be nice to think I could have a drink with my best friend, without either of us worrying about whether we're ignoring someone more important, more interesting, more pressing. When she lays her BlackBerry back on the bar, I pointedly stash my phone in my purse.

"Kevin called me," she says. "He said to watch the news."

I wave the bartender over and ask if he can switch one of the TV's to CNN. Since they're not screening any major sporting event, he obliges. It's the top story. And there's Kevin—on CNN!—looking like a BBC anchorman in a fabulous pink shirt and purple tie. Unfortunately the violet tones underscore the circles beneath his eyes. We're both so impressed that it takes us a second to realize there's no sound. The banner at the bottom of the screen reads, "Councilman: I never trafficked child pornography." Angela calls the bartender back over, but by the time he figures out how to activate the closed-captioning, they've moved on to another story.

"So if he never trafficked underage girls, but just somehow tangentially benefited, that makes it okay?" Angela muses as CNN goes to commercial.

"The feds might give him a pass if they can't prove he was an active participant." Marvin explained this to me today, but it was probably in the papers, too.

Marvin claims that whoever they catch is in deep shit regardless, because the international trafficking and Internet distribution make the crimes federal offenses. Not that the state of New York should turn a blind eye if the feds don't jump all over this. Anyone involved in something so vile should be held accountable, especially someone as high-profile as the Councilman. The fact that his biggest donor and oldest friend was just hauled off in handcuffs doesn't give me a lot of confidence in O'Malley's innocence.

Angela must be thinking the exact same thing. "O'Malley already lost my vote."

"Yeah, mine, too, though I'm not eager to tell Kevin that. I'm hoping he doesn't ask. Or at least asks you first."

"He probably will, but only because you two are fighting. You're always his first choice." The bartender looks our way and Angela tells him she wants to switch to wine.

"We have a cool connection that other people don't get. It doesn't mean he likes me that way."

"I can't talk about this anymore. It's too irritating." The bartender brings us both fresh wine glasses and pours generously from the bottle of Oregon pinot noir I'd been drinking. Angela, who seems inexplicably unstoppable in her quest to strike every one of my raw nerves, asks, "Did you pick an apartment yet?"

"Not yet."

"Why not?" she prods in a lilting tone.

"I want to look at a few more."

"If you say you're waiting for Oscar to ask you to move in, I'm going to slap you."

"That's not it at all. It's only been a couple of weeks. I'm not even thinking anywhere remotely close to those lines." I'm protesting way too much, and I feel my ears and cheeks redden. Even lubricated with alcohol, I'm smart enough not to voice my real feelings to Angela. She'd probably march me right out of the bar and into a psychiatrist's office. Fortunately, the bartender picks this very moment to serve the antipasti tray she ordered while he was fumbling with the TV remote. It's decadent, especially on top of the third round of drinks, and Angela catches me wincing as I contemplate our bill. She softens and says, "I ordered it, I picked this place, and I'm getting the check. You need to save your pennies for your move."

Which makes me feel relieved and inadequate at the same time.

Oscar is waiting at my place, right before eleven, when I step out of the cab. I thrust a wad of ones at the driver, who peels away from the curb like a teenage boy with a week-old license. Oscar looks delicious with his tie and top button undone and the faintest hint of stubble on his face. He scoops me towards him with his free hand and plants a kiss on my mouth. He tastes like a dirty martini.

"Successful dinner?" I ask.

"Highly. I just landed the biggest account of my career." He's beaming.

"Congratulations. What account is it?"

"A company you've never heard of."

My face must show disappointment, because he says, "You've never heard of it because it's the largest holding company in the alcoholic beverage industry. Which is one of the few businesses thriving these days. So I feel like celebrating, and patronizing my newest client. Do you have any bubbly upstairs or should we go buy some?"

"There's a bottle in the fridge I've been saving."

As we slip through the door, he pins me against the wall and kisses me hard. His free hand grasps both of mine and holds them to the paneling above my head. His new briefcase hits the floor with a thud. His mouth pulls at my lower lip and his hand finds its way up my shirt. His lips move to my ear lobe and he whispers, "You have no idea how sexy you are," just as the door swings open and Kevin walks in and jolts me from my ecstasy. I see him in full focus, underneath the unforgiving fluorescent lights of the foyer. His faces flushes and I feel mine start to burn. I think I hear him mutter something along the lines of, "Christ, Zoë, you *have* a room," before Oscar disentangles himself from me enough to stick his hand out and smoothly say, "Oscar Thornton."

Kevin, visibly unwilling to be the smaller man, grudgingly shakes hands. "Kevin O'Connor."

"Great to meet you. I've been telling Zoë she needs to go public with me and introduce me to her friends. Why don't we have a drink next week?" I love how unruffled he looks, even though his tie is un-done, I messed up his hair a little, and he clearly wasn't thinking about meeting anyone two seconds ago. He's still so manly. So in control of himself at every moment.

"I'm jammed until after the election. Maybe sometime in Novem-ber, though." Kevin steps towards his mail box, clearly determined not to walk up the stairs with us.

"I'll call you tomorrow, alright, Kevin?" I say, as I take Oscar's arm and make motions to move along.

"Sure," he says flatly. "Nice to meet you."

Oscar remarks on the stairs that the campaign looks like it's kick-ing Kevin's butt, and he doesn't even know the guy.

"He's like you. He's one of those lucky people who loves his job, but unfortunately, in this particular election, he's getting way more than he bargained for."

Oscar's big career coup must whet his appetite beyond its normal levels, because he has most of my clothes off before we get beyond my tiny kitchen. He leads me straight to the sofa and we do it on top of this month's *Vogue*. I push Janice Broadwick's college file out of the way just in the nick of time. I try to enjoy the moment, but all I can do is pray that Kevin can't hear anything. Hopefully he's got *The Daily Show* on.

When Oscar collapses in a sweaty heap on top of me, I wait a minute or so and ask if he still wants champagne.

"Sure, but I'd love a shower first."

"No problem." I ease myself out from underneath him and wrap a throw blanket around me. I get him one of the good guest towels from the linen closet. Thankfully, he doesn't invite me to join him. Even though we're going at it like rabbits almost every night, I'm not ready to be totally naked with him yet. By which I mean I'm not ready for him to see me with wet hair *and* no make-up. Maybe soon, but not to-night. I had too much to drink at Per Se, and I have the sneaking sus-picion that I'd look more haggard than I'd like without my war paint.

When I hear the water start running, I pad over to the kitchen to get the champagne. Just because I've had too much wine doesn't mean we can't have a teeny drink to toast my boyfriend's success. Hmm. Boyfriend. I wonder if that's what Oscar is. We haven't had that talk, and Angela's admonitions start ringing in my mildly drunk head.

Of course he could have someone else, but I have no easy way to find out, short of asking him and therefore appearing totally needy and insecure. My eyes settle on his BlackBerry on the kitchen counter. Would it be so bad to steal a quick peek? I pick up the device and see that it requires a four digit code to unlock. I'm suppressing the urge to try a few obvious combinations when I hear the water turn off. If Oscar is indeed my boyfriend, I'm sober enough to realize he won't want to continue in that role if he catches me rifling through his contacts. But who locks a cell phone?

The little voice in my head cautions me not to question my man's silly quirks. She says I should be thankful he doesn't have a lucky shirt he never washes, or an irritating need for friendship with all his ex-girlfriends. She warns me not to be nosy. For once, I listen, abandon my musings about Oscar's possible extra-curricular love life, and retrieve the bottle of Veuve Clicquot that I've had stashed in the fridge since before Brendan left. I haven't been in the mood for bubbles, but that's changing.

Oscar emerges from my cubby-hole sized bathroom with the towel wrapped around his waist. I pop the champagne and pour us each a glass. "Congratulations," I say, with a broad smile, as I step closer to him. He sips the bubbly but his eyes dart to his BlackBerry. Maybe I moved it down the counter a bit and he knows I was looking at it. Or maybe that's paranoid.

I swear something in his expression darkens. For one ugly instant, my mind flashes back to his throttling of Reiner, and I wonder if my too-sexy-to-be-true new lover might just possess a bit of a nasty streak. The little voice in my head snaps at me to stop concocting drama. She says if I stopped to look, I'd see Oscar beaming at me. So I should stop behaving like a damaged, paranoid crazy person and enjoy the moment. She adds, unnecessarily, that tens of thousands of pretty, smart women would kill to be in my shoes right now.

"You know, on the way over here, I was thinking there's nobody I'd rather celebrate with." He sets down his glass and scoops me up in his arms. I gaze up at him and wonder how I got so lucky as he plants a lingering kiss on my mouth.

THIRTEEN

Niles Townsend calls me midway through the morning, right as Sybil drops an over-stuffed document mailer, bearing the stamp of a bicycle courier service, on my desk. I've been waiting to hear from him with a mix of anticipation and nausea. He's returned from Cutler's Los Angeles office. The firm left me a voice mail sometime over night that they're preparing an offer for him. If I can convince Niles to accept, the commission will stave off my looming down-market move for at least half a year. Of course, if I leave my place, I won't have to dread facing Kevin daily. Which until recently was an unforeseeable wrinkle.

"So how did it go?" I try to sound as un-invested as possible, but I'm holding my breath.

"You know, I really think they're a fit."

I exhale. Not audibly, I hope.

"That's great, Niles. I'm sure you know they're very excited about you, too."

"The thing is, Zoë, their number isn't where it needs to be."

I don't respond for fear of saying the absolute wrong thing. In my day to day life I work with associates who are happy to toil for six-figure salaries that start with a one. In fact, given the headlines these days, the ninety-plus hours a week junior attorneys snivel way less about their gold handcuffs than they did a year ago. In contrast, Cutler & Boone has offered Niles Townsend, who's barely past forty, an equity partnership starting January 1st, and annual compensation in the amount of $1.2 million. As Carol would say, he ought to be showing us a bit more gratitude. And I can't say I disagree. There's just something fundamentally wrong with a person who whines about seven figures when most people are grateful to be employed at all. Impeccably mannered, but hopelessly self-absorbed Niles surely doesn't realize I've spent dozens of hours going over his revenues and experience with half the people he's met, in what I view as a successful attempt to justify his salary expectations.

"Susie and I think they need to find me another $200,000."

"That would put you out of line with what other partners with your level of business make. You know they can't do that."

"If they want me, they will." He sounds like a spoiled kindergartener. "That's what Susie says, and I agree."

"Niles, Susie isn't exactly an objective party here."

"She's my most trusted adviser." I ignore the not-so-subtly implied dig at me. I can tell this conversation is going nowhere good, so I defuse the situation by promising to see what I can do.

Carol's standing over me when I hang up. Her make-up looks okay today, and she's not frowning or snorting air through her nostrils. All good signs. "I hate when the wives meddle," she says. "Do you think you've got this?"

"Absolutely."

"What's your plan?" She folds her arms across her chest and drums her bejeweled fingers against her elbows.

"I'm going to call Cutler, tell them Niles is really close to saying yes, gush about the synergies for a few minutes, ask them to split the difference, and sell that to Niles."

"You mean sell it to Susie."

"Right."

"I've taught you well. Let me know if you need help closing. I don't want to lose him." Evidently satisfied that I haven't torpedoed a huge fee through my woeful incompetence, she turns her attention toward New Girl, who is unabashedly reading her Hotmail messages. Carol lurks over her victim's desk for a full minute and a half, unnoticed. When New Girl signs off Hotmail and swivels in her chair, she actually squeaks and jumps. Carol, satisfied her mere presence has scared the daylights out of the next person she'll fire, heads back to her office.

When I hear the door slam behind her, I decide it's safe to open the package. It contains a pile of legal documents. At first I think there's some mistake, but then I look more closely. The papers are copies of a contract for sale, a deed, condo documents, and a settlement statement for the purchase of my apartment. Oscar has bought my place from Brendan's dad for almost a million dollars. He closed last week.

And he gifted it to me this morning before boarding a flight to Los Angeles, which lands in two hours.

After I've dragged Marvin across the street to Starbucks, plied him with coffee and sworn him to secrecy on his grandmother's grave, his clandestine flask, and a stack of Bibles that mean nothing to him, he confirms my analysis of the contents of the envelope.

"Nothing says l-o-v-e *love* like Manhattan real estate," he says.

"This is insane. Last week I was wondering if we're an official item and now he's buying my place?"

"Well, we've known from the get-go that your white knight's a fan of the grand gesture. The move with the flowers was the stuff of Hollywood."

"I can't accept it."

"You can and you will."

"I can't. I could never repay him." I know I'm not an expert on how functional male-female relationships should work, but I'm pretty certain that Oscar's latest move is well outside the usual realm of normalcy.

"Fear not, honey. He doesn't expect remuneration in kind." Marvin grins lasciviously.

"Don't. This is serious."

Marvin refuses to let it go. "I wonder how many blow jobs a Murray Hill flat is worth? Thank God you don't live on the Upper East Side, girl."

"You're really not helping." He's actually starting to tick me off. I don't need his lewd commentary. I need to figure out what to do when Oscar lands in an hour and switches on his phone. "Even if he wanted to get Brendan off my back by purchasing the apartment, he didn't have to give it to me. Why did he do that?"

"That's where the grand gesture comes in. He doesn't want to be your landlord. He wants to be your hero." Marvin takes a too-big swig of his coffee and winces as it burns his tongue. "I wish I could find a gay Oscar. That would solve so many of my problems."

I love Oscar's manliness, but I'm not sure I want to be cast as the damsel to his knight. I let the remark slide and go for the other opening Marvin provided. "Except you like younger men."

"Ah. There's that. I guess I should get back to it, if I'm going to have to sweep some unsuspecting boy-child off his feet with a flat in TriBeCa."

"As if. But Marvin, thanks for keeping this between us."

"Of course. You know I love a secret." He picks a piece of lint off his monogrammed cuff and says he has to get back to the office for a noon meeting with a litigator who fears confrontation.

Oscar's phone remains shut off, so his plane must be late. After the fourth or fifth attempt to reach him live, I leave a voice mail saying I'm floored, speechless, and generally blown away by his generosity. Then I add that we need to talk about this as soon as possible. For the rest of the afternoon, I jump a little whenever my phone rings, but he doesn't call. Not unusual. If he landed late, his day will have gotten going without him and he'll be racing to catch up.

Tonight Kevin's tarnished, but still alive, candidate will speak at a fundraiser for the Feminist Majority. Angela's going, and though I pleaded poverty when I got the invitation several weeks ago, now I'm wondering if I shouldn't take a page out of my new boyfriend's book. If I show up, personal check in hand, Kevin will have to accept my grand gesture of contrition. Right? Because he won't know about Oscar's ludicrous gift to me. Yet.

I send Angela an email saying I'm in. *Vogue* bought two tables and hopefully I can squeeze in at one of them. Otherwise I might be facing a less appetizing evening. I could end up choking down rubber chicken at a table by the kitchen, surrounded by militant mullet-sporting biker-chicks. She shoots a message back saying no problem, and that they actually have one more place because half the office has been felled by some early season flu, so I should round up another warm body if possible.

"Marvin?" I yell over the grey cubicle dividers.

"What?"

"You want to spend two-hundred-fifty bucks on abortion rights tonight?"

"Why?" he yells back. The Town Crier shushes him.

"There will be at least a couple of hot male models at the table?" I mean to say it persuasively but it comes out sounding doubtful. Marvin must not pick up on the nuance because he hollers that he's in. Maybe it will be okay, even if Angela doesn't bring along any eye candy of the male variety. Marvin always says he doesn't get enough wear out of his tux.

Oscar finally calls as I'm in the cab on the way to the fundraiser, sporting my trusty black dress yet again. I've stashed a personal check in my borrowed-from-*Vogue* Valentino clutch. It's written out for the minimum donation. For a second I thought about going higher, but I elected not to cross that fine line which separates a grand gesture from a foolish and desperate act.

"Hi, beautiful," he says when I answer. "Did you think about me today?"

"Of course I did. All day long while I listened to disgruntled associates re-hash their personal problems." That's what they do now; they frame their complaints by proxy. It's out of vogue to whine overtly about their working conditions in the middle of the Great Recession. So they snivel about their private lives instead. "How could I not? But Oscar, it's just too much. I can't accept an entire apartment from you."

"Why not?" I'm surprised that *he* sounds so genuinely surprised.

"Because it's worth seven figures and I—I don't even know where this is going. Or what we are. Or whatever."

"So just because we haven't bestowed a label on our relationship means I can't buy you a present?"

"Come on. We both know this isn't a normal present. And I'm not saying we need a label. I mean we should get to know each other better."

"But I know you well enough to see that this is what you need, so it's what I want to give you."

The cab pulls up to the W Hotel and the driver sticks his hand out for payment. A few yards ahead, Angela's disembarking from her own taxi, smoothing a hot pink silk number that gives her cleavage a major boost and cascades in an avalanche of ruffles from her hips to her knees. "We are so not done discussing this," I tell Oscar reluctantly. "But I have to run. I'm late."

"You know, you could take the easy road and say thank you. That's really all I need."

"Well, thank you then. But I'm still not accepting it. I'll call you later." I hang up and silence the ringer before he can object again.

Marvin comes out of nowhere, resplendent in his Armani tuxedo. He plants air kisses on both my cheeks and Angela's. "Where are all the beautiful boys?" he twitters.

"Upstairs, waiting for you, of course." Angela doesn't miss a beat. Nor does she find it odd that twenty-one-year-old hotties regularly respond to middle-aged Marvin's advances. He has just enough money, pedigree and gravitas to bed them. By the time they realize Marvin's not in it for the long haul, they've also discovered that maybe he doesn't possess enough of those three enchanting qualities anyway. Consequently Marvin hardly ever suffers an unpleasant break up.

The three of us make our way through the modern lobby and up one flight to the ballroom. It looks like a solid turnout. Maybe the fact that it's early in the week helps because people don't have as many competing obligations. We join the steady stream of donors inching towards a reception table, where a large punch bowl is already half full of checks, some tastefully veiled in plain envelopes, and others, like mine, unapologetically flaunted.

Kevin is at the table, looking over the shoulder of the pretty girl greeting guests and taking cash. He looks nervous. Angela says he told her that the campaign is pretty much wagering O'Malley's political future on tonight's speech. When he sees us next in line he comes around from behind the table and doles out air kisses. Maybe it's my imagination, but his token of affection seems icy and distant, like he's greeting some garden club acquaintance of his grandmother's. "Thanks for showing up. You ladies look lovely."

"Thanks. I guess my little black dress has risen to the occasion yet again," I say, as Angela surveys the crowd. A smattering of panache— probably the *Vogue* folks and other media people. A fair number of women in black dresses that are nice but not quite right, possibly because they feel inexplicably entitled to wear them straight off the rack. And a healthy representation of women who look like they might prefer to be men. By which I mean they've applied the invitation's black tie directive to themselves.

Angela glances pointedly at this last group, bats her false eyelashes and swings her hips so the ballerina skirt of her dress sways playfully. "Someone has to put the feminine in feminist."

"You're terrible," Kevin says.

Angela shakes her head and her earrings, a cascade of crystals and fresh water pearls by Dior, sparkle. "There's nothing wrong with being a lesbian. But isn't the beauty of *liking* women that you'd appreciate the beauty *of* women?"

"There's no accounting for taste." I cringe as this crosses my lips. It comes out sounding like a dig. What I meant to say is that maybe we should be enlightened enough to practice a little live and let live.

Kevin waits until the reception girl's attention is focused on checking in a group of five couples, then hisses at both of us, "Could you two please try to mumble though the next few hours without pissing off any group of the Councilman's key constituents?"

"Relax, Kev," Angela coos, but then can't resist adding, "The stress is getting to you isn't it?"

"I'm fine."

"If by fine you mean you've morphed into a judgmental, self-important prick, then yes, you are." Wait. I just said that out loud. Damn it.

Before I can utter anything to redeem myself, the Councilman appears, looking surprisingly pulled together. Kevin introduces Angela and me but then whisks the candidate off somewhere to go over his remarks one last time.

"Let's go find the bar," Angela says. "I think we're in for a long night."

"We could sneak out now. They have our money," I suggest hopefully, as we edge towards the alcohol.

"I can't leave the magazine's table looking abandoned. That would not be good for my career." She checks over both shoulders to make sure nobody's listening to us. "And, between you and me, it sounds like my boss's job might be opening up. She thinks she's all discreet, but *everyone*, even people in other departments on other floors, knows that she's seriously considering taking her maternity leave in the new year, and then resigning."

"Wow. That would make you what? Their number two person in shoes?"

Angela beams. "And all other accessories."

"So when do you find out?"

"Not until March or April, but *her* boss is sick to death of people opting for part-time or getting out altogether, just because they have children, and she's told me I'm in line for the next good spot that opens up."

"I guess you're reliable that way. She doesn't even have to worry about a serious boyfriend diverting your attention from *Vogue*."

A woman bartender in a dopey outfit featuring a men's waiter jacket and black bowtie sighs loudly because we don't order fast enough for her liking. She frowns with disapproval as she starts mixing our Stoli-Raspberry tonics.

"Can you make one more, but stronger?" Marvin's familiar voice asks from over my shoulder. "Did I mention earlier that you two look fab-u-lous," he fawns, before asking where we're sitting.

"Over there with the hot gay men." Angela flashes a flirty smile at Marvin.

"Good girl." Marvin nods his approval and stirs his drink. "I might need another of these before we face the cheap chicken."

Someone behind me clears her throat deliberately in that irritating way some people use to attract another's attention. She does it a second time, and when I turn to look, there's a familiar face, out of context, and I scramble to place this older woman in an elegant black and white dress. It's Trudy Bainbridge, from the opera. Her lips are outlined in crimson, which makes her mouth look enormous, and her eyelashes are fluttering at me rapid fire. "Zoë, *darling,* what a pleasure to see you again," she says, in a more affected tone than she deployed the other night in the presence of her husband. "Have you met my dear, dear friend, Olivia Sevigny?"

FOURTEEN

Olivia? Oscar's Olivia? Of course I haven't, and I don't particularly relish the opportunity to do so, but it's too late. A thin, olive-skinned beauty with a regal face and an incredible purple dress is already extending her hand. "It's nice to meet you," is all I can manage. She has highly defined collar bones, and flawless arms and shoulders that belie hours of torture at the gym. I steal a glance at her ring finger. She's sporting a diamond the size of a dime. Both Carol's rocks look like trinkets in comparison. She wears no other jewelry, except for a gold pendant that dangles suggestively just below her breasts.

"The pleasure is mine," she says, in an accent that sounds neither quite French nor Spanish. Any hope that this would be a coincidence—that Trudy would be in the company of a different Olivia—vanishes. As does any hope of immediate extrication from this situation. While I stand there, stupefied, and wonder what's expected of me, especially since this is now the second time in as many encounters that Trudy Bainbridge has caught me blinking vacuously, Angela steps in, introduces herself and Marvin, and begins gushing over Olivia's clothes. "I love the more sophisticated look in the new Cavalli collection, and this dress looks like it was made for you," she purrs.

"Thank you. I think Roberto's show was the most exciting in Milan this September. Don't you agree?" Angela, who is always on the prowl for kindred spirits, swoons as the second "*r*" in *Roberto* rolls off Olivia's tongue. I decide in that second, perhaps irrationally and unfairly, that I don't want anything more to do with Olivia. I'm not sure whether she's a threat, or whether she just makes me feel inadequate and off my game, but either way, I don't like it.

Trudy asks me and Marvin whether we're long time supporters of "the cause." I tell her yes, which is technically true in that I'm a lifelong feminist, just not a check-writing one before tonight. I try in vain to shoot Angela a look that says, please wrap it up. Trudy, oblivious or unconcerned with my distress, starts to explain that her family foundation is partnering with the Feminist Majority to fund several girls' schools in Afghanistan. Which is indisputably cool. Trudy starts explaining how Olivia has been *instrumental* with the PR, and I feel a flush of shame. It somehow seems wrong to hate her for being stunning, or for being an adulterous bitch who broke Oscar's heart, if she's donating her time to such a worthwhile project.

Mercifully, a waiter interrupts and asks that we start making our way to the tables.

We snake through the tightly packed tables and find ours, by the stage in the see-and-be-seen section of the room, and two tables over from Olivia, whose presence here tonight has unnerved me way more than it should, seeing as things are over between her and Oscar. I expected she'd be sophisticated and attractive, but did she really have to be drop-dead gorgeous? I suddenly wish I'd worn something with more panache.

Seven of Angela's fashionista friends are already seated, and I see that she didn't misrepresent the talent to Marvin at all. Two of the men are beautiful, in a juvenile, slightly underfed way. I do a double take thinking I know one of them, and then realize I've seen him, larger than life over Times Square, wearing only his underwear.

Marvin leans in and whispers in Angela's ear, "Thank you."

"You're welcome, sweetie," she says in a normal conversational voice. Then she whispers to me, "Look at him sucking in his tummy."

"Why do guys like that agree to do an event like this?"

"They make huge bucks advertising in women's magazines, so we sell it to them as an easy way to give back."

Marvin slides in and introduces himself to the underwear model and his friend, who's presumably also a male model of some ilk. Surprisingly, the two young guys don't appear the least bit put off by the intrusion of this middle-aged man, who's blessed only with average looks. I park myself on Marvin's other side, which means I'll have his back for company, and Angela sits to my right.

"Your new friend back there is Oscar's Olivia," I hiss into her ear.

Her eyes widen. "Are you sure?"

I nod.

"Too bad. I like her. I don't suppose you'd be alright with me being her friend?"

"Not a chance." Maybe this is lame, but I can't stomach the idea of my best friend consorting with the enemy.

"I know. But I had to ask. What a shame." Angela leans backward in her chair to take a closer look at my boyfriend's ex-wife. We can see her in profile. Her hair is swept into a loose bun at nape of her neck. She has an easy elegance about her that I'm sure men find irresistible. And even with her clothes on, it's obvious she has an incredible body. I can see why Oscar was despondent enough after to losing her to swear off dating.

Angela starts introducing me to the other *Vogue* staffers, but before she gets all the way around the table, the room erupts with the industrious buzz of simultaneous whispering. It starts in the back and sweeps over the space like a wave. Within seconds, word has spread to the farthest reaches of the ballroom that the Councilman's wife is here.

Holly McDonough O'Malley marches into the room in her no-nonsense black dress with her head held high, but she's not fooling anyone. She looks like she's accidentally bitten into something rancid and cannot bring her well-bred self to spit it out. Her eyes sport tremendous dark circles and it seems she went a bit overboard in trying to cover up the worry lines that have no doubt deepened in recent days. The result being that her make-up looks crusty. Little lipstick flakes flutter around the edges of her narrow mouth and as she passes our table, I notice she's got her hands clasped together to prevent them from shaking. At forty-five, the presumptive future lady of Gracie Mansion never seemed old to me, but it's like the events of the past week have aged her ten years. I wonder whether Oscar looked that haggard after Olivia left him for the film maker, if he wore his bitterness and betrayal on the outside for all to see. I wonder if he knows she's back in New York. Does that change anything? Could she be the one he talks to behind closed doors in the middle of the night? My stomach lurches and my palms start to sweat. I fidget with my napkin and wonder whether people will notice that I look stricken.

My quick survey of the room confirms that all eyes remain on Holly O'Malley, who has taken a seat at the table next to her husband's. All eyes, that is, except Marvin's. He's completely focused on the reason he came tonight, and, inexplicably, the boy toys are listening to his life story with rapt attention. I've heard the whole thing before, probably a dozen times. He's going to tell them about his early, life-changing sexual experiences with an upperclassman in the boat house at boarding school.

Immediately after the waiters serve the first course, Kevin heads to the podium to introduce the Councilman. I've never heard him keep it so short and sweet. Under the unforgiving lights, his expression is nearly as dark as Holly O'Malley's.

The Councilman takes the stage, looking surprisingly relaxed and in charge. Polite applause greets him. He thanks everyone for coming and cuts straight to the chase. "Many of you have been reading the news and wondering whether to believe the things they've been printing about me."

People start whispering when he pauses for a breath, but the room falls silent again as soon as he continues. "Let me say this clearly, and unequivocally. I abhor *all* exploitation of women and children. Especially children. And in recent days, I've done a lot of research on the subject. My campaign has been working around the clock on this, and I believe there exists no better forum than this dinner to unveil my latest initiative."

I glance over at Kevin. A tiny hint of a smile is forming at the corners of his mouth.

O'Malley clears his throat. "The average age a girl enters prostitution, or any segment of the adult entertainment industry, in New York City, is twelve. *Twelve.* Most of you probably didn't know that, because the days of the Manhattan streetwalker are largely past. Tourists come to New York, and they don't see the adolescent girls with half-dead souls selling their bodies. Which is a good thing for our local businesses, but it also makes it a little too easy for the average person to ignore this blight on our city."

Judging by the expressions around the room, this is news to most people here.

O'Malley pauses for a moment to let the fact sink in. He must have nerves of steel. I bet most candidates in his position would not willfully keep the audience focused on any kind of exploitation of young girls.

The Councilman consults his notes and keeps going. "Make no mistake: the oldest profession in the world is alive, well, and thriving right under all our noses. And the fastest growing segment of the oldest profession is the sale of teenage girls. So let's not lie to ourselves for one second longer. The overwhelming majority of these girls and women are *not* entrepreneurs. They are controlled by pimps who beat them down, isolate them from everything and everyone familiar, force them to turn tricks for hours on end every night, and take all the money they earn. They control who these girls see and speak with, and what they eat for lunch. Despite what the music industry, and several legitimate but misguided feminist organizations would have you believe, there is nothing glamorous—or good for women—in prostitution."

I glance around the room. Many people are silently nodding as they listen.

"Because of the Internet, all prostitution, but especially child prostitution, has moved indoors, into the shadows, and most of all, into hotel rooms. My predecessors may think they've cleaned up the problem, but they've just brushed it off 42nd Street and into the Executive Suite.

"So what can we do about it? Our great city wastes millions of dollars every year prosecuting *children*, stuffing twelve-year-olds into over-crowded jails. After these kids serve their weeks or months, we release them back onto streets, with no direction, education or means of support. And then we act surprised when they turn up with the same pimps who lured them into prostitution in the first place."

O'Malley has everyone's full attention. People are actually leaning forward in their chairs, waiting to hear where he's going with this.

"We need a complete change of course. We must go after the adults who profit from the vicious abuse of our children. Adult men pimp these girls, these *children*, to adult customers, many of whom are well-to-do, middle-aged, *educated* men who pay the pimps good money to—let's be honest here—sexually assault minors. And what happens to these johns? What does the greatest city on earth do to punish these predators? I'll tell you what we do. We fine them a hundred bucks and clear their records if they manage to stay out of trouble for one year."

Stunned whispers emanate from a few tables, but O'Malley keeps going. He looks around the room and makes eye contact with select reporters.

"Under my mayoral administration, all of this will change. I'm rolling out a plan, here, tonight, to protect young girls from the worst kind of exploitation. As your mayor, I will propose new legislation so we can stop jailing kids and instead get them the help they need. I will champion funding for prevention programs, to mentor at-risk kids, to keep them out of the sex industry. And I will use every ounce of political capital I have left to change the laws of this great city so the pimps and johns, grown men who permanently damage innocent kids, go to prison." He pauses and stares straight into the lone TV camera in the room. "And if you pay for sex with a minor on my watch in New York City, I will do everything in my power to make sure you will have to register as a sex offender. I don't care who you are, or how outwardly upstanding you look."

Applause starts in the back of the room and rolls through like strong surf. Soon everyone is on their feet. The Councilman stands at the podium and beams. I glance at Kevin. He's clapping madly off to the side of the stage. He looks like a man reprieved. His candidate just won back my vote, and judging by the standing ovation, I'll have lots of company at the polls. Even his wife looks impressed.

I feel so sorry for Holly O'Malley. Anyone can see she loves her husband, but she's smarting from the shame he's caused. And though she's probably not as easily distracted by his bold campaign tactics as the rest of us, her desire to believe in him, to believe he really didn't know where his money was going, is written all over her exhausted face. When the applause dies down enough for O'Malley to keep talking, he makes the interesting tactical decision to recognize her.

People start murmuring again. Angela whispers that men never know how to quit when they're ahead. The Councilman had everyone in the room, and everyone who'd hear the sound byte later, focused on the new sex offender registry. How can someone with so much political savvy allow himself to steer the discussion back to his own personal problems? The only explanation I can think of is that he's actually innocent, and desperate to have us all believe him.

The Councilman asks his wife to stand up. She does so, but with the deer-in-headlights look in her eyes. She waves at the crowd and sits back down as quickly as possible. Flashbulbs go off from every direction. This wasn't scripted. I glance at Kevin. He looks alarmed.

The Councilman goes on for a full minute and a half about all the things his wife has done for women in general, and for the Feminist Majority in particular. Then he motions to a junior campaign volunteer, some freckle-faced kid who's probably not even out of college yet. The intern scampers up to the podium with some kind of plaque and foists it towards his boss before scurrying away.

"I decided to go off the script tonight," the Councilman says. I hear Kevin groan. More flashes go off.

"I know the organization has its own awards to present tonight, and I in no way want to upstage them, but I thought that my wife was due some recognition. Holly McDonough O'Malley has worked tirelessly to advance the standing of women in New York and all over the United States. She's championed a wide variety of critical issues ranging from day care reform, to equal access to health care and contraception, to ovarian cancer awareness. She's served on too many task forces and committees to enumerate here. She's always led with grace, poise and level-headed intellect. While doing all this, and raising our daughters, she's been the best wife a man could ask for. She's been my most trusted adviser and constant confidante. And I want to thank her for standing by me during this tumultuous time for me personally."

Angela nudges me and points at Kevin. He's turned a pale shade of green, almost the color the Crayola people call sea foam. In the back, reporters who would never have bothered with this event, if not for the hope of catching something as audacious as this, scribble furiously on their note pads.

The Councilman invites his wife to join him. She appears riveted to her seat and looks like she might vomit. He waits a moment, adjusts his tie, and asks a second time. Holly O'Malley gets up slowly, as if being reeled in by some invisible thread. The Councilman smiles his best proud family man smile as Holly takes a tentative step towards him, then stops, bursts into tears and makes a mad dash to the exit. She knocks into a few guests along the way. Cameras flash madly and a couple of the reporters try to sprint after her. The room erupts in a low roar. Angela leans over and whispers to me that the Page Six writer, a slightly-built brunette whose face is somehow pretty and forgettable at the same time, is already on her cell phone.

I look at Kevin. He's got his head in his hands. I wonder if this is the final coffin nail. The Councilman's campaign for the most prominent mayoral office in the land was supposed to rocket Kevin's career to the national level. It looked marginally salvageable on the Sunday morning talk shows, and tonight's speech should have corralled thousands of straying voters back into the O'Malley fold.

But tomorrow everyone who matters in the world of political consulting will be asking why the Councilman's campaign advisers allowed their candidate to adjust his personal settings to self-destruct mode, mere seconds after delivering what should have been a watershed speech. If the media decides to focus on the rift between O'Malley and his wife, and what caused it, Kevin will be lucky if his next gig is with a second tier candidate for an upstate Congressional district. Even though he's been a twit lately, I feel a pang of sympathy for him.

The Councilman takes this moment, while the attention is briefly diverted elsewhere, to wrap it up and yield the stage to Trudy Bainbridge, who will kick off the presentation of awards. Hardly anyone pays attention. I spend the rest of the evening studying Olivia surreptitiously, for clues and insights about her true character and her relationship with my man. She gives me nothing. She sits and listens politely and claps when everyone else does. The bitch.

FIFTEEN

Marvin waltzes in at quarter after nine the next morning, wearing a ridiculous ear-to-ear grin and bearing Starbucks for everyone. He balances two cardboard cup-holder trays on one arm and distributes thirty or forty dollars' worth of caffeine to our colleagues before stopping at my desk. I thank him for the coffee and ask, "Well, which one? Blondie-boy-next-door, or dark, brooding underwear model?"

"Both." He says it with forced nonchalance. "And they're both underwear models." Marvin's got that tired but sated look about him, and his navy blue tie is flecked with happy little green frogs who look like they're leaping for joy.

"Nice."

"They were way more than nice."

"And I don't even get a thanks for inviting you?"

"I'll pay you back when you really need it sometime."

Across the bullpen, the Town Crier catapults out of her chair and squawks, "She's on the elevator!"

"Incoming. That's my cue," Marvin saunters off in the direction of his desk. "People! Try to look busy! And awake! And important!" he yells on his way there. He does it for fun, not because he's in charge or anything.

Carol stomps into the office with a cell phone pressed to each ear. Her blue eye shadow has been applied in two uneven cerulean blazes over, around, and inadvertently under, each eye socket. She's yelling into the phones alternately, demanding to know what the hell is going on. A few months ago, Carol stunned all of us by announcing that she would open a west coast office. Broadwick & Associates already has a sizeable presence in Washington, D.C., but that's a short hop away. Carol regularly swoops down on her D.C. staff on the early shuttle, without warning, to make sure everything is running to her specifications. Marvin claims she has hidden nanny-cam devices down there, so she can watch them on closed circuit television, and presumably fly down the moment she spies anyone running amok. Office legend has it that she stashes them inside the awards she distributes at each year's holiday party, since she expects the recipients to display these tokens of her recognition prominently. But Los Angeles is a different matter. Any way you book the travel, you basically lose an entire day or night with the trip. Which makes it challenging, even for a slave driver like Carol, to keep her staff under her thumb.

She's worked herself into such a lather that she's apparently forgotten which incompetent imbecile she's speaking with. She holds one of the phones directly in front of her mouth and brays, "WHO is on this call? WHO is on the phone?"

When it seems that nobody replies within a nanosecond, she flails the first phone maniacally in one hand and repeats the exercise with the second. She then mashes both phones to her ears and waits for a response. Tiny beads of sweat percolate on her forehead and dampen her professionally blow-dried coif. "Who is on the fucking phone?" she bellows once more, before emitting a guttural, animal growl.

Evidently the person on the other end of the call has managed, probably by merely existing, to piss her off beyond the ability to form words. Carol flings one of the two phones at the wall behind her assistant's desk. She throws her weight into the pitch and it sails from her fingers with surprising speed and misses the secretary's head by less than a foot, before leaving a ding in the sheetrock.

"Nobody wants to fucking work!" she yowls at all of us, but no one in particular.

New Girl says, "It's only six thirty in the morning out there." It must be the extra shot of caffeine Marvin brought her. It's killed her brain.

A collective gasp escapes the cube farm.

Now, if this were a happy, on the meds, beautiful make-up morning, Carol might let a thoughtless yet offhand remark like this slide. But any moron can see it's not that kind of day. "What did you just say?" Carol exhales loudly through flaring nostrils.

"Nothing." New Girl's voice wavers.

"I didn't hear *nothing*. Zoë! Did you hear *nothing*?"

"No, ma'am." I wince as I say it, but it's better to throw New Girl under the bus than to lay down in front of it myself.

"That's what I thought. Thank you." Carol smiles what she must think is a benevolent smile in my direction, but it looks more like her usual sadistic grin to me. "New Girl!" she barks. "Who signs your checks?"

"You do." The poor thing is shaking. She can barely manage a whisper.

"Right. So if I sign the checks, and those lazy idiots work for me, then they can damn well make themselves available when it's convenient for me. If they don't want to start before nine, then they should move to New York, right?"

"Right," New Girl squeaks.

"And they should also be thankful to have jobs in this economy," Carol booms.

"Exactly," New Girl nods earnestly.

"Nobody was asking you." Carol stomps through the bullpen and slams her office door shut behind her.

All remains quiet until about ten after ten, when red roses arrive from Oscar. The card says he misses me already. They're gorgeous, but I can't risk their *feng shui* implications after New Girl sparked Carol's wrath, so I stash them under my desk. I call Oscar to thank him but his phone rolls to voice mail.

By lunchtime, the color has failed to return to New Girl's face and Marvin has sunk from post-coital euphoria into morning-after regret. "Because I bedded both of them, that means I can't call either of them, right?"

"I can't say I'm an expert on gay sex etiquette, but if it looks like a one-night stand and quacks like a duck, or whatever they say..."

"Why do I do this to myself?" he moans again.

"Because you're a guy. Even though you're a lovely gay one, you've got enough of that commitment-phobic wiring. You pick young, tight-bodied hotties over age appropriate adults every chance you get. You can't help it."

"Maybe more therapy would help me."

"You already go twice a week. Who can afford more?"

"Asks the girl with two nice commissions in the bag, Niles in the home stretch and, oh, what was yesterday's big development? Right. You have no mortgage."

"Keep your voice down. The whole office doesn't need to know that." Although I presume they do already. "Oscar has more resources than most people. He's really into me, and I'm crazy about him, so that makes it acceptable." I'm not sure I believe my own speech, but I hope I'm mitigating the image of myself as a kept woman. And if we do end up living happily ever after like I hope we will, people will stop keeping score, right? Although, after meeting Olivia, I'm feeling insecure and inadequate. I can't believe that when I see Oscar tomorrow I now have to tackle not only the issue of the apartment, but also the re-appearance of his ex, who, at least to the casual observer, appears to be the perfect woman.

"Hmm. Remind me what they call a sugar daddy's other half?" Marvin asks, almost snidely.

I shoot him what I hope is an icy glare.

"Shut up, Marvin. You're sounding too much like Kevin. I can't deal with two of you."

"He's still in a snit?"

"So it would seem. After last night's debacle, I could hear him on the phone through the wall, yelling at someone."

"The Councilman's still going to win."

"I'm not so sure. This morning's paper had the poll down to a ten-point gap."

"Kevin's not just sulking about his career. Although with the former child porn actress speaking on prime time tonight he'd be totally justified." Marvin says this breezily and examines his cuticles to avoid eye contact.

"What's that supposed to mean?"

My phone lights up before he can answer. I tell Marvin I need to grab this. "Yes?"

Sybil's chirpy voice tells me she has Susie Townsend on the line.

"Put her through." My mouth goes dry. I know Carol sometimes talks to the wives, and I joked about, or rather I *thought* I joked about it, just yesterday. Now that the moment is upon me, I have no idea what to say to Angela's insane cousin.

"Susie! Hi! How nice to hear from you." I wince at how strained I sound.

"Zoë, I just wanted to call in person and tell you how pleased I am that you've been so helpful to Niles. He's so excited about joining the Cutler firm." I hold my breath and wait for the but.

"He came back from California all ready to pack up his office, but…" There it is. "They're low balling him."

I have to hand it to Susie. She's got nerve.

"Nobody wants to see him get the highest possible compensation package more than I do, and I've gone back and asked them if there's anything else they could do for your husband, because he's such a rising star, but I can't go in there screaming that $1.2 million is a low-ball number."

Neither is the $300,000 Broadwick & Associates would collect as the fee. Or the $150,000 which would be my share. I'm momentarily distracted by the thought of the largest commission I've ever had the potential to earn. Ironic that I'm on the cusp of such a windfall the day after Oscar removed my biggest financial burden.

"I don't care whether you consider it a low-ball number or not." Susie snaps me from my musings. "Niles and I need another $200,000, and Angela said you could deliver it."

"Did she?"

"Well, not in so many words, but she said you're the best. You aren't about to prove her wrong, are you?"

"It's not so much about my ability at this stage as it is about Cutler's pay scale. If they give Niles another $200,000, he'll be more highly compensated than any other partner at his business level."

"What's wrong with that?"

"It practically guarantees two things. No raise in the next couple of years. And a fair dose of resentment from the home grown lawyers who think it's unfair the lateral makes more."

"I don't give a hoot about their feelings!" Susie's indignation is palpable even through the phone line. I wish I could feel her pain, but I can't.

"Susie, this move makes sense for Niles. Not just because it's more money on day one. The Cutler firm has a stable of Fortune 100 clients that Niles can mine for business. Nobody in the firm does precisely what he does except a senior guy who's retiring at year's end. Niles will inherit those billings. His own book should grow exponentially over the next five years and his compensation will increase accordingly, well beyond the two hundred thousand you're fighting for now. Quite frankly, I cannot imagine a more perfect career move for your husband." I'm not sure where I'm pulling this from, but I think it sounds good.

A gong clangs in the background. "That's my masseuse," she announces. "I have to dash, but just find the money, Zoë. Angela promised and I think you know I can't have any additional stress with the baby making project underway. So just call when it's all set, okay?"

The line clicks and she's gone before I can respond.

"Zoë!" Carol booms behind me. I jump out of my chair. Not figuratively. I literally launch several inches into the air and land with such force that my chair wheels backward and almost plows down my boss.

"Yes?" I can't mask the fear in my voice.

"That was fucking great. You have managed to learn something from me after all."

"Um, thanks, Carol."

"Where are we? Is he close?"

"He's there. His wife is putting on the brakes. She has no concept of the upside or the long term opportunity."

"They never do. If she's like the rest of them, Susie Townsend doesn't understand finance beyond using her Platinum Amex at Barney's. She swipes the card, takes her purchases, and sends the bill to her husband's office."

"Maybe I should tell her that after Niles spends a year or two at Cutler, she could get a Black card."

"Not a bad idea." I'm shocked to receive this much positive (or at least non-negative) input from Carol. "Here's what we're going to do. They're going to find him another $150,000. They're going to pay it as a signing bonus so it doesn't rock their compensation scale and ruffle feathers. Nobody needs to know except Niles and the compensation committee."

"I'll call the firm right now and suggest it." I spin towards my phone but Carol places a bejeweled hand on my shoulder.

"No need. It's all done. Sell it to Niles. Make sure he accepts. Today, preferably." She turns to leave and spins back towards me to give me the closest thing she can muster to a compliment. "And Zoë. When you close this thing, remember to bill them on the signing bonus."

Wow. The fee on Niles' signing bonus alone is as much as I'd make for placing a junior associate. Maybe I need to consider, seriously, whether my soulless, socially useless, took-it-because-I-couldn't-think-of-anything-better job could turn into my career after all. Maybe I've got a talent for this profession. Maybe the lucky break I got when Angela sent Niles my way will catapult me into the upper echelon of headhunters. *I* could become one of the few must-know placement consultants in the city, instead of riding Carol's custom-tailored coattails. Then everyone would stop criticizing.

Like countless other Americans, I watch the former child porn actress tell her story to an overtly disgusted Barbara Walters during a nine o'clock special with limited commercial interruptions. The poor girl, identified only as Ekaterina, may have turned eighteen, but she could easily pass for four or five years younger than that. She has a dead look in her eyes and she's way too thin. She tells Barbara Walters, in surprisingly good English, about how some man in Belgrade told her he could take her to the U.S. to work in a restaurant. Her parents are dead, and she needed the money, and the man was charming. She and two other girls, whose whereabouts remain unknown, realized something was very wrong when they landed not in San Francisco, as promised, but in Saigon, where he took their passports. He then handed them over to an overweight, brown-toothed Asian man. He herded them into a van that was labeled as a resort shuttle but smelled of cigar smoke. They spent two nights holed up under armed guard in a seedy apartment with broken plumbing, on the outskirts of the city. She never saw the charmer from Belgrade again. On the third evening her captors injected her with something that made her achy and groggy, and put her on what she believes was a chartered jet, along with three "very young looking" Asian girls. She realized they'd landed in Mexico when they were driven to the California border by yet another man. He pointed a gun at them and ordered them not to talk with the border guards. If questioned, they were supposed to say they were with a church group. Ekaterina thought surely the customs officers would notice something was amiss, but they rolled right into San Diego without so much as a second glance from anyone, because the men had procured fake U.S. passports for their human cargo.

From there, Ekaterina doesn't remember much about the rest of the trip. She says she thinks she was drugged again because the next thing she knew, she'd woken up groggy in another filthy, windowless apartment. Barbara Walters bats her eyelids rapidly and looks suitably disturbed. After the first commercial, Ekaterina recounts weeks of beatings, starvation rations and drugs, and her eyes become deader as she walks through the details. She's not sure how long they held her captive before they forced her to start making the movies.

The whole thing turns my stomach.

Despite making the naïve and tragic mistake of trusting the man in Belgrade, the girl seems astute for her age. She knows her cooperation helped the authorities arrest the men directly responsible for hurting her and exploiting her, but she figures someone behind the scenes—someone more outwardly respectable—was financing the venture. And she also supposes that the European accomplices who trafficked her and her friends in the first place will probably get away with their crimes. So if by coming forward, even though it's embarrassing, she can help stop the money from flowing to these people, she says it's well worth it.

Just when I'm wondering how Kevin can criticize *my* job when he's the right hand man for a person supposedly involved in this scandal, Barbara Walters, as if trying to underscore my point, wraps up the segment by naming a few prominent men suspected of benefiting from the sales of the movies. Of course Councilman O'Malley's name comes up. His attorney has sent a statement, insisting that the Councilman admits to "a passive investment in the *legal* adult entertainment industry." He says his client, "like many New Yorkers, supports the rights of consenting adults to watch explicit films, but he does not condone the use of underage participants in any part of the production process. He urges his detractors to read his new initiative to prevent the exploitation of girls just like Ekaterina, and to prosecute the people responsible for committing such heinous acts."

I switch off the tube and get ready for bed. Oscar calls from Los Angeles as I'm settling under the covers with my book. He's through security and he has some time to kill.

"At least you'll make your flight. I miss you."

"I miss you, too. My bed at the hotel was so cold and empty."

Something inside me gets all molten and gooey, but I steer my mind back on track. "Oscar, we really need to talk about the condo. I'm blown away by your generosity, but I can't accept it. It's way too much."

"Yes, you can, and I don't want to talk about it in public, okay? Did you see the hooker interview?"

I ignore his abrupt segue and tell him I did.

"Everyone is talking about it, even out here. That O'Malley has balls, saying he's going to register most of the adult film industry as sex offenders when he invested in the stuff himself."

"That's not what he said, and maybe he didn't know his money was going to *child* porn. And if this scandal is what it takes to get a serious politician to talk about trafficking, then maybe it's a good thing."

"He's never going to get rid of prostitution. Or porn. There's way too much demand, and it's impossible to police because of the Internet."

"So you're saying it's okay because it's everywhere? Isn't that kind of backward?"

"Don't be so naïve, Zoë. Men are pigs, and there are always going to be girls who are happy to oblige them. Not everyone grows up in a safe little bubble in Wellesley, Massachusetts."

Ouch. That was harsher than necessary. What happened to the mushy Oscar I had on the phone two minutes ago? I take a breath and remind myself that he got up yesterday before four, flew to California, and did nothing but sit in meetings and traffic for two solid days and evenings. Plus he still has to face the red eye tonight. I decide to change the subject. "I can't wait to see you," I purr into the phone. If the little voice in my head could do so, she'd roll her eyes.

A security announcement blares in the background. It drones on for what feels like an eternity about unattended packages. When it finally stops, Oscar's voice has softened. "Sweet dreams. I'll call you when I land."

He's gone before I can say anything else. I turn off the bedside lamp and lie in the dark completely awake. I have to ask or I won't sleep a wink. I sit up in bed, pull the covers up around me, turn the light back on and dial.

"Hey again, beautiful," he answers, sounding pleasantly surprised, his tirade about my sheltered upbringing seemingly forgotten. "What's up?"

If I don't just blurt it out, I'll lose my nerve. "I met Olivia at the dinner. She was with that Trudy Bainbridge woman."

I hear Oscar draw a sharp breath. "And?"

"Well, you said she went to live in Paris, and now she's here, and she's gorgeous and amazing..." my voice tapers off.

"And you're feeling insecure?"

"Uh huh." I'm so ashamed. What was I thinking, starting this conversation?

"Zoë, listen to me. I can't keep her out of New York, but I can keep her out of my life. I have no desire to see her any more. I don't even see friends we shared. She's in my past. You're my present. Okay?"

"Do you miss her?" I cringe at myself. Obviously if he was pining for his former wife, he wouldn't be buying me real estate or indulging this conversation.

"Nope." He says it with such unhesitating certainty that I feel myself start to relax. "Now why don't you try to get some sleep? One of us should and it's not looking good for me. I hate the damn red eye."

I toss and turn most of the night, despite his reassurances about our solidity as a couple. His cavalier attitude towards an issue I find upsetting makes me feel even more unsettled. Though I suppose he has a point about men being pigs and prostitution being unstoppable, the Ekaterina interview haunts me. I can't imagine what it must be like to be junior high age, and desperate enough to sell yourself to complete strangers.

Oscar calls when the red eye lands at LaGuardia, just after seven. I'm on my way out the door to the gym. He wants to know if he can swing by and take me out for an early breakfast. He's already in the cab, approaching the midtown tunnel. I consult my watch: Not nearly enough time to get there, work out, get home and make myself presentable before he shows up. The tiny voice in my head mutters that I shouldn't be so available all the time and that I ought to make better use of my health club membership. I silence it, reasoning that I haven't seen Oscar since he lobbed the real estate bombshell at me. Besides, I've missed him. He's only been gone two days, but it feels like a week. We're still in that heady new relationship phase, where you spend countless hours making delicious discoveries about each other, and I can't get enough of him. Plus, I feel sheepish about wearing my insecurity on my sleeve last night and I rationalize that it's best to get past that as soon as possible. So I untie my sneakers, remove workout wear unsullied by sweat, and head for the shower, excited by the thought that he'll be here in under an hour.

I'm feeling very decadent sitting down to breakfast at eight-fifteen on a work day, with the handsomest man in the place, while all our fellow urbanites scurry in for coffee and bagels to go. The waitress, a tired Chinese woman with more gray hairs than black, and an unfortunate mole on her forehead, pours our coffee. She splashes some onto the Formica table and wipes it away without saying a word before whipping out her pad and asking, "Ready?"

"So how does it feel to be a full-fledged homeowner?" Oscar asks with a smile, when the waitress retreats towards the kitchen with our order.

"It doesn't feel real."

He stirs an entire packet of sugar into his coffee but doesn't say anything. Because the silence makes me nervous—yeah, I know it's irrational—I rush to explain myself. "It's like I said on the phone. I can't believe how generous you're being, but I can't accept an apartment from you."

"Why not? I have the money and you need a place to live."

"If only it were that simple." I reach across the table and put my hand on his.

"Why isn't it?" He looks genuinely confused. Could this possibly be normal in the elite socio-economic circles Oscar inhabits? No way. I know lots of very privileged people. Nobody buys real estate for non-family members. As if intentionally adding to my surprise, he says, "It's not like I had to get a mortgage. Seriously, Zoë. I'm not stressing over it and neither should you. Manhattan real estate is one of the few sure things in the investment world."

Right. That doesn't explain why he'd buy real estate *for me*, although it explains the speed of the transaction. He didn't need to wait for financing. How on earth lucrative is life at Takamura Brothers?

Instead of asking such a rude question, I tick off the responses I composed in my head at work yesterday. "It's not that simple, because I can't possibly repay you. I feel like I'm taking advantage. And it sort of makes me feel like a kept woman. You know, the kind who hardly ever leaves the boudoir and who wears garter belts and negligees all the time."

"That last part can be our little secret." He smiles and something inside my chest softens. I can't help it. After the ego-bruising Brendan debacle, it makes me happy that this hot, wealthy, successful guy wants me, for whatever reason. The waitress reappears and unceremoniously dumps two omelets in front of us. "Enjoy," she orders in heavily accented English, before leaving us again.

Oscar unloads a stunning quantity of Tabasco sauce on his breakfast. "I want you to be happy. I've got a decade on you in terms of age, so I have more resources than you do. I really don't see why this is a problem."

I poke at my omelet with my fork. In my head, this conversation went differently, but now I realize, I didn't hash out the logistics. He bought the place and now I can either live there on his charity (weird), foist rent on him (unlikely), or make a stink and insist he sell it or rent it to a real tenant (which would render me homeless and possibly single). Faced with this absence of anything resembling a plan, I decide to stall for time. "I guess I'm a bit floored. Nobody has ever done any-thing even remotely like this for me before. It's taking a bit to digest."

Oscar glances around the restaurant. None of the harried cus-tomers are paying any attention to us. "I have a confession to make. I've put it off, because it's not something I share with people, but I feel like we could have something real and you deserve to know."

I hold my breath and wait. He's going to tell me something that will force me to end it. I wish I could go back in time and prevent this conversation, because I've fallen for him and I don't want the rug yanked out from under me.

Oscar says, "You know how I said my parents died and I was raised by an aunt and uncle?"

I nod. It's an awful story. His parents died in a head on collision caused by a drunk driver. They were on their way home from a wed-ding. Oscar and his sister went to live with an older aunt and uncle who took them in out of obligation. He shared all this on our fourth or fifth date, when I asked about his family. He made it clear he didn't like to talk about it. I can't say I blame him.

"I lied." Oscar said. "And for that I apologize. The truth felt too embarrassing."

"You're talking to the girl who failed to notice her fiancé was gay. For over a decade."

"This is worse. My parents belonged to the Fundamentalist branch of Mormons. You may have heard of my father, Warner Parks. He was all over the news a few years ago. He's serving thirty years for sexual assault on a minor, polygamy and a bunch of lesser offenses. My mother was the second oldest of his four wives. She died giving birth to what would have been my ninth full sibling when I was elev-en. When I was twelve, three of the elders came for me in the middle of the night and drove me to a campground near the Grand Canyon. They left me there with a canteen of water and a bag of trail mix."

I am speechless. I've read about this group in publications as di-verse as *National Geographic* and *Marie Claire*, so I know they're no-torious for dumping their extra boys (it's an ugly practice needed to sustain the multiple-wives-for-each-old-geezer thing), but I've never met anyone who's even known anyone from that community. And evidently I'm dating a survivor of this cult.

Oscar watches me digest the information for a moment before continuing. "I bounced through a couple of foster homes until I basically hit the lottery and landed with the headmaster of a private boys' school in Scottsdale and his wife. They took me in and somehow sorted me out. They let me change my name. I was Luke before. I picked Oscar, because when I first arrived *The Complete Works of Oscar Wilde* was on the nightstand in what became my room, and no one from the FLDS was named that. Stupid, right?" He shakes his head. "But I guess it suits me as well as any other name. I had tutors for every subject. I played soccer. I managed to make a few friends, probably because I was such a goddamned novelty. Richard and June—those were their names—they helped me apply for the scholarship to the University of Colorado, which turned out to be my ticket to the life I have now."

"Wow. Oscar, I don't know what to say."

"Nobody does. So I don't usually tell anyone. Olivia knows, and Seiji, my friend from B school. And two of my college friends. That's about it. Anyway, Richard and June died in a car wreck, when I was seventeen and a half. Their daughter, Jennifer, she's forty-eight now and an art teacher in Sacramento, managed to get custody of me for the six months until I turned eighteen. She's the one I call my sister. My biological family is dead to me. Before I left for college, I changed my name to Thornton. Partly to honor Richard and June, but I had planned to do it anyway. Before the accident, I mean. I didn't want people hearing about Warner Parks in the news and making the connection."

He pauses to glance around the restaurant. "Which brings me, after that long and arduous detour, back to your apartment. Don't worry about the money. I made a small fortune when I sold my story right after business school. Ever hear of a book called *Surplus Boys*? It was on the bestseller list for months. It's basically my memoir, as told to a friend of Jennifer's who ghost wrote it. She changed all the names at my insistence. Too many kids in my situation weren't nearly as lucky as I was. It felt wrong to lord my triumphs over them. Most of the extra boys never even finished high school, and I know at least two who died of drug overdoses. I have a half-brother serving time for a string of burglaries. One girl who ran away, she was my cousin and she was barely fifteen, hanged herself in her foster family's basement." He shakes his head as if trying to erase the mental image. "Anyway, I brought you a copy."

He reaches in his briefcase and pulls out a hardcover book with a dusty desert road on the cover. A quotation from a review on the back calls it *a look inside one of the most sinister and secretive cults in modern America... a riveting read... a powerful message of hope and redemption.*

I'm glad Oscar trusts me enough to tell me all this. Though I can't help wondering if anybody can be as well adjusted as he seems after enduring such a horrific childhood. Doesn't that kind of trauma stay with a person? I feel out of my depth as I leaf through the first pages.

"Zoë? Are you okay? You don't hate me now, do you?" His face contorts with worry and I realize I've checked out of the conversation. It's the first time since meeting Oscar that I've seen even a flicker of insecurity from him. I'm embarrassed to admit it's reassuring. If he has moments of self-doubt it means he's not insufferably perfect.

"Of course I don't hate you. I'm glad you told me." I reach across our untouched omelets and touch his hand.

"Good." He smiles. "So I know you'll tear through the book and waste your day researching the FLDS, but just promise me that we won't have to talk about it all the time."

"Of course," I say, though I suspect it might be a challenge.

Oscar takes another scan of the restaurant. "One of my colleagues is at the counter," he whispers. He launches into small talk without missing a beat. "How are things at the office? You know, we had a co-op meeting last night, and I was sorry to miss it. I would have loved to meet the famous Carol Broadwick."

"She doesn't go to those things. She sends one of her lawyers." I can't believe the ease with which Oscar changes gears. I wonder what really goes on in his good-looking head. Does he obsess over me like I do about him? Does he think about me while sitting in traffic, or between meetings, or for no reason at all?

He's mopping up the remains of his omelet with a triangle of toast, seemingly oblivious to my silly obsessing, when my phone buzzes. Carol. "Speak of the devil," I say, throwing caution to the wind and letting her roll to voice mail. My stock is high enough with the Niles Townsend deal pending to put her off until I leave Oscar's earshot in a few minutes.

Oscar takes care of the check at the counter on the way out, and I feel a familiar twinge of guilt about not paying my way, even though the coffee money means nothing to him. His car is waiting. He's heading downtown but offers to drop me first. I decline, since the subway will be just as quick at this hour, but mainly because I don't want to call my boss in front of him. His kisses me goodbye and disappears into the traffic.

When I call Carol back, she, as usual, doesn't pause for pleasantries. "It's done. He accepted." I can't see her, but I know her eyes are gleaming the way they always do when she's counting her money.

Even though I feel like squealing and jumping for joy, I force my voice to stay level and professional. "That's great. I think this move will catapult Niles' career."

"Plus the client is happy, happy, happy," Carol practically sings. She's not raising her voice, or berating me for savoring a success while neglecting the pipeline for the future. It's bizarre. Then she says something even more out of character. "Nice job, Zoë." She hangs up as I'm stammering, "Thank you."

"When it rains, it pours," Angela says moments later, once I've related the details of my brief but momentous conversation with Carol. "It doesn't matter if you're talking about men or job offers or money. A little action always attracts more."

"I was hardly rolling in it before today. I've only placed two junior people since Brendan left, but luckily, placing Niles puts me in another league altogether. I can't thank you enough for sending him my way."

"Don't mention it. And don't change the subject. I wasn't talking about you making placements. I meant, now that you have no money issues, because you're not planning to pay rent to Oscar, more money will come your way. That's always the way it goes."

"Interesting theory."

"It does explain why the rich keep getting richer," she muses. "Anyway, Susie is thrilled. She was all worried that she'd overplayed her hand when she called you and demanded more money. She says Niles would murder her if he knew, and she wasn't sure she could get away with playing the hormonal card on this one."

"Good thing I was smart enough not to mention it to him." My other line beeps. "Have to take that. It's the man himself."

I switch over and say congratulations before Niles has the chance to say anything.

"Thank you," he says. "But I'm afraid we have a logistical problem."

This stops me dead in my tracks. A heavy set man in a blue suit crashes into me on the stairs to 33rd Street Station, sloshes coffee on his hand and curses me, the Starbucks people, and Jesus, before barreling past me into Manhattan's underworld.

"What kind of logistical problem?" I try to ask as levelly as possible, but I'm sure he can detect the waver in my voice.

"My firm wants me gone today. In fact, I'm standing on the sidewalk outside my old building with my secretary. They had security escort us both out."

I start to exhale. "Remember? We talked about this. Firms remove their ex-partners unceremoniously all the time." I had given Niles a heads up that this could happen, and I told him to download his contacts, somewhere other than his work issued BlackBerry, to take with him before giving notice. Junior associates may get cakes and going away parties, but defecting partners almost always get ejected immediately. Even the stodgiest law firms operate with lightning efficiency when it comes to locking people off their computer networks and confiscating their communication devices. "Didn't you warn your poor assistant?"

"She knew something was up with me, but for some reason, she never assumed she would be part of the deal. When I asked her last night to follow me to Cutler, she was surprised."

"Yeah, I'm sure nobody enjoys being manhandled by security. But listen, Niles. I will take care of everything. I'll have the Cutler people send movers over today to pack and deliver your office. You'll be up and running this afternoon. I'll let them know you're on your way now."

"Um, Zoë, could we hold off on that for a few hours?"

My stomach lurches. I rack my brain for the prefabricated speech I most dread delivering: *What To Say When the Candidate Changes His Mind (After Accepting an Offer from One of Carol's Very Important Clients).*

I'm about to explain to Niles that he cannot march back into his old firm and throw himself on the mercy of the managing partner. He's damaged goods. He's thought about resigning, and indeed has resigned, once. The other partners will never look at him the same way again. And for that matter, why would he want to go back upstairs? They just forcibly removed him and his secretary, a loyal servant of nearly two decades, from the building in front of hundreds of gawkers and passersby who might or might not know them.

Before I can say any of this, Niles hisses into his phone, "Susie's ovulating."

"Again?" It comes out before I can stop it.

"I guess it happens every four weeks or so. And I need to be there this afternoon at three."

I feel like asking him why the hell he didn't take care of this, err, personal matter, and resign this evening *after* their doctor's appointment. But of course I don't. Instead I say, "I'm going to hold off on telling the Cutler folks you've resigned until this afternoon. They'll either send the movers tonight or first thing in the morning, but probably tonight. That should give you plenty of time for your appointment, and your secretary can take today off to recover from the shock, or have her nails done, or whatever."

"You make it sound simple." Niles Townsend, a hotshot securities litigator who could have gone to work at almost any firm in the entire United States, suddenly sounds like an unsure little kid.

"That's because it *is* pretty straightforward. And I do this for a living," I say brightly.

"I'm not so worried about the movers, actually."

"Then what is it?"

"When I get anxious, or have a stressful day, I can't, well, you know..."

Oh, God. Don't say it.

"...perform." He says it. Out loud.

And then, because I am a moron, I say, "I'm sure you'll rise to the occasion."

Silence on the other end of the line. Then, "You did not just say that."

SIXTEEN

"You did not say that to the poor bastard." Oscar pauses with his wine glass midway between the table and his mouth and looks at me with an expression that manages to convey both amusement and disbelief.

"I'm afraid it came out before I realized what I was saying." I swirl my own wine, taking care not to swish red stains over the rim and onto the white table cloth. True connoisseurs twirl their wine to bring out the bouquet. In my case, it's more of a nervous habit that I've come to view as the adult version of peeling the labels off beer bottles.

"What did he say?" Oscar leans in across the table. It's a louder than usual night at normally serene Anissa. As much as I want to be out with my guy, I desperately want to get home and tear into *Surplus Boys*. I thought about starting it at lunch, but I decided I want to read it in one, or at most two, sittings.

"Silence. For like a minute. Then he changed the subject. But the worst part was that he called me back a few hours later to say that he couldn't perform this afternoon, and that he had to go back tonight because his wife had already taken the trigger injection, or something like that, and she had threatened to castrate him with an ice cream scoop if she stuck herself again for nothing."

"Thank you for sharing that lovely image. I have to say, I feel for the guy."

"People wish they had his problems. He's sniveling about making $1.2 million dollars and having an orgasm in a cup, when his poor wife is half insane on hormones." This latest bit of perspective came from Marvin, whose sister is doing the IVF thing. It sounds like about as much fun as being stranded at some Godforsaken Midwestern airport on a layover with Carol. On a Friday night. Of a three day weekend.

"That's colorful," Oscar says, and I immediately regret phrasing my thoughts so crassly. I forget he's still sort of new. I should have my interview manners, and vocabulary, in use. Or should I? We're sleeping together more nights than not, and he just presented me with an entire apartment, which hardly qualifies as a normal early-in-the-relationship gift. I know I'm a dating novice, but shouldn't we be letting our real selves shine through at this stage? I'm starting to feel a bit pathetic about not knowing how to proceed. It's as if we're simultaneously settled down and newly dating. To an objective observer, our arrangement must seem a bit unorthodox.

But it appears to be working for me and Oscar, so instead of steering into dangerous terrain by introducing a potentially toxic topic, I do the cowardly thing. "Sorry. I was just repeating the way Marvin, my colleague, explained his sister's experience with the fertility medicine ordeal. So, anyway, because of Niles and Susie's treatment schedule, I had to do a tap dance and explain to the increasingly anxious recruiting director at Cutler & Boone that the firm's newest partner would report for duty tomorrow, bright and early, instead of today, as originally announced. I justified the delay by calling a friend who works in the hiring department at a firm downstairs from Niles' old one. I explained the whole tawdry situation and asked her to book all the service elevators for the afternoon so Niles' movers couldn't start until later."

"Ingenious, my darling." Oscar laughs out loud. The skin around his eyes crinkles like it always does when he's smiling, and I can't help thinking that my guy is so much more attractive than the emaciated underwear models Marvin bedded at the Feminist Majority fundraiser.

I accept his compliment graciously and don't add that I must really be learning something from Carol. As recently as a year ago, such a ruse would have never crossed my mind.

Oscar tops off my wine just as the waiter returns with our fabulous looking, *Gourmet* magazine cover-worthy food. He presents my swordfish, a perfectly grilled steak balanced on some potato creation and topped with grilled asparagus, and the woman to my left, who looks about my age and isn't dressed like the type who eats in Manhattan's finer restaurants on a regular basis, makes a loud and snide remark about my dinner being "a complete environmental disaster."

"I thought that was sea bass." Oscar doesn't look up from his plate, but he says it loudly enough that there's no mistake he means for her to hear. She says nothing, and feigns fascination with her poached pear salad. Oscar prods, "Isn't it sea bass that's over fished?" Still no response. The woman reaches for the pepper as Oscar asks, "And Atlantic cod, if I recall correctly?" I can't decide if I should be happy he's sticking up for me, or worried that he's escalating a scene.

The woman's face starts to flush. I sit frozen and hope Oscar shuts up before she notices his veal, which honestly bothers me a little, too. Just when it appears he's about to needle our dinner neighbor into an unseemly confrontation, something across the room catches his eye. I turn around to see whatever he sees and there's Olivia, looking gorgeous in a fabulous green wrap draped over a simple black sheath. With thousands upon thousands of eateries in this city, she has to be here? She's with a slim blond man slightly her senior, and she hasn't noticed us watching her. Oscar stiffens as the hostess marches them towards our table. The former couple greet each other tersely and Olivia introduces her new husband, Jean-Luc. She looks so enamored of him, that I want to jump for joy. I may not be the most perceptive person ever, but it's obvious Olivia has no designs on Oscar.

Oscar stands halfway up to shake hands. "Congratulations," he offers gruffly. "This is my girlfriend, Zoë Clark."

"We've met, as you probably know. How lovely to see you again, Zoë." I'm not sure whether Olivia means to sound patronizing, and in the moment I don't really care. I smile, offer my hand and get through the so-nice-to-meet-you with Jean-Luc before the emotional side of my brain hijacks control from the rational side, and the little voice in my head loses her head and starts gushing at me. "Girlfriend! Oscar called me his *girlfriend*! So we're official. No dating others. That's what girlfriend means. The apartment was a grand gesture, and now he's publicly introducing me this way. To his ex-wife. This is *huge*."

I'm so lost in my private moment of jubilation that it takes me a second to catch up to the fact that everyone else looks uncomfortable and ready to move along.

"We're meeting the Bainbridges," Olivia finally announces, as if it's important for Oscar to know that.

"How nice for you," Oscar says, acidly. I study my plate with too much interest and wonder why Olivia seems hell bent on lingering when it's clear neither half of the former couple is enjoying the interaction. Jean-Luc looks to the hostess for an escape route, and she leads them to a table out of our line of sight.

"Sorry about that. I didn't realize she'd suddenly be everywhere. It's like no place is safe," Oscar says. He stabs at his dinner. "I'm better off without her, but it still feels weird that she's just installed her new guy into *our* old life, like he's version 2.0 or something."

"I don't know what to say."

I'm trying to find a tactful way to phrase the question of whether "girlfriend" means no sleeping with other women. I'm ninety-nine per cent sure it does, but it would be awfully nice to be certain.

Oscar, however, has warmed to the theme of his past. "I guess I shouldn't be surprised she's seeing the Bainbridges. We met them at a cocktail party at Seiji Takamura's house five or six years ago. Trudy and Olivia hit it off. Trudy sort of adopted Olivia as a daughter she'd never have, but the four of us used to get together once in a while." He pauses for a second, and I can tell he's visualizing this snapshot of domestic contentment from a life he's lost. He catches himself. "Anyway, Olivia kept them in the split. As you can see."

He pauses for a bite of his dinner. I'm wondering how to steer the subject to monogamy when Oscar starts telling me about his first golf outing with Bradford Bainbridge. He tells me he felt out of place because he wasn't wearing plaid pants. But I'm only half listening. Instead I look into his eyes, as if transfixed on whatever he's saying, and try to memorize my boyfriend's features. It seems so weird. While I haven't exactly led a chaste and pure existence, it's been ages since anyone but Brendan held the boyfriend moniker. Only when the waiter returns to clear the plates do I realize that I've once again allowed Oscar to duck an obvious opportunity to share more about his past. I tell myself that's an issue for another day. Tonight, I'm going to enjoy this milestone in our relationship. As the dessert menus appear, I excuse myself to go to the ladies' room, which turns out to be an orchid-filled oasis that features incredibly flattering lighting.

I'm touching up my lipstick when Olivia appears beside me at the marble sinks. I feel every muscle in my body stiffen as she steps closer and pouts at her reflection in the mirror. I notice we're both wearing Amarige, which has been my default perfume forever. Is it possible my new boyfriend likes me because I smell familiar? The little voice in my head snaps at me to stop being ridiculous. I'm about to ask Olivia to excuse me and slip out of the restroom when she says, "You seem like a nice girl."

Okay. What am I supposed to do with that? Thank her? Why does she think I need her approval on my niceness, or any other trait? She evidently takes my silence as license to continue talking. She pulls a small hairbrush out of her bag and asks, "Did Oscar tell you why we separated?"

"Because you dumped him for Jean-Luc." I try to say it plainly, but there's an edge in my voice.

"Not exactly." She brushes her brunette mane. "Oscar became successful beyond his wildest dreams." Olivia replaces the hairbrush in her bag and starts touching up her eyeliner.

"You expect me to believe you left your husband because he got rich?" It's not that I want to converse with her, but this is so weird, I can't help myself.

"No. I left my husband because his personality changed after he became wealthy. At first I thought the money was wonderful. It gave him confidence and a degree of freedom to take risks in his career. But something snapped inside him. He wasn't the same man I married. He started seeing call girls. I gave him a pass the first time. I told myself it was a boys-will-be-boys thing, as women say when they wish to excuse the infantile behavior of their men. But the second time I caught him, I left. I realized he has too many issues because of his past. You should ask him about his family, by the way. He's running away from who he is, but he can't shake his demons and he will always deal with them by acting out. Or at least that's the conclusion I reached. You're of course free to judge for yourself."

She pouts at her reflection and reapplies her burgundy red lipstick.

I feel my cheeks start to burn. "Why are you telling me this?"

"Because, like I said, you seem like a nice girl." She snaps her alligator clutch shut and blithely wishes me a pleasant evening before slipping out of the restroom.

I stand there for at least five minutes and panic silently. She's lying. She wants to punish Oscar for some reason, and she thinks turning me against him is an easy means to that end. Or maybe she feels like an idiot for leaving Oscar, and she's making up nasty stories to make herself look good. That must be it. Oscar has everything going for him. He can't possibly need to pay for sex. It's preposterous.

When I return to the table, Oscar asks if I'm alright.

"Something's not agreeing with me." This is, strictly speaking, not a mistruth.

"Let's get the check and go home, then. I'll make you some tea and tuck you in."

Half an hour later, I'm sitting up in Oscar's king size bed with my hands curled around a mug of chamomile tea, which does not seem like the kind of thing a guy with a seedy second life would have on hand. He settles in next to me and grabs the remote, but before aiming it at the TV, he asks, "So what did Olivia say in the bathroom that spooked you?"

"Is it that obvious?"

"Yeah."

"It's too ridiculous. I'm embarrassed to repeat it."

"It can't be that bad. What did she say? Did she tell you I was a so-so lover, because I think I've demonstrated that's not the case." His expression is playful, as if whatever his ex and I discussed must be inconsequential.

"No, nothing like that. She told me you made more money than you'd ever imagined and it changed you."

He nods slowly, and replaces the clicker onto the nightstand. "I invested in Bainbridge's hedge fund and it did well. She'd never say so, but it bothered her that I was suddenly richer than she was. I never understood the big deal." He looks genuinely puzzled, like he's trying to figure out a riddle that should be obvious but isn't.

I know if I stall I won't have the gumption to raise it again. "Olivia said you broke up because you started seeing prostitutes," I say tentatively, and scan his face for a reaction.

Oscar laughs out loud and shakes his head. "Wow. She always was creative. I have to give her that. Though I'm not sure why she feels the need to drag me through the mud. I'd think she'd want to leave well enough alone."

"So it's not true?" I prod, because he hasn't said those words exactly.

Oscar leans over to look me in the eye. "Absolutely not true. I do not, and have not *ever*, paid for sex."

I let out the breath I'd been holding. "I didn't think so, but she was so matter of fact about it. And then I got to thinking about the conversation we had after the O'Malley scandal hit the news."

"Just because I think something should be legal, doesn't mean I indulge in it. I feel the same way about pot, but I haven't touched the stuff since college."

"Right. I'm sorry I said anything."

"Relax. I understand. You had to ask." He leans over to kiss me. "So are we okay?"

"We're more than okay." I beam at him, thrilled that he apparently has zero interest in prostitutes and pleased with myself for having the maturity and fortitude to tackle a tough question head on.

"So should I quit talking now and let you dive into your book?" he asks playfully.

The next morning when I emerge from the Beresford's distinctive entrance at just before six-thirty, Oscar's driver is waiting to shuttle me home so I can change and face another day at Broadwick & Associates in attire that won't draw negative commentary from my boss. Carol is so rarely happy with me—satisfied, yes, but happy is unheard of—that I want to keep the honeymoon going as long as possible. Which probably means three or four days. By then, some other big deal will close, which will cause transference of her praise to another employee, or, more likely, some small catastrophe will befall the office, which will make my little triumph seem meaningless.

Most of midtown is still sleeping, or at least hitting the snooze button. We pass a few joggers, and several coffee carts, but Oscar's driver ferries me home in no time. I unwind my scarf and remove my sunglasses as I shuffle upstairs. My kitchen clock says 6:45. I could easily get to the gym this morning. Maybe if I showed up now and then, they'd stop sending me snarky emails extolling the benefits of physical exertion and reminding me that my metabolism slows with lack of exercise. I turn the key in my lock, pleased with myself because I'll easily make it to 7:15 spin. For almost the whole hour, as I pedal and sweat, I think about Oscar and how wonderful he is.

I stayed up until almost three reading *Surplus Boys*, and though I'm exhausted, my mind is racing. Oscar amazes me. He grew up in a house with four "sister-mothers" and their thirty-eight children. His father once wielded a good deal of power in the FLDS, but he couldn't stay out of trouble with the authorities, so his influence waned during the course of Oscar's childhood. Oscar watched a dozen of his sisters married off in tears to gray haired men; he witnessed his older brother repeatedly raped by an uncle who had a thing both for blond boys and exhibitionism; and he realized that even as his father's star fell in the church, his mother (herself a fifth generation multiple wife) was unwilling to stop the church elders from banishing her sons by going to the police. His mother's betrayal seems to have hit Oscar the hardest. He thinks she knew the elders would send him away early on, because through some fluke of genetics, he looked like a black sheep. The cult prefers conformity in all things, behavioral and physical. Oscar admits, towards the end of the memoir, that he would probably be incapable of maintaining a normal relationship with anyone if his foster family hadn't been so incredible.

He hadn't met Olivia at the time the book was published, but he was confident he'd go on to have a normal family life. The book isn't as seedy as I expected—it recounts awful events but doesn't dwell on lewd details –and several chapters do nothing but extol the virtues of Oscar's foster family.

Instead of spooking me, reading Oscar's memoir sort of reassures me that Olivia's behavior is what my mother would call "sour grapes." The more I come to understand Oscar, the more certain I am that Olivia must regret leaving him. So his past is unorthodox. Arguably, surviving it has made him a stronger person. She's probably just realizing this. Oh well, too late for her. At least Oscar doesn't seem interested in rekindling their romance. If only Olivia would hurry up and fly back to Europe where she belongs, my life would be perfect, I decide as I stand under the hot shower.

My early workout must have great karma, because things hum along smoothly all day. So smoothly, in fact, that I actually pause around four in the afternoon, right after the snack cart lady rolls through our floor with her contraband trans fat-laden wares, and wonder whether I'm experiencing some kind of cosmic calm before the storm.

Niles and his secretary have completed their move and he's up and running as a partner at Cutler & Boone. I've spent the day calling associates he'd like to bring with him. There are three, plus a junior partner, who is slightly less likely to move. If any or all of them go as follow-ons, we get to bill on them. At a slightly reduced rate, but it's a windfall I hadn't allowed myself to contemplate until today. And I get to arrange all their interviews without Carol breathing down my neck, because she's flown down to DC to terrorize her neglected Washingtonian employees for a change. I'd forgotten that she was going to be gone today, until I saw Marvin on the way in, suit less and sporting a sweater. He wouldn't dare do that if the boss lady hadn't left the tri-State area.

After weeks of maternal goading, I've gotten it together and purchased a plane ticket to Florida for Thanksgiving. I got a direct flight for under $300, way less than I expected to pay. My mother practically hyperventilated with excitement because I told her I *might* be bringing someone for them to meet. Nothing is definite, but Oscar didn't seem against the idea when I floated it last night on the way home from the restaurant.

I hadn't planned on asking him until he mentioned that he and his ex had a few of the best holidays ever with those people we met, the Bainbridges. He asked where I go for Turkey Day, and I told him. I even mentioned that since my mom went vegan over a decade ago, it's been Tofurkey for everyone, unless my brother's gang comes in from San Francisco. My sister-in-law, after enduring one Clark family holiday on what she called starvation rations, now arrives at all family functions bearing her own provisions, which last time included an obscenely large bird. She spent most of the rest of the weekend transforming the leftovers into vats of divine-smelling soup, which she sent home with everyone. Unfortunately, airport security confiscated my share.

Oscar surprised me by saying it all sounded charming and wonderful, so before I realized what I was doing, I asked if he wanted to come for the holiday weekend. He said he'd love to, but he'd have to check on some things at work, and he'd let me know by tonight.

Part of me is freaking out, because while I want him to come, to make us more public, or more official, or whatever, the other half is afraid. Maybe he won't like my family, or they won't like him, and the whole thing will be a disaster culminating in a break up at the holiday dinner table, right before my mom serves her homemade vegan pumpkin pie with non-dairy whipped topping.

Today, though, I'm feeling so Zen about everything that I think it'll be fine either way. If he comes, that's great, we'll make it work, and if not, there's always Christmas. That is, I'm Zen about it until just after five, when Oscar emails me that he's in, and his secretary is booking his ticket right now. We're going to fly out with the mad rush on Wednesday night and return Sunday morning. Three full days in the Florida sun with Oscar. And my parents. And my brother, his wife and their twins. I feel a stress headache brewing as I email him back that I'm so happy he can make it. Then, feeling sick to my stomach, I call Angela.

"He's coming home with me for Thanksgiving." I announce, not caring if the whole office hears me. Half my colleagues are out having manicures or getting a head start on happy hour anyway. This office is a perfect case study in what happens when some tyrannical figure rides a group of self-motivated, smart, driven individuals relentlessly. She transforms them into exactly what she fears most: opportunistic slackers who take advantage when her back is turned.

"Really? Did you tell him about the Tofu?"

"Yeah, he knows all about the menu and he still wants to come."

"Wow." Angela doesn't know quite what to make of this development. "Do you think he's going to ask your dad for permission to marry you or something?"

"No. Don't be dumb. Wouldn't you think he'd discuss that with me first?"

"Right. Just like he discussed the apartment with you. Zoë, this is huge."

"I know."

"It's also potentially relationship ending."

"I know that, too. You're not really helping here, Angela."

"Sorry. You've stepped outside my realm of expertise. You know I don't do long term monogamy. And the last four guys I've been with were European, so Thanksgiving was off their radar. Thank God. It would be tough to choose whom to bring home otherwise."

"People wish they had your problems. What are you doing for the holiday anyway?"

"We're all going to my sister's in DC, since she's pregnant and my mom doesn't think it's safe for her to travel. She's only four months, and she knows mom is being ridiculous, but we're all humoring her."

I'm about to agree that her mom is overly cautious when my phone beeps with an incoming text. "Hang on one sec." I check the screen. "New Message Kevin."

It asks, somewhat cryptically, "What's your deal?"

"I guess Kevin's trying to talk to me again. Maybe I should call him."

"You think?" Angela is gone before I can answer her.

Kevin's phone rings so long that I start to compose a curt but not overtly rude voice mail message in my head. Just when I'm about to hear the recording, he picks up. "We need to talk."

"Alright." I hope I sound flat, but not too bitchy. I'm mad, but I miss him. He's been a constant presence for over a decade now, and I am having a hard time imagining life without him in it.

"Don't be mad, but I just heard about the condo. I'm afraid you're way over your head with this guy. You barely know him and he's buying you real estate? What kind of deranged nutcase does that?"

"He's not a nutcase. He's generous, and thinking long term."

"Fine. Maybe 'nutcase' is too harsh. But you need to consider that Oscar might not be the knight in shining armor you think he is."

"I see. And since you've never exchanged more than, oh, seven words with him, I'm dying to know what you base this on."

He starts to say something but I cut him off. "For the record, I feel like Oscar *is* my knight in shining armor, if you want to use that antiquated term. He makes me feel loved and, I don't know, safe, somehow. He's the best thing that's happened to me in ages. So why can't we just agree that you and I are done discussing him?"

"Because I'm your friend and I'm worried about you."

"You could've fooled me."

My lower lip starts to quiver and I feel the waterworks start. "It really makes me crazy, Kevin, that you can't be happy for me. Ever. If I do well at work, you say my job is beneath me. If I'm happy with my new boyfriend, you try to convince me what we have isn't real. And frankly, I'm kind of tired of it. Especially since I've been your number one cheerleader since we were eighteen years old and eating Ramen noodles in the dorm." I pause to take a deep breath through my mouth, because my nose has gotten stuffed up. "When you were working seventeen hour days stuffing envelopes, thinking you'd never get noticed, and *everyone* else, including your girlfriend at the time, said give up and go to law school, I told you to hang in there. When you almost purposely screw it up with every woman you date, I always tell you it's their loss. Even though you're too old to be such a dog, and you're starting to be an affront to single women everywhere. For Christ's sake, even Brendan saw it. There're always two standards. One for you and one for everyone else. And guess which is the unattainable one. So fuck you, Kevin. Don't call me anymore, unless you want to apologize and start acting like a real friend."

When I hang up, the phone falls to my desk from my shaking hands. Maybe it should feel cathartic to let loose and express myself, but instead it feels sickening. I take a cursory look over my shoulder to make sure I'm alone. I am, except for New Girl, who's hunched in her cube, trying to slog through the fifty cold calls Carol decreed she must log each day until further notice. I put my head down on my keyboard and sob, as quietly as possible.

It takes me a full ten minutes to register that this is at least the second time in recent memory I'm crying after talking with Kevin. I can't believe how nasty he's being, and I'm mad at myself for letting him get to me. I doubt Angela's right about his feelings for me, but maybe it's one of those territorial male things. He might not want me for himself, but he doesn't necessarily want anyone else to have me. He's doing the human equivalent of running around me and peeing on my feet to mark me as taken and make me smell bad, in case anyone else comes along. Which makes sense, since most men are basically dogs. I latch onto this thought and it makes my tears stop as I start to contemplate an unpleasant possibility. Can Kevin be the true friend I've always believed him to be, if he's urging me to ditch a man I'm crazy about?

SEVENTEEN

Angela's ever-shrinking eyebrows knit together in concentration as she positions two perfectly executed twists onto the cosmopolitans she's mixed for us. Ernest and Algernon look on from their customary post on the opposite counter. She long since gave up on her foolish battle to keep them off certain furniture. She's got a live-and-let-live attitude towards her cats, and she says she uses it to cull men. Guys who complain about paw prints near their food don't last long. It's a funny quirk for someone who's so meticulous about most other things in life. Such as the presentation of our cocktails.

Finally satisfied with the positioning of garnish on drinks nobody but the two of us, and her cats, will see, she admires her handiwork before passing me my cocktail. "Here's to a man-free night," she grins.

"Cheers." Angela's concoction is stronger than I expected, and my first sip burns the back of my throat on its way down. "But why are you suddenly anti-male?"

"I feel dated out," she says as she sinks onto one of her barstools. "And I'm kind of happy Oscar has another business trip. I'm afraid you're morphing into one of those girls who only has time for her friends when the man in unavailable."

Fair enough. Angela may have a more active dating life than any other woman I know, but she always makes time for her friends. Sometimes she double books an evening, and sometimes she's rushed, but if you really need her, she'll leave whatever hot young trader, automotive parts heir or European prince she may happen to have in her bed hanging, and rush right over.

"Sorry. This thing with Oscar, it's still so new and intense. It's a big change of pace for me." I'm not sure I need to solicit forgiveness, but I'm doing it anyway, as a prophylactic measure.

"Don't apologize," she says, as if reading my mind. "Just don't disappear on me totally. I don't have that many real friends."

This is true. Angela *knows* practically everyone in New York. But she's so much more complicated than she looks. Most people don't get her, or, more often, they presume: beautiful girl, great smile, works in shoes, not much substance. As a result, her inner circle is limited. Its core consists of me, Kevin, and this girl Karen she grew up with, who now lives in Connecticut.

"What's wrong?" I ask, because it's so unlike her to say down-beat things. With Angela, everything is normally bright and bubbly.

"I'm probably just over-tired, and afflicted with monster PMS. My boobs are killing me this month," She slides off her bar stool and we take our drinks and move to the couch in her small living room. Ernest and Algernon, delighted to see two laps where usually they have only one, leap up to join us. Angela arranges her drink and her cat and says, "But you and Oscar have got me thinking. Maybe it's time to stop dating like my life depends on it. Maybe I've already dumped Prince Charming because I didn't get to know him well enough to realize who he was. Does that make sense?"

"Sort of."

"I don't know how to step off the treadmill without careening backwards, splayed onto the floor. Ouch." She flails her arms for dramatic effect and forces a laugh.

"It's simple. You just stop taking gifts from age-inappropriate admirers and notorious international playboys, and instead go out with guys you can actually talk to, you know, people with real relationship potential."

She frowns at me. So I add, "Come on. There's nothing that says one of your suitors isn't the one. You need to give the promising guys more time, and weed out the Reiners of the world."

"You're right." Angela pointedly admires the enormous cocktail ring on her finger. She's the only person I know who can carry off big jewelry while wearing yoga pants. "I have enough baubles and I get great freebies at work."

"You're incorrigible."

"Yes, I am. But don't think for a second that I'm about to let your crack about taking stuff from older men slide. Didn't a certain guy with more than a couple of years on you just furnish you with an entire apartment? Which, by the way, is *such* a new money move." She rolls her eyes and I can't tell if she's being facetious.

I shrug sheepishly. It's such a new development that I failed to focus on my own blatant hypocrisy while dispensing advice. "Touché, I suppose, but I had no idea how much money he had, so you can't say I started dating him for his income."

"That's right. You went out with him because he's hot. Very, very hot." She smiles broadly.

I laugh. She's not far off. Hot and interested in me, and that's all it took to hook me. And sometimes I can't help but wonder if it's normal for him to be this into me so fast. It all feels too fairy-tale-perfect. So much so that I'm a tiny bit afraid that I fill an immediate vacancy in his life more than a longstanding hole in his heart. Which would fit his over-achiever profile. I don't like to dwell on that, because it makes me wonder slightly too much about what I want from our fledgling relationship. Besides exclusivity. I've been hedging on whether to solicit Angela's opinion on the whole call girl thing, but now I decide to broach it.

"So we ran into Olivia again at Anissa."

"She's suddenly everywhere, huh?"

"So it would seem. She cornered me in the bathroom."

Angela jumps ahead of me. "Do you think she wants to steal Oscar back?"

"I don't think so. She gave me this whole 'I'm telling you this because you seem nice' spiel and then said the real reason they divorced was because Oscar was seeing call girls." I'm embarrassed to say it, even to my best friend.

"Yikes."

"Exactly. So I asked Oscar and he denied it."

"That was ballsy of you. I'm impressed. But do you believe him?"

"I think so. But why would she make it up?"

"It's a convenient way for her to make his life difficult. Oscar is running around blaming their divorce on her, so she's getting even. Not that Olivia's motive really matters. The real question is whether you trust your boyfriend or not."

"I'm not very confident in my ability to read people lately."

"You could always indulge in some harmless fact finding," she suggests, almost hopefully, as if she's eager to partake in a little secondhand drama.

"Maybe. I don't know. That's not the kind of relationship I want."

We eat our Chinese take out, kill a bottle of pinot noir, and watch the *Sex and the City* movie (again) before Angela brings up the tap-dancing pink elephant on her coffee table. "How long are you planning to avoid Kevin?" she asks without looking at me. Instead she makes herself busy with uncorking a new bottle of wine.

"Until he decides to move out of the building?" I'm only half joking. After I told Kevin off on the phone the other night, I asked Marvin, who practiced law for three years during his life before Carol Broadwick, and who is therefore my go-to guy for all questions legal, if there would be a problem with me selling the place Oscar bought me. He told me that I'm the owner, I can do what I want, but if I want to avoid an unpleasant "taxation event," he suggests I live there for two years before selling.

"Seriously. Are you going to the party Tuesday night?"

Right. The election. Which is now too close for the pundits to call, so they'll have to conduct actual voting and wait for the count before releasing the balloons and confetti. Though I suppose they do that anyway, even if everyone expects a landslide. Angela prods again, "Well?"

"I wasn't planning on it after the other night, and I doubt Kevin wants me there, either."

"I really wish you could work it out." She reaches over to refill my wine glass.

"Me too, but he's pitted himself against Oscar and he seems hellbent on making me feel like a horrid human being. So, as much as it stings inside to say this, I'm done. The next move is his and it had better be a sincere apology."

Algernon readjusts himself on my lap and continues purring, without regard to my human angst. His paws knead my thighs contentedly before his green eyes close to upturned slits and he falls asleep.

"Your cat snores," I say, and reach for my refilled wine.

"Don't change the subject. Kevin feels awful, too, you know." She sounds like she's getting stuffed up.

"Well, he should. He's been doing his best to put me down and I've had enough."

"He's been driven to temporary insanity by jealousy. And he's not so much judgmental, as protective of you. He just expresses it all wrong."

"Angela?" Not having Kevin as a daily part of my life is finally taking its toll. A lump is forming in my throat. I force myself to swallow it and resolve that another will not take its place.

"What?"

"Promise me you won't say anything to Kevin about what Olivia said to me. I don't want to give him more ammunition."

"You're no fun," she pretend whines, but I know my secrets are safe with her. It's one of the best things about Angela. Despite her love for gossip, frivolity and drama, she can be the most discreet person I know. At least when reminded.

On Tuesday night, at twenty-eight minutes past ten o'clock, the Associated Press calls New York City's most closely contested mayoral race in decades for Councilman O'Malley. He marches to the podium and claims victory with neither his wife nor any of his daughters at his side. The margin of victory is just under one percentage point, and TV's talking heads predict a recount, but it's obvious none of them expect the result to change. The pundits say he put himself over the top at the Feminist Majority dinner. His promise to fight child exploitation turned out enough women who wouldn't have otherwise bothered to vote.

I watch the revelry on the tube, in my flannel pajamas with the sheep on them, and the Totes slippers with treads that my grandmother sent me the Christmas before she died. It's safe to lounge in my secret single outfit tonight, with Oscar halfway around the world in Tokyo. It's also safe to do a little research on his ex. I've had my laptop out all night, but I've found nothing remotely unsavory about Olivia Sevigny. All Google comes up with are a few articles about her charity work with the Afghan girls' schools. I give up around eleven and shut my laptop in disgust, just in time to change the channel and see Kevin giving an interview.

Kevin sounds like he's reading bullet points from the spin team. He tries to wrap it up by saying, "The Mayor-elect looks forward to working with citizens from all boroughs, and from all walks of life, to make the best city in the world even better."

The surprisingly plump reporter purses her lips and asks about the pornography scandal.

"The Mayor-elect abhors all abuse of children and his administration will work tirelessly to protect the city's most vulnerable citizens. He looks forward to working closely with law enforcement, to bring those who exploit minors to justice."

The reporter scowls. "What about Mr. O'Malley's alleged ties to the adult film business?"

Kevin answers in a tone that sounds way too sober for election night. "Like many New Yorkers, the Mayor-elect owns stock in a company, which has a subsidiary, which in turn owns another subsidiary that is the target of the current investigation. The Mayor-elect has absolutely nothing to do with the corporation's day to day activities and he does not participate in its management."

"Shouldn't the Mayor-elect have vetted his investments more carefully?"

"As this campaign has repeatedly noted, he plans to divest his stock holdings to avoid any appearance of impropriety, before taking office."

The reporter, visibly disappointed that she can't elicit one candid comment from the newly elected mayor's battle-weary aide, sends the broadcast back to her anchor.

In one of the shots panning the ballroom at the Marriott Marquis, I see Angela, looking marvelous in a kimono-inspired dress with her hair skewered into an elaborate up do, held in place with just sticks. And hairspray, I imagine. She's got a date in tow, an olive-skinned Roman heartthrob named Claudio, whose family somehow married into an enormous stake in one of those mind-boggling Greek shipping fortunes. She told me his vital statistics over the weekend. He's getting his MBA at NYU so he's local for at least the next year and a half. And he's our age, which I thought sounded like a good development, until she snidely reminded me that I was still an infant when Oscar was finishing the fourth grade.

I glance at my cell phone on the coffee table and briefly consider sending Kevin a congratulatory text before switching off the TV and padding to bed.

The next morning, on my way to the office on the early side for a change, I step out of the stairwell and see Kevin at the mailboxes. He's in last night's suit minus his tie and he has about a week's worth of mail spilling out at him. He's flipping through his bills and hasn't seen me yet. Maybe I should just go back to the stairs and wait five minutes. No, that's stupid. He lives across the hall. I'm bound to run into him. But should I say something? Nod good morning? No. He's in the wrong. He needs to make the first move.

I march into the foyer purposefully, convinced I am the aggrieved party, who should be allowed to pass without delay. Kevin looks up when the door opens. His eyes are red and exhausted, but the worry lines aren't as severe as they were last time I saw him. I'm fully intending to give him the silent treatment and brush past when he stops me dead in my sneakers.

"Look what I got." He holds up a tasteful ecru envelope with the words "Mr. Kevin O'Connor and Guest" brandished across it in the thick black ink of an expensive calligrapher.

"You're not actually going to go." It comes out before I can stop it. Maybe we're fighting. But still. He can't possibly be angry enough to go to Brendan's wedding.

"Of course I'm not going. Are you talking to me again?"

"I'm sorry, I'm late for work. Excuse me."

"Bullshit."

"What?"

"It's not even 7:30 and you're wearing your Nikes." He motions at my feet. I loathe the working girl look, and Carol doesn't like her people coming in with sneakers where their pumps should be, but I prefer looking like a dork to wrecking my real shoes when I decide to get some refreshing Manhattan air by walking the commute.

"I have an early meeting," I lie.

"Fine." He shoves the unwieldy bundle of mail back into his post box and slams the door shut. An avalanche of third class junk will cascade down onto the mailman if Kevin doesn't empty it before they deliver today's batch. "I'm walking with you."

This throws me for a second, but obviously I can't stop him from following me onto a public sidewalk. And I doubt he'll keep it up for more than a block. Two at the most.

We walk out the doors of our building in preposterous silence and I set off up 37th Street at a good clip. He falls into step beside me. At the intersection of 37th and Lex, he says, "I'm sorry."

"Sorry for what?" I know I should be pleased to hear any apology, especially a straightforward one, but part of me suspects that Kevin's male brain, perceptive as it is, hasn't figured out exactly how pissed I am.

"For tearing into you lately. About your job and Oscar and everything."

Wow.

"Did Angela put you up to this?"

"No, but I'm sure she would have, if I'd allowed her to venture an opinion."

We walk the next long block in silence, which is surprisingly not nearly as awkward at it should be. When we come to Madison, a taxi careens through a red light at high-speed chase sequence speed. We retreat onto the sidewalk with a dozen other pedestrians. A mustachioed construction worker behind me yells obscenities after the driver.

Maybe I should take the high road, accept Kevin's apology and move forward. For so long, I've assumed he knows me almost as well as I know myself, and now his crazy reaction to Oscar's existence has put that in doubt. I wish I didn't care, but I can't help myself. I have to ask what's going on in his head. "Why have you been such a jerk?"

"It's complicated." Kevin runs his hand through his hair and tousles it inadvertently. A renegade lock skims down his forehead. I will not forgive him because he's adorable.

"Not to me." I focus straight ahead.

"Alright. I'm just going to say it. I think you've lost your mind over this new guy and I'm kind of worried about you."

"Oscar makes me happy." Kevin doesn't need to know my fleeting misgivings.

"I don't think you're ready."

"That's none of your business." I think I feel my blood actually starting to simmer. I can't believe his audacity. He's managed to nullify his apology in under three minutes. "I know Oscar doesn't fit into our happy little post-collegiate family like you wish he would, but I'm planning on keeping him around, so you need to get over yourself and deal. And if you care about me at all, you should be happy I'm so happy."

"You went from sweat-pant-wearing, bad-candy-devouring, spinsterhood-dreading despair, to utter elation, in under two weeks. Most people don't make that leap without the help of prescription medication," Kevin says, more cautiously. "I think some friendly concern is warranted."

"Right. I forgot. Your concern has seemed so friendly lately. If you can't muster any enthusiasm for me, then maybe you ought to leave me alone. It seems to me you have enough on your plate with the transition, and the future mayor's sex-capades still in the news, and whatever girl is in your bed on any given night."

I'm almost certain Kevin will say something snide, then shake his head, shrug and turn towards home. Instead he grabs my arm and pulls me to the edge of the sidewalk, so others can pass. We're halfway down the block from my building, next to a popular coffee cart. I see Marvin rushing in early, consulting his watch at every other stride like the White Rabbit. He must be late for someone somewhat important, because he doesn't usually move that fast. He nearly trips over his untied wingtips on the way through the revolving doors.

"Zoë," Kevin says, in a more serious tone than he deployed before. "Please, *please*, be careful with this guy. If something or someone seems to good to be true, it usually means there's something off. And with his ex back in the picture, a little caution seems warranted."

"She's back in New York, not back *in the picture*," I snap.

"Defensive, aren't we?"

My gut says he's spewing melodramatic nonsense, but my brain argues that Kevin has no reason to create more waves, so I try to soften my tone. "You honestly sound like my father, when I was in the ninth grade and I brought home a perfectly nice guy, whose parents happened to live on the wrong side of the tracks. My dad couldn't find anything wrong with him, but he forbade me to see him outside of school because he just 'seemed wrong for me.'" I consult my watch. "I have a meeting. I have to go."

"So are we okay?"

"You tell me." I spin on my sneakers and speed-walk the last few paces into the sanctuary of our lobby.

I spend the half hour I meant to use clearing my inbox hunched in the ladies' room, trying not to hyperventilate. I have every right to be furious with Kevin, but the insistent little voice in my head won't stop buzzing. Am I so head over heels about Oscar that I'm setting myself up for a gigantic hurt that will make the Brendan debacle feel like a minor bruising? Or maybe I should take a leap of faith and trust my guy, because most of the time, I think he's the best thing that ever happened to me. We're so drawn to each other. And then there's the offbeat romantic comedy circumstances of our meeting. It makes me believe we must have crossed paths for a reason.

When I force myself to emerge from the lavatory, Angela's on my voice mail, with a full report on Brendan's wedding invitations. "Please don't freak out," she says. "But I think he used the same ones you and your mom picked out. They have the same tiny splashes of hand-painted color."

Surprisingly, I'm not freaking out at all. While I felt a fleeting stab when faced with the evidence this morning, there's something reassuring about the finality of Brendan's wedding. It closes that chapter of my life and allows me to move forward unburdened. I feel a sudden surge of empathy for Brendan. This has to have been gut-wrenching for him, too. He lashed out because he felt powerless and overwhelmed by what should have been a liberating experience—calling off our engagement to be his true self.

Since things seem to be working for both of us on our separate paths, maybe I should let the bitterness go and wish him well. I feel the muscles in my neck and jaw start to relax as this realization takes root. I'm logging onto the Williams Sonoma website to buy Brendan and Steven a wedding gift when Marvin interrupts me to ask about a client visit we're doing later today. By the time we're done talking about actual work, I've decided that forgiveness is healthy, psychologically speaking, but gift-giving probably constitutes overkill.

At nine in the evening, I step out of a cab in front of Oscar's building and pull my long winter coat more tightly around me. There's a bitterness to the chill this evening and it feels so raw that it might even snow overnight. I hope not, because I'm teetering on my highest black heels and I didn't pack anything more sensible.

I stand at the desk feeling less certain about my decision to drop in as the concierge rings up to Oscar's apartment to announce my arrival. What if he's dead asleep after the long flight? What if he's not even here? Or worse, here but not alone? The little voice in my head reminds me that the whole point of showing up unannounced is to ease my fears without going through the icky exercise of snooping.

It feels like forever before the concierge says I can head on up. I hold the elevator doors for an old woman in a wheelchair and catch her looking me up and down. I hope it's not obvious I have nothing but lingerie under my coat. Because if it is, and it turns out to be a bad time, or worse, he's not alone, I think I'll die of humiliation. I shouldn't have gotten so carried away with my make-up either. I study my reflection in the elevator mirrors and wonder whether I overshot sultry and achieved slutty instead. My heart starts racing. This was a phenomenally lousy idea.

I think my sigh of relief is audible all the way down the hall when I step off the elevator and Oscar's standing in his open doorway, obviously fresh out of the shower in his bathrobe. He's grinning at me like he's won the lottery.

"Wow. Look at you." He kisses me and then pulls away, looks at me with raised eyebrows and a mischievous grin and peers under my coat. "Very nice." He takes my arm, pulls me through the doorway and leads me towards his bedroom. "How was your trip?" I ask, as I teeter down the hall half a step behind him.

"Long and busy, but productive." He undoes my coat, pushes it off my shoulders and looks at me appreciatively. I've abandoned my usual undergarments for a risqué black lace teddy that made the salesgirl blush, and the tiniest matching thong they had in the store. I've completed my sex kitten look with silk stockings held in place by actual garters. He spins me around to get the full effect before leading me down the hall. We tumble onto his bed, groping like frenzied teenagers. I start to slide under the covers, but he stops me and says, "Not so fast. You went through all this effort and I want to see you." He guides me on top of him. "This is the best surprise. I missed you, you know." He reaches up to play with my breasts through the lacy fabric.

"I missed you, too." He's looking up at me lustily and the little voice in my head is telling me to enjoy the perfect moment, but I can't help myself. And it's not the call girl thing, because I've decided that's bullshit. All I can think about is Olivia. Instead of feeling like the sensual seductress I was in the cab over here, I feel like a pathetic imposter. Why would he want to settle for me when he could presumably have her?

And what if Olivia came to New York because she wants Oscar back? That would give her a motive to scare me off with the stupid call girl story. Maybe they've already discussed getting back together, and her besotted behavior towards Jean-Luc was merely theater. Maybe I should ask Oscar, casually, if he's run into her again. The little voice in my head screeches at me to refrain from mentioning his former spouse while straddling him in bed.

I'm so engrossed in this new nightmare scenario that it takes me a second to realize that Oscar's stopped touching me and he's waving his hand slowly in front of my face, asking "Hello? Are you still with me?"

"Totally," I murmur, and lean down to kiss his neck, thinking that I've ruined the moment, but Oscar smiles devilishly and says, "Good, because I've never wanted you so badly." He rolls me over and slides on top of me and we have mind blowing sex that far exceeds any expectations I had when I decided to drop in. The whole time he seems so into me, so present, so singularly focused on making me happy, that by the time we're both lying breathless, tangled in the sheets, I'm convinced that my insecurity over Olivia is just my imagination running amok.

EIGHTEEN

On Saturday night, Angela puts on a slinky red and pink Cavalli dress, throws down her Amex, and celebrates her thirty-third birthday in style with a party for thirty-three friends. She makes her entrance at Cipriani's with her new Roman lover, Claudio, on her arm. Because Angela said it was all she wanted for her birthday, Kevin and I have temporarily put aside our differences to toast the start of her thirty-fourth year on the planet together. We're flanked by Oscar, who's jetlagged and trying his gentlemanly best to pretend he's not slightly smitten by my glittery, infectiously bubbly best friend, and by Lily, who eats nothing but a single boiled shrimp all night. Without any cocktail sauce.

It's Oscar's big debut with my friends, except for that night when he clocked Reiner, of course, and I'm nervous about him talking to Kevin. I so badly want it go well, so Kevin can quit criticizing. I told both of them that I bet they'll like each other. Advertising and politics have some overlap, after all.

When the waiter asks if he can offer us an aperitif, Kevin wonders aloud why Angela's spending this kind of money.

"She says it's because, on the other 364 days of the year, men buy her food and drink. She's giving back." I laugh.

"Except none of her benefactors made the invite list."

"So she's paying it forward. Which is her prerogative." I raise my glass. "Drink up, O'Connor."

"Cheers." Big, genuine smile. Maybe whatever disturbance was in our force has passed.

Kevin empties his glass and gets up to go to the men's room. I snuggle closer to Oscar in my chair, stroke his arm and ask playfully, "Can you do something for me?"

"What's that?"

"Make nice with Kevin. He's afraid you're some dirty old predator."

"Right. Sounds like exactly the man I'd want to spend the evening talking to."

"He's just being protective. In a brotherly way. Think of him as my older brother."

"My high school girlfriend's older brother once chased me off their porch with a hunting rifle."

"This isn't Arizona."

"Fair enough. I'm sure I'll win him over with my countless charms." He kisses me on the cheek. Kevin's at the bar. Oscar goes over to join him. I catch myself holding my breath. After forcing myself to exhale, I turn my attention to Angela and Claudio. He's telling us about their failed Vespa-driving lesson last night in Central Park.

"This one is dangerous," he says with a grin, as he pulls a beaming Angela onto his lap. She looks even more radiant that usual.

"You didn't tell me that your scooter had a manual transmission." She counters playfully.

"You should have seen her. Right into the bushes and over the top, and she leapt right up from the ground, dusted herself off and said that was only a rehearsal."

"Your Vespa doesn't sound long for this world," I say.

"I'm afraid you're right," Claudio says, with exaggerated solemnity. He is stunning, but he's got something more, a charisma that money and education can't purchase or cultivate. You have to be born with that kind of charm.

Maybe this guy has something Angela's other rich Europeans don't. Claudio has been in the mix with a couple of other guys for over a month, but for the past few weeks, she hasn't seen anyone else, and he scored date status for this birthday celebration. That's as close to a traditional boyfriend as I can remember Angela having since college.

Kevin and Oscar arrive back at the table with fresh drinks, and I'm thrilled to see they're discussing baseball as if there's nobody else in the room. When Oscar gets up to talk to a friend of Angela's from the magazine he knows through work, Kevin leans over and whispers in my ear, "He's alright, I suppose. I'm sorry I was an ass."

Maybe Kevin's second or third cocktail, tossed back on top of his second or third glass of Prosecco, poured tonight in lieu of champagne as Angela's one nod to the grim economy, has lubricated his conscience. Whatever the source of his softening, I'll take it. I jump up and give him a huge hug. "You have no idea how happy that makes me."

He hugs me back. Maybe it's that simple. Maybe our tiff has ended as abruptly as it began. I hope.

Lily begs off after the dessert tray she doesn't touch comes around. She has an early photo shoot, and she's due in the make-up artist's chair in under five hours. Kevin walks her outside and puts her in a taxi. I'm surprised he's not going with her, but maybe she's serious enough about her work that she's banned him for the night.

Angela is making the rounds, saying good bye to some of her guests, and trying to rally her core supporters for an after-party elsewhere. I'm so happy that Oscar actually found lots of people to talk with, besides the super model at our table, that it doesn't bother me at all when he says he has to call it a night. He hasn't gotten a decent block of sleep since before his trip to Asia. It's somewhat surprising that he's still upright and coherent. I'd be toast.

I go with him to get his coat, because mine is on the same hanger. The attendant is nowhere to be found so Oscar goes behind the counter and reclaims our outerwear himself. He kisses me good night and tells me he just needs a power nap. "Come by after the festivities," he murmurs, as he drops his key in my palm.

Wow. I wasn't expecting that. A key must mean we're kicking it up *another* level. He trusts me to come and go from his place on my own. That's huge.

"You sure you won't be dead to the world? You won't attack me as an intruder in your sleep? Clobber me to death with the bedside lamp?"

"That depends how you go about waking me up." With a big flirtatious smile, he buttons his coat, pulls on his gloves, and kisses me once more before striding out to face the unseasonably cold autumn air. I watch him go, still feeling his kiss tingle on my mouth and thinking I even love the way he moves. He has the manliest gait.

When Oscar disappears down the hallway, I snap myself out of my happy love-haze, check that my scarf and gloves are still stashed inside my sleeve, and turn to leave the coat room to re-join the party when Kevin appears in front of me. "Zoë?"

"Yes?" I say absent-mindedly. I'm still tasting Oscar's kiss and I'm stunned he gave me a key. I wonder if it's just for tonight, or if he means for me to keep it.

"I can't do this anymore." Kevin says, and his voice sounds like he has something big on his mind.

"Do what?" I start to ask, but before I can spit it out, one of my closest friends, who was too mad to speak to me until very recently, has pushed me back against the counter and he's kissing me. Hard. Like he means it.

My brain lurches into overdrive. The one time I contemplated hooking up with Kevin was many years ago, after I came back from that ill-fated trip to Belize with my Australian adrenalin-addicted transitional man. I thought there might be something nice about being with someone whose quirks are already familiar, who's smart, reliable and always there. A known entity. But I never went there, mainly because I assumed if we had that kind of chemistry, we'd have acted on it years ago. I figured kissing Kevin would be like kissing my brother. Platonic. Disgusting.

But it's none of those things. Kevin's kiss is insistent, hungry, and not taking no for an answer. And even though I'm still fingering Oscar's key, I feel myself kissing the best guy friend I've ever had back.

Like I mean it.

Claudio clears his throat loudly and turns to look out into the corridor while Kevin and I unlock lips and step away from each other. "Everyone is ready to go," Claudio says. He's located the coat check girl and she slides behind the counter and takes his ticket.

The remains of the party pile into three cabs. I make a point of taking a separate car from Kevin. He goes with the birthday girl and I hop in with some of Angela's girl friends from the magazine. I stare out the window and watch Midtown whiz by and wonder, quietly and incoherently, what I've just done, whether it means anything, and what happens next for me and Oscar.

Angela's new beau reserved space for her after-party at the Rose Bar in the Gramercy Park Hotel. I perch on an upholstered chair designed by someone famous and stare at the Warhols. Claudio tells us that they recently refused entry to Paris Hilton, which to him is reason enough to patronize the place.

After the waiter takes our order, Angela leaves her post at Claudio's side and drags me into the ladies' room. Once we've checked that no one from our party is within ear shot, she says, "Told you so."

"Told me what?" I'm not sure why I decide to play clueless. News obviously travels fast.

"Don't be coy." She whips out a lipstick and pouts at the mirror. "Claudio told you?"

"Of course. He thinks there should be no secrets between lovers, which is total bullshit, but he's an awful gossip. He said he cleared his throat twice before you guys noticed."

"He's exaggerating." I feel my ears redden. The bathroom attendant hovers a few feet down the counter. She's taking her time stacking clean hand towels, and obviously hoping to hear something good. Who can blame her? It's got to be a horrible job, even in an immaculate marble bathroom like this one.

"So? How was it?"

"How was what?"

"The kiss. Don't play dumb."

"It was nice. Really nice."

"Who started it?"

"He did, but I didn't exactly push him off me." I turn away from the mirror where I'd been playing with my hair, trying to arrange the highlighted pieces to best frame my face. "What am I going to do?"

She pauses with her eyelash curler in mid-air and says, "You don't necessarily have to *do* much. Not yet. Kevin knows all about Oscar, and Oscar doesn't suspect a thing about Kevin. You could date them both for a few weeks and see how you feel. Even if you choose Oscar, which I don't think you will, by the way, Kevin will be okay because you were open about it from the beginning. And if you dump Oscar, it really doesn't matter what he thinks of you dating Kevin."

"Why do you think I wouldn't choose Oscar? We're well past the point of dating other people. He gave me a key to his place tonight."

"So fine. Tell Kevin you're sorry, but you're in love with Oscar and you can't do this right now."

"I can't do that to him."

"If you loved Oscar, you could."

One of the girls from *Vogue* sashays into the bathroom. Angela gives me a look that says she thinks she's gotten the last word in under the wire.

When we get back to the table, Claudio is talking nonsense about inviting all of us to spend next August at his family's villa in Capri.

"Are the taxis really all convertibles?" One of the *Vogue* girls asks.

"Of course. And the rest are boats. You'll have to come stay. We have the most amazing chef."

The girl's eye lashes are batting wildly by the time Angela reappears like a fast rising electrical storm and displaces her new would-be rival from the perch next to Claudio. I've never seen Angela so besotted. It can't be just Claudio's looks. She's not as easily plied by chiseled abs, soulful eyes and a winning smile as the average female. Some of her short timers actually tend to be wealthier than they are handsome, but with their resources, they can make the best of whatever the genetic lottery awarded them.

More drinks arrive and the conversation becomes increasingly inane as the *Vogue* girls toss back too much wine and gush about a trip to Italy that will never happen. Kevin sits between them, studiously avoiding eye contact with me. When Claudio gets up, I slide in next to Angela and say, "I didn't know you had it so bad."

"He's wonderful, Zoë, but I don't know."

"What do you mean you don't know?"

"I'm not really a monogamy kind of girl."

"That's because you never date anyone you actually like enough to be that way. You go for the guys who can show you a good time, but if you take away the glitzy gifts and big nights out, there's nothing left. I love you, Angela, but you do have a tendency to fall for the same smoke and mirrors tricks over and over again."

The little voice in my head wonders whether I'm guilty of falling for a similar type of substance-free glamour myself. She's speculating, somewhat loudly, that Angela and I suffer from the same fear of true romantic intimacy. I tell her to shush. This isn't about me. It's about my friend.

"I'm not falling for them if I'm the one who does the dumping," Angela says finally, as if she's really been thinking this through.

"Fair enough." I don't want to sail into treacherous waters so I ask, "What do you suppose it is about Claudio?"

"He checks all the boxes I normally require, of course, but the thing is, he *gets* me. It's like we're on the same wave length. He knows what I'm going to say before I say it. And I can't stop thinking about him. Like yesterday, when I was going over the proofs for the January feature on Jimmy Choo, a not-so-little part of my brain was trying out my last name with his."

"Your name, if you wanted to change it, would go with any Italian name."

"I know! It must be a sign that we're meant to be," she says jokingly. "And I have this destructive urge to tote him home to meet my family."

"So now you know how I feel about Oscar." I stir my Stoli Raspberry tonic.

"But do you? Even now that you know I wasn't off the mark with Kevin?"

"Kevin and I need to talk." I hear myself try to say this with conviction, but the truth is, I'm unsure what I really want to say to Kevin.

"I don't think talking is what he has in mind," Claudio says as he re-joins us. He waits expectantly for me to slide over a chair so that he won't have to sit three feet away from Angela.

Sometime before two, the birthday girl decides she's had enough to drink and Claudio gets the check. We all reach for our wallets, but he waves us away, looking almost insulted that we would foist our dollars on him. Of course, he's a rich man made even richer by the exchange rate. I'm curious as to what three hours for a dozen people in the Rose Bar costs, but I'm not drunk or rude enough to ask.

Kevin comes over to me. "Share a cab?"

I open my mouth to say I promised to go to Oscar's when the party broke up, but what comes out is, "Alright." I can always ask the cab to make two stops, or, better yet, I could go home first and get my overnight stuff. I don't want to be wearing my dress and stilettos again in the morning.

We kiss Angela and Claudio goodbye. She raises one eyebrow and gives me a knowing look. When Kevin's attention is elsewhere, I hiss at her, "It's not going to be like that."

"Of course it's not, honey," she says playfully. "Call me in the morning, okay? And thanks again for a great birthday."

Kevin and I settle into the taxi for the quick trip home. As the driver pulls away from the curb, Kevin looks out the window on his side and says, "So it seems that my secret is out."

I don't know how to respond. I suppress the urge to come up with something pithy and pointless to fill the silence and wait for him to say more.

"I didn't mean to tell you that way." He's still looking out the window.

"Well, technically, you kind of *showed* me. Although, if we're being honest, I'm not completely clear on what exactly you hoped to communicate."

I've been staring straight ahead but now I turn to look at my friend. I've always thought he was cute, no, better than cute, but in a totally different way than Oscar. Oscar is classically tall, dark and handsome, and judging by the looks he gets on the street, that's not a matter of opinion. Kevin's one of those guys who's better than average looking to begin with, but his charm makes him even more attractive.

He finally turns his head to meet my gaze. He takes a deep breath. "I love you Zoë. I have for a long time, and not in the just-friends sense. I thought I was being so painfully obvious about it, but in retrospect, maybe I wasn't. And now you're with Oscar and it's literally tearing me up inside." He looks away again.

Wow.

"I don't know what to say. But at the minimum, I can say it wasn't obvious. You've been seeing Lily, and I thought that was going well, that you'd graduated to more than the odd date and lots of casual sex. And you've been so angry with me."

"That's because I've been a big wimp."

"So what's changed?"

"I started to see Oscar might have some staying power, and of course, all the drinks tonight gave me some courage."

"Maybe you're just beer goggling me. Won't you feel sheepish in the morning?" I force a laugh, but I know there's no putting his big announcement back in its tidy little box.

The cab pulls up to our building before he can answer. The little voice in my head warns me not to rock the boat with Oscar. I should take Kevin's ten bucks and tell the driver to take me to Central Park West. But I can't. I let Kevin pay and slide out of the car. He takes my hand as a group of drunk guys commandeers our cab, and leads me through the entrance and up the stairs. He holds the door for me and we step out of the stairwell into our shared hallway.

"Your place or mine?" he asks with a smile.

NINETEEN

"Kevin, I can't." I say it after he's swung his door open and led me through it.

He flips on the lights. They make the tiny foyer too bright, especially for the late hour. "Because of him?"

"Yes. I'm sorry."

Kevin looks away from me and asks, "But you want to?"

"I don't know. Yes. No. Maybe if we'd had less to drink. Or more to drink. I just don't know, so I think the best thing to do would be to call it a night, and for me to go home."

"You mean go to his place." He still won't look at me.

Despite my best efforts to squelch them, tears start to leak from the corners of my eyes. They make my worn-too-long extreme lengthening mascara sting and itch. When I wipe my eyes, an ugly black smudge appears on the back of my hand. "What am I supposed to say? What do you want me to say?" I sound stuffy and borderline hysterical.

"Zoë, come on, don't cry." He reaches out and envelopes me in his arms. I take a deep breath, will myself to demonstrate a little composure, and try not to sob into his shoulder. It's a good thing his wool overcoat is black cashmere. It probably won't show cosmetics stains.

"Do you want a cup of tea or hot chocolate or something?"

"Okay." I shrug my coat off my shoulders and hang it with his on an over-crowded hat stand that takes up most of the entrance. I follow Kevin into his familiar kitchen and realize I haven't been inside this apartment since I started dating Oscar. Even though the timing of my new boyfriend has coincided with Kevin's busy season at work, normally I'd at least have been by for a late night beer now and then.

The kettle starts to screech. He pours two cups and mixes in the little packets of instant hot cocoa. Both mugs bear a (fortunately) rejected mayoral campaign slogan supposedly penned by an intern whose parents were major contributors. O'Malley: A Shiny Future for the Big Apple. As he hands me one, Kevin says, "This is not how to-night had played out in my head."

I put the mug down and hop up to sit on the counter. For a sec-ond, I watch Kevin contemplate sliding in next to me, but he situates himself on the other one, opposite me in the small galley. I slide a lar-gish pile of unopened mail out of the way. Not that it was interfering with my comfort, but it gives me something to do for a second be-cause I still have no idea what to say.

Kevin breaks the silence again. "Leave him."

"Please don't do this. Maybe I should go. I need time to think." It's the truth. Everything is happening too fast and I'm starting to feel as if I'm watching my life speed by as if hijacked, instead of steering it myself. I slide off the counter. My dress rides up my thighs and I pull the fabric back down.

Kevin hops off his counter and takes both my hands in his. "I don't know if I can handle being just friends anymore." He's no lon-ger avoiding my gaze. His green eyes are staring right into mine. "And when you kissed me back tonight, it didn't feel like you were doing it out of sympathy."

"Of course it wasn't sympathy. But you have to admit, you caught me off guard."

"I've always enjoyed the element of surprise." He tries to muster a laugh.

I slip my hands out of his grasp. "I really should go. Let's talk tomorrow, if you want, when both of us have less drink coursing through our veins."

"The alcohol hasn't intensified my feelings. It's just given me some much-needed liquid courage."

"Are you sure?"

"Positive."

"So if you had these feelings towards me, then why on earth did you encourage me to go out with Oscar in the first place?"

"If you remember, I wasn't egging you on all that enthusiastically. Angela was. It was obvious you were flattered and excited, and rightly so. I thought there'd be no harm in you having a little fun. And God knows I didn't want to slide in as the transitional man. Not that I thought of it this way at the time, but, you know, in hind sight, I gam-bled. I bet that you'd have one or two dates max with this mystery ad exec, and that would be that."

"Wow." It's all I can think of to say. Then, "What about Lily?"

"Friends with benefits. Nothing more."

"For her, too?"

"Her idea. Or requirement, more like it. She has some serious boyfriend in Ljubljana."

"Interesting. But it doesn't lessen or change what I have with Oscar. I love him, and I think he loves me. We've just kicked things up a notch. He gave me his key. But now I feel like a big idiot for screwing things up by drunkenly kissing you." I wonder if I really have messed things up. It's one stupid, boozy, over-tired little slip, so perhaps there's no need to come clean to Oscar. It would just hurt him, right? And it's not like I'm going to let it happen ever again. "I feel like I need to see where we're going. Kevin, I am so sorry. You're the last person in the world I want to hurt. Please believe me."

"I do," he says, grudgingly. "But I don't want to see you get hurt, either, and honestly the guy gives me a weird vibe. It's like he's too good at playing Mr. Perfect or something."

My head is already swimming. And for some reason, my earrings are starting to hurt. They've become unbearably heavy. I unclasp the over-sized chandeliers and lay them on the counter. I rub my ear lobes and look up at Kevin. "At least now I know why you can't be objective." I feel a stress headache, the kind normally induced by Carol, coming on. "It's really late. We're both exhausted. Let's not do this anymore tonight." I start moving towards the door.

He takes my arm and spins me to face him. "Just promise you'll consider one thing, okay?"

I blink at him blankly. I wasn't lying about feeling exhausted. Or overwhelmed by tonight's developments.

"His career may be taking off, but his income can't possibly cover his lifestyle. The guy has no mortgage on your place, and none on his pad in the Beresford, either."

When I frown, Kevin adds, "That stuff is public record. I didn't snoop anywhere but the registry of deeds."

"Not that it's any of your business, but he made some good investments, and got in and out at the right time." This is what Oscar tells people who ask nosy questions about his finances. He says people would harp too much on the truth. They'd think he was some sort of inbred freak show attraction—his description, not mine.

"Of course he did," Kevin says snarkily. "You know, I actually talked to him tonight, to try to figure out what's so great about him, and all I could think is that there's something shifty about the guy. There's something in his eyes that I don't like. And he was asking me all about the O'Malley investigation. It seemed sort of classless."

I feel my cheeks flush red again. "Now I think you sound paranoid *and* pathetic." My eyes narrow. "Oscar is the classiest man I've ever met. I know him well enough to promise you that." I glare at Kevin. He'd better get the message that this subject is closed.

"What can I say?" Kevin looks defeated, and slightly stunned to boot. His persuasive gifts rarely fail him. "Most of me hopes you're right, but if we're being honest, part of me hopes he's a total creep."

My throat is tightening, like my clothes are constricting me. Suddenly I can't wait to be free of my favorite little black dress. I shove my way past Kevin and lunge towards the door. He reaches out to grab my arm.

I brush him away. "I need to be alone. To think." I sprint out the door before he can stop me. I'm so beside myself that it takes me three or four tries to get my key into the lock. Once inside my apartment, I slam the door behind me, slide both the deadbolt and the chain shut—something I hardly ever bother to do—before leaning back against the doubly-secured door and slumping to the ground.

I sit there for a few minutes, expecting to cry but just feeling dazed and empty. Did we just have a friendship-ending conversation? My phone vibrates in my little satin evening bag. Oscar. For the first time since we've been dating, I let him roll to voice mail. He doesn't leave a message. Seconds later, the phone vibrates again and I answer.

"It's lonely over here. Are you still out partying?"

"No, I just walked in the door."

"Now that's not entirely true. I don't see you here."

"I meant my door. I thought I'd let you get a decent night's sleep for a change."

"Come over."

"It'll be four by the time I get there."

"So?"

I'm so cooked that I feel like it might be a better idea to say good night and crawl into my own bed, but I hear myself say, "I'll see if I can find a cab."

Naturally, the one time I wish for taxis to be scarce, one pulls up as soon as I step onto the sidewalk and raise my arm. I spend the entire ride so conflicted that I feel like my head might explode. I love Oscar, so why did I cheat with Kevin? Not that everyone would agree that a kiss constitutes cheating, but to me it does. If Oscar kissed another woman, I'd be furious, jealous and generally beside myself. Every time the taxi stops and goes, I flounder between guilt and exhausted indifference. I'm completely unsure whether I should throw myself on his mercy for being such an inadequate girlfriend, or leave well enough alone. As the taxi turns onto his block, I decide to do what Angela would do—proclaim a kiss just a kiss and say nothing. I can always change my mind later, when I've had the benefit of a few hours of distance. And sleep.

The Beresford's twenty-four hour doorman admits me. I ride the elevator up and knock on Oscar's door. No answer. I knock again. Nothing. He must have fallen back asleep. Maybe I should go home. But then he'll call again if he wakes up and notices he's alone.

I use the key I was so excited to receive only a few hours ago to let myself in. I kick my heels off and make my way down the hall with my overnight bag, which I keep almost constantly packed these days, slung over my shoulder. Sure enough, I hear soft snoring coming from the bedroom. I slip into the master bath and close the door before finally peeling off my dress and stockings. I scrub away my party face, slather on some cream, brush my teeth and pull on a little black night gown before emerging. He hasn't changed position at all. He's spread out on his back, one arm flung overhead, snoring louder than before.

I start to climb in beside him, then realize I will hate life in the morning if I don't drink some water. I guzzle a glass in the kitchen and refill it to take with me to bed. I'm about to switch off the lights when I notice Oscar's phone resting on the granite counter. Its screen taunts me with "New Message—Krystal Klein"

Who the heck is Krystal Klein? Olivia's warning, and Oscar's unequivocal denial, flash back to my mind's eye. The idea starts to take root and I know I won't be able to purge it with plain will power.

No. If I snoop, I'll find nothing, and I'll feel like a tremendous jackass for violating his trust. Maybe my imagination has run away from me because of sleep deprivation, booze, and my traumatic interaction with Kevin.

If I trust Oscar, which I do, or at least I really, really want to, I shouldn't need to delve any further. Though isn't there a chance, however miniscule, that I'm wrong? Wouldn't it be better to indulge a tiny bit of psycho-chick behavior now, in order to assure peace of mind later?

Don't gamble, I tell myself firmly. Oscar is everything I didn't even know I wanted, and now can't imagine living without. It's not just the grand gestures and romance. He's older and wiser. I feel like I can learn from him, that he can show me the world and teach me things, cheesy as that sounds. He's not too good to be true, and he's given me no indication that I have competition. If I want to know who Krystal is, I should ask him, and trust him to tell the truth.

The little voice in my head needles me about how wrong I was about my former fiancé. She says Oscar can still be older and wiser and wonderful beyond description, *after* I've satisfied my doubts, however preposterous they may seem.

I flip the pendant lights over the counter back on. If he comes to investigate, I'm just here for a drink of water. My heart starts pounding in my chest as I pick up his phone. Of course it's locked. I try 0-0-0-0.

Still locked.

1-2-3-4.

Nothing.

4-3-2-1.

What other combinations are obvious? I try Oscar's birth year, 1-9-7-0. Maybe his birth date. I enter 0-4-2-7, already feeling frantic about what numbers to try next.

The keys unlock.

Why am I doing this? My heart feels like it's going to burst right through my rib cage. Even if he's hiding something, there's no guarantee that his phone holds an explanation. I'd be furious and hurt if someone did this to me, but I can't stop myself.

I should try. That would be the decent thing. Trust him, love him, and march back to bed. And never think of this again. I place the phone down and silently make my way back towards the bedroom. He's still sleeping. I start to climb under the covers once more, but the self-destructive urges in my psyche get the better of me. As soon as I close my eyes I see this Krystal person, and in my imagination, she's a gum-snapping bleach blonde bombshell with huge breasts spilling from a pink bustier. I slink back to the kitchen, rationalizing that, if I learn anything incriminating, it will absolve my guilt over hiding the kiss I shared with Kevin.

I unlock the phone and play the new message. A chirpy voice says, "Hi Oscar. It's Krystal. I wanted to let you know that Hideki wants to reschedule your Monday morning meeting for Tuesday. If that's a problem, send me an email and I'll try to find a better time. Otherwise, have a good weekend."

I exhale as I realize Krystal is his secretary, whom he's always referred to as Chris. I didn't make the connection because the spelling wasn't what I expected. My shoulders relax out of my ears as I scroll through his recent calls. I account for nine of the past fifteen. The rest look business related, based on the fact that they're to men, some with Asian names, and all with numbers labeled "office." I feel a rush of relief when Olivia isn't listed among his contacts. In the interest of thoroughness, I replay his saved messages, and start to feel really lame as I realize they're all from colleagues and clients. Why didn't I trust Oscar? Let alone my own instincts? It's toxic to live my life as if everyone has a secret as big as Brendan's.

I'm trying to figure out how to save Krystal's message as new when something moves in the hall. Oscar's up and out of bed. Frantic now, I hit delete and restore the phone to its spot on the counter. My heart feels like it's going to pound through my chest.

I'm hovering without purpose by the barstools when the overhead lights flip on. Oscar leans against the wall of the corridor, folds his arms across his naked chest, and looks at me through surprisingly alert eyes. "What are you doing?"

TWENTY

"Bumping into things like a total klutz. I'm still buzzed from the after-party. I should get to bed before I hurt myself." My explanations spew out like a spray of bullets. I must sound guilty beyond any reasonable doubt.

The muscles in Oscar's face relax visibly. "Sorry. I was sound asleep and I heard you in the kitchen. I'm not fully awake. Let's go back to bed."

I can't believe that's it, because honestly, if I caught him—or even *suspected* I caught him—rifling through my things, I'd be livid. My hands are still shaking. When I raise my glass to take a drink, I miss my mouth and water splashes down my chest.

"You are still drunk. I hope you don't develop a bed spinning problem."

"Yeah, I guess I lost track of the champagne."

Except I'm not feeling the slightest bit intoxicated. As I slip between Oscar's over-priced sheets and he curls up behind me with his arms around me, I stare at the clock. Ten after four, and I'm wide awake. Not Oscar. Maybe I just imagined he looked awake in the kitchen. His breathing gets deeper from the moment his head hits the pillow and he's back to sleep in no time.

Thank God it's Sunday morning. If I could nod off now, I could easily get four or five hours. Maybe more. But I know I'll be lucky to manage a cat nap, because my mind is racing. Maybe this is really it. He's The One. It's time to accept that I'm the luckiest person I know because I'm falling in love with a brilliant, wonderful, gorgeous guy who apparently adores me, too.

Of course he probably wouldn't think quite so highly of me if he knew I was snooping. Or kissing Kevin. I resolve to purge all self-sabotaging impulses. Immediately. But what if it's too late? What if he finds out about either of last night's transgressions? I feel panic brewing in my chest and force myself to focus on my breathing in an effort to stay calm, but my mind spins with insecurity until the clock reads almost seven and weak daylight starts peeking under the edge of Oscar's shades. He rolls towards me and his arm fumbles under my tiny night gown, but he's not fully awake. He grabs at me like I'm a stuffed animal and settles back to his slumber. I must nod off, too, because when I open my eyes, it's twenty after ten and Oscar's no longer in bed.

I untangle myself from the covers. As I step barefoot onto the hardwood floor, I decide I should bring some slippers over here. I'm wary about colonizing Oscar's bathroom too soon, but if he gave me a key, it must mean it would be alright if I left a toothbrush here. And some face wash. And night cream. And maybe a spare lipstick and mascara. Right. Maybe now I'm getting too carried away in the opposite direction. Still, I wish he'd offer me a shelf in his medicine cabinet. Maybe he doesn't want me that settled in. Or maybe it's just not something his male brain thinks about. What's our deal anyway? Was the key just a matter of convenience for last night? Or does it mean he's sure about me? I tell myself to stop obsessing over stupidity and walk to the window. I raise the shade and look out onto a gray, drizzly morning. Maybe I should go back to bed. Instead I pad into Oscar's study. He's dressed and focused on his laptop, with an empty coffee mug on his oversized and extremely manly mahogany desk.

The whole office is more masculine and traditional than the rest of the apartment, and it's my least favorite room. It's not as bright as the kitchen and living room, and two walls are covered with dark bookshelves, which in turn contain hundreds of hardcover volumes ranging from *War and Peace* to a recent biography of Warren Buffett. Oscar displays his diplomas on the remaining wall, along with an oil painting of a hunting scene I don't much care for. The best thing in his study is an antique globe that stashes a bar.

"How long have you been up?"

"A couple of hours. You were dead to the world."

"Sorry. Do you have a lot of work to do?"

"Yeah. This presentation needs to be perfect by tomorrow and right now, it's a stretch to call it mediocre. At best." He reaches for the dregs of his coffee.

"Want a refill?"

"Sure."

I take his mug and head for the kitchen. The coffee smell helps me fight the urge to crawl back under the covers. I can't believe there's no fallout from my phone surveillance. Still, that was stupid of me. I gambled with the best, and really only, adult relationship I've ever had, to listen to a mundane work message. If he knew, he'd never trust me again. Not that he should. I feel doubly dirty for spying on him after the kiss, which in and of itself could be grounds for breaking up. One thing seems clear, even through the haze of my hangover: I need to get a grip, before I destroy the best thing that's ever happened to me.

I pour myself some coffee, drop a splash of milk into it, and check my phone. Angela wants to know if I can have lunch later. I take Oscar's coffee to him and perch on the corner of his desk. He rests his hand on my thigh but doesn't turn his eyes away from the computer screen. He looks stressed.

"I should have never delegated to this new kid. My boss insisted we hire him, but he's never worked with a beverage account before. Now I have to do three weeks' worth of work in two days." Oscar rubs his temples. "He's not a bad guy, but he surfed his way through UCSB, and then decided he wanted to be in advertising. So he spent his early twenties in some second-tier shop in New Jersey, and he thinks just because he's put in the time, he's ready to run a major account. And sadly, that's not the case. I wish it were. It would make my life easier."

"That sucks. But maybe he'll grow into the job." I don't sound convincing. One thing I've learned as a headhunter is that nobody wants to make a hire who needs on the job training. It doesn't look like Oscar is going to get to leave his desk anytime soon. Unfortunately. I wish we could spend the day lounging around, or wandering in and out of book stores and coffee shops, or seeing a movie. Stuff established couples do on weekends. Maybe this is the price I pay for being with a career over-achiever. No lazy Sundays.

I notice Oscar's passport sitting on his desk by my leg. I pick it up and start flipping through it. "You get around."

"Yeah, mostly I see airports and conference rooms. Very exotic stuff."

I turn the page and squint to make out an especially foreign-looking visa. "Phnom Penh? When did you go to Cambodia? I've love to see Angkor Wat. Do you have pictures?"

"I went for a day to see a Japanese client's bottling plant," Oscar says in a tone that's neither nasty nor encouraging of further light conversation.

"That's too bad." I restore his passport to its place on the desk. I should find something else to occupy my time this morning. I hate feeling like I'm underfoot.

"Since you're obviously slammed, I'm going to take a shower and leave you to it, if that's okay." It's not what I want to do, but I'm not pathetic enough to spend the day puttering in his apartment, waiting to see when and if he finishes his work.

"Of course it's okay. I'm tempted to blow all of this off and join you in there." His fingers trace little circles up my leg. It sends a shiver up my spine.

In that moment, all my negative suspicions of him from last night evaporate. I was over-tired, tipsy, thrown by Kevin's bombshell, and therefore susceptible to foolish suggestions. "I wish we could just lie around together all day. I've missed you. Or rather, missed being alone with you." I hope I sound sincere, and not whiny. I don't mean to be whiny.

Oscar pauses to look at his watch. He runs his hands through his hair and lets out a muffled growl of frustration before spinning in his seat and looking me in the eye. "I wish we could spend the whole day together, too." He glances at the clock on his computer. "Maybe I've got time for just a little fun. I'm totally screwed anyway."

He gets out of his chair and leans over to kiss me.

"I have coffee breath," I protest.

"Who cares?" He shoves his laptop out of the way and pushes me down onto his desk. I stop worrying about my coffee breath when he drops to his knees on the Persian rug and buries his face between my legs.

Angela stabs at one of the grape tomatoes in her salad as if she's trying to bludgeon it to death. "I can't believe this is how it all goes down."

I can't tell from her tone if she's ticked, or confused, or merely fishing for more information. Before the food arrived, I gave her the minute by minute recap of last night's events. But Kevin had gotten to her first. He woke her, and Claudio, at nine this morning. Angela said he sounded so unhinged that she left Claudio in her bed with the cats and went out for a bagel with Kevin.

"Why did he have to do it now?" I moan. Instead of assaulting my food, I'm plowing the lettuce around the plate with my fork.

"Duh. Because for him, the timing couldn't be better. You've moved past Brendan. Kevin's done with the hellacious election cycle, and he figures Oscar is new enough to be expendable." She decapitates an asparagus spear and pops the top in her mouth.

"Do you think our friendship is over?"

"Not necessarily. But I would say it's severely damaged. Kevin has a fragile ego, like all guys do. You need to talk to him, before too much time goes by and everything gets too weird."

I nod noncommittally. "What if I'm doing the wrong thing by picking Oscar? I can't trust myself post-Brendan. Do you think I'm doomed to suck at relationships forever?"

Angela's face wrinkles with concentration for a moment. "You can't think like that, because you never know, do you? You just have to do what feels right and take a leap of faith. People waste so much time stressing about the road not taken. It's kind of dumb. There's never any way to tell what would have happened."

"What about the kiss?"

"What about it?"

"Should I tell Oscar?"

"I see no need to hurt him if it was a fluke. No offense, Zoë, but you're practically a relationship rookie. You're going to make a few minor mistakes."

"You're right. Why make a big deal out of nothing? Now I just wish I was sure Oscar is who he seems."

Her heavily lined eyes narrow. "What do you mean by that?" She puts down her silverware and leans in to listen more closely.

"I need you to tell me it's ludicrous. I have no evidence, or even a rational reason to suspect, that he's doing anything wrong. But I can't shake the feeling that it's all too good to be true. Like I'm not supposed to be this happy or something, and I'm setting myself up to get my heart shredded to pieces because he's going to leave me for someone better."

Angela ponders this for a moment and says, "Yup. You're being ridiculous. I don't get that vibe from him at all. From what I've seen, he's only got eyes for you."

I stir the lemon slice around my Diet Coke with my straw. "I suppose I could always just ask him, 'Oscar, are you screwing anyone else?'" I say, in a tone I'd use to ask my brother's kids if they're up to something naughty. "But seriously, we've never had lunch together, even though he's across the street. Maybe he's having nooners right under my nose."

Angela laughs out loud. "Maybe you need to find a job that allows you to express more creativity. Clearly your imagination has been driven to desperation by the lack of stimulation in your workplace. But if you want to know for sure, why not dig around a little?"

"I went through his phone last night, or this morning, rather, when he was sleeping." I'm embarrassed to admit it, even to my closest friend.

"And?" She looks annoyed I didn't spill this crucial intelligence earlier.

"His phone log makes a compelling case that he has no time for anything but work and me. So why can't I stop obsessing?"

Angela's fork stops in midair. "Because you really like him. Which is why I think you should stop looking for drama. But if you can't manage that, you should get a peek at his computer. You know, trust, but verify." She sounds totally serious.

"Really?"

"Absolutely. You have this nagging feeling that something's wrong. The seeds of doubt are going to keep sprouting, unless you do something about them. You're just torturing yourself if you abandon your espionage without squashing your suspicions."

"Oscar almost caught me this morning."

"Then you'll need to be more careful," she says, as if it's the most obvious thing in the world.

"So, to summarize: I need to have a potentially friendship-ending talk with Kevin, and then I need to gamble with this great thing I have with Oscar by snooping again."

"Sounds right to me, except I'd rather you called it a friendship-*altering* talk, instead of a friendship-ending one. I don't want our happy little threesome to dissolve. It would suck to have to see you guys separately. Just promise me you won't put it off. You'll talk to him soon. Like today."

"I'm such a jack ass."

"Yes, you are. Now do you understand that you should have listened to me? But no. You thought I was nuts when I said good old O'Connor had the hots for you."

"Fine, you were right."

"Good. I'm so glad that's resolved. Now on to the next event: Want to see what they have for dessert?"

We order a chocolate brownie, smothered in ice cream and hot fudge, ostensibly because Angela has decided to extend her birthday celebration. The waitress, a large woman with alarming orange lipstick and angry furrows in her forehead, takes some of the wind from our sails when she sniffs that it must be nice to be skinny girls who can eat dessert. Angela frowns and asks me if we should go for the fruit cup. I tell the waitress we're sticking with the sundae, and mentally downgrade her tip while we watch her waddle away to fetch our ice cream.

As we dig into the gooey heap of calories with our sundae spoons, Angela says, "So enough about *your* dramas. I have a bombshell of my own."

"Oh, yeah? What's up?" Maybe she got that long-awaited promotion at the magazine. God knows she works her ass off for them. Or maybe she's going to tell me she's joining the ranks of the monogamous and officially boy-friending Claudio.

But her face suddenly looks more serious. She rests her spoon on the edge of the dish and looks over both shoulders, as if double-checking we know nobody here.

"I think I'm pregnant."

TWENTY-ONE

"Oh, Angela," is all I can think to say. I reach across the table and touch her hand. "Talk about burying the lead. Are you sure?"

"I'm ten days late and I'm exhausted. I've been pushing the possibility out of my mind, but it's seeming increasingly likely."

I feel my eyes roll, involuntarily. "But have you taken a test?"

"Not yet. I can't bring myself to buy one. I walk into the drug store, stand in that aisle for ten minutes, then buy something else, like soap or a toothbrush, and scurry out of there. I've repeated this exercise at least two dozen times this week. I'm set for toiletries for the next twenty years."

"Do you want me to go buy one for you?"

"Can you just come with me?"

"Of course. We can go right now, if you want. I don't know how you got through lunch, not to mention your party last night, acting as if nothing's wrong. I'd be a basket case."

"I guess I've got a talent for compartmentalizing my life."

Angela suddenly looks smaller and meeker, somehow, than I've ever seen her. Underneath her perfectly applied façade, she looks like a scared teenager. I don't know what else to say, so I push the now-forgotten brownie sundae around with my spoon and flag down the waitress to bring us the check.

"How can this be happening?" Angela asks in a quieter voice than usual. "Infertility runs in our family to the point that I'm shocked we have a family. All three of my maternal cousins are killing themselves with that IVF thing."

Well, I guess she knows about Niles and Susie. That answers one, suddenly trivial, question.

"My mom had three miscarriages before she had my sister." She stares despondently at the mostly uneaten dessert.

"But then your sister got pregnant on her honeymoon." I don't mean to sound argumentative, but the sooner she knows if she is or isn't, the sooner she can decide what she wants to do.

"I had blocked that out." She puts her elbows on the table, rests her face in her hands and blows her bangs, a new and instantly regretted development, out of her eyes.

The put-upon looking waitress reappears and deposits our bill on the table. We both wait until she retreats again to say anything.

"Seriously, Angela, you're getting ahead of yourself. Sometimes stress can throw your cycle."

"Not when you're on the pill."

"You don't know that."

"Yes, I do. And I also know I missed three pills when I went away for a weekend and forgot them on my bathroom counter. I'm such an idiot. I realized it five or six blocks from my place, but I didn't bother to go back for them, because I thought the relevant window of time had passed for the month. I guess I was wrong."

Forty-five minutes later, Angela pees on a stick in her bathroom and makes me stand in there and wait for the results, which the instructions say can take up to five minutes. She paces in her narrow hallway. Ernest and Algernon join her. They look surprisingly anxious, considering they normally don't care about anything but the presence of Angela and canned food, and their feline brains can't possibly process the present drama.

The little blue plus sign forms almost instantly. "I think you need to see this," I say, tentatively.

Angela comes in, tears already welling, and confronts the evidence. She stares at the test stick on the counter for a moment, then picks it up and flings the offensive piece of medical technology into the trash.

"Are you going to tell him?"

"I don't know."

"What do you think Claudio would say?"

"I have no idea. We're not what you'd call a long-established couple. I don't even know for sure if he's seeing anyone else." She lets out a little laugh and dabs at her eyes with her fingertips. Her eyeliner smudges downwards. "But at least I know he's the only candidate. Some months in my not-so-distant past, I wouldn't even have that."

"Well, you don't have to decide today. Whether to tell him, I mean. Or anything, actually."

"Shouldn't all the alcohol I've put away over the past few weeks make me miscarry?" Angela says, suddenly sounding hopeful.

"I doubt it. I think it just causes birth defects."

"Thanks. That's really comforting." Her face is starting to turn white.

"Come here." I open my arms and constantly composed Angela allows herself to fall into a big hug.

"Let's keep this between us for now, okay?" she snuffles into my shoulder.

"Of course."

Angela disentangles herself from me so that she can step back and look me in the eye. "That means don't share with Oscar."

"I would never. Don't worry about that for one second. Your personal life is none of his business."

Monday morning arrives with alarming punctuality, and without any progress on the mystery of my boyfriend's true character, or Angela's pregnancy dilemma, or my now-eclipsed drama with Kevin. I have to put all of it out of my head for the next few hours anyway, since Carol has decided to "reward" me for closing Niles Townsend by having me tag along with her and Marvin to a pitch meeting with Walker Smythe, the investment banker whose son she made me coach pro bono a few weeks back.

Honestly, I shouldn't be so flip about this development. It means Carol believes I have a future here, which is more than a lot of her employees can say. It's just that I've seen firsthand, how fast she can take away whatever she sees fit to give, which makes it difficult to put a lot of stock in my new favorite child status.

It's only 8:30 in the morning, but Carol has whipped herself and Marvin into a frenzy. If all goes well today, my boss will get to bed Walker Smythe and, equally importantly, Silverblum Gatz will give Broadwick & Associates an assistant general counsel spot to fill. And if that happens, Marvin will become the point person for the account. Which means he will have to dazzle them with the quality of people he sends over, or Carol will never get another Silverblum assignment again.

Marvin fully understands the need to bring his A game. He's even abandoned his traditional whimsical ties in favor of bold blue stripes,

in honor of the occasion. Carol knows Marvin appreciates the importance of this meeting, but she can't help herself. She appears hell bent
on spending the time before we need to leave making him crazy. She's
standing over his desk, yelling at him to rearrange Power Point slides.
She points at the screen and shouts cryptic instructions at him, even
though she's less than two feet from his ear. Every once in a while, she
jabs at the screen with her index finger if he doesn't move "this" or
"that" fast enough.

Carol performs a similar futile exercise before every major meeting. She screams and yells that the presentation sucks, and this is
somehow not only news to her, but also not her fault, even though
she authored almost every word of every bullet point personally. Her
normal *modus operandi* is to spend an hour tweaking the presentation, and then make one of us scramble, in the three minutes before
we need to get out the door, to restore it to its original state. Carol
developed Broadwick & Associates' new client pitch over the course
of several years, it works like a charm over ninety per cent of the time,
and everyone, even New Girl, who has not yet been allowed to interact live with an actual client, knows it needs very little in the way of
improvement.

Not until it's twelve minutes before we absolutely have to be in a
cab to have any hope of making it downtown on time, does Carol start
shrieking at me to pull up the pitch presentation on my computer and,
"Fucking fix the fucking cluster fuck Marvin has made."

Because I knew this was coming, I have the file open on my
screen already. I don't have to fix anything, actually, since the changes
she ordered Marvin to make are on his computer. Carol, for all her
business acumen, holds only the weakest grasp on the workings of
modern technology. She can't fathom that if her presentation has been
tampered with, the changes don't automatically appear on all versions
of the document. But I know better than to try to explain this to her.
I move the mouse around for a moment and then pronounce the presentation "fixed."

She barks at Marvin to print it out. I am not allowed to print
anything. I stopped taking this personally when I learned that only
Marvin holds this sacred privilege, and that he has to log every letter, file and document he puts to paper. This policy has nothing to do
with conservation, but rather with Carol's paranoia and previously
noted lack of computer savvy. She thinks, by preventing her employ-

ees from printing anything, she's insuring that we will never carry any confidential client information out of the office. Nobody in the history of the firm has had the male anatomy necessary to enlighten her that it would be really easy for any one of us—even useless New Girl—to email Carol's entire proprietary database out of here in about two seconds.

While Marvin prints the original version of the presentation, I finally focus on Carol's face. I can't believe I didn't check earlier. Maybe I didn't want to risk eye contact, because her mood was so obviously manic and vile. And now, when we should be heading to the elevators, I wonder if I have a professional obligation to tell her that she's applied her trademark blue eye shadow expertly over one eye, and slopped it garishly over the other. I've never seen this happen before, although Marvin once mentioned a sighting of the same phenomenon about six years ago. Never mind what incomprehensible statement her make-up makes about her mental state. We can't possibly allow her to go to Silverblum Gatz looking like that, and I can't believe Marvin hasn't noticed, or more likely, is pretending not to have noticed. As the senior person, shouldn't he be the one to tell her she needs to look in the mirror?

Of course I chicken out. Marvin and I follow our asymmetrically blue-eyed boss down to the street and cram into the back of a cab for the stop and go ride to Wall Street. Maybe she'll whip out her compact and fix her face in the car. No such luck. Instead she gets on her cell phone and starts barking nonsensical orders at some registered nurse unlucky enough to be looking after Carol's infirm but not utterly incapacitated mother. Evidently the moldings in her room at assisted living offend Carol, and she wants them replaced. Today, naturally. Marvin and I listen to this for a good five minutes before I work up the nerve to mouth, "Did you notice her eye shadow?" When Carol looks out the window at the passing storefronts lining Fifth Avenue, I gesture frantically at my own eyelids.

"What can we do?" Marvin hisses at me.

I shrug.

"We're meeting a bunch of straight men. They won't notice," Marvin says.

I'm not so sure, but before I can do more than shrug again in response, Carol claps her phone shut and begins rooting around in her purse. She's muttering under her breath about the idiots at the old folks' home, and that it's no wonder people lose their minds while living there. As the cabbie accelerates to beat a yellow light, she holds up a full-sized bottle of Bulgari perfume, which strikes me as an odd thing to carry around in a $10,000 Birkin bag.

Before I realize what's happening, she's doused—not just spritzed, but fully drenched—both herself and me with the perfume. And while it's a nice scent, it's not a weak one, and I'm pretty sure it's going to clash with what I was already wearing. Marvin coughs dramatically, and the driver starts cursing Carol in his native tongue. I can actually see the cloud of fragrance hanging in the air over the backseat. Marvin rolls his window all the way down, and hangs his head out like a dog, while the cold air rushes in.

When we finally pour out of the taxi in front of Silverblum Gatz, Carol tips the driver less than a dollar. Sometimes when she does that, and she does it almost all the time, Marvin will slip the driver a couple of bucks, but this meeting is too important. He can't risk triggering a tantrum. The cabbie speeds off with an effusive and obscene hand gesture aimed in our general direction.

The offices of the most prestigious bank in the world are plain and unremarkable, compared to the lavishly decorated law firms we frequently visit. We go through a main reception desk to get to Walker Smythe's secretary, an old battle axe of a woman in gray, whose breasts have sunken to stomach level and whose no-nonsense glasses perch on the tip of her pointy nose. She ushers us into a medium-sized interior conference room. That's also not par for the course; our law firm clients love to show off their views, so we always get put in the best boardroom space available. The idea is that we'll gush to the recruits about the real estate.

The secretary leaves us, only to return almost immediately with a tray of coffee and Walker Smythe and two other bankers in tow. We stand up to shake hands. Carol sucks in her non-existent stomach and shamelessly arches her spine so her boobs thrust forward as she greets Walker Smythe. If he notices, he's enough of a gentleman not to let on. Which, come to think of it, would be a rare thing in a heavy-hitting finance guy. They tend to be a pretty crass bunch. I also assume, admittedly based on stereotypes of rich older males, that Walker Smythe is not the kind of man who'd notice a woman his own age coming onto him. Especially one whose eye make-up resembles something from Picasso's blue period.

After brief introductions, one of the bankers looks pointedly at the clock on the wall. I surreptitiously study Mr. Smythe, whom Carol pronounced "dreamy" a few weeks back. He's got a strong chin, deep set eyes, and an overall distinguished air about him. He also sports manicured fingernails and what appear to be tweezed eye brows. I wouldn't say he's dreamy, or even handsome, but then, to Carol, power and money hold way more sex appeal than any particular physical attribute.

Marvin launches into the presentation. He looks capable and in control as he ticks off the firm's successes. When he starts to explain how Broadwick & Associates goes about screening its candidates, Walker Smythe cuts him off. He produces a piece of paper from his inside coat pocket and slides it across the table to Carol, who has managed, while Marvin was extolling her professional victories, to unbutton her blouse one more hole.

"We want one of these guys," Walker Smythe says. "So that should make it easy." His two partners nod curtly in agreement.

Clients give us wish lists all the time, and most of the time it's an awkward moment, because we have to explain that they're aiming way too high. Carol sometimes tells them it's like dating. You have to stay in your own league. That line hardly ever goes over well at first, but usually the clients admire her chutzpah, so it works out for us. But any problem with over-reaching is virtually impossible in Silverblum's case.

Carol smiles her most confident smile and says, "I'm sure any of these men would be thrilled to get a call from Zoë, saying Silverblum Gatz wants to talk to them. She will get started immediately. Marvin will call your assistant with a status report by the end of the week, and if you want, you and I can discuss any changes you want made to the list then."

"That sounds fine," Walker Smythe rewards Carol's smile with a business-like nod. Uh-oh. She's not going to like that.

It may not sound like much, but *I'm* going to get to make the first round of calls on their wish list. This means—without question—that my boss trusts me enough to let me interact with some of the most senior, talented and influential people in her contacts list. Carol would never let me navigate a candidate through Silverblum's fourteen-stage interview process by myself, and Marvin has earned enough battle scars to be the client relationship point person, but this is still a *big* leap for me. I fully expected to be relegated back to placement of junior associates after she made an exception for Niles.

Normally, the next phase of the meeting would be the most important, especially since I'll be making the initial calls. It's when the client explains the "sell" for the firm, so we know what to say when we talk them up, but that's not necessary here. I glance over at Marvin, and he's flipping through his notes, obviously wondering if he should just wrap it up. He opts to do so, and before we know it, we're in another soon-be-be-underpaid taxi, heading back to midtown. Carol should be ecstatic. She's holding a list in her bag that confirms she, and not any other headhunter, has won one of the city's most coveted assignments, but instead she's stewing.

"Marvin!" she barks. "Is he gay?"

"Is who gay?"

"Walker Smythe."

"No, I don't think he is."

Wow. That's brave of Marvin. If she'd asked me, I would have ventured a maybe. Marvin can afford to be bold. He closed a firm record of four deals last week, and was rewarded with a more ergonomically correct chair, plus immunity from persecution for at least two weeks.

"Then what's his problem?" my boss demands.

Neither of us responds. We're only in the forties. We're stuck in here for twenty more blocks. One of us will have to speak. I'm sure she's surmised his problem already. I'd wager almost anything that twice-divorced Walker Smythe dates significantly younger women. But I really, really, *really* don't want to say this to Carol, even though it's cruel of her to put her employees on the spot about her personal affairs.

"Zoë, what do you think his problem is?"

I take the wimpy way out. "Maybe he thinks it's important to keep things professional. I mean, this is a big search he gave us, sorry, I mean, gave you."

Carol scrunches her face into a childlike look of extreme concentration. I think she actually holds her breath while she processes my theory because when she exhales, it comes out as a thoroughly unladylike grunt. Her age might not be in her favor, but Carol's frequently masculine body language sure doesn't help her case, either. I would never say this aloud, though, even if drunk *and* questioned at gun point.

"I'm going to take him to lunch at Peter Luger and find out for sure," she says, suddenly a picture of poise. Her ability to change her mood in a fraction of a second never ceases to surprise me, but this latest plan strikes me as flawed. At best. Carol may be petite and impeccably attired, but she's like a piranha around a good steak. I've seen her devour a side of beef more than once, and it doesn't make for an attractive tableau.

Obviously I smile and nod and say nothing.

Imminent steakhouse debacle aside, I want to grin from ear to ear, but I know better. Carol might read such a brash display of positive emotion as a mark of mental instability. How ironic. But the truth is, I'm feeling great about the morning. We got the account and I received a major vote of confidence from my employer, in front of an incredibly important client. As a kind of added bonus, Carol's mood has been moderated by her fantasy about a lunchtime seduction. When I return to my desk, recharged and ready to tackle the Silverblum wish list, there's an unwelcome, subject-less email from Oscar waiting for me.

It says, simply, "We need to talk."

TWENTY-TWO

By eight o'clock, I have stopped puttering in my apartment, pretending to straighten up stacks of magazines, re-organize the contents of my medicine cabinet, and sort through a week's worth of junk mail. Now I'm just spinning in my tiny kitchen. I called Oscar as soon as I saw his message, but he said he was swamped and he'd come by after work tonight. Which could mean anytime between half an hour ago to four hours from now.

We. Need. To. Talk. The four words most dreaded by the entire English-speaking female dating population.

Naturally, I spent the bulk of the work day obsessing about what could be on his mind. And I've assured myself, repeatedly, almost like a mantra, that it cannot possibly be the phone. If he knew I'd snooped, he would have said something on the spot, or at least over the weekend. Maybe there is someone else. Just because Olivia seems happily in love with her new husband doesn't remove the possibility of cheating for good. Or maybe he's decided it's all going too fast and he wants to put on the brakes. I floated this theory by Marvin, my third choice sounding board, since Angela has bigger problems of her own and it's too damned awkward to ask Kevin. Not that he's in a position to offer objective advice anyway.

Marvin thought that men who buy real estate for women don't usually decide to slow things down immediately thereafter. I grabbed onto his reassurances enthusiastically. Then he said, "Of course, he *might* have met someone else. He meets people every day. It's a possibility you have to consider."

I could have smacked him for stating the obvious so bluntly. But that has to be it. My insides are churning, and I feel my skin heating up, like I'm about to break a sweat. How could I be so stupid? How could I let myself fall so hard and fast for someone older, richer, way more experienced, and generally a shade or two more refined and therefore perhaps out of my league? Yesterday I was wondering if I could trust him, but now that there's a real chance I might lose him, I can't handle it.

When the buzzer sounds, I nearly jump out of my skin. With shaky hands, I turn my deadbolt and admit my (soon to be ex?) boyfriend as soon as he knocks. He scoops me right up in his arms and plants a big kiss on my lips before taking a step back and asking, "Are you feeling okay? You look a little green."

"I think I ate something funny at lunch," I fib.

He takes off his coat and hangs it on my overflowing row of hooks. He's got his suit jacket on, but he's removed his tie and unbuttoned his collar. "You have any wine open?" he asks.

Hmm. Either whatever he has on his mind is minor, and I've been worried for nothing, or it's so major that he thinks I need a drink to stomach the news.

I grab a bargain bin bottle of shiraz from the counter and hold it out for Oscar's approval.

"Looks fine to me."

I pour two glasses and we move to the couch, because my kitchen really can't accommodate two un-entangled adult humans at once. I curl my legs underneath me and he sits with his head propped on his hand, which is resting on the back of the sofa, and looks at me. It's a relaxed pose.

"We need to talk about Thanksgiving."

"What about it?" I ask, as levelly as possible. While part of me is relieved he didn't say we need to discuss our entire relationship, if he's about to bail on our first out-of-the-city outing, not to mention meeting my parents, I think I hear brakes squeaking.

My face must show my alarm because he adds, "I'm still coming to Florida with you. It's just that I can't stay the whole weekend, because of a business trip that just came up. I'll need to fly out of Miami Saturday, instead coming home with you Sunday, like we'd planned."

A little half-laugh, half-snort slips out before I can stop it.

"What?" Oscar looks confused. His forehead wrinkles and he tilts his head to try to get a better read on my face, just like a puppy dog does when trying to understand what the people are on about.

"That's it? The whole we-need-to-talk is about a twenty-four hour change in travel plans? Seriously?"

"Well, yeah. I figured the holiday weekend is important to you."

"Of course it is, but I'm not a complete psycho. I work for a crazy lady, remember? I know better than anyone that work things come up, sometimes on weekends. You're so busy and important," I say, more playfully. "You can't help it," I lean over to kiss him.

"So you're not mad?"

"About Thanksgiving, no. Honestly. I was actually starting to worry about what we'd do down there, trapped indoors with my family, if we got unlucky and it rained all weekend." I pause for a second, and the little voice in my head cautions me to let the other thing slide. I ignore her insistent pleas.

"But if we're being honest here, I am a little peeved about your whole 'we need to talk' thing. Don't you know those four little words strike fear in the hearts of women everywhere?"

He laughs. "I guess you're right. I didn't give it a second thought. I'm a guy, remember? I had something I needed to talk about with you, so I said so. But, if you'll allow me the opportunity, I'd like to redeem myself with four other little words."

I think I feel the world start spinning slightly faster as Oscar leans over, cups my face in his hands, and says, "I love you, Zoë."

Angela phones me during the late morning, when I'm between meetings. I step into an empty conference room to take her call, and I have to bite my tongue, literally, to keep from sharing this most startling and wonderful development in my life. I mean, I'd worked myself into a lather thinking he was going to break up with me, and instead he says the magic words and cements our status. I need to put a stop to all the worrying and self-doubt. Oscar and I are going to live happily ever after. I told Brendan when we were engaged that I'd never change my name, but I'm starting to think that Zoë Clark-Thornton *does* have a nice ring to it.

Angela cuts right to the chase and her leaden tone goes a long way towards yanking my head out of the clouds. "I went to the doctor to confirm it. Of course their test came back positive."

"I'm sorry." I stop short of asking if she's thought about what she's going to do. It seems better to let her talk.

"You haven't heard the worst part of my morning. They said I should have an exam. I can't imagine what they expected to see in there, but I guess it's standard protocol. So my regular doctor is out, taking her first vacation in two years or some such nonsense. The nurse says her partner could squeeze me in, so I say, okay, because I can't really take another morning off work this week."

She stops for air and keeps explaining. "So I go in the room, and get half naked and sit on the table with the horrible paper drape over me and the doctor knocks. I'm not sure why, but I suppose I was expecting a woman."

"I don't like going to a guy, either."

"Well, maybe some old, gray-haired professorial-looking guy would be alright, in a pinch and everything, but this guy was gorgeous. He had sparkling green bedroom eyes, dimples when he smiled, and there was something so manly about him. He reeked of sex appeal. So I shook his hand and took a deep breath and went to lie back, but then bolted right back up and said, 'No way. You're way too cute. I can't do this.'"

"You did not!" Despite the seriousness of my friend's predicament, I'm laughing out loud. Had I been in her place, I might have *wanted* to do the same thing, but I probably wouldn't have had the presence of mind to do so.

"I did, and he looked at me for a minute, then asked if I was serious, and I said yes, and please find me another doctor. So then he got a little red-faced, but he said okay—I mean he has to listen to the patient, right?—and I waited there, half naked and freezing, while he went to find me someone else."

"Wow."

"Yeah. So of course these places book up months in advance. Eventually they found this female nurse practitioner with poor skin tone and cold hands to check me out. I caught her staring at my ring finger. Judgmental bitch. So anyway, everything looks normal down there and I left with a prescription for both prenatal vitamins and an informational leaflet about the abortion pill, which, if I decide to go that way, I need to take at the doctor's office sometime within the next month."

"Which way are you leaning?" I try to ask as gently as possible.

"I haven't decided. Neither route seems all that tempting. What do you think?"

"I think listen to your gut."

"What if your gut was telling you everything happens for a reason, but on the other hand, you were thinking, it's just not the right time? What then?"

"I don't know."

Angela exhales loudly into the phone. "That's the problem. Neither do I. For the first time in my life, I'm truly confused about what I want."

TWENTY-THREE

When I get home at eight, Kevin's nowhere to be found, but Angela's waiting on the sidewalk outside my building, bundled in a black cashmere coat, without any of her usual flamboyant accessories. She looks lost and somehow small and timid, adorned only with modest pearl earrings.

"Why didn't you use your key?" The temperature is dropping fast. My mother will be despairing over the first hard frost, which will kill most of her garden. She calls me the morning after every year, as if the mass murder by Mother Nature of her eggplants, raspberries and carrots is somehow surprising. Every fall I tell her she should avoid the carnage by leaving for Florida a month earlier.

"I didn't feel like going home to get it."

Once upstairs, I instinctively reach for a bottle of wine, but then catch myself and put the kettle on the stove instead. Angela chatters nervously about her uneventful work day until it screeches. I pour us two cups of tea and we settle around my little table, which would seat four in a pinch, assuming I cleared a month's worth of junk mail off it.

She wraps her hands around her mug, stares into her Darjeeling and says, "So I've officially gone off the deep end."

"I doubt that."

"That's because you haven't heard how I spent most of this afternoon. You know how I'm still struggling with whether to tell Claudio about the baby?"

I nod.

Angela exhales and swipes at her abhorred new bangs. "Today I consulted the stars. I Googled our astrological compatibility." When I don't register a big reaction to this revelation, she says, "It turns out two Scorpios can be a *great* thing, so that would weigh in favor of telling him. One of the sites I checked even used the words 'sublime' and 'legendary love affairs.'" Her eyes widen as she tells me this.

"Okay, I don't mean to burst your bubble, but that can't possibly be true of all Scorpio couples."

"It's not. One site said that when it doesn't work out, it's usually because the couple spends too much time planning and not enough time doing. Clearly not an issue in our case. Whatever you think about all of it, you can't say I planned this." She pats her non-existent belly.

I've got nothing against recreational chart consultation, but it seems to me like an odd methodology for reaching such a major decision. "I know you're upset, but let me play Devil's Advocate for a minute. How do you know these astrologers don't gush about how wonderful every possible combination of signs can be?"

"Because I checked. I went through and read the pages for me and at least six of my exes. More than once. And it was freakishly spot on." She stares back into her tea and her hated bangs flop forward into her eyes again.

I reach across the table and put my hand on hers. "You're leaning towards having the baby, then?"

She nods, but can't seem to form the word yes. She's obviously fighting back tears. "Five years ago, it would have been a no-brainer for me to have an abortion. I wasn't anywhere near mature enough to have a baby, and I was just starting out in my career. And while I don't think this timing is fantastic, there's an insistent little voice in my head that says maybe this is my chance. I know so many women at work who can't seem to meet the right guy, but whose biological clocks have taken over their lives. And then we have my cousins. They have met the right guys, but they're too old or whatever, and the system's just not working right for them. And then, there's something that seems nice about being a mommy at a relatively young age. Not that I gave that much thought until yesterday or so, but it's just one more small thing. So if I decide I'm having it, I obviously should let Claudio know sooner rather than later, so that he can figure out whether he wants to be involved."

"I suppose that's right."

"But I'm scared of losing him. I'm terrified that once I drop this bombshell, he'll either disappear back to Italy, or have a tantrum and demand I get rid of it."

"He can't make you do anything you don't want to do. It's your decision. If Claudio wants to check out and you decide to go it alone, you know you have a phenomenal support network. And who knows? He might surprise you."

Although business at Broadwick & Associates maintains a frenetic pace during the fall months, a day or two before Thanksgiving the phones always fall silent. Carol goes through her usual holiday tradition, namely hyperventilating over the slowdown, which while predictable to every other person in the legal industry, always throws her completely off her game. She's one of those self made successes who, whenever she closes her eyes, pictures herself ninety days from the street. The upside is that her paranoia keeps her motivated.

Carol has earmarked the Wednesday before Thanksgiving to go through her daughter's college applications with me. When I asked if Janice ought to be present for the meeting, Carol looked at me like I'd been recently lobotomized, then snapped that *her* Janice had much more pressing obligations.

Oscar told me last night when I was nearly hyper-ventilating about this meeting, that the most stressful thing about working in advertising is showing new clients a potential campaign for their product. The client can torpedo weeks and weeks' worth of work with a single frown. Or the client might like the concept, but not the details, such as price, market reach or a thousand other variables. Oscar says when he goes into one of those meetings, he has to be prepared to tell the client how much it will cost to run their detergent ad during the evening news in two dozen different media markets. Not only that, he has to be able to project the number of viewers in each city and anticipate their reaction. Which can mean tweaking the presentation slightly for each audience. Which is sort of what I've done with Janice's applications, on a smaller scale, of course.

Laid out before me on our largest conference table are materials ready to mail to Wellesley, Duke and each of the Ivies, except Yale, which went out for early decision. Carol has blocked four full hours for this meeting. I can only presume she wants to pick apart every minute detail. Fortunately, I'm properly fortified with extra coffee.

My boss charges into the conference room like a storm trooper and immediately assaults the blinds. They come crashing down so no nosy colleagues can see us from the corridor. I steal a glance and note that her make-up looks good today. Lucky break. Carol flings herself into the chair at the dominant end of the table. "Let's see what you've done."

At my fingertips, I have detailed talking points about why I answered each question the way I did. I also kept records, complete with postmark dates, of when each of Janice's transcripts and letters of recommendation went out to every school. I am as ready as possible to deflect her inevitable barrage of questions. And not that Carol cares, but I'd forgotten how exhausting it was to apply to college. The materials laid out before us easily represent more than a hundred hours of work.

Carol leafs through the Harvard application with what strikes me as remarkable calm and detachment. "I like you, Zoë," she says, without looking up from the essay she's skimming. "You remind me of myself as a young woman."

People talk about falling out of their chairs with shock, and I've always thought that's a stupid hyperbole, but I actually catch myself grabbing the arm rests. I have no idea what I'm supposed to say. Probably thank you would be the most appropriate response, but I'm too scared to form words. If Carol sees herself in me, then is it possible I could end up as unhinged as her?

She turns the page and keeps talking. "I was young, smart and high energy, but directionless, and my first husband swooped down from his corner office and swept me off my feet. He was charming, refined, and worldly—all the things I wanted to be but couldn't quite afford. He was seven years older than me, devastatingly sexy, and it seemed like he had everything all figured out. I lost myself in the heady days of a new relationship, and stopped thinking. He was older and wiser. Before I knew what was happening, I'd lost my sense of self. My life revolved around him, my dearest friends went on the back burner. I started skipping out of my entry-level job at a PR firm early every night, because it seemed so inconsequential compared to Reid's work. That was his name. Reid Chatham."

Carol looks up and stares into space for a moment. I've let my painstakingly prepared talking points flutter to the table. Why is she sharing such personal details? Carol Broadwick never talks about her private life, unless it's to brag about her kids or curse her most recent ex-husband. I've never heard anything about this Reid person before.

"I let myself get lost in the greatest love affair of my life, and before I knew it, Parker was on the way. We got married and after Parker was born, Reid insisted that I stay home with him. When I complained of isolation from adult humans, he hired a nanny, a nineteen-year-old English girl named Gwendolyn Strathmore. He ran off with her four months later and left me unemployed, broken-hearted and solely responsible for the well-being of one very colicky infant son." I can't be sure, because she stops talking, but I think I hear a catch in her voice, like she could cry.

"I'm sorry. I had no idea."

"It was all for the best. I hid in the bedroom for a week, lost and paralyzed by panic and simple exhaustion. Then I picked myself up and started pounding the pavement. A friend of a friend introduced me to legal search. Within three years, I'd spun off my own firm. When I met Evan and Janice's father, I promised myself he'd never get to me like Reid did, and that I'd never give up my own ambitions for a man again."

She puts down the Harvard application and asks to see Princeton. "Your alma mater," she remarks with a smile. "You're a smart girl, Zoë, and if you don't screw up your life, you're going to go far."

"Thank you." Even though she's dealt me yet another back-hand-ed compliment, I feel I have to acknowledge it. Carol has never been this calm, rational and *open* for such a sustained period of time. And equally importantly, she's not running me through the ringer over every detail of every page of every application. I hold my breath and wait for the proverbial other shoe to drop.

She opens the Princeton file and flips to the essay section. "Some sadistic fuck composes these questions."

That's for sure. Carol blinks at the page and stares in disbelief. I could recite the question she's reading verbatim, even though I can't see the page in front of her. I racked my brain for days over how to compose Janice's answer. The Princeton admissions committee want-ed to know: "Using the quotation below as a jumping off point, tell us about an event or experience that helped you define one of your values or changed how you approach the world." When I first saw the quote, I wondered whether the whole essay question was a joke. The lines, pulled from some obscure poem, deal with unanswerable ques-tions and smooth rocks washed up by the surf.

Carol looks up from the nonsense I've written, which relies heavi-ly on Janice's two hours of experience volunteering at a homeless shel-ter, and says, "I'm not done yet. Listen to me very carefully. This older man, who's turned your world upside down and made your financial worries go away…"

I look up and meet my boss's gaze. I'm about to ask how she knows that when she says, "Don't look so surprised. I know everything. Anyway, I'm going to give you advice, whether you want it or not, alright?"

At first I don't nod or give her any affirmative answer. It's so unusual for her to ask permission before holding forth on any topic that I've been conditioned not to react to her questions. Safer to assume they're always rhetorical.

"Don't ever surrender control of your financial future to a man. When Reid left me, I got nothing but child support, and the 'right' to live in what I thought was my house for six months. And it's not like I didn't have a decent lawyer. My parents put a second mortgage on their home in Long Island to pay him for me. But it turns out Reid had everything squirreled away in trusts that I didn't understand—and wouldn't have cared about anyway—because I was so dippy and in love. I signed all sorts of papers early in our marriage, because he said he was protecting our future. I didn't bother to ask questions, and I didn't realize until it was too late, that the whole time, he had been securing his own nest egg. Not ours."

Wow. Carol Broadwick was dippy. Surely not in this lifetime. When she pauses to shake her head and presumably marvel at her own naiveté, I feel like I need to say something. But I'm not so stupid as to try to nudge the conversation in my own direction. What she craves now, like always, is praise.

"Even though he treated you horribly, you became an enormous success in your own right."

"I did, didn't I? But my point to you, Zoë, is that it would have been so much easier for me if I'd had some of my own money to throw into the business at the get go. Instead I saddled myself with debt and left my toddler with strangers every day, and dragged him into the office with me on weekends. So it kills me to watch one of my brightest stars start down the same road that almost derailed my life."

I'm one of her brightest stars? That's a new development. It occurs to me that she's neither cursed nor criticized for at least ten minutes. That must be a record. Then, as abruptly as she digressed, Carol shifts her focus back to Janice's college applications. Our moment of personal connection has ended, but her review seems cursory at best, and we're finished in way less than the time she allotted.

She watches as I carefully arrange each package into its pre-labeled FedEx mailer, and when I say, "I guess that's it, then," and get up to leave, she hands me an envelope.

"Whatever you all say about me, you can't say I'm not a woman of my word."

Inside is a personal check, not a C.R. Broadwick & Associates one, from her to me, for $10,000.

I relate most of the details of my *tête-à-tête* with Carol to Oscar, in the car on the way to LaGuardia. We've got time for the long version, since we're sitting in brutal traffic. I leave out her overt warning about him. Instead I go on and on about how I get her now that I know where she's coming from, and while I've never begrudged her hard-won success, I've never liked the woman. Maybe that's about to change.

Despite everyone's (alright, mainly Kevin's) admonitions that my job lacks social utility, my primary complaint has never been with the substance of my work. I actually don't mind talking to stressed out lawyers whose careers are the most important thing in their lives, day in and day out. But I have spent years living in real and palpable fear of my boss. I don't want to develop a twitch like the poor Town Crier, whose face ticks uncontrollably whenever Carol invades her space. Maybe this conversation is a defining moment for me. Instead of passively hoping to succeed, I need to take a page from Carol's book and be more assertive. Maybe not psychotic like her, but at least more proactive professionally. For the first time in ages, I see my future ahead of me and I'm not overwhelmed. I'm actually kind of excited.

As I hold hands with Oscar in the back seat of the black sedan, I wonder if I'm wrong to take him home so soon. We've only known each other for a couple of months, and it's been less than half a year since my break up with Brendan, whom my entire family had embraced as one of their own. Even though everyone knows his sexuality drove our split, and I certainly garnered heaps of sympathy, maybe it's too soon to ask them to welcome a new man.

Oscar sets aside my doubts by saying exactly the right thing. "I'm proud of you. You're finally coming to grips with the fact that you're great at what you do. And you do it in the shadow of a crazy lady, with a great deal of grace, as far as I can tell. I think it's fantastic." He leans over a gives me a quick kiss. I feel myself starting to glow.

He looks calm and collected, not at all like an anxious boyfriend being dragged home to Mom and Dad for inspection. His ease should put me at ease, but it doesn't, and I'm not sure why. It must be normal anticipatory anxiety about the weekend.

Oscar's BlackBerry beeps and he consults his watch before scrolling to the new message. "We should be fine, even if it's gridlocked all the way out to Queens." While he reads email, I notice he's brought his scratched up briefcase. Even now that he's bought a replacement, he's still attached to the original. That's so sweet, I think as we pull onto the Tri-Borough Bridge at a snail's pace. I'm so content being with him that I don't even mind the traffic jam. How pathetic is that? Especially since he's ignoring me at the present moment, typing madly with his thumbs. I stare out the window and watch a blinding orange Corvette inch along beside us.

Oscar makes me happy, deliriously so at times, but I can't seem to relax and enjoy my good fortune. I'm too worried about whether I'm good enough for him, despite the fact that he's given me no reason to be insecure. I waste so much time thinking about what I'm wearing, and what I'm saying, and whether he thinks I'm smart and beautiful and sophisticated enough. Sure, I go through the motions of being his settled in girlfriend, but I hate when he sees me without make-up, or with my hair not blown dry, or my clothes not quite right. He's never seen the comfortable shirts I sleep in when I'm alone, and I don't invite him in my apartment without launching a massive clean up first. I'd die if he ever opened one of my closets and saw all the things I deem too common for his eyes.

Which is ludicrous, because everyone has that stuff. Even Oscar, I presume. He's just got more storage space than the average city dweller, which lets him hide it better. So I should stop trying to undermine myself. Everything is great. I should not be searching for a problem where there is none. He obviously thinks I'm good enough, so maybe I ought to believe it myself. The weekend will go beautifully. Everyone will say we're made for each other, and when we get back to New York in three short days, things will be different. Easier. More settled. More solid.

TWENTY-FOUR

My mother greets us in the chaos of Thanksgiving Wednesday at Miami International Airport, dressed in her usual ensemble of diamond earrings, immaculate coiffure, billowy dress made of hemp or some other politically correct fabric, and Birkenstock sandals, circa 1982. Not that they've changed the design much over the decades, but I think it's kind of noteworthy that my mom, who spends $75 twice a week to have her hair blown dry, keeps having her old sandals repaired. I stopped noticing her self-contradictory sense of style years ago, but maybe I should have been more thorough in my pre-flight briefing to Oscar. I catch him doing a double-take. He tries to cover by removing his jacket and commenting to me about the weather, even though we're inside the air conditioned terminal.

Mom comes hurtling at me for a big hug, then lurches back suddenly as if shocked. "Did you get your breasts done?" she demands in a loud hiss, that lets everyone within twenty feet know that she's visibly horrified by the thought of her own flesh and blood going under the knife to have inorganic pouches of perk inserted.

"No. Mom. God. What are you thinking?"

"They feel pretty fake to me," she presses the issue.

"Mother, I did not have a boob job. I'm wearing a good bra, that's all. And now that you've totally embarrassed me, this is Oscar."

Oscar struggles to stifle a laugh and extends his hand. "It's a pleasure to finally meet you."

"You *are* every bit as good looking as Zoë claimed. Which is surprising, because I was afraid she might be getting a bit desperate." Mom's eyelids flutter. She's a pretty lady, even though she's spent most of the past sixty-five years baking her skin in the sun. She has huge blue eyes with flecks of green that none of her kids were fortunate enough to inherit, cheekbones like a cover girl, and every month she has her hair painstakingly restored to its original honey blonde color.

Under the tent-like garments she lately favors, she's disguising a great figure to boot, from swimming at least a mile a day, every day. Sadly, while I can always predict what she'll look like, even if it's been a long time between visits, I can never guess what will fly out of her mouth at any given moment.

"Mom, please. Where's Dad anyway?"

"He went looking for a Starbucks."

"Dad puts away seven or eight cups of coffee a day," I explain to Oscar.

"I see nothing wrong with that," Oscar says, just as Dad appears down the hallway. He's balancing one of those cardboard cup holder trays as he pushes upstream against the throng of deplaning travelers.

He reaches us and sticks out his free hand to Oscar before greeting his only daughter. The steaming coffees list precariously to the left but miraculously don't fall. Oscar shakes Dad's hand and relieves him of the tray.

"I expect a man like you would drink black coffee," my father says in a tone I'm sure he thinks is his man-to-man voice. Oscar accepts the *grande* black graciously even though I know he usually drinks it with three blood jolting sugars.

"And green tea lattes for the ladies." Dad looks to Mom for affirmation. I make a face and protest that he knows I love coffee. It's been one of my major food groups since high school.

"It's healthier for your ovaries, darling," my mother says, as she foists the unwelcome beverage at me. "At your age, you can't be too careful."

"Mom!" I hiss. Oscar stifles another laugh. I consult my watch. We are less than ten minutes into an almost 72-hour visit. I take a drink of my parentally hijacked hot beverage and almost spit it out. It's that foreign. "What the heck is in this?"

"Soy milk, darling," my mother trills.

Of course. I keep forgetting that the vegan thing means non-dairy creamers. I make a mental note to dash to the grocery store for real milk before anyone needs further caffeination. And maybe I'll stop at the liquor store on the same trip. God knows I'm ready for a drink.

As we start to push through the crowds towards the exit, my mother takes Oscar's arm and begins earnestly explaining about the horrors of the American dairy industry. "They used to get seven or eight years out of a cow, and now they normally cull them after two," she laments. Oscar, to his credit, doesn't venture an opinion. He arranges his face into a suitably sober expression and nods solemnly.

Once they're safely four or five paces ahead, my dad takes pity on me and offers to switch drinks. I wouldn't normally take him up on this, but it's the only way he can find to rebel against the tyranny of his wife, and I can't bring myself to take that away from him. He grins conspiratorially as I relieve him of his high test coffee.

We're not quite in the driveway when my brother's kids stampede out to meet us. They've recently turned five and I, being the prejudiced aunt who sees them two or three times a year, think they're the most gorgeous little beings ever. Ben sports what looks like his Halloween costume. "Auntie Zoë! I'm a pirate!" he calls happily.

I roll down the window and give him my best arrrggh before he adds, breathlessly, "And Courtney's going to walk the plank!"

"No I'm not and you can't make me!" Courtney starts to make her own dash towards me, blonde banana curls streaming underneath a glittery pink tiara. She's tripping over the folds of her princess dress but somehow managing to stay upright.

As I step out of the car, Ben swings his pirate sword to keep his sister at bay so that he can pounce on me first. "Auntie Zoë! Come see my pirate ship!"

"No! Come see the castle first!" Courtney squeals, as she tries to muscle her way in. After I manage to sneak in quick hugs and kisses, each of them seizes one of my hands, and united in their task for the moment, they start to drag me towards the front door. I glance back at Oscar apologetically. He smiles and shrugs and looks uncharacteristically indecisive about whether to join the children's pirate expedition, or to stay behind and risk whatever line of questioning happens to fly out of my mother's mouth. Maybe he regrets coming already.

Ben stops short on the front step. "A coconut hit Daddy's rental car yesterday and made a big dent," he reports, suddenly solemn. "And then Daddy said a very bad word."

"That's too bad," I say, "But at least it didn't hit a person."

"That's what Mommy said."

My brother, Scott, has registered our arrival. "Hey, sis." He plants a kiss on my cheek and asks, "So aren't you going to introduce your new man? He must be either brave or severely limited to come here for the weekend."

"I'm hoping for brave. I hear you had a coconut incident."

"Yeah, it took me four hours to sort out a new rental car, with the holiday weekend."

"Auntie Zoë!" Ben pleads. "Let's go!"

"You go see the pirate stuff, I'll help Oscar with the bags," Scott says.

We step into the foyer and one of my father's paint by number projects, a large homage to Rembrandt, greets us. Thank God I told Oscar about Dad's hobby. He said it sounded harmless, but this particular example of his early work might be enough to force a re-evaluation of that opinion.

Ben and Courtney stop, drop to the floor and exchange their sneakers for slippers. Another quirk of Mom's that I failed to warn Oscar about. Though if he's planning to stick around, he might as well get used to the craziness now. I kick off my own boots, and trade them for the least offensive available option, rubber flip flops. Laurie, my sister-in-law, who I'm sure brought her own slippers, yells hello from the kitchen.

"Let's go say hi to your mom on the way to the castle," I say to the kids.

The kitchen, which normally has so little to offer it propels me to seek fast food outlets I'd never patronize in New York, looks as if it's been transformed into a set for Martha Stewart's program. That is, it would look like their set if every inch of wall space weren't covered with examples from Dad's paint by number still life period. Most of these, his early works, clash with each other. Mom says he likes the kits because he's colorblind. I always thought she was joking, but now that I see the arrangement of finished work, I understand that she's been right all along.

Laurie rolls out dough for pie crusts, next to several overflowing bowls of perfectly cored, peeled and sliced apples of various varieties. I know this because each one is labeled. Laurie is one of those women whom other moms love to hate. She has two rambunctious children, but her house is always immaculate and the meals are always to die for. And she does it all while looking an awful lot like a modern take on one of those fifties TV commercial housewives who smilingly pushed their vacuums around in dresses and high heels. Laurie used to work as an associate in one of San Francisco's biggest law firms, but she gave it up when she ran out of maternity leave, and as far as I know, she's never been happier.

My mother doesn't get it. She thinks Laurie should "apply herself." Laurie and Scott think Mom should mind her own business, and that Mom's just bitter because she never had a career and she wishes she had it to do over. It always makes for at least one tense exchange per holiday.

By the time Laurie and I have gotten through the basics, such as how the flight was, the kids are squirming to get me out of the kitchen before I'm sucked into adult conversation. Laurie asks if I'd like a glass of wine, and I say I'd love one for the road.

"Pirates only drink rum!" Ben protests.

"We can pretend it's rum."

"Okay." His face wrinkles in concentration for a moment, then he says, "I'll have one, too!" A split second later, he remembers to add, "Please, Mommy."

"Only grown up pirates get to bring drinks upstairs," Laurie says. I see a glimmer of protest spark in Ben's eyes but he decides not to push what he must recognize as a bad position. "And Aunt Zoë's going to need one as soon as she hears about the sleeping arrangements."

"What sleeping arrangements?"

"Scott and I are at the Hyatt. Your mother plans to put Oscar in the guestroom and have you bunk with the kids."

"You can't be serious."

Laurie rolls her eyes. "She thinks it's positively *immoral* for the grandkids to see their Auntie shacked up. But don't freak out. Scott already booked you guys a room, weeks ago, when we first heard about this. You're welcome to drive over to the hotel with us later."

"My mom will lose it if I don't sleep here."

Laurie shrugs, as if that's part of the point, and reaches for the wine bottle. Normally it would annoy me to hear my sister-in-law criticize my mother, but in this case, I can't say she's wrong. Mom should be thrilled I'm serious enough to bring my new guy home. And since she's so worried about my biological clock, she shouldn't be so judgmental about my sex life.

My new boyfriend, my brother and my parents catch up to us as Laurie pours me a generous glass of wine. Oscar has sportingly traded his Ferragamo loafers for worn gray slippers, which Dad has probably tried to toss several times in recent decades. I manage quick introductions before the kids start pulling at me to get moving. "Want to come see a pirate ship?" I ask Oscar again, thinking it might not be best to leave him with the adult members of the Clark family.

"And a castle!" Courtney corrects my invitation.

"Absolutely," he says, with a huge smile in my direction.

Upstairs, I'm so surprised when Oscar gamely drops to his hands and knees to access the ship and fort crafted from old sheets and sofa cushions, that I stand there for a second, taking in the whole scene, before Courtney re-commandeers my full attention to the castle tour.

Evidently Oscar likes children. We've never discussed the kid question, probably because we never really see any children in New York. Maybe it's something I need to bring up, assuming we survive this visit. I've always pictured myself with kids, at some vague point in my distant future, but certainly not on Angela's stepped up timeline. What if Oscar is in more of a hurry? He does have a decade on me. I wonder if this is a deal breaker for him. If it is, wouldn't he have told me right off the bat?

Later, I take my mother aside and tell her that there is no way, since I am over thirty years old, and I have this great new man who gave up his holiday weekend to be with me, that I am sleeping down the hall from him. When I was upstairs playing pirates, I ran through various scenarios in which I explained to Oscar that my hippy mother was really a prude, but none of them were appealing enough to re-create in reality. Mom puts up surprisingly minimal fuss, probably because she knows I'm more than willing to make good on my threat to join my brother and his wife at the Hyatt. Either that, or she sees Oscar as her fastest possible route to more grandchildren. Without further drama, Oscar and I shuffle our belongings upstairs to the guest room, which houses a perfectly serviceable, though quite squeaky, queen sized bed.

I open my suitcase and start hanging my clothes for tomorrow in the closet, in hopes of not having to iron. Oscar takes out his laptop and asks whether I mind if he checks his messages before heading downstairs.

I tell him no problem, but my expression must say I suspect he's willfully hiding from my relatives. Not that I would blame him, if he'd known them for more than about half an hour.

Oscar sighs. "I'll be right down, if it's so important to you. Just let me answer a few emails." He pulls me towards him and plants a kiss on my forehead. Maybe under the correct circumstances, that would be cute, but in this moment, it feels patronizing and dismissive. I try to remind myself that his work demands a huge commitment of his time, even if everyone else is in holiday mode. I, once again, need to stop creating issues where none exist.

As I head back downstairs, I hear Laurie grumbling to my brother that it's not fair, since my mom never let them co-habit under her roof, prior to their engagement.

Dinner feels roughly seventy-four hours long, but in reality lasts only about ninety minutes. Basically, in lieu of normal conversation, my parents take turns interrogating Oscar. Dad's questions about his career, and what he thinks about the market downturn would be bearable, if Mom didn't chime in at every opportunity to make wholly inappropriate inquiries, such as whether Oscar wants children.

My normally cool, self-possessed guy blinks like a young doe in headlights. "I suppose so, yes," he finally says, as neutrally as possible.

This is all the validation my mother needs. "Well, you shouldn't put it off, you know," she trills. "Zoë's not getting any younger, are you, darling?"

I feel my face burn red. My dad asks whether anyone would like more mahi. Scott says he'd love some, and volunteers to go retrieve it from the grill.

My mother smiles like a criminally insane person and bats her eyelids madly at me. "Mom, *please*," is all I can think of to hiss.

Oscar decides to ignore the moment of colossal Clark family dysfunction and remarks that the squash is excellent.

"I am so, so, *so* profoundly sorry," I tell him three long hours later, when we're safely locked in the guest bedroom.

"Your mom's something. I know you warned me, but I don't think I was prepared."

"She's had a filtering problem all her life, but it seems to get worse with age. Plus she's been lobbying for me to have babies since I graduated college."

"But she's got two grandchildren already."

"She loves Ben and Courtney to pieces, but my brother's kids are still a bit like a consolation prize for her. Not that she'd admit it, but she desperately wants me to reproduce. I think she thinks it would give us some kind of sacred earth-motherly bond."

Maybe this line of discussion is the opening I need. Maybe he'll say something about wanting children eventually, and we can have a heart to heart talk about our shared hopes for our shared long-term future.

No such luck.

"Well, at least she's not boring. Although now that I've seen what you'll be like in thirty years…" Oscar says playfully, and kisses my ear-lobe. I snuggle closer into the nook under his arm, close my eyes and drift off thinking I'm the luckiest woman in the world.

Because my brother is a kind man with a good soul, he has reserved a tee time that requires Oscar and Dad to leave before breakfast, there-by avoiding the lumpy flaxseed porridge my mother would try to push on them first thing in the morning. I get up early, too, to make sure Oscar gets out of the kitchen with plain old coffee, instead of the Asian virility tea with which Mom threatened him at dessert last night. The plan succeeds, mainly because my mother is momentarily distracted by her sun salutations.

As I close the front door after Oscar and Dad, who looks like he's about to start apologizing as soon as he's sure his spouse is out of ear-shot, I exhale for what feels like the first time since we landed. Laurie will arrive any moment now, and she'll want company in the kitchen. Ben and Courtney will be vying for Auntie time, and Mom will spend the morning wringing her hands about the evils of the food indus-try. Which in Laurie's case means she's preaching to the converted, because I know my sister-in-law has procured a vegetarian-fed, hu-manely raised "happy" turkey from a small, local farm.

I go back upstairs and jump in the shower, but instead of the hot, steamy cascade that used to fall from an over-sized shower head in this bathroom, I get a trickle from some foolish low-flow faucet. It takes three times the usual amount of time to rinse the conditioner from my hair and I decide that this is one of Mom's environmental "improvements" I could live without.

I wrap myself in a towel, slide my slippers back on my feet, and pad back into the guestroom. Oscar's briefcase rests propped against the closet door. I move it to retrieve my clothes and see that it's the undamaged replacement he bought himself around the time the O'Malley scandal broke.

I stand in Mom's kitschy guestroom, hair still dripping wet, and try to wrap my head around the fact that Oscar switched bags some-time during the course of our journey. Which unquestionably quali-fies as abnormal behavior. My heart starts racing. What is he up to?

I have to know. Of course, if I look inside, I'll probably find nothing and end up feeling like a creep. I must have dreamed I saw the other briefcase in the car yesterday.

Except I know I didn't.

I try to reassure myself that my unease is an understandable result of being burnt by Brendan. If I think about things rationally, I wouldn't expect to uncover anything weird in Oscar's luggage. Supposing I believe Olivia's tawdry version of events—which I don't anymore—it's not likely he'd pack evidence of his infidelity on a trip with me. So I can't even articulate why the bag is calling me to look inside.

Other than the possibility that he switched it with someone when he went to the men's room at the airport. That's the only time he's been out of my sight. But what then? Is my guy a CIA operative? How sexy would that be? Or could he be some kind of high end drug mule? The little voice in my head demands to know where I come up with this stuff.

Why am I plagued by such nosy, immature urges? And if I peek now, where does it end? Do I rifle through his underwear drawer next? Or in the deep recesses of his bathroom closet? Or under his bed? Why can't I trust him? He's been nothing but wonderful to me. I should extend him the same courtesy and assert some control over my imagination.

I'm about to take the high road when the little voice in my head eggs me on. She says peeking will reassure me that he's a great guy, just like when I snooped in his phone. And I won't be able to relax until I *know* he's not hiding anything. Which means I'll be silently embarrassed at my unbecoming behavior for the rest of my otherwise perfect life with Oscar.

That seems like the lesser evil.

The briefcase feels heavier than it looks as I wedge myself in the chair and hoist it onto my lap. I make a silly deal with myself: I'll try his birthday, which unlocked his phone. If that doesn't work, I'll abandon this pursuit once and for all. I arrange the dials on the clasp. The lock remains shut. Hmm. It can't hurt to try one more combination. I adjust the dials to my birthday and the clasp springs open. Wow. I'm not sure why I attach great meaning to this development but I do. So much so that I leaf through the files on top almost absentmindedly, mulling if his use of my birthday means he's decided I'm *The One*.

As suspected, all he's carrying is a small pile of business documents, his laptop, which I can't open without the password card he carries in his wallet, and this month's *Food and Wine* magazine. I set it all on the end table, taking care to keep the pile in order. I'm already berating myself for my slimy behavior when I notice a pocket in the bottom of the briefcase.

The compartment is small and snug, and I have to wedge my hand between the leather lining to produce its contents. It yields an unsealed letter sized envelope and an Andorran passport. Interesting. He must have procured it during his marriage. I flip through the stamps. He's used it in Andorra, Cyprus, and a bunch of islands in the Caribbean, over the past five or six years. And just this Monday, he was issued six-month, multiple-entry visas to Cambodia, Laos and Vietnam.

I realize I've been holding my breath and force myself to exhale as I open the envelope. It takes me a second to register what's inside.

I'm holding a cashier's check, drawn in U.S. dollars on some bank in Phnom Penh, made out to CASH, in the amount of $500,000. It's wrapped in a sheet of paper that contains a series of wiring instructions, but doesn't mention any financial institutions by name. There's just a long list of account numbers.

My hands start to shake and my jaw drops. Who carries that kind of money? Certainly not upstanding young executives with normal incomes and traditional bank accounts, even if they've made brilliant investments along the way. I'd be an idiot if I didn't smell something off. Very off. The sudden sound of small feet pattering in the hallway makes me jump.

"Auntie Zoë! Come play with us!" Courtney demands.

"Mommy says you have to, if you don't want to help in the kitchen," Ben adds.

Normally it would grate on me that Laurie presumes to tell me what I need to do, but I'm distracted enough to let it slide. "I'll be there in just a minute." I stare at the number in shock. Half a million dollars seems like an awful lot of spending money to bring along on a weekend to meet my family.

A chill shoots up my back and I pull my towel more tightly around myself. What the hell is Oscar doing on the side? Because it's pretty clear he's up to something. Takamura Brothers doesn't pay him that well, and they certainly don't compensate their executives with foreign cashier's checks. Kevin's warning echoes in my head. Does he know something he can't share? No, that's ridiculous. Kevin was motivated by simple, old-fashioned jealousy. Oscar can't possibly be involved in anything below board. He's so upstanding and clean cut, and besides, when would he have the time? When he's not at work, he's with me.

Except when he's not. If I thought he had time for another woman, I can't tell myself he doesn't have time for a clandestine business venture.

Just because he tells me he's at a meeting, or a client dinner, or the gym, doesn't mean it's so. There are just enough bizarre little details to raise my antenna. Maybe the story about replacing the damaged bag is horseshit. What if he's always had two? And what if he's been swapping bags with someone right under my nose? And why would he need a second passport to travel to *Southeast Asia*? My heart starts racing and a knot forms in my stomach and pulls itself tight.

No. My imagination must be going places it has no business exploring.

The children rap on the door again. "Nana! Auntie Zoë is too *slow!*" Courtney yells.

I re-pack the briefcase and obsessively check and re-check that the files are in the exact same order I found them, even though I know I didn't re-arrange anything. As I pull my clothes on, I have an idea. The clock on the night stand shows that the guys have only been gone an hour. Plenty of time. I re-open the case, and empty the secret compartment again. The kids tackle me as I step into the hallway. "Santa's going to be in the parade!" Ben announces, with wide eyes and a huge, dimpled smile. "Come watch with us so we don't miss him!"

"It's going to be a while before it's Santa's turn. He's always the big finish. Auntie Zoë needs to go in Grandma's study to make a copy and then I need to dry my hair, and then I'll come down. I promise. Why don't you go check on the parade? Maybe they have something fun on right now."

"Okay," the twins say in unison and stampede off in the direction of the stairs.

My mother's study features an almost un-navigable labyrinth of boxes, books and piles of loose paper, arranged in towers like skyscrapers in a small-scale city all over the floor. Mom may have never held a job outside the home, but that hasn't stopped her from joining every committee, social movement, and neighborhood outreach organization she could find. Her desk isn't much better. The laptop almost gets lost in the other chaos. So many plants line the window sill that they block much of the natural light, which means most of them look a bit anemic.

I move a stack of literature on sustainable farming off the printer/scanner/copier and place the wiring instructions on the glass. It produces a single photocopy at what feels like a glacial pace. I repeat the exercise with the check and the photo page of his passport. I grab the originals and the copies and dart back to the guest room before anyone has a chance to way-lay me. My fingers tremble as I restore Oscar's treasures to their hiding place. I check four times that the briefcase is resting in its exact original position by the closet, before folding the photocopies and stashing them inside a box of tampons.

So this is how my fairy tale romance ends. I try to steel myself as I dry my hair, rolling each segment out with my wiry round brush, just like I do almost every morning before work. Something is seriously up. My prince charming has been less than forthcoming at best, and at worst, he's a common criminal. God knows what he's doing to rake in that kind of money, but he's obviously hiding something major. Why did I have to bring him here? Why couldn't I wait to confirm or deny my fears first, as Angela, even in the midst of her own crisis, so wisely advised? I'm surprised I don't feel more unhinged. Or maybe that comes later, after the initial jolt dissipates.

All I feel is a sort of crushing emptiness, a loss so out of nowhere that I can't begin to process it yet. I'm not getting stuffed up, or teary, or even lumpy in the throat. I take a deep breath and watch the color start to drain from my face in the mirror. I have to pull it together. If my happy ending is about to be torpedoed, I want to be the one to decide that. Not have it unravel in a flood of hysteria in front of the whole family. I need to decide whether to push through the weekend with a cowardly smile and pretend all is perfect, or end things immediately. Though that sounds messy, and therefore so *not* tempting, it might be the most reasonable course.

TWENTY-FIVE

I'm over the stove, stirring gravy under Laurie's zealous supervision, when I decide there's no way I will be able to wait through the entire long weekend for answers. I need to know what Oscar's up to. A large, possibly pretzel shaped, knot has formed in my stomach, and despite my best efforts at willful denial, I know I won't think of him the same way, at least until I get some answers. I'm already bracing myself to learn something I'd rather not know. The little voice in my head taunts me, saying she knew he was too good to be true all along.

When my mother floats into the kitchen to start assembling the salad that will constitute the centerpiece of her holiday meal, I foist the wooden spoon into her hands, and dash upstairs, still sporting the floral apron Laurie fastened around me earlier. I raid the box of Tampax for my photocopies and hole myself up in Mom's study again. This time I double check that the door locks behind me before placing the first sheet of paper on the scanner. I don't know why my heart is pounding. Oscar isn't expected for another couple of hours, and my female relatives seem unlikely to leave the kitchen and inquire about my emailing activities.

Once the document appears on the desktop, I log into my Gmail, attach the new PDF file to a blank message and write, "Kevin, Will explain background later. No time now. Found this in his briefcase. What do you suppose it means? Thanks in advance. Zoë." My hand hovers over the mouse. Of course I could be way off. Maybe my imagination has gotten away from me. Also, I'm not sure why I'm turning to Kevin for help. Probably because he was the first person to articulate any doubts about Oscar. And because he has an incredible network of connections who seem able to find out anything about anyone. Anything unsavory, at least.

I click the send button without allowing myself to reconsider all the potential fallout from my chosen course of action. With a great deal of willpower, I make myself log off, double delete the PDF, and restore the copies to their hiding place.

When I rejoin Mom and Laurie in the kitchen, Mom is bemoaning Laurie's plans to use real butter and cream in the mashed potatoes. She can't abide the thought of such "morally bankrupt" products in her home. The kids have given up on the parade and are chasing each other around the island, wielding carrots as swords and giggling maniacally. Some member of the rat pack or other croons over the stereo. My heart rate starts to slow back to normal as I begin cleaning a mountain of green beans. At least I'm exploring my fears. I'm not going to bury my head in the sand. If Oscar isn't who I think he is, I'd rather know as soon as possible. So why do I feel like I've been punched in the gut?

Kevin calls just as I hear the men coming back through the front door. I duck into the downstairs guest bathroom and answer. "Wow," he says, in lieu of any greeting. "Zoë, I really have no idea what any of this means, but we need to look into it. Today, if possible."

Suddenly weeks of tension on my part towards Kevin dissipate. We may be going through an awkward phase, but he's still in my corner. Why did I ever doubt that? "I didn't know what to do. I felt like the biggest heel for snooping, but then I found the passport and the check, and spying suddenly felt like the lesser evil." I make a concerted effort to keep my voice down. This house has the paper-thin walls often featured in new construction.

In the background, I hear his mother yelling that she is sick of slaving for her thankless family, and some of her useless children had better come lend a hand in the kitchen and pronto.

"Do you need to go?" I ask, thinking, please don't cut this short.

"I'm sure my sisters are on it, plus it's her own fault for giving the housekeeper the weekend off. So listen to me. Let's forward this to Angela. Her sister's husband will be able to make sense of the banking information way faster than we could on our own. He's got the FBI's full resources, whereas we have a hunch."

Why didn't I think of Angela's brother-in-law? Maybe because I thought my problems can't possibly merit interrupting a federal agent's turkey dinner. My stomach's in knots. The sooner someone tells me what this is all about, the better. If my mother allowed antacids in the house, I'd be chomping on them like candy right about now. I hear Scott telling my mom it would have been nice of me to warn them that Oscar is a scratch golfer, and wonder if they can hear me as clearly out in the hallway.

Kevin's mom shrieks again that this is the last holiday she's hosting her ingrate relations. "I've got to dash," Kevin says. "I'm forwarding this now and I'll call you if I hear anything. And do me a favor. If Angela calls you first, it would be nice if you'd allow me into the loop."

"Absolutely. You're the best."

There's a brief silence that's long enough to make me think the call dropped, then Kevin asks, "Do you mean that?"

"Of course."

"That's the nicest thing you've ever said to me."

I doubt that's the case, or at least I certainly hope it isn't. Mrs. O'Connor yells again that they're going out to eat next year and she doesn't care if it's Chinese food, McDonald's, or the take-away counter at the Food Giant. Kevin says a hasty goodbye before I can spit out anything else.

I take a deep breath and force myself to leave the relative safety of the guest bathroom. I drape my arms up on Oscar's shoulders, and wonder whether he'll notice any change in my attitude towards him. "How was your golf game?"

"Great, though I feel bad about beating your dad on his home course."

"I'm sure he was happy just to get out and play." I wonder when I'll get a chance to speak to him in private. Probably not before dinner. I remove my hands from his shoulders and ask if he'd like a beer.

"That man of yours is gorgeous," Laurie gushes when I run into the kitchen to get Oscar's beer. "And it must be serious, if he's here for the holiday."

"I guess you could say that." Even I can hear the sudden lack of passion in my voice, but she apparently doesn't.

"Has he thrown out the L-word?"

"Yes, as a matter of fact, he has." I wince at how smug I sound reporting this, as if it's an achievement in its own right, regardless of where things go from here. I flip the tops off two winter ales, one for Oscar and one for my brother. My mother probably won't let Dad have one now, if he wants wine with dinner.

"So do I hear wedding bells? Is he it? Is he *the one*?"

Laurie's directness catches me off guard. I can't remember the last time she and I talked about anything except her kids, and my mother's special brand of crazy. Though we don't normally discuss our personal lives, and my world appears likely to implode again, I decide it's best to answer her question. She doesn't need to be alerted to a problem at this stage. I'm still hoping, irrationally and against a strong circumstantial case to the contrary, that there's an innocent explanation for everything.

"I don't know. I thought maybe yes, at first, but now I wonder if it's all going too fast. But he's perfect, right? Smart. Handsome. Successful. Driven. Generous. Into me." As I tick off each remarkable quality, I hear the enthusiasm in my voice wane. "And I'm not getting younger."

"Please stop with the I'm-so-ancient nonsense. You've been spending too much time listening to your mother, who's spent her whole life in suburbia, where women settle down younger. None of your New York friends are in a huge hurry, right? There's nothing wrong with putting on the brakes if you feel like it. More women should do it, but they're afraid. I think it shows guts and smarts to take the time to make sure it's right. I have so many friends who got married because the guy checked the right boxes and they felt like they were on the train and it was therefore too late to 'do better,' whatever that means. So take your time. Get to know him. Get to know what you guys are really like as a couple. Then decide if he's your future. Not before." She catches herself talking more than stirring, chopping or basting. "Sorry. I'm getting preachy. It happens when you have kids. You hear yourself sermonizing like you're somebody's mother or something." She laughs at her own silly joke.

"No, it's totally okay. It's actually the best advice I've heard so far. Thank you. Seriously."

"Don't mention it." She reaches for her potholders and turns her attention to the contents of the oven. Whatever she has in there with the turkey smells wonderful, and our conversation has given me more perspective than she could imagine.

By shortly after six o'clock, my mother and sister-in-law have laid out a holiday table that's equal parts Norman Rockwell tableau and modern political statement. Laurie's perfectly roasted poultry spills artfully arranged oyster stuffing next to an enormous platter of tofu, marshaled into shape by a recycled Jell-O mold from the 1970's that somehow made the trip, decades later, from Wellesley to Key Biscayne. Rival bowls of mashed potatoes, vegan and non, stare each other down from opposite sides of Grandma Clark's silver candelabras, which Laurie undoubtedly polished on arrival, before unpacking her bags or feeding her kids. Laurie's gravy, which I feel like I spent much of the day stirring, floats shunned in its boat at the corner of the table farthest from Mom. Dad keeps glancing at it longingly. In the middle of it all, in a sort of gastronomic demilitarized zone, enough roasted vegetables to feed the greater Miami area, including the Keys, bridge a tenuous peace. They may not be universally local, as both my mother and Laurie would prefer, but at least they're devoid of harmful pesticides that could pulverize the children's livers. Mom and Laurie seized upon this area of agreement yesterday and it should be enough to make the holiday meal copasetic. At least I hope so. It would be really nice if Oscar could get through Thanksgiving dinner without witnessing a family meltdown. Even if he and I are destined to part ways after the weekend.

Oscar and I take our seats to Dad's right, where we're graced with a full-on view of one of his latest masterpieces: a giant paint-by-number rendition of Van Gogh's "Starry Night." It's a vast improvement over the unfortunate series of junior high portraits of Scott and me that used to occupy this wall of honor.

It takes a while to get everyone settled, because Courtney decides she wants to sit between me and Grandma, which requires a re-shuffling of places and mashed potatoes. Dad raises his glass and wishes everyone a happy Thanksgiving.

We're about to start passing the food when Oscar clears his throat and says he'd like to make a toast. I'm not sure why exactly, but my mouth goes dry. Scott catches my eye across the table and shoots me a look that asks if I know what this is about. I hope the face I shoot back says I have no idea.

Oscar gets out of his chair and turns to my mother first. "Thank you for graciously welcoming me into your home, and for preparing this enormous meal, which I'm sure will be delicious." He diplomatically nods in Laurie's direction as he says this last part. He clears his throat again. I wonder if it's a tick I never noticed before. "I hope this is the first of many dinners I'll have at this table."

Mom smiles at him. Dad mutters under his breath that the food isn't getting any warmer. Ben asks if he can have a drumstick. I exhale, thinking that's it, he's conveyed a lovely sentiment, which starkly contrasts Brendan, who never did anything beyond the minimum dictated by acceptable manners and his strict upbringing. But wait, why isn't Oscar sitting down yet?

"To that end," Oscar continues, "I hope you don't mind putting off the feast for just another minute or two, because I have something I'd like to ask Zoë."

I feel the world stop turning for a second. It lurches to a halt and my stomach gets whiplash. Is he drunk? No. He can't be. He has ingested one beer, maybe two at the most, all afternoon. I swear nobody breathes as we all watch Oscar, as if in slow motion, reach into his pants pocket and retrieve a small velvet box. Suddenly I feel a dozen eyes riveted on me. Even the kids have fallen silent, sensing something noteworthy afoot.

Oscar turns to me and takes my hand. I feel outside myself, as if I'm watching the whole scene from off-stage somewhere.

"Zoë, the past two months have been amazing. You've made me feel alive again in a way I didn't think possible. I don't want this ever to end. Will you marry me?" He pops open the box and the ring inside is blinding and embarrassingly large, if such a thing is possible. Just like I knew it would be as soon as he pulled it out of his pocket.

The king of the grand gesture strikes again.

"Are you out of your mind?" It flies out before I can stop it. I clamp my hand over my mouth, but of course it's too late. Oscar looks as if I've spit in his eyes. My family stops looking at me and they all stare downwards, at their empty plates, each adorned with a gold linen napkin, expertly folded by my sister-in-law.

Dad finds his voice. "Why don't you two go talk in the kitchen?" He makes the suggestion with way more enthusiasm than the moment warrants.

I'm out of my chair before anyone can say anything more. Oscar follows right behind me, ring still in hand. I slam the kitchen door shut behind us.

"Not exactly the response I expected, or hoped for."

"Not exactly a question I expected to field this weekend, and in front of my family, to boot. Oscar, it's only been a couple of months, and it's not like we've ever discussed the long-term future. So you can't blame me for feeling blindsided."

Even as I make this off-the-cuff appeal to reason, a pit grows in my stomach. Oscar doesn't seem the type to take rejection, and public humiliation, in stride. Because I blurted a no, without stopping to consider anything beyond a gut reaction, I'm probably going to spend the rest of the long weekend hiding in the guest room, crying over him saying goodbye. The little voice in my head snipes that Oscar might be a criminal, so she won't abide any tears. But whatever happened to innocent until proven guilty? Maybe I'm all wrong about him. Maybe it's a ridiculous misunderstanding and there's a logical explanation for the passport, and the money, and the banking directions. The worst part is, now I'll never find out.

"When you know, you know. I'm too old for silly games." He's pouting now, and the ring has, not surprisingly, made its way back into his pocket.

"That seems sort of unfair. If a woman starts planning a wedding less than three months into a relationship, men say she's out of her tree."

"I've never said that about anyone."

"Fair enough. But you know what I mean. It's too soon for me. I did the whole engagement thing before. A part of me is still reeling from that not working out. And, if we're being honest, I'm confused as to why you'd be willing to rush to the altar again, when that approach didn't work out for you the first time." *And a bigger part of me suspects you might be a felon.* The little voice in my head tells me to go ahead and pat myself on the back for not verbalizing this last piece.

"I think your arguments about timing are just a hedge. You're everything I want in a wife. You're beautiful, smart, fun, and you still have this youthful wide-eyed innocence I find irresistible. We're great together. Don't you see that?"

How can *he* not see that we've been existing in a happy little bubble for two? It all feels idyllic because we haven't allowed real life to interfere with our fun. Maybe if I hadn't been so busy enjoying my new guy high, I might have sensed weirdness. I so desperately want to erase the briefcase and its contents from my memory, to pretend we aren't over even as we stand here discussing more ordinary reasons to delay marriage. I want to keep moving down the path we were on as if my trust in him hasn't been shaken, to plan but not rush a future together.

In the deepest part of my gut, I know this will never happen. But I don't want to face it in this moment, in my parents' kitchen, with my brother's perfect nuclear family listening through the door. So I take a non-confrontational route out of the conversational corner.

"I haven't met any of your friends, let alone Jennifer, who's the only family you've got. You hardly ever mention her."

He frowns. I switch gears. "And I don't know about you, but I have lots of quirks you might find annoying. You just haven't seen them yet."

His expression brightens slightly. "What quirks?"

"I love anchovy pizza."

"Not a deal breaker."

"I'm terrified of hot air balloons, even though I've never set foot in one."

He grimaces. "You'll need to do much better."

"I like to sleep in old sweatshirts and wool socks. Fuzzy, thick wool socks." My voice is playful. I can't help it. He still makes my heart do crazy cartwheels.

"The socks could be a problem." He steps forward and wraps me in a bear hug.

I extract myself from his embrace before he can go in for the kind of kiss that would wither my resolve. "I guess, if we're being brutally honest, what I'm trying to say is, I'm not sure if we're totally meant for each other. And I need time to know for sure, before accepting another proposal." The little voice in my head cheers. She's shrieking with joy that I've found my backbone. His cavalier listing of wide-eyed innocence as a top virtue helped with that. I never realized that our age difference is such a huge selling point for him. That suddenly bothers me.

"So I can't persuade you to elope to Anguilla this weekend? We're practically halfway there."

I look him straight in the eye and realize I have no idea what to say. A barrage of questions about the briefcase's contents probably won't meet with an indulgent reception right now. He must think I'm reconsidering his proposal because he adds, "It's gorgeous down there, and I was so sure you'd say yes, I grabbed your passport from your desk last time I slept at your place."

"I'm sorry. I can't."

Oscar sighs loudly. His eyes look defeated and he seems deflated, which I suppose is entirely understandable. It would be weird if a rejection didn't affect him, right?

"Let's go back in there so everyone can eat," he says, with what I can tell is forced brightness.

"Are you sure you want to face them?"

"Absolutely. They should see I'm not going anywhere."

Wow. That went better than any sane person could have predicted.

Oscar crosses the small space between us, cups my face in his hands and kisses me gently on the mouth. It's a nice kiss, but that electrifying, have-to-have-him feeling that his mere passing touch used to elicit is gone. "Don't be too shocked if I ask you again. I bet I can wear you down." He smiles broadly, but it's forced. His eyes give him away. "Now let's get back in there and face the music."

My family, naturally, pretends like they haven't spent the entire time we were gone straining to hear our conversation. Laurie rockets out of her chair to start re-heating serving dishes, now that the coast is clear in the kitchen.

"Auntie Zoë, are you getting married?" Courtney demands. She looks adorable in her blue holiday dress with lace trim, and several ringlets of her hair tied back in a matching bow perched jauntily on top of her head.

"No, honey, not anytime soon."

She sticks out her lower lip and pouts. "Grandma says if you get married, I get to be the flower girl." She shoots an accusatory look at my mother, as if she suspects she's been victimized by an adult fraud.

"If and when I get married, of course you can be the flower girl."

My niece grins. Her whole face and demeanor change in an instant, in that way only a child's can. God, I envy her ability to shift gears like that. My hands are shaking as I reach for my wine glass. Even though that conversation went as well as it possibly could have, it's going to stress me out for weeks. The little voice in my head has already stowed away her cheerleader's pom-poms and she's nagging me with self-doubts. She wants to know if I've just turned down my big chance at happiness. She's listing Oscar's virtues and telling me I'm an idiot for not saying yes. Circumstantial evidence doesn't make him a criminal. He could easily work for the CIA, she argues. He's perfect for them: highly educated, with no family ties. The little voice also admires Oscar's chutzpah for asking in front of my family. A guy who had the smallest doubt about his feelings for me would never go out on that limb. The little voice wants to retract her earlier statements. She thinks I may have fucked up utterly.

TWENTY-SIX

It doesn't take Oscar long to have a change of heart over his decision to take my big, public rejection of him in stride. He's gone after Laurie and I have cleared the dinner dishes, but before Mom serves dessert. I have no idea if he's checking into a hotel, or making a beeline to the airport to catch a flight back to New York. But more troubling than that, is that I can't figure out whether I'm heartbroken or relieved at his hasty and premature departure.

As soon as he's out the door, all hell breaks loose. It appears unlikely that my family, who dazzled me with their collective, unexpected ability to hold it together in the face of such drama, will talk about anything else for the rest of the weekend, or indeed the entire holiday season. My mother, not surprisingly, offers the most vocal critique of the afternoon's events, which is all negative, at least as it pertains to her only daughter. She practically wails that I'll never have an opportunity with a man of "such quality" again. By which everyone assembled takes to mean handsome, rich and successful. Laurie snidely points out that maybe Mom shouldn't focus on material goods and outer beauty if she's trying to force her "neo-hippie ideals" on the rest of us. Dad fails to come to my defense. Instead he takes advantage of the distraction I've created to scarf some unauthorized apple pie that Laurie baked with an old-fashioned lard crust, topped with a generous scoop of non-soy ice cream. My brother makes a lame attempt to diffuse the situation with unfunny humor.

"At least now Zoë won't end up divorced," he tells my mother with a patronizing pat on her hand. "And you won't have to shell out for a wedding."

I suppress the urge to tell him to screw himself, and instead opt to go hide in the bathroom. Secure behind the locked door, I check my phone. Two missed calls from Angela, but no message. Her phone rolls to voice mail, but before I can exit the sanctuary of the guest bath, she calls me back.

"Definitely suspect, and of great interest to the authorities," she announces breathlessly.

"According to your sister's husband, you mean?"

"Of course. I haven't shown anyone else. And Max said he might want to talk to you himself, once he does a little research. He says the accounts on the list are some kind of double blind accounts, where the bank doesn't even know the customer's identity. It sounds shady to me, but evidently it's legal. When money hits one account, it gets immediately divided and portions get wired out to other accounts, where they get re-divided and re-wired elsewhere, and so on. If he deposits the foreign check in a foreign bank, he can avoid reporting the income to the IRS, but still be dealing with a legit financial institution. And if he wires it onward through these blind accounts, those banks won't have records of him showing I.D. to make the initial deposit."

"So that explains Anguilla."

"You just lost me. Dare I ask what else is going on down there?"

"He asked me to marry him and I turned him down. So he left, right after dinner. Briefcase in hand."

"That gets a big wow." I can see Angela shaking her head in disbelief, trying to wrap her brain around this latest development. I can also tell she has no idea what to say, or even what to ask. Instead of waiting for a question, I give her a summary of recent events here in sunny Key Biscayne, to which she has nothing to add but a series of wows. I can't stand to re-hash it all yet, mainly because I can't decide how I feel. Instead I try to divert attention by asking how things are going at the Mancuso family gathering.

"So far, so good. My mother is so obsessed with my sister's pregnancy that she hasn't noticed I've been carrying around the same glass of merlot all afternoon."

"I guess that's in the positive news column. Talk about stealing your sister's thunder. At her big holiday entertaining debut, no less."

"Yeah, she'd never get over it. Everyone would be talking about my pregnancy, because it's so juicy and scandalous, whereas her future bundle of joy was respectably conceived in church-sanctioned wedlock. But I'll tell you this: sobriety sucks."

"I imagine it does."

My mother starts banging on the door. "Zoë, honey! Are you alright in there? You aren't sick, are you?" This last part sounds almost hopeful, as if it would please her that Laurie's cooking poisoned someone.

"Are the natives getting restless?" Angela asks.

"I think I've got a few minutes before they ram down the door. So are you going to spill the news?"

"I haven't decided. I might tell my sister. She'll be okay, no matter what I choose to do. I can't tell my parents until I'm sure I'm having it."

I don't know if she means to say *until* instead of *unless*, but it sounds to me like her mind is made up and she hasn't quite accepted or internalized that fact yet. "So you're still weighing your options?"

"My boss loves to tell me that in life, there's the plan and then there's what happens. I think I might be too old to have an abortion. What if this is my chance and I blow it? It's not like I planned this. I'm years away from actually planning for a baby, since I haven't even identified a potential husband. Whereas you've had two proposals in the last year and a half, if my math is right. But I look around the office and see all these women who gave their twenties and thirties to their careers, and now they're single and forty-something, and it's too late for most of them."

I wait a second to make sure she's done. "Whatever you want to do, I'll support you. Like a thousand per cent. But I don't think you should look at this as your one opportunity for parenthood. It's not like it's game over anytime soon. If you want to keep the baby, for whatever reason, I think that's great. You don't need to justify it to anyone, or make any rationalizations about career, or age, or anything like that."

"Really?" Angela's voice sounds like a little kid's again.

"Absolutely. You'll be the chicest pregnant woman in the city."

"Thanks, babe. You're the best. Now I just have to work up the gumption to tell Claudio. Which will be tough, since the liquid courage option is off the table."

"When are you going to talk to him?"

"I need to get it over with. I'm going to kill myself with stress if I put it off. So I guess I'll do it as soon as I get back home."

Angela's brother-in-law, Special Agent Max Friedman, calls sometime after ten, when my family has called it a night and my brother and Laurie have tucked in their kids upstairs and snuck out to the hotel.

He goes through this long and unnecessary explanation of who he is. Then he apologizes profusely for interrupting my holiday. I tell him it's fine. I'm so anxious to hear whatever he has to say that I can't bring myself to engage him in any more polite small talk.

"So it sounds like you have a boyfriend with unexplained wealth and unusual travel habits. I assume you're familiar with the controversy surrounding the new mayor?" he says.

"Oscar is mixed up in the mayor's pornography ring?" I should be prepared for bad news. It's not like my mind hasn't already detoured in a similar direction. A dry, metallic taste settles in my mouth, and the world starts to tilt under my feet again.

"Well, we're not exactly referring to the situation as the 'mayor's porn ring,'" Max says. "Anyhow, we suspect your friend started out as more of a paid liaison than a key partner. We think they approached him because he had the perfect excuse to travel to Asia. He works for one of Japan's most prestigious firms, which means he has legitimate business all over the continent. Plus, when he started, he would have been young and hungry."

I want to ask about a thousand questions, but I can hear Max warming up to his topic so I let him keep talking.

"Thornton fits the profile: he grew up middle class and wanted to catch up to all the privileged kids as fast as possible. So when his path serendipitously crossed with the right person, he took a huge gamble and invested in a criminal enterprise. He probably told himself he'd only do it for a little while, but the money was beyond his wildest dreams. And the person who brought him in almost definitely put the screws on him to stay in. So now your friend is over his head. Or that's my theory, and that's all it is at this point, a theory."

When Max finally pauses to breathe, I ask, "Who do you think it was? I mean, who lured him into the trafficking business? If he is indeed involved?"

"I can't say. I'm sorry, I'm getting way ahead of myself."

"Okay, but can I at least ask you, is it a crime to invest in adult entertainment?" I mean to sound skeptical, or at least defensive, but my question comes out flat. I cannot wrap my brain around the fact that I am on the phone with a federal agent and we're talking about Oscar. My Oscar. Who wanted to marry me a couple of hours ago. It feels like Max and I are discussing fictitious characters. And like I'm a spectator instead of a participant.

"It depends on the kind of adult entertainment. It's a crime to invest knowingly in the exploitation of minors. What we try to do in a case like this is establish a pattern. We're not talking about one seventeen-year-old who slipped through the cracks. That's sad when it happens, but it's rare that we'd prosecute those, and even rarer that we'd get a conviction. But in this case, we suspect a knowing and concerted effort to recruit younger and younger girls for the productions. Which makes an enormous difference to our level of prosecutorial interest."

"It's so vile."

"Yes, if what we suspect is true, it is completely vile. But the fact is, it's rare for us to get a conviction on child porn charges. We're more likely to try to prove tax evasion. Or money laundering, if we're lucky."

I swallow hard. I'm no expert, but these do not sound like insignificant charges. There has to be some enormous misunderstanding. Law enforcement makes mistakes. Oscar could *know* unsavory people, maybe even have business dealings with them, and not *be* one himself. That happens all the time.

Max interrupts my train of thought. "Does your boyfriend routinely leave his briefcase unattended?"

"I'm not sure he's my boyfriend anymore, after today."

"Fair enough. But assuming you two patch things up, do you think you could get back into the briefcase?"

"I can't promise, but maybe."

"Or better yet, does he leave his laptop lying around?"

"Sometimes."

"Can you get access to it when he's not there?"

"Technically, yes. He gave me a key. But it's a doorman building, so someone will always know I was there."

"Let me give this some more thought. I'll be back in touch soon." We hang up. I don't know what to think. I feel disloyal, justified, pleased with myself, and horribly ashamed all at the same time. Oscar swept me off my feet. I thought I had found true love, with a wonderful, non-commitment-phobic guy. The real deal that every single woman in every bar in New York hopes to find, whether she admits it or not. And now, just when we should be settling into the next, more comfortable stage of our relationship, Oscar stuns me with a marriage proposal I never asked for. On the very same day I start to wrap my mind around the frightening fact that he—my supposed great love—

is actually a criminal. And a particularly revolting kind of criminal at that. How did everything blow apart so fast?

I push through an uneventful Monday back at work by forcing myself to get organized. I spend all available downtime between meetings and calls ruthlessly purging and re-cataloging old files, and sending boxes to off-site storage. I even disinfect my keyboard and phone by drenching them with the better part of a bottle of Lysol that Carol keeps in the kitchen for her intermittent germ-phobic episodes. I do all this because I'm not ready to face another break-up. Even if it's the right thing.

My body feels as if all my nerves have sprouted out through my skin. It doesn't help that Max forbade me to mention anything about the investigation to my family, so of course they're thinking, poor Zoë—she's screwed it up for herself again. As Laurie rather insensitively put it, it might have been nice for me if I could have been the dumper, instead of the dumpee, for a change. Dad came to my defense and said I did just that, by turning down Oscar's proposal. It sure doesn't feel that way, though. Not even three solid sun-filled days at the pool did anything to improve my mood. I read the same page of my book about a thousand times without following the story at all, listened to sad songs on my iPod, put on a smile for my niece and nephew, and generally felt more pathetic than I thought imaginable. At night, I lay awake and listened to the ticking of the old wind-up clock on the nightstand and practically felt the bags forming under my eyes.

I thought it would be a relief to get out from under the parental roof and back to my regular life, but instead I feel empty. And stupid. I'd never felt so much like a failure as I did last night, when I admitted myself to the apartment chosen by Brendan and bought by Oscar. Not only can't I get it right with men, it's starting to hit me that I'm pretty lousy at taking care of myself, too. Which makes me feel stupider. I'm making more money now than ever before, so whatever the reason I can't get out of my own way, it's not financial.

As a matter of fact, the only bright spot I have right now is my job. I don't want to go home when everyone else starts clearing out shortly after seven, but I've got no better offer, and I don't have my gym stuff with me. I can't even do any more work on the Silverblum wish list, because they're still scheduling initial meetings with the first three lawyers I recruited for them. They were basically tripping over each other's wingtips to secure an audience with Walker Smythe.

It's pouring cold fall rain outside, and I'm drenched to the skin halfway home from the subway, even though I remembered my favorite oversized yellow umbrella. At least the weather matches my mood.

Oscar is waiting at my door. I'm rarely speechless. It's not a trait that would serve me well in my chosen profession, but he's so unexpected, and I'm not sure if he's here to fight or make up. I can't even form a hello.

"Can I come upstairs?" he asks. He's soaked, too, despite carrying a golf umbrella.

I nod, completely unsure of whether I should be ecstatic or annoyed to see him.

Safely inside my apartment, we shed our sopping coats. He's waiting for me to speak first. "What do you want?" I ask, abruptly. My voice sounds edgier than usual.

"I'm sorry I put you on the spot. The weekend didn't go the way I'd planned. Not even close. We'd be lounging in the Caribbean right now if it had. I cleared my calendar, which was no small feat. And even though I should have thought twice about asking you at your parents' dinner table, I've got to say, I'm a bit stunned you turned me down."

He's apologizing, in his own way, but it irks me that he didn't stop to consider that I have a job and a life, too. Even if nothing else was wrong, I couldn't have blown off work to go to Anguilla for the week without notice. Carol would have told me not to bother coming back. But is that enough of a reason to slam the door in Oscar's face? I like that he's successful and confident. Whether or not he focused on my end of the logistics, he did plan to clear his schedule to be with me. Which also might mean he's up to nothing sinister. If he's involved in some massive illegal enterprise, he probably can't check out of his life for over a week. Besides, he's so careful about hiding his past. Why would he risk the scrutiny that would result if he got caught committing a crime? I must have misunderstood something that's none of my business.

The little voice in my head, who's been so conflicted all weekend, barks at me to stop making silly rationalizations. The FBI would not be involved if the allegations weren't extremely serious. Oscar probably flew to the Caribbean without me this weekend, strolled into a bank, and deposited that enormous check with his Andorran passport. A surprise honeymoon would have just improved his cover story. Instead of beating myself up, I should be glad I was bright enough—or lucky enough—to detect a problem. At least I wasn't blindsided by the police banging on the door at midnight. They would have hauled Oscar away, and left me in the bed, scrambling to cover myself and make sense of what just happened. Alone.

"Zoë, say something. Are we okay?"

"Yeah, we're okay." I manage a smile. He doesn't need to know that he's on double secret probation.

"So okay that I can spend the night?"

"Of course."

The little voice in my head groans and scolds me for thinking below my belt.

I silently snap back that she's got it wrong. Now that I've opened the briefcase and spoken to Max, I want a look at Oscar's computer. If he's involved in something unsavory, I want to see for myself. Maybe because it would give me a sense of control over how it all ends. She sighs and mutters something along the lines of, "*Okay, Mata Hari.*"

The little voice shuts up when she sees I can't bring myself to have make-believe make up sex with Oscar. I tell him my period came early and he falls asleep before John Stewart comes on.

Angela's email hits my BlackBerry during the first commercial break. Claudio took her to Pastis, and she broke the news before their table was ready, over an untouched glass of Veuve Clicquot. She says at first he looked confused, then he smiled and gave her a huge hug, right in front of everyone, and ordered himself a scotch, which he doesn't normally drink. She thinks the news began to set in an hour or so later, when the waiter cleared the soup, because he started to get a bit white in the face. It took him until the arrival of the dessert menu to ask if she'd thought about what she was planning to do. She told him she wanted to have it, and he said his family would insist they get married. As he took care of the check, he suggested that Angela take a few days to consider if that's what she really wants.

I write back: "Glad you told him. It must be a relief, at least somewhat. You don't have to marry him because his parents would expect it. Or because of whatever yours would want. You don't have to do anything because of anyone, actually. I'd give him a day or two to digest the bombshell, see if he's in or out, and go from there."

I scroll back through my reply before hitting send. It's a sudden, almost seismic role reversal for us. Angela usually dispenses the advice that I eagerly accept. It feels strange, and also kind of good, to be in the opposite role.

An epiphany, which I imagine by definition is supposed to come as a beautiful illumination, instead hits me like a blinding flood of search lights, as soon as Oscar gets out of bed to leave shortly after six in the morning. Even if, as I've been hoping against all reason, Oscar hasn't done anything illegal, something is not right. In this rare moment of pre-dawn clarity, I concede to myself that the primary problem could be one of several things.

The most obvious possibility is that, after our first couple of dates, Oscar hasn't much cared what I think about anything. He's lavished me with attention, but made no attempt to solicit my opinion on us, or where we're going. He kind of steam rolls ahead, certain his chosen course will be right. Some people might say it's old-fashioned, charming and romantic, but now, in the absence of any mind-altering post-coital glow, I think it's off-putting. It's like Oscar has this slot in his life to fill, he's decided to place me in it, and he's assuming I will go along with all of it, happily.

Another possibility I consider as I hoist myself up, fish my slippers from under the bed, and pad to the kitchen to make coffee, is that maybe we had too much spark and not enough substance. Which would explain why my initial suspicions revolved around the possibility of another woman, despite a complete absence of evidence of one's existence. I imagined he had somebody somehow superior to me, who could give him whatever it was I lacked. Perhaps our initial connection wasn't much more than a physical one, we tried to pretend it was more, and now it's run its course. Which I guess would be the easiest scenario to deal with, if he hadn't just presented me with an apartment, not to mention the ring I rejected over the weekend. There's no way it was worth less than $25,000.

I wait for the coffee to brew before letting my brain contemplate the worst case scenario. Oscar might truly be leading a double life. I've watched enough tabloid television, particularly in the weeks right after the Brendan break-up, to know that it happens. Some criminals look like criminals, but many others fool everyone, sometimes for decades. Everyone has seen those interviews with neighbors, who say they're shocked, they had no idea. That could be Oscar. Or all this could be my imagination running amok. Still, it's easier to wrap my brain around the more sinister possibility after seeing the check for half a million dollars and the extra passport.

And if I'm convinced he's *capable* of something so reprehensible, I suppose I have my answer, whether he's actually guilty or not. It's time for the two of us to part ways. As if the other, more common reasons for moving on aren't enough.

By the time I reach to refill my coffee, it hits me like a ton of bricks. I'm not even sad about the looming break up. Disappointed, yes, but nowhere near devastated. What I feel, more than anything, is an insistent curiosity. I need to know whether Oscar is up to something rotten. I'm not sure why, if I'm planning to cut him out of my life. Maybe it's a desire to know if I've once again grossly misjudged a romantic interest. Or maybe it's mere, cheap, garden variety fascination with the criminally seedy. Or a little of both. Either way, it means I can't give him the it's-not-you-it's-me speech quite yet.

That night, I lie awake into the wee hours while Oscar snores softly beside me in his king size bed with the luxurious Pratesi sheets I'll probably never experience again. At a quarter to three, I slip out, wrap myself in the fluffy pink bathrobe he bought me a few weeks back, and fish his wallet out of his pants pocket. My heart feels like it's about to burst through my ribs as I remove the computerized security card that generates a new password every few minutes. I replace the wallet and slink down the dark hallway into his study. It takes what feels like five minutes to slide the door shut without a sound. I tiptoe across the room and switch on the desk lamp before settling into the leather chair and moving the mouse. The screen lights up and asks for a password. I type in the twelve digit code from the card and Oscar's desktop pops up. The Internet Explorer history shows he checked three email accounts yesterday: his work one, his Gmail, which I use most of the time, and a Hotmail account. I click on that one and hold my breath. I can hear my heart thumping.

The computer thinks for a second. It can't possibly be this simple. Except it is. "Welcome, TS45JQ7!" flashes on the screen. "You have no unread messages."

I freeze for a second and listen. No sound, other than the white noise hum of the heater. I grab a pen and scrawl the login name on my left palm. I exhale and click on his inbox, which is empty. The Drafts folder, however, contains 127 messages. The first shows $4,500 hitting some bank account. The second shows a $7,300 deposit into a different account. There are no transaction comments or details listed, other than today's date.

I keep reading. There are dozens of emails showing various amounts between $1,000 and $9,999 entering and leaving various accounts, all today. I start to do the math in my head, but the numbers get staggering.

I scroll down to the messages dated yesterday and the day before, and count twenty-three, which seems like a lot of emails to have in progress.

They're all innocuously titled and many have unnamed attachments. The first several contained short cryptic missives, like "Units 7347 -7353 transferred to residence BT. Confirming 23:45 travel 12/12," and "Units 8413 and 8414 from KL to BH 12/14 at 4:50." I have no idea what I'm reading, but its appears unrelated to Oscar's work in advertising. I open the first attachment. The PDF displays several pages of naked full body photos of girls, most Asian, but some white, each staring listlessly at the camera and holding a card with a number. At least two of them can't be very much older than my niece. I feel vomit creeping up my throat as I hurry to click the message shut and pray the image won't be seared in my mind forever.

With shaky hands, I click on sent items and trash, but both are empty. The only other messages in the account are spam ads for cheap Cialis in the Bulk Mail folder.

I click back on the Drafts folder and mark all the messages as unread. I'm signing out when the door swings open.

Oscar stands in the doorway, looking especially imposing in the dim lighting. "What the hell are you doing in here?"

TWENTY-SEVEN

"Checking email," I say. "I couldn't sleep." I reach for the mouse to sign out, but Oscar's across the room before the screen changes.

"You mean you're checking *my* email." He's trying, and failing, to keep his voice level. And probably cursing himself for not closing out of the account. Or for choosing such an inquisitive girlfriend.

I want to say something that makes him the villain, but I appear to have lost the ability to form words. Oscar's ears burn bright red and the veins on his neck bulge. I wonder again if his violent streak could ever be directed at a woman. I can't believe my stupidity and impatience. Why couldn't I have come here to look around sometime when he was at work?

Because I was over eager, of course.

Oscar folds his arms across his chest and glares at me. His liquid brown eyes seem to harden. "Aren't you going to say anything?"

"I think you're up to something illegal," I blurt, stunning myself. "You have *way* more cash on hand than any other ad exec in Manhattan, and last weekend, I heard from a reliable source, that you could be involved in that big sex trafficking ring."

"You can't possibly believe that," he says, almost dismissively.

"Judging by what I just saw, I think it might be true." I fold my arms across my chest defensively.

I can tell by the look on Oscar's face that he wasn't expecting an answer even remotely close to the one I just recited. As if to underscore my point, he says, "And I thought you might be snooping for evidence of another woman."

"Well, I wasn't. Should I have been?"

"No. I'm not in the habit of proposing to one girl while keeping another in the wings."

"How gentlemanly of you. So did you really buy my apartment with money from child porn?" I'm surprised at how bold I sound, since I'm still wondering whether he could get angry enough to throttle me.

"I'm good at my job, Zoë. And whatever else you saw was spam." I can tell by his voice that he doesn't truly expect me to buy this.

"Most people don't store their spam." I wince as this comes out, and half expect him to lunge at me, but evidently Oscar's too calculating for that. I can tell he's trying to figure out what, if anything, I could possibly know.

Before he can re-group, I push myself out of his big leather chair and say, "I think I should go." My voice wavers and I feel tears coming on. I expect him to reach out and grab me, or block my way, but he lets me walk right past. I grab my purse off the kitchen counter before dashing out the door.

"I have side deals with clients that are over your head."

Wow. I guess now I'm sure he was never with me for my intellect, because even if I bought this dumb excuse about side work, I don't think—at least I hope—I'd never stay with a man who claimed something to be beyond my mental capabilities. Anger and indignation move in and push out any residual sadness I had left. There's nothing left to say.

I bolt for the hallway.

My heart is racing by the time I reach the elevators, only thirty feet down the hall. I pound on the call button, as if that will make it arrive faster. I can't believe he hasn't come after me.

I'm sick to my stomach by the time the elevator doors close. The graveyard shift doorman looks more than a little surprised as I fly through the lobby, out onto the sidewalk. Only then do I recall that I'm barefoot and wearing a bathrobe. A very fluffy feminine one at that. The street is eerily calm, quieter than I've ever seen it. A light but steady drizzle sparkles against the street lamps and adds a rawness to the already chilly fall air. Only a few cars pass, and there's not a cab in sight. Not that most taxis would stop to pick up a crazy lady in a robe, even if it's accessorized with a Marc Jacobs bag, and even if the whole scene is playing out in New York.

I try the cab company whose number is programmed in my phone. The woman who answers warns me of a ninety minute wait. I consider walking for about half a minute. That would be foolish at 3 a.m., even with shoes and without the cold rain. Sheepishly, I do something I've never seen anyone under fifty do: I go back inside and ask the doorman if he can find me a ride.

He tries his best to look unfazed and professional, as if there's nothing strange about having one of the residents' girlfriends come down half naked in the middle of the night and ask him for assistance. While he calls some undoubtedly overpriced car service to ferry me home, I call Angela's brother-in-law. He answers on the second ring, sounding totally asleep.

After apologizing profusely for waking him, I tell Max about the email account, and recite the login name scrawled on my hand. "I'm sorry I don't know the password. He's at his computer now, probably deleting stuff."

Max says he's looking into it as we speak, and sounds about a thousand per cent more alert by the time he asks, "Where are you now?"

"In the lobby of his building."

"Good. Don't go back upstairs. Catch a cab home and call me when you get there. And thanks for the tip."

When I hang up, I feel a hand grip my shoulder. My whole body tenses. Oscar has pulled on some clothes and followed me down here.

"I think you should come back upstairs. We need to talk this thing through." He's arranged his expression to look contrite, and he's obviously determined to make the doorman think we're having a routine lovers' spat. As if to underscore his intent, he says, "There's no need to make a scene."

"I should go home."

"I really wish you'd come back up." His hand slides from the top of my shoulder to my arm and he digs his fingers in so it hurts. A lot.

"Let me go," I hiss. Inexplicably, the doorman picks this exact moment to disappear from the lobby. I have no idea whether he's ducking into the men's room, making some kind of security rounds, or mistakenly thinking we desire privacy, but we're suddenly alone. Oscar readjusts his grip on my arm and drags me towards the elevator.

I don't know why I don't scream. Maybe it's too unreal. This is Oscar. The same mushy, romantic Oscar who swept me off my feet in September, who sends me flowers at work and cooks me gourmet meals, who met my family and proposed marriage less than a week ago. I don't find my voice until the elevator doors slide shut and we start our ascent. When I open my mouth, what comes out is a blood curdling wail I didn't know I was capable of emitting.

"These cars are soundproof." He's doing his best to sound bored and blasé, but his eyes betray him. Oscar is furious. "So scream all you want."

I'm not sure what I'm thinking, or maybe I'm not thinking, but the next thing I know, I'm kicking my now suddenly very ugly boyfriend in the shins. He starts to yowl but catches himself just as the elevator stops and the doors start to slide open. As he grabs my arm, it suddenly occurs to me that this is a high end building. They must have security cameras everywhere. If I can stall long enough, or act distressed enough, sooner or later the bored night watchman will notice and lumber up here to investigate.

Instead of allowing Oscar to guide me out of the elevator, I drop to the floor and sit on the carpet, cross legged. "I'm not following you anywhere. If you think you're going to drag me into that apartment again, you can forget it."

Oscar is obviously fighting to keep his anger in check. He draws a deep breath, exhales loudly, then squats so we're at eye level. "Zoë, it's just *me*. I don't know what your imagination has cooked up in the middle of the night, but whatever you think, it's way off. Now could you please get up and come inside before all the neighbors hear us?" He tries to force a conciliatory expression.

"I don't believe you." While I'm disinclined to tell him I looked in the briefcase and found his secret stash, I'd think the emails alone would be enough to alert any normal person to a potential problem.

"Fine." He pushes himself off the floor, then in one motion bends down and scoops me up. I kick and punch at him as he carries me the short distance to his door. I try to squirm out of his grasp, but he's got a surprisingly secure hold on me. I aim my foot between his legs and manage to hit my target on the second or third try. He curses me under his breath and starts to bend forward in pain but catches himself and manages not to drop me until we're through his door. He slams it shut behind us.

"Security just saw that whole performance." I clamber to my feet and close my robe, which had flapped open during the trip from the elevator. "If you wanted to kidnap me, you'd be better off doing it in my lower rent building." My voice starts to waver. I want to sound confident, but I'm unsure. Maybe nobody noticed the spectacle in the elevator and hallway. Or maybe the man downstairs doesn't get paid enough to care.

"I don't care if Joseph saw our little lovers' quarrel or not. I'm much more interested in why you've been snooping through my emails." He's managed to back me against a wall so I can neither dash to the door, nor move further down the corridor into the apartment. I can't believe any of this is happening. It feels utterly surreal.

"Snooping is the lesser evil here." I try to say it with confidence, but I'm squirming, trying to create more distance between his face and mine. I can feel his breath on my skin, and for the first time ever, it repulses me.

"I beg to differ. I think trust is important, no, not important, *essential*, to a relationship and you just blew it."

"No, Oscar, I didn't blow it. I did what I had to do to find out the truth."

"What truth?"

Either he's unconvinced I know anything, or he's taking some kind of strange delight in making me say it out loud. "You're profiting from the exploitation of innocent, defenseless children."

The blood vessels over his temples throb more violently and his face grows even redder. "That's an awfully serious accusation you're throwing at me."

"I happen to believe it's true."

"Not that it's any of your business, because we are so over, but I've made some strategic investments over the years. Some of them include interests in companies that distribute adult entertainment. But I'm not a pervert, and I'm not doing or even condoning anything depraved or illegal. I thought I knew you, Zoë. I thought you knew me."

A large shot of adrenalin has kicked in from somewhere, and I realize I'm no longer feeling scared. Whether that's reasonable or not, I'm unsure. "People who invest in legitimate companies do not ferry second passports and suspicious checks around in their briefcases. Or exchange said briefcases with contacts in public places, as if you're playing some stupid spy game. Or take bogus business trips to Southeast Asia. Or maintain numbered accounts overseas."

The color drains from his face as I watch him realize that I've snooped beyond his Hotmail account. Before I process what's happening, he grabs me by both shoulders and jams me against the wall. Hard. Then he gets in my face and through clenched teeth, asks, "What did you see? How long have you been spying on me, you wretched little bitch?"

"I saw enough to know you've been living a lie." The tears are welling in the corners of my eyes and I will myself not to cry. My heart is pounding and I realize that Oscar is probably not merely capable of physical violence. He seems likely to perpetrate it against me at my next misstep.

"You'd better be prepared to get a lot more specific than that." He readjusts his grip on my left arm and starts to twist the right arm back. It hurts and the tears well again. I'm starting to shake and I hate myself for it, even though it must be a perfectly normal and legitimate reaction. The little voice in my head chooses this exact moment to pipe up and tell me I am an idiot. In case I needed any clarification.

Oscar waits for me to volunteer something, but I can't seem to choose or form the right words. "You'd better tell me what you saw. Right now."

"I don't need to tell you anything. You know what you have in your own briefcases. And it seems pretty damn disingenuous for you to get all holier-than-thou about me *snooping*, when you've been involved in something so unspeakably disgusting for years."

The slap across my face hits me completely off guard. My fingers fly up to my cheek and the tears suddenly dry up. No man has ever raised a hand to me in my life and, but for the sting, it feels unreal now.

"I mean it, Zoë. I want to know exactly what you think you saw, and when."

I'm too stunned to comply, even if I wanted to. He's going to hit me again. For some reason, I suspect it will hurt more than the first time. I don't know what to do. I feel paralyzed, both physically and mentally.

Oscar looks stunned, too, as if none of this is going remotely close to how he would have imagined. An insistent banging snaps me from my state of shock. In the half second it takes us both to process that the noise means someone is at the door, a booming male voice with Staten Island undertones demands, "Open up. NYPD."

Oscar releases his hold on me, readjusts his bathrobe, runs his hands through his hair and exhales loudly before opening the door. Two uniformed officers push past him into the foyer. A man and a woman in suits, maybe detectives, follow a few steps behind. The older looking of the two regular cops speaks first. "Ma'am, are you Zoë Clark?"

I nod.

"We got a tip from another law enforcement agency that you might be in danger."

I blink vacuously at my rescuers, unsure what to say or think. I pull my robe more tightly across my chest and wish I knew how much time had passed since I hung up with Max. It must have been a while, because I doubt he's one to sound an alarm over nothing.

"Ma'am, we have a few questions for you. Do you want to get dressed?"

I nod again and turn for the bedroom just as the tears start to well.

Behind me, I hear Oscar make motions to follow. One of the cops stops him. "Oscar Thornton?" he asks.

Oscar answers yes in a tone that conveys a high degree of irritation.

"You're under arrest," the officer informs him. I don't dare turn around. I hear the clink of handcuffs as the other cop starts to read Oscar's rights. They sound exactly the same as they do on television. The woman detective escorts me to the bedroom so I can pull some clothes on. When we emerge, the uniformed cops have taken Oscar away.

"All set, ma'am?"

"Yes."

"Because we'll need to seal off the apartment and wait for the judge to issue a search warrant."

This can't be real. My world can't possibly be imploding again. How many times can this happen? My karma can't be that horrendous.

The pair I presumed to be detectives turn out to be FBI agents. We sit down on Oscar's kitchen stools, where I first allowed myself to consider the possibility that he might be the man of my dreams, and they ask me all the same questions I've already answered for Max. After we go through all that, they ask detailed questions about what transpired tonight. They've already procured the security tape from downstairs. It's after five when they decide I don't know anything else of interest and put me in a taxi.

I can't decide if I'm wide awake or utterly exhausted by the time I let myself into my apartment. Maybe I'm not totally out of it, because the first thing I notice is that my plants could use some water. I realize that while I won't be able to sleep, there's no way I'll ever be able to do anything at work today but damage my career. I've never, even after my break up with Brendan, taken a true mental health day, and I don't feel the slightest bit guilty as I dial Carol's assistant, but by the time I hear the beep, I've decided I'll just go in late.

After leaving the message, I see seven missed calls from Angela. The last time she tried, at quarter to one, she left a voice mail. "Hey it's me," her familiar voice chirps. "I have big news. Call me. I'll be up at six." She sounds upbeat, like it's good news.

Six o'clock is only ten minutes away. I have to admire Angela's stamina. From what little I understand, most pregnant women would not be able to be stay up after midnight and then haul themselves out of bed in time to hit the first spin class of the day.

Suddenly I feel really icky. I undress and pour myself into the shower, and try to relax under the steam and almost-too-hot water. After pulling on my favorite flannel pajamas and poodle slippers, I glance at my watch and decide it's safe to call Angela back. She sounds surprisingly chipper and properly caffeinated when she answers on the second ring.

"I got your message," I say. "You won't believe the night I had."

"You won't believe the night I had, either." She's talking fast, to make sure she gets to share her news first. Maybe it's fair, since she's the one who was stalking me all night. But she can't possibly have anything as big as the nightmare that is now my life.

"I got a marriage proposal, and I promised to think about it and let him know today."

"What do you mean, *you're thinking it over*? I thought he made your heart do cart wheels. Maybe you do love him. And isn't a marriage proposal usually one of those questions you answer on the spot? Didn't you say the other day that Claudio is your ideal guy, or something to that effect? Are you sure this isn't some kind of conspiracy by your pregnancy hormones to torpedo your happiness?" I don't mean to push her, but I'm seriously, and I believe legitimately, worried that Angela's instinct to run from commitment is not serving her well in this particular moment. Once I start peppering her with questions, I can't seem to stop myself until she cuts me off.

"Claudio didn't ask me. Kevin did."

TWENTY-EIGHT

"Excuse me?" The world turns under my feet and I almost drop the phone as I grab the kitchen counter for support. "Why would Kevin ask you to marry him?"

"I know, shocking, right? He said because we're friends who could get along well enough, because my baby should have a father in its life, and because you'll never have him anyway."

This sounds so unlike either Kevin or Angela that I have to suppress the urge to scream that aliens have taken away my friends. Instead I ask, with as little trepidation in my voice as I can manage, "Was he drunk?"

"A little, but Zoë, seriously, *don't* worry about it. What seemed like a plausible idea at one in the morning sounds preposterous now that I'm talking about it with you. It's my hormones. They're making me a lunatic."

"Well, that's good, at least. I mean the part about seeing clearly now, not about pregnancy making you nuts." I realize I've been holding my breath. "So you're not marrying Kevin. What about Claudio?"

"That's what brought on the whole Kevin side-drama. Now that Claudio's had a few days to digest the news, he thinks he's happy, but he keeps saying that his family will be scandalized. I got the vibe that part of him wants to stick around, but just as large a part of him feels the urge to bolt."

"So what does that have to do with Kevin?" Claudio's behavior doesn't sound like a complete disaster to me, especially considering they're not what you'd call a longstanding couple. But now Angela sounds nearly despondent. I should be more sympathetic. Her life has suddenly disregarded all her carefully laid plans and she's having to adjust at light speed. Still, I'm thrown by the whole threatening to marry Kevin thing. Which she's not going to do, so I need to get over it. And quickly. It was his drunken stupidity, combined with her crazy hormones, and it means nothing.

"I told Claudio to let me know when he's sure he's happy."

"Don't you think that's kind of harsh? You just totally changed the guy's life. Whether he stays with you or not, he'll have this little kid here in New York. And if he decides he's going to be involved, he'll have to kiss his carefree bachelor existence goodbye."

"My life is changing way more than his," Angela says, suddenly sounding irritated. "I've checked with a lawyer, and even though Claudio has that huge trust fund, if he decides to leave the country, I have virtually no chance of seeing a penny in terms of child support. NYU might not be enough to hold him here if he gets the impulse to bolt."

"But if he thinks the baby is good news, though unexpected, maybe he's not about to disappear."

"We'll see. I wonder if I'll hear from him today. Anyway, when he said he had to leave after dinner, I felt so lost and *empty*. Like nothing I've ever felt before. When you didn't answer, I went over to Kevin's. After he tossed back five beers while watching me sip herbal tea, he threw out the crazy idea of us getting hitched. And I laughed at him, but in the scary hours of the morning, it started to seem less frightening than single motherhood. You know I've had the recurring single mom nightmare since college. But I'm going to tell him no. Today. As soon as we hang up. So please don't freak out. Claudio might still come around and when and if he does, I'll face a tougher question."

"What's that?"

"I'm scared of doing it alone, but I'm also scared of tying myself down to him so fast. It's been a wonderful couple of months, but that's all it's been. We haven't had a chance to see what happens after the honeymoon phase."

"Well, maybe it's good that babies take nine months to make."

"Right. Can you believe it's almost 6:30? I'm sorry to drone on and on. It's like I can't stop myself lately. What happened with Oscar anyway? I feel like the world's biggest heel for not asking sooner."

I can't help myself. As soon as Angela's up to date on the drama in my life, and I'm dressed and somewhat caffeinated, I march across the hall and bang on Kevin's door. I have no idea what I should be feeling. The Oscar disaster alone would be enough to overwhelm me and send me into a tailspin, but the news of Kevin's proposal to Angela is almost too much to take. There's an icky, selfish thought shoved into the far recesses of my brain and it's becoming more persistent. I don't want anyone else—and *especially* not my best friend—to have Kevin, because I'm not totally clear on how I feel about him.

I knock again. A muffled but grumpy "I'm coming" emanates from within. Kevin appears seconds later in flannel pants and a Princeton sweatshirt. His hair shoots in seven different directions. "I haven't slept at all, so you'd better have coffee."

"I just made some. I'll get you a cup."

"Black, please." He rubs at his eyes.

"I know." I disappear back into my apartment and return with two mugs to find Kevin starting his own coffee maker.

"I'll need more than one," he explains, as if it wasn't perfectly obvious. He downs about half the cup I brought before facing me. "I know what you're thinking."

"Really? Because I'm thinking you've lost your mind."

"Yup. That's pretty much what I figured. See? I know you better than you think." He laughs nervously.

"Insanity seems like the only plausible explanation. First, you go out of your way to try to sabotage my fledgling relationship, and then you tell me you love me, and a couple of short weeks later, you're *proposing* to Angela."

"I regretted it as soon as I heard myself say it. If she'd said yes, I would have had to back out."

"Obviously." I'm suddenly sick of standing, hovering in each other's space. I cross the room and settle into one of his big leather armchairs and curl my legs underneath me. He follows and plops down on the couch. We stare at each other for a moment, and sip our coffees.

"I don't know what to say," we finally say, in unison.

"So, really, Kevin, what was going through your mind?"

"A drunken, over-heightened urge to help a friend. She seems so scared and, I don't know, lonesome and overwhelmed, that I impulsively tried to make it better, and of course, only managed to make it awkward."

"She'll get over it. There's not much Angela can't get past, and I suppose she was flattered."

"That's good, at least. I don't know, Zoë. It's not like my parents were the best role models for healthy relationships. My dad has always treated my mom like part trophy, part staff. She's scared of him to this day. So there was this nagging feeling in my mind, that if the great love of my life is unattainable, maybe I should settle for a great friendship. I told myself a good partnership could grow out of it."

I have no idea what to make of the love of his life comment. Wow. I wonder if he truly believes that. I do the cowardly thing and ignore it. "Don't you think we're all way too young to settle for less than the real deal? And did you think for a second Angela, of all people, would be the settling type, even in the midst of her baby crisis?"

"When you put it that way, I feel like even more of a jack ass." He stares blankly into his coffee. He looks so defeated, and I don't know—embarrassed, that I feel a surge of pity. I hoist myself out of the armchair and sit next to him on the couch.

"Well, I'm a jack ass, too, if it makes you feel better. It seems your bad feeling about Oscar was right."

I try to sneak into the office sometime not too long after ten, without drawing attention to myself, but it's hopeless. The online version of the *New York Post* has a short piece on Oscar's arrest and everyone's buzzing about it. Marvin and Jessica swarm me before I can get my coat off, and New Girl hangs back behind them, eager to be included in the drama, but unsure of how to insert herself. Mercifully, Carol is out at meetings until lunchtime.

Marvin has thrown caution to the wind and printed the piece. He's reading from it with all the ardor of a revival tent evangelist. "Takamura Brothers rising star Oscar Thornton, once one of *New York Magazine*'s 'Forty to Watch Under Forty,' was arrested by federal agents early this morning for his alleged part in an international human trafficking ring, in which Mayor-elect O'Malley's fundraising chief, Burton Smealey, 53, has already been implicated. Authorities believe Thornton, 42, played a pivotal role in managing the finances of the syndicate, which bought underage girls, some as young as seven, from contacts in Eastern Europe and Southeast Asia, and sold them into sexual slavery in the U.S. Many of the girls were lured with promises of lucrative restaurant jobs, and instead found themselves making adult films or working as prostitutes in cities including New York, Los Angeles and Chicago. The FBI alleges that Thornton, who holds an M.B.A. from Columbia University, was responsible for the collection and distribution of profits through an intricate network of offshore accounts, located mostly in the Caribbean. They also contend that Thornton played a key role in facilitating the syndicate's expansion into Southeast Asia, by setting up a network of front companies to facilitate both trafficking girls and laundering profits. The details remain hazy, but law enforcement believes that each of the fronts was semi-autonomously managed, but owned by various off-shore subsidiaries of a larger shell corporation started by Smealey. The ring's management apparently used an anonymous email account to communicate on day to day matters, by storing unsent messages in the drafts folder. Thornton, Smealey, and their key contacts abroad could log into the account, review the contents, and reply to each other without sending a single message."

Disgusting, but clever.

"Why?" Jessica wonders aloud. Her brow wrinkles in confusion. "Why would a gorgeous hot shot like him risk it all to get involved in something so seedy?"

"Arrogance and greed," I say quietly, but loudly enough that my co-workers hear me. There's no other logical explanation. He thought he was smarter than the police. He thought he'd get away with it, especially with his tidy cover story about making his fortune in a friend's hedge fund. And if I know Oscar at all, I bet he was able to convince himself that his role wasn't so bad. He wasn't personally perpetrating physical harm on these girls. Just setting up the infrastructure and reaping the profits. My stomach turns with disgust at my own blindness, which was at least partially willful.

I rip the paper from Marvin's grasp when he pauses to take a breath. My eyes scan the page frantically, but it yields very little new information, except that the Mayor-elect will make a statement at noon.

As I reach the end of the article, Marvin asks, "Are you hanging in there? You've had a rougher time in the love department lately than anyone I know. And that's saying a lot."

"Strangely, yes. I am okay. I'm too horrified to be devastated. I actually feel relieved that I learned the truth now and not months or years down the road. But tell me, if someone as outwardly perfect as Oscar turns out to be a two-faced misogynist Neanderthal, how am I supposed to trust anyone? Should I just forget about dating, get a bunch of cats and take up needlepoint?"

"I think you need to get a hold of yourself before the Boss Lady comes back and sees you unraveling." He glances over his shoulder and lowers his voice. "Can I offer you a Xanax? Because I was thinking of indulging myself." Marvin reaches for his top drawer, brandishes a bottle of pills, and pops a couple without water. I'm not sure what's stranger: that he thinks I need a sedative or that he has them readily available at the office.

"Um, no thanks. I'll be alright."

We refresh the *Post's* webpage, and there's a file photo of Burton Smealey's arrest several weeks ago. I wish I'd looked at it more closely the first time. They nabbed him on his way into his Wall Street office building. The arresting officer is relieving him of his briefcase, which looks identical to Oscar's.

The refreshed article reads, "Off-shore banking records seized from Mr. Thornton link him the largest child sex trafficking ring ever uncovered by the FBI." It also says that Oscar has been talking as part of a pending plea deal. Smealey supposedly recruited him to the venture at a bachelor party for a mutual friend, where they engaged in a lengthy conversation about "the profit potential of certain areas of the sex trade." The FBI believes Oscar's business acumen, language skills and frequent travel to the Far East enabled the enterprise to grow its revenues into the *hundreds of millions.*

At least that clears up any doubt about why my well-paid, seemingly well-adjusted ex would risk his career and reputation for a life of organized crime.

The final paragraph says Smealey concentrated his recent efforts on recruiting new investors, none of whom were known to each other, or even to Oscar, but all of whom were allegedly "high net worth individuals with a lot to lose."

Interesting. Maybe Oscar was honestly surprised when news of O'Malley's investment in the ring broke. Or perhaps he'd gotten a heads up. Not that it matters now.

The FBI source goes on to say that the key players often transferred cash and information by swapping briefcases in crowded public places. *Like airports. Or the opera.* Their immaculately choreographed arrangement of high- and low-tech communications served them well, allowing them to operate undetected for years. I feel an odd combination of pride, over my small role in exposing Oscar, and shame, because I didn't catch on sooner.

The rest of the article is re-hash of earlier developments.

Minutes later, an unnamed spokesperson from O'Malley's transition team says that although Mr. O'Malley denies any "willful unlawful activity," he will step aside "because doing so is in the best interest of the city." So that's it. Kevin will have to reinvent himself with some other, hopefully cleaner, candidate. Probably in some other, hopefully less scandal-plagued, city.

I try to throw myself into my work, but it's hopeless. My cell phone rings off the hook. After telling the fifth reporter that I have no comment, I turn it off. I stop answering my office phone and I instruct Sybil to tell everyone I'm away from my desk. When I check my voice mail, the first message isn't business related.

"I am sorry to bother you during such a difficult time," Olivia Sevigny says formally, in her distinctive accent. "But I felt I had to ring you. To tell you I had no idea. About the children. I would never have kept such a thing private. I am very sorry for you, and I wish I could have warned you." I feel a minor twinge of guilt as I delete her message, for assuming the worst about her when she tried to warn me about Oscar's penchant for prostitutes.

Carol storms in at 11:30, barking at her assistant to order her a turkey sandwich with extra lettuce and tomato, and some kind of specific mustard that the deli messed up last week. She plows through the bullpen and launches into one of her stock speeches, bemoaning her perception that nobody does any work when she's out of the office. She snaps at New Girl that she'll never be able to pay back her draw if she doesn't start making more calls, but her assault is tempered compared to her usual ardor, and when I steal a glance, I note that it's a good make-up day. At noon, she even lets everyone cram inside her office to watch O'Malley give up Gracie Mansion.

O'Malley reads a statement vehemently denying any direct involvement in the trafficking of minors. He regrets not asking more questions when money invested on his behalf by his long-time friend and fundraising chief, Burt Smealey, posted "eye popping returns." He says he should have taken action when Mr. Smealey borrowed money from the campaign to travel to Asia with Mr. Thornton. O'Malley claims he now regrets choosing to remain silent. "I gave an old friend the benefit of the doubt, based on the sage counsel of a trusted priest, and for that I ask your forgiveness." He adds that he expects to be exonerated by the ongoing investigation.

"That fucker has balls of steel," Carol barks from behind her desk. She has the clicker poised to turn off the TV the moment the special report ends.

I think O'Malley looks like he's trying way too hard to appear contrite, a perfect portrait of a man who's merely sorry he got caught. Off to the side, Kevin spends most of the speech studying his wing-tips. At least that way, the camera can't hone in on the enormous black circles around his eyes.

O'Malley keeps his remarks brief, and ten minutes later, we're all filing back into the bullpen.

"Zoë, hang back a second."

I freeze. My brain flips frenetically through recent events at work as I struggle to realize what I could have done to rattle Carol. I can't think of anything. I've been doing well at work lately. And Carol never harps on the past. Only the here and now, and my here and now looks damn good, if I may say so. I have three commissions invoiced and pending, and seven good candidates out interviewing, despite the lackluster economy. None of the Ivies have rejected Janice yet. She should love me right now. "Close the door," she instructs.

I do as I'm told and take a seat in one of her new visitor chairs. They were deliberately ordered with short legs, so Carol can look that much more imposing from her perch behind her desk.

"I'm sorry about your boyfriend," she says, without looking up from her email.

"Thank you."

"It's better to find out now. Trust me on that." She looks away from the screen and studies me for a second. I fight the urge to fidget as I watch her size up my outfit, my haircut and my body language. "I have an opportunity to present to you," she says finally.

Not what I expected. Besides I'm wary, based on experience, of "opportunities."

"Carleen in the D.C. office is leaving us at the end of January."

I don't know what comes over me. It must be residual stress. I interrupt my boss. "Carleen Caputo is opting out?" I'm incredulous. Carleen has been with Carol since the D.C. office opened, some ten years ago. She's the company's top producer, and Carol trusts her more than she trusts anyone.

"Carleen Caputo *Cavendish* is opting out. She got pregnant and fucking lost her mind. She even took her husband's name and, between you and me, the guy is such a total fucking *noodle*." Carol shakes her head in disgust. "So I'm offering you her job. I'd need you down there right after the new year, to learn what you could about running the place before the last of Carleen's brain cells commit suicide."

"Wow. I don't know what to say. You've caught me way off guard, but of course, I'm flattered. Really, really flattered. But I have to ask, why me?"

Carol shifts effortlessly into sales presentation mode. "Because you've managed to have a great year end, in spite of the train wreck that is your personal life. Because I think you're level-headed and loyal enough to manage the place, with a lot of guidance from me, of course." She arches her eyebrows at me from across the desk. "And because you don't have roots here. You could move, and I venture to guess, you might even benefit from a change of scenery."

"Why not Marvin?" I'm not sure why I blurt this question, but it comes out.

She smiles without parting her lips and I can tell she already asked him. "Marvin's elderly parents live here in New York. Their declining health makes it a bad time for him to contemplate a move." She recites this reason as if he made her memorize it. "Plus he drinks too much."

So she knows about the flask. Not surprising. I'm beginning to think nothing gets past Carol Broadwick. Perhaps she's not as deranged as we all presume.

Carol waits to see if I'll verbalize any reaction, and when I don't, she studies her manicure pointedly and says, "And also because Janice has been accepted early to Yale, which obviously reinforces my faith in your ability to come through under pressure."

Wow. That's the biggest compliment she's ever thrown my way. I'm slowly developing a whole new respect for Carol. Of course she realized all along that the college application assignment was the project from hell. And now I can finally exhale, because a skinny letter, or its modern email equivalent, isn't going to derail my entire career.

"That's wonderful news," I finally manage to say. "Please congratulate your daughter for me."

"Of course. But can we talk about business now?" This is rhetorical. She knows I have no input about the direction of this or any conversation between us. "It's a great opportunity I'm offering you, Zoë. You'll get to develop management skills and cultivate a whole new stable of clients. You'll work harder, but you'll make more money. Washington, with all its regulatory work, is far more recession-resistant than New York City, which is not a bad thing. D.C. is the fucking promised land of legal recruiting. I'll give you until the end of the week to decide, but I'll tell you right now, you're a fucking idiot if you don't say yes."

I thank her profusely for her confidence in my abilities and promise to give her an answer by Friday. As I let myself out of her office, her comment about possibly benefiting from a change echoes in my ears. A fresh start would make sense on several levels. It hits me for the first time that, whatever happens, I'll have to move out of my apartment. If it's even legally mine. For all I know, the police might seize it, like they confiscate yachts and sports cars purchased with drug money. I have no idea how all of that works.

More than the apartment, though, it might be healthy to put some distance between myself and the two men with whom I inextricably associate that particular piece of mid-market Midtown real estate. Maybe it's time I take a break from dating altogether. I've never been alone in my adult life, and while I should be reeling from the collapse of my affair with Oscar, I feel strangely liberated. Yes, I read him wrong. Just like I read Brendan wrong. And Kevin, for that matter. I completely misinterpreted his feelings when to everyone else, they were plain as day.

Maybe I won't be able to read anyone correctly until I figure out what it is *I* want from a man. In the cases of both Brendan and Oscar, different as they are from each other, I tried to make myself fit with men whose resumes and outward appearances suited the job description I thought I had to fill. And with Oscar, there was the added factor of the sex haze. I was so thrilled with our physical chemistry after such a long drought, that I ignored other signs of incompatibility. I'm ashamed to admit that I'd be engaged to a child pornographer if I hadn't opened his briefcase. And though it turned out for the best, I'm equally ashamed that I had to spy on my almost-fiancé, because I was so unsure and insecure about him and the whole relationship.

It's time for me to confront the crux of the problem. I never figured out what I needed from Brendan or Oscar, or even what I had to give. I'm going to do myself the biggest favor of my life, and give that question some major consideration before throwing myself back out there.

So as unlikely a savior as Carol might be, I find myself considering her offer as I return to my desk and check for urgent messages. Leaving New York wouldn't be running away since there's a lucrative and interesting job opportunity at the other end. Wow. That's a first. I've never let myself admit that I find my job, nutty as it is, *interesting*. Maybe there's a real career path in this company for me after all, and with my personal life in shambles again, it does seem like an auspicious time to explore that possibility. I'm going to channel my energy into making something of my professional life, instead of feeling like a lowly drone. By the time I've finished listening to my voice mail messages, I've decided the only variables preventing me from hurrying back into Carol's office and telling her yes right this minute are Angela and Kevin. I wonder, if I tell them the big news tonight, whether they'll try to persuade me to stay, or encourage me to go for it.

I stay at work out of fear that reporters have swarmed my apartment. The news is all Oscar and O'Malley, all the time. Around noon, a breathless anchor on CNN breaks the story about Oscar's polygamist background. My office phone rings off the hook to the point that I reach under the desk and yank the cord from the wall. It's not like I'll get any work done anyway. I watch clips of the live coverage on my computer with all my colleagues hovering over my shoulder. Various television shrinks speculate on the permanent psychological damage Oscar's upbringing could inflict. A legal analyst raises the possibility that his childhood could form the basis of an insanity defense, while another psychiatrist holds forth about sociopaths who lead outwardly upstanding lives. Evidently, the overwhelming majority of such criminals suffered abuse at the hands of their parents. There's a report that the major booksellers can't keep up with the flood of orders for *Surplus Boys*, before yet another television shrink comments on the common maladjustments of people rescued from cults.

Around three in the afternoon, I overhear Jessica telling someone, "Ms. Clark has no comment. She asks that you please respect her privacy during this difficult time." She clicks over to the other line and repeats her statement. The Town Crier seems so happy in her unofficial role as my press person that I decide to leave her alone, at least as long as she sticks with the no comment script.

About an hour later, Sybil appears at my desk. She tells me she has a woman claiming to be Oscar's sister on the line.

TWENTY-NINE

I sneak into an empty conference room to take the call away from my colleagues' ears. Jennifer Thornton sounds more saddened than surprised by the charges against her foster brother. She tells me that she and her mom were always afraid Oscar was hopelessly screwed up by his demented childhood, but her father insisted from the start that Oscar was bright and innately charming enough to overcome his rough start. "Dad always said Oscar would go far, because he possessed an academic's soul and a fanatic's drive," she says, in a mournful voice.

Jennifer catches herself sounding weepy, regroups, and tells me Oscar went through years of intensive therapy as a teenager. Multiple experts told her parents that he displayed signs of difficulty relating to women in a healthy way. She tries to explain what one physician labeled Oscar's extreme Madonna-whore complex. "Anyway, the real reason I'm calling is because I plan to testify on his behalf, when and if his lawyers mount an insanity defense. I'm hoping I can convince you to do the same. What he did, if it's true, is disgusting. But I still think, maybe because I've known him so long and watched him struggle, the whole situation is more tragic than anything. I spoke to him a half hour ago. He'd love to hear from you, to explain as best he can. I suppose he also wants to apologize. I know it's a lot to ask, but please think about it. He's not the monster they say he is on TV. You must know that." She's getting choked up again.

I promise to consider her request, but I know when we hang up that I won't call Oscar. True, he's a victim of an unspeakable childhood. That may explain why he lacks a moral compass, but it doesn't excuse his actions. At least not in my mind. I'm shocked at how clear things suddenly seem.

And how unequivocally over.

Still, I'm surprised to feel no yearning for whatever explanation Oscar might offer. Nor do I crave an apology, though I suppose I deserve one. All I feel in this moment is an overwhelming desire to put him in the past, into a little box I can shove to some back corner of my brain, so that I can forge forward with my life.

Oscar's attorney calls as I'm getting ready to head home. He leaves a message asking to arrange a time to talk. I take a deep breath, press delete, and close that calamitous chapter of my romantic life. I imagine if there's a trial, I might be required to testify. Until then, I'm washing my hands of Oscar. There's nothing I can do to change what he did or make any of it better.

"You totally blew off his lawyer?" Kevin asks incredulously on Thursday night. The three of us have gathered at Angela's for pizza, because she's been craving it almost every day since the baby news broke, and she says being in a bar or restaurant with everyone drinking around her feels like torture, not unlike electrocution or water boarding. Of course she's being melodramatic, but I feel like it's okay to indulge a pregnant woman. Even if she's only very newly pregnant and can't play that card with anyone but her closest confidantes.

"It was cathartic," I say, as I take what I hope is a surreptitious sip of my Chianti. Staying out of bars in solidarity with Angela is one thing; she can forget about me abstaining altogether.

"So are you going to talk to the press?" Angela asks.

"I don't think so, but I haven't totally ruled it out." The reporters who staked out my building mercifully disappeared after I gave them nothing but silence for two days, but I've received a couple of calls at work, from the producers of the major news shows, offering to pay me for an interview. The Town Crier has told them I'll get back to them.

"Boss-zilla must hate that you're the center of attention all of a sudden," Kevin says.

"Fortunately, I'm in Carol's very good graces these days."

"How so? Did her precious Janice get into school?" Angela manages to pull her attention away from her third slice of pizza, which she's been devouring like some starving orphan who's never seen food besides gruel.

"Actually, yes, she'll be going to Yale in the fall, but there's so much more." I fill them in on the job offer in Washington, and how

I'm leaning towards accepting it. Truth be told, I know I'm going to take it, first thing tomorrow.

"So sad for me, but how fantastic for you!" Angela squeals. "And my sister's already down there, so I'll get to visit both of you for the price of one."

Kevin, not surprisingly, sounds slightly less enthused. "It does sound like a big step up, but are you sure you want to become middle management? You'll have way more interaction with Carol, even if it's over the phone."

"Maybe I'm a lunatic for being an optimist, but I think Carol and I understand each other a lot better than I thought we did. I have this Zen-like sense that it's really going to be okay. Not that I don't have a ton of stuff to do before January. Like finding an apartment, and figuring out the status of my place."

"Whether you're moving or not, you should get a lawyer. I bet you have a solid case that the apartment is yours. You didn't do anything illegal, you just exhibited extraordinarily bad taste in men," Kevin says.

I don't want to escalate, so I laugh and stick my tongue out at him. Juvenile, I know, and not befitting someone who's about to become management, but I do it anyway. It works. He rolls his eyes and laughs.

Angela has stopped to digest before reaching for a fourth slice. "Not so fast with the condemnation there, O'Connor. If the Oscar disaster hadn't come to light when it did, Zoë might be tempted to turn down the best thing that's ever happened to her professionally. So maybe everything happens for a reason." She pats her non-existent belly as she says this, and turns to me. "The hot male attention was good for what was ailing you this fall, but it had to end unambiguously, not just fizzle or fade, for you to move on. So I think it's all good, just like my news is all good."

"What news is that?" I ask. She can't possibly have anything that trumps the baby. Wait. She must mean the baby. Why did I have to say that?

"Claudio and I are moving in together. He came over last night and we had a long talk, and I really think he wants to give us a try. He's going to come live here for a couple of months, and if things go well, we'll start looking for a bigger place in time for the baby's arrival. He says it's his life, and if his parents are scandalized, that's their problem, and anyway, they'll come around when *il bambino* makes its entrance. He says he won't even mind sharing the bed with Ernest and Algernon."

"Wow. *You're* going to do the domestic bliss thing and I won't be here to witness this earth-moving event." Angela's beaming as I say this. I don't think I've ever seen her look so content. It's strange how fast things can be turned upside down. Mere weeks ago she was single-mindedly career obsessed.

"I know. Tragic, isn't it? But I don't care how driven and successful you become, I need you to swear to me, on a whole stack of Bibles, that you'll come up and host my baby shower. I can't bear the thought of one of Mom's friends running with it. It would be so suburban. And there's no way I'm allowing any dumb games or measuring of my girth. I want a classy, champagne cocktails type of affair."

"Don't lose sleep over that. I wouldn't dream of letting anyone come near your stomach with a measuring tape. And if someone tries, you can always knock them out with one good swing of your favorite Fendi."

Kevin says, "Alright, this is getting way too girlie, even for me, and I'm kind of used to you guys. Do you have any beer, or did you purge it when you got the big news?"

"There should be a couple hiding in the back of the fridge. By all means, take them off my hands. I don't need Sam Adams calling me in the wee hours of the night."

"Do you believe everything happens for a reason?" Kevin asks as we're walking home. It's an unusually warm and pleasant night for early December, so when he suggested saving six bucks and stretching our legs I was fine with that. Especially since Angela was ready for bed well before ten. She may be a happy, glowing pregnant lady, but she's a sleepy one, too.

"I suppose. Believing that gives a certain sense of order to all the chaos."

"Because I didn't want to say anything tonight, and I'm not sure exactly why not. Maybe it's because I don't have an offer in hand yet, but now I feel like spilling my news."

"Well?" We're paused at an intersection three blocks from our building, waiting for the walk sign.

"I'm interviewing in Washington. I've got appointments next week for three Congressional chief of staff spots and another for communications director for the Democratic Senatorial Campaign Committee."

"Wow. That's great. And here you were, all worried you'd be banished to the northern reaches of the great State of New York to run a campaign for some creepy gun-toting county coroner."

He grabs my arm and turns me to face him. It's obvious he's got something else on his mind. "I think your offer from Carol is a sign. Maybe we should move together, try to make a go of us."

The light finally turns and gives me a legitimate reason to look away, because I'm really not sure whether he's going to make me scream or cry.

"Not even a week ago, you were proposing to Angela," I remind him, and yes, I mean to say it every bit as snidely as it comes out.

"Temporary insanity?" he asks, with the hopeful and ever-so-slightly goofy grin that's won him his way with countless women in the past.

"It sure was insane," I agree. "And we're all entitled to a little bit of crazy from time to time, but it still didn't feel so nice for me to hear that news."

"I'm so sorry for any pain I caused you, Zoë. You have to believe me. The last thing I'd want to do is hurt you. But it was making me crazy, thinking that you'd never want me, and it feels like high time to stop sleeping around, and Angela needed someone. And while I'm apologizing, I might as well add that I feel awful about all the digs I've made at your career over the years. It would be totally wrong for me, but it suits you and that's awesome. There are worse things than finding jobs for lawyers. In fact, it appears I wasted a good chunk of my time trying to fulfill the political aspirations of a liar, thief and pervert." We've stopped at our building and I start fumbling in my bag for the keys. He puts his hand on mine and says, "Wait a second. Let me get this out."

We step aside to let the elderly couple who live in the penthouse pass. Interesting. We're home from a night out at the same time as a pair of octogenarians, one of whom totes an oxygen tank.

Once the door shuts behind them, Kevin takes both my hands and says, "I love you. More than I've ever loved anyone, and I'm pretty sure, based on your behavior at and after Angela's birthday party, that you at least feel something for me. We've been friends for so long, and we're so in tune to each other. We owe it to ourselves to give us a chance. What better way than a fresh start in a new city?"

"A fresh start sounds almost divine to me, and I'm really happy that you're probably going to live there, too…"

Before I can devise how to phrase what I need to say, he kisses me. Despite my best intentions, I find myself kissing him back, and it feels right and comfortable and tremendously exciting, all at the same time. Even though he tastes not-so-faintly of winter lager. He pulls away for a moment, and looks at me as if trying to read my reaction before cupping my face in his hands and kissing me again. For a second, I let myself go and enjoy the moment. He somehow manages to extract his keys from his pocket and let us into the building. He leads me up the stairs, hand in hand, and I start to think, maybe this feels right because it is right.

It could be the insistent and utterly unromantic fluorescent lighting in our hallway, or perhaps it's the little voice in my head shrilly shouting, "Brakes! Brakes!" Or perhaps I just reach somewhere within myself and find the resolve I had ten minutes ago on the sidewalk.

We're standing in the hall, between our apartment doors, and he's clearly waiting for an invitation into mine, because he's put his own keys back in his pocket. He looks at me with slightly confused eyes and I think, he is *so* adorable. And smart and kind and loyal and an extraordinarily adept kisser, among many other great things.

But he'll also be all those things in a month or two. And, the little voice in my head says matter-of-factly, he'll still have all his not-so-wonderful points, like he's a workaholic, and he's moody, and his relationship track record isn't anything to write home about. I tell her to shush and kiss Kevin again. He holds me close and I feel the bulge form in his pants.

I force myself to pull away.

Kevin looks at me lustily. "Did I ever tell you how beautiful you are?"

Something inside me melts, and aches to kiss him again and lead him to my bedroom for what would promise to be an amazing night. We could see where we go in the morning.

But I know if I do this now, I'm plunging head long into something that can only be forever or end very badly. I'm not a relationship genius, or anything close to it, but this I know for sure: If I start dating Kevin, we will either get married or suffer a horrible break up that will result in neither of us wanting to speak to the other ever again.

And maybe I'm up for that risk, but not today.

"This is so hard to say, because, right now, I want you so badly it hurts." I'm thankful I only had one glass of wine. If I was drunk, I might be in bed with him already. "I'm not rejecting you, or saying never, but I need a little time, and not just to rebound from the Oscar nightmare, because I know that's what you're thinking. I need to learn to stand on my own, live independently, and see what that feels like. I've never done anything without a man holding my hand. This summer doesn't count, because I did nothing but hide and wallow, and I'm not about to make that mistake again. I jumped into a whirlwind romance with Oscar when I wasn't ready, because he fell into my lap and I was so excited to have what I thought was my first really mature relationship." I shake my head and marvel at how clueless I was.

"It's alright. Everyone makes a wrong turn now and then. You just have to keep moving forward."

"You're right, but I've also figured out that it's very hazardous to hunt for a new relationship while still heartbroken over the old one." I force a little laugh, hopeful this last remark will lighten the mood.

Kevin tries to smile, but his eyes still look sad. "You're not really hunting. I'm here. You don't have to sniff me out and stalk me like I'm some unwitting prey animal. God knows you do enough of that at work. You don't need it in your love life." When I don't respond, he asks, "Seriously, what do you need to feel more comfortable?"

"I don't think I need tons of time, but I do want to make the move by myself, find my own place and get my feet wet in a job I'm really excited about. Then we can see. I'm thrilled you'll be coming down there, too, and you may think this sounds nuts, given everything I just said, but I have a good feeling about us. Just not right this minute."

I hold my breath and wait for his response. Part of me braces for a minor tirade about my need to grow up, or seize the day, or whatever. Kevin surprises me, though. He takes a deep breath, exhales and says, "None of that makes me feel great right in this particular moment." He glances below his navel and flashes me his most flirtatious smile. "But it's the smartest thing I've ever heard you say. Take whatever time you need. I'll be here. Or there. Or, you know what I mean." He gives me a quick kiss on the lips before forcing himself to turn and go into his own apartment, by himself.

With the security chain fastened and my boots kicked off, I take a lingering look around the apartment I was so scared of losing when Brendan called off the wedding, and realize I don't care at all that I'm not going to live here anymore. I pour myself a glass of wine, but before I even take a sip, I dial Carol's voice mail. I know she'll check it tonight and again very early in the morning. "Hi Carol, it's Zoë. It's not an emergency. I just wanted to let you know that I'm thrilled to take the job in D.C. Thank you again for giving me this opportunity, and I'm looking forward to discussing the details."

When I hang up, I don't even need to go look in the bathroom mirror, because I can feel myself smiling from ear to ear. And it feels extra wonderful, because this time, it's not because of anything some guy has done for me. I've realized, perhaps slightly belatedly, with over three decades on the planet, that I have the power to make myself happy. I raise my glass and toast a new beginning.